THE GOLDEN GIRLS' GETAWAY

JUDY LEIGH

Boldwood

First published in Great Britain in 2021 by Boldwood Books Ltd.

Copyright © Judy Leigh, 2021

Cover Design by Debbie Clement Design

Cover Photography: Shutterstock

A CIP catalogue record for this book is available from the British Library.

Paperback ISBN 978-1-80162-334-6

Large Print ISBN 978-1-80162-336-0

Harback ISBN 978-1-80162-333-9

Ebook ISBN 978-1-80162-337-7

Kindle ISBN 978-1-80162-335-3

Audio CD ISBN 978-1-80162-328-5

MP3 CD ISBN 978-1-80162-329-2

Digital audio download ISBN 978-1-80162-331-5

Boldwood Books Ltd
23 Bowerdean Street
London SW6 3TN
www.boldwoodbooks.com

For the NHS, with so much thanks...

THE GOLDEN GIRLS' JOURNEY

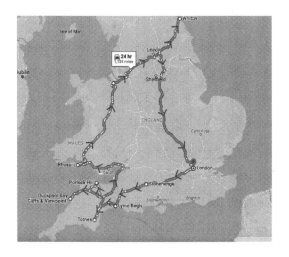

1

London was alive with the early morning rumble and bustle, despite the cold March weather; red buses shuddered by, fumes spluttered from the exhaust pipes of lines of cars. On the pavements, pedestrians were on the move, collars turned up against the wind's bite, shoulders hunched. The breeze huffed and puffed, scuffing up litter at the kerbside, whirling dust in the air, as people rushed towards their separate destinations, faces expressionless, heads down, pushing against the bluster. The young postal worker, Sonia, her bag weighing down on her shoulder, was about to shove the mail through the shiny letter box at 104 Drayton Mews when the door was swept open and a slender woman in a dressing gown, huge curlers in her blonde hair, thrust out a hand.

'Anything for me today?'

Sonia, who wore a brown face mask and matching khaki shorts despite the chilly morning, gazed up from the bottom step at the elegant woman who faced her, ringed fingers clutching a mug of steaming coffee. 'Just one letter for you, Ms Goldman. The others are for 104A and B.'

Vivienne Goldman took the letters, curling her lip as she studied the top one. 'Oh, it's only a bill. I always hope for so much more.' She offered Sonia her warmest smile. 'But thank you.'

Sonia's eyes shone. 'I thought you were great last week in *The Edge of Edgeware*, the scene where you were in the pub and you spotted your Joe chatting up the barmaid and you called him a legless Casanova. Everyone in our house cheered when you poured beer down his trousers.'

Vivienne smiled graciously. 'I don't write the script – but it is great fun being Maggs. I've had the role for so long now, sometimes I wake up in the morning and I'm not sure if I'm Vivienne Goldman or Maggs Pryor.'

'I think she's wonderful – we all do.' Sonia heaved her heavy bag onto her back; there were many more streets to traipse along before it would be empty.

Vivienne waved a hand. 'You have a lovely day, now,' and closed the door. Once inside, she gazed at the letters and muttered, 'Three brown envelopes, one each. That's the winter electricity quarter. Gwen and Mary won't be up yet...' The fourth letter was for Mary, a white envelope emblazoned with the letters NHS in blue. Vivienne placed the mail on the shelf in the hallway and rushed up the stairs, a sprightly leap for a woman in her early seventies, and disappeared into her flat.

Half an hour later, Vivienne came down again, swathed in a dark woollen coat, sunglasses on her face, her sleek hair a blonde helmet that touched her shoulders. Her stomach grumbled: she'd had a coffee but nothing more; she could grab a bite on set or just do without – it was always better for the waistline to abstain, she reminded herself grimly. She set off at a smart pace down the street, turning onto the main road, the wind tousling her hair in a way she hoped made her look windswept and interesting. There were a few pedestrians, the usual endless stream of cars pausing, then chugging away from the traffic lights. The grocery shop had just opened, trays of fresh vegetables placed outside; next door was the baker's shop, the warm aroma of pastries and fresh bread drifting on the air. The tube was five minutes' walk away: she'd be in costume and make-up by nine. Vivienne delved into her pocket and pulled out the silk face mask, looping it around her ears, covering her nose and mouth. She increased her pace; good timing and reliability were everything in her profession.

* * *

Gwen Prichard lay in bed, staring up at the ceiling. There was no sound from the flat above; Vivienne would have left already, on her way to the TV studios. Gwen sighed: Vivienne was so lucky to be still working at her age. Filming was back on again now, after a layoff of several months. Even though Vivienne had complained that the new lockdown storylines avoided physical contact, and the action had to be done at a social distance, at least she went out. Gwen gazed up at the cracks in the ceiling and wondered what she would do today, other than walk around the flat, watch television, take a bath, make tea, the same things she had been doing for a whole year now. Lockdown had affected her in more ways than she could have thought possible, a single woman in her early seventies living in a ground-floor flat in London, with only the soap actor above to talk to, and Mary in the basement below for company when Vivienne was out. Gwen liked Vivienne and Mary a lot, they were great fun, but her own life was empty in comparison: she felt like the limp slice of ham in the sandwich. Lockdown had been a cold, lonely time. But at least she had her voice. And the guidelines meant that their landlord had to remain outside on the pavement each time he called round, which was a blessing in itself. Gwen was grateful for that.

She slipped from beneath the duvet and padded in pyjamas to the window, pressing her nose against the polished glass, watching. It was bleak outside: a blank sky, an empty street, a single parked car opposite. A teenager wandered past, not in school uniform, of course: it was all home education these days. In this case, home education meant that the poor kid was being sent to the shops. There was no sign of Vicente de Lorenzo, the landlord. Gwen was relieved: she knew he was passionately in love with her. He called round several times a week to declare the depths of his feelings – he had been doing it for almost a year now, bringing gifts, words of love, even serenading her from the doorstep. That was the only good thing about the restrictions – she could refuse to let him in, especially since he always stood too close to her, and without a mask. He didn't want to hide his face, as if he believed his moustache was his most attractive feature.

Gwen shook her head, making her dark hair fall loosely from the clip that had held it back. She had endured a year of endlessly gazing through this window, the same drab sky, the same drab life. But summer would be here soon, and Gwen intended to do something with the sunshine months. She had no idea what, but until a plan formed, she would sing, as she did every day. Even now, at seventy-four, her voice was strong, the practised polish of a professional for over fifty years.

Gwen inhaled once, twice, then launched into her scales, her voice rising up and down, a bubbling brook of pure notes. She breathed from her diaphragm and sang again, louder. Then, as her voice warmed up, she launched into the terrifying two-octave aria in D minor, Mozart's 'Queen of the Night' from *The Magic Flute*. Gwen raised her arms, encouraging the notes to rise and fall, to rebound against the walls and bounce off the ceiling. She hit the top note, F6 above top C; she was imperious, stern and regal, then plaintive and full of sorrow.

Gwen paused and silence filled the room. It was her constant companion, but she decided to chase it away again. She closed her eyes, imagined herself in a recording studio, the swell of a full orchestra behind her, and she opened her mouth, allowing the purest and most delicate notes to emerge as she sang Henry Purcell's 'Nymphs and Shepherds'.

Gwen crooned in her pyjamas, her voice as clear as running water, lifting her fingers, urging the pastoral clan to come and play, her voice sweet as springtime. Then a repetitive thudding came from below, a broom handle banging on the ceiling from the basement, and a voice thick as a demon's growled, 'You can come away yourself and take your fecking nymphs and shepherds with you. Holy mother of God, Gwen, it's not breakfast time yet.'

Gwen dropped to her knees. 'It's ten o'clock, Mary. I'm not being funny, but every self-respecting human being is up and about by now.'

The demon down below grunted something like, 'Jaysus, Mary and Joseph...'

'And you shouldn't really blaspheme,' Gwen retorted. 'It's not nice, is it?'

Silence returned, and with it, Gwen's solitude. She wondered if she should have breakfast or make a batch of Welsh cakes from her mam's ancient recipe that always reminded her of her childhood in Llanclawdd and take them down to the basement to share with Mary. It might cheer them both up. Gwen smiled fondly: Mary was a live wire, who was usually wonderful company, but she wasn't always tactful. She often grumbled about Gwen's singing, especially early in the mornings. Vivienne often said that Mary's mood depended on how much ale she'd consumed and, as Gwen knew well, Vivienne was partial to a glass of wine or two herself. Gwen sighed. She liked both of her neighbours; she was so grateful that they all shared the same house. The solidarity, friendly greetings, the occasional shared meals and cups of tea felt like a life saver. But Vivienne was so poised and self-assured; Mary seemed so fearless. Gwen knew she was different, she had so many doubts about herself. Being sociable could be demanding, and that made it harder to blend in.

* * *

Mary Molloy struggled into her coat, out of the door and padded up the steps to the road, ignoring the pile of letters on the shelf in the hall. Her head, warm in a woollen hat, white hair sticking out, was bent forward against the stiff breeze that was funnelling through the street. A shopping bag containing only her purse clutched in her hand, she made her way steadily past the other houses, all doors closed. Dust accumulated by the side of the road, shuffling along the kerb in the breeze like tired feet. A pigeon scratched at the side of the road, wings tucked in, its beak stabbing at gravel. Overhead, the London sky was pale as a new piece of paper.

'I don't like the lockdown, not one little bit,' she muttered between clenched teeth. 'I used to have my breakfast out – I liked a sausage sandwich with ketchup and a cuppa in the mornings...'

The wind made her eyes water. She swung her shopping bag and hummed a little tune, something she'd heard recently about 'Nymphs and Shepherds'. She recalled Gwen singing from the upstairs flat earlier that morning and Mary made a soft sound of contentment. 'Ah, she has a lovely voice, that one,' Mary mumbled. 'I should tell her so more often. She's a good sort. I'll invite her round for a cuppa later.'

She had reached the main road, a long parade of shops where people in face masks ambled along and gave each other a wide berth. Noisy traffic blew out fumes and dust. Mary gulped a mouthful of diesel.

'Essential journeys, my arse,' she grumbled as she delved into her pocket, tugged out a light blue face mask and pulled it on. 'A year ago, they'd have thrown you out if you'd gone into a shop wearing one of these – they'd have thought you'd come to rob the place.'

The idea made her laugh. She stopped outside a shop, Chandra's Convenience Store, and wandered in, pausing to look at the fruit and vegetables. She pressed a pineapple with one finger. It was firm and resistant. She hadn't had pineapple in a long time, so she picked it up. A smiling man in his late twenties took it from her hands. 'Just this today?'

'Ah, no.' She rubbed her chin, then squirted hand sanitiser everywhere, missing her fingers completely. 'Let me have a tin of the chickpeas and a punnet of the fresh okra and a bunch of coriander. Oh, and I'll be needing a little bag of basmati rice.'

The shopkeeper placed her purchases on the counter. 'Curry again tonight, Mary?' he quipped. 'Is that what keeps you looking so well?'

'Oh, but I do love a curry.' Mary's hand plunged in her shopping bag for her purse. 'I like a good bhuna. Or a steaming madras.'

Ravi raised his eyebrows. 'Here, try this...' He handed her a tin of coconut milk. 'Add some of this to your curry. It will enhance the flavour. On the house. I can't sell the tin – it has a dent in it.'

'Oh, you're a superstar, Ravi. I might just make a triple portion and invite the neighbours to dine at my basement residence. We could all do with cheering up. Or...' She winked. 'I might just eat nothing but curry myself for three days. You know it gets better with age, a good curry...' She snorted mischievously. 'Just like a good woman.'

'I'll take your word for it.' Ravi took the money she offered. 'You have a nice day now, Mary.'

She loaded her bag with her shopping, and squirted the hand sanitiser again. The liquid shot across the counter in the opposite direction. 'God bless you.' Mary hugged her bag and stepped out, leaning into the March wind, pushing herself towards home.

2

Vivienne, wearing a grey mackintosh and a grey curly permed wig, folded her arms as she stood outside the makeshift betting shop. The cameras closed in, hovering over her frown, her unhappy face.

Inside the betting shop, a short stocky man with tousled white hair and a battered denim jacket was furtively handing over money to a tall man behind the counter. Two other men, also in their later years, were watching, mouths open. The short stocky man raised his eyebrows anxiously. 'This is for the 3.30 at Newmarket, Roy; Golden Pond, to win.'

Vivienne stepped into the betting shop, slamming the door, standing back, her voice shrill. 'Joe!' Her accent was more Lambeth than her usual rounded tones. 'Joe, what on earth do you think you're doing here?'

The stocky man's face was earnest. 'Maggs, we need the money.'

Vivienne put her hands on her hips. 'How much have you got there?'

'Fifty pounds...' Joe trailed off.

'You took it from behind the clock? That money was going

towards this week's rent – I saved it from my wages, cleaning the pub. You can't have that.'

Joe stayed where he was. 'Golden Pond's a cert, Maggs. At 20-1, we'd make a killing, love...'

'The only killing round here's going to be me killing you, Joe Pryor. I'll skin you alive. Just put that money back where you found it...'

'Too late, Maggs...' Joe glanced at the tall man behind the counter, who pointed up at a TV screen. He muttered, 'I've placed the bet. They're off.'

A voice called, 'Cut,' and the five bodies in the betting shop relaxed as one, their shoulders dropping. Vivienne scratched her head beneath the heavy wig and spoke to the actor playing Joe, all trace of the accent gone. 'That scene's done, Robin – what's up next?'

'The one where the horse falls at the final fence. The one where Maggs loses her cool with Joe.'

'I don't know, this lockdown acting...' Vivienne sighed. 'In normal times, I'd be over there, grabbing you by the throat, screeching in your face. Now I have to lose my rag at a distance.'

'But you do it so well, Vivienne.' Robin Pettigrew, the stocky actor playing Joe, gave an exaggerated gesture of relief, a hand to his brow. 'I remember when we came to blows over Tania the barmaid, I had a bruise on my arm for weeks.'

'Sorry, Robin.' Vivienne laughed. 'It's the curse of playing the hard-boiled old couple, terrible together but worse apart.'

He nodded. 'We keep winning the awards, though, the most popular soap couple, the most loveable rogues...'

'I got an award for the woman most men wouldn't want as a wife or mother-in-law,' Vivienne complained cheerfully. 'I seem set to be the miserable whingeing old biddy for ever...'

'Hey,' a deep male voice called over. 'Have you got time for a coffee, Vivi?'

Vivienne turned round to see a broad-shouldered man in his early seventies, wearing a donkey jacket, ruffling thick curls frosted with white. She smiled. 'Lennie, my favourite window cleaner. Yes, come on, let's go get some caffeine in our veins.'

Vivienne and Lennie Lindo, who played Delroy Pickett, walked over to a small room where tea and coffee urns were steaming, and paper cups were piled next to packets of sugar and an opened bottle of milk. Lennie strolled with the confidence of a septuagenarian who had been recently voted the older woman's number one pin-up in a TV poll. Slender and muscled beneath his window cleaner's garb, he reached out for a cup, filling it with black coffee, handing it to Vivienne in a smooth practised movement before pouring a cup for himself. He took a gulp and then smiled, showing even white teeth.

'So, Vivi, how's life?'

She pulled a face. 'I can't complain – I'll be better when I take this damned wig off. It's boiling hot in here – I thought we had to have ventilation everywhere to keep the virus at bay.'

'Ah, I almost forgot.' Lennie took a step back. 'Social distancing has to be observed at all times. Which, I must admit, is easy when you're on the set, up a ladder cleaning everyone's windows.'

Vivienne agreed. 'And Joe is safe because Maggs can't punch his lights out, although I did throw beer over him several days ago.' She sighed. 'What I'd give for a passionate storyline, though.'

'It's overrated, I can tell you.' Lennie sipped black coffee. 'There are times when I'm bored with being the stereotypical man with his top off and his trousers down, who sleeps with every middle-aged husband's wife.' He put on a mock-West Indian accent, taking on his character, Delroy. 'Oh no, you buss me again, Mr Dobson. All fish does bite, but di shark always get di blame.'

Vivienne had not touched her coffee. 'I recall that scene – you and George Dobson's wife, Carol, in a compromising position next to the beer barrels and the boxes of crisps in the basement of the pub.'

Lennie shrugged. 'It's a hard life, being a gigolo...'

'It's even harder being the old crone, I promise you,' Vivienne retorted. 'I've played some of the most wonderful roles during my career: Kate the Shrew, Maggie the Cat, but now it's daft grannies, hags or witches, or all of them at the same time, that's Maggs Pryor.'

'And what about me?' Lennie's eyes blazed. 'I just get racial stereotypes, comic roles, flippant fools, criminals, dads of criminals, randy window cleaners. I'll never play Hamlet again. Even King Lear's out of my reach – I'm old enough now, but who ever saw a Lear with Jamaican parents?' He rubbed his temples. 'And I'd love to play Lear.'

'You deserve so much more, Lennie – you're so talented.'

Lennie inched forward, his social distance temporarily forgotten. 'And you're so talented, radiant, and lovely, Vivi.'

She looked away, thinking, then she asked, 'How's the latest girlfriend? Marlene? Arlene?'

'Charlene, and we lasted a month.' Lennie gazed at his workman's boots. 'I can't settle for anyone nowadays, too many memories of all the good times with you to make anything meaningful again.' His face was sad as he put down his cup, the coffee unfinished. 'We should get back together, Vivi. Me and you. Like we were before...'

'That was three years ago, Lennie. A lot of water has flowed under the bridge. That ship has sailed.'

'I hear lots of liquid metaphors, Vivi... but you still float my boat.' Lennie laughed. 'You're the only one...'

'You'll always be very special to me, Lennie.' Vivienne shook her head. 'But that's because we know each other inside out. We have separate homes, separate lives now. This isn't the time for us to consider getting back together.'

'Then when?' Lennie's eyes were soft with emotion.

'I don't know.' Vivienne put down her coffee. 'Come on, we'd better get back on set. You and I are sewn into the fabric of this soap opera and there would be no *The Edge of Edgeware* without Maggs or Delroy, but the directors want more thrills-and-spills drama than ever from us now.'

'I know.' Lennie adjusted the donkey jacket around his shoulders. 'We have to cheer up the viewers, showing them that our lives during lockdown are even worse than theirs. Let's give them some action.'

Vivienne's expression was tender. 'Sometimes I miss you, Lennie.'

'That gives me hope, Vivi. Maybe when this madness is over...'

Vivienne shook her head sadly. 'No, we're best as friends now. Come on. You must get back up your ladder and peep through Carol Dobson's window and I have to give Joe Pryor a good socially distant rollicking for losing my rent money on the horses. Back to being stereotypes the public love. I think our days of any substantial roles to get our dentures into are well over.'

Lennie didn't move. 'I wish I could hug you.'

'These are strange times.' Vivienne rubbed her scalp beneath the wig. 'But it will all be over soon. We've had our first jabs, we oldies, and by the summer, who knows, we might even be back to normal.'

They walked back towards the set, a metre apart. 'I hope so,' Lennie muttered. 'But then, I hope for so many things nowadays...'

* * *

Gwen breathed in the aroma of frying onions and garlic. Her sensitive nose could recognise cumin, other spices, probably garam masala. Below in the basement, Mary was cooking up a storm. Gwen gazed at the clock on the wall; it was well past five o'clock and she hadn't made the Welsh cakes from her mam's recipe yet, the recipe that had been handed down through six generations. She hadn't even cooked breakfast or lunch. She'd munched an apple, drunk five cups of herbal tea, chewed a handful of walnuts. She wasn't even sure if there was food in the cupboard; the delivery came once a week and she seldom ventured out to buy groceries.

She'd been down to the community centre three weeks ago for her vaccination; that had been terrifying enough, so many older people in face masks shuffling through corridors. She'd worried all the way home about side effects, about what would happen if the vaccine made her ill, if she'd be alone at home feeling like death, but she'd only had a slightly sore arm the next day.

Gwen wondered what it would be like to be normal again, and to go out. She'd promised herself she'd join a choir, but the truth was, it had been so long since she'd done anything sociable, she'd forgotten what normal was. She had a cuppa with Vivienne upstairs every few days and Mary invited her in for bhajis last week and insisted on playing every song from the back catalogue of the Dubliners, which had lasted into the small hours. Then she'd asked Gwen to sing 'The Irish Rover' and 'Seven Drunken Nights' and was appalled that Gwen didn't know any of the words. But Mary and Vivienne were always so positive and welcoming: Gwen was grateful for their company.

The aromatic scent of curry seeping through the floorboards made Gwen's stomach growl. She wondered if she shouldn't go downstairs to Mary's flat and compliment her on the mouth-watering smells. If she had a bottle of wine, she could take it with her and offer to make an evening of it. Some light chatter was what she needed, in truth, and Mary always lifted her spirits. Gwen sighed: she'd done nothing all day again. Even reading a book was difficult during these times. Apathy bred more apathy. She was losing the knack of living.

Gwen did what she always did when life scared her, she reverted to what she knew best. She unclipped her hair, the smooth black mane tumbling to her shoulders, stood tall, folded her hands, attempted a few scales and then launched herself into Cherubino's aria, 'Voi, Che Sapete', from *The Marriage of Figaro*.

When she had finished, she listened to the silence, hoping that Mary might bang on the ceiling again with her broom. It would be a conversation of sorts. But Mary was in the basement flat's kitchen cooking, probably listening to the Dubliners. Gwen thought about singing 'Voi, Che Sapete' again, but the song made her feel sad: she too had so much love to give but no one to give it to.

She needed a song that would lift her spirits, and she searched the list in her brain for something raunchy. She could think of only one sexy song from the early seventies, when she'd been a young singer with the Swansea City Opera. Not that she'd ever have sung such a song in those days; she was too busy playing beautiful tragic heroines in extravagant costumes, singing with handsome barrel-chested men in fantastic outfits or dark suits. Now, she took a deep breath and began to bawl 'My Ding-a-Ling' by Chuck Berry in her best operatic soprano voice. She concentrated on meaning: she made each line suggestive, slowing the pace, making the notes of the rudest words resonate. Then there was a sharp banging at the door and Gwen stopped and caught her breath.

Gwen crept over to the door and cracked it open. She recognised the small white-haired woman outside who was frozen in a statue shape, her hand to her ear, listening.

'Mary. What is it?' Gwen's heart leaped: Mary was going to invite her to dinner.

'He's at the door, the mad auld fella again,' Mary hissed. 'He's after you again – he's been at it for months. He's besotted with you. Can't you just give him a kiss, Gwen, and perhaps he'll go away? Or invite him in and make a proper night of it.'

'Who?' Gwen gasped, and then she knew. She felt her chest heave in a sigh, and it wasn't one of love. It was such hard work finding excuses not to talk to the landlord. He was a nice man, harmless, always showering her with compliments, but he wouldn't give up.

'It's the handsome Mr "just call me Vicente" de Lorenzo, our lovely landlord.'

'Oh, dear.' Gwen's hands flew to her face. 'Can't you just tell him I've gone out?'

'You never go out. Besides, I told him to stay where he is on the bottom step. He was after coming in, but I told him he has to maintain social distance,' Mary whispered. 'He insisted he wants to see you now. And...' She lowered her voice. 'He's got a big bunch of flowers in his hand. It's not looking good.'

3

Gwen stood at the door, Mary positioned just behind her shoulder, taking in every detail. Vicente de Lorenzo was wearing his smartest suit, a red dickey bow tie, his dark hair slicked back, brown eyes glowing behind his huge spectacles, his moustache waxed. He thrust a bouquet of roses and lilies forward and gave a little bow. 'For you, Gwen: beautiful petals, just like you; they are perfect, like your wonderful voice.'

'Take the roses, Gwen,' Mary urged. 'Shove them in a vase. You can give the lilies to me: they smell lovely and the basement could do with freshening up.'

Gwen held the flowers stiffly, not moving. 'Mr de Lorenzo,' she murmured.

'Just call me Vicente, please,' he beamed. 'May I come in?'

'No, you can't.' Mary pushed forward. 'You've no mask on your face and I don't want to catch the coronavirus.' She folded her arms and winked at Gwen. 'We've all paid the rent for this month so there's no need for you to be here again, bothering us.'

'Gwen, dearest lady...' Vicente began. 'I've come to see how you are. These are difficult times. I wanted to check that all was well. I think of you – I worry night and day if my Gwen is all right.'

Gwen wasn't sure what to say: she was out of practice with social chit-chat, and men in smart suits showering her with flowers made her feel awkward. She replied, 'I'm fine, thank you very much,' and pressed her lips together.

Vicente de Lorenzo was not short of words. 'I have just bought a new camping van, for when all of this is over. I want to get out of London, travel the countryside again, see the sea, feel the sunshine on my skin.' He grasped Gwen's wrist, the one holding the flowers. 'And when I bought it, I thought of you, of love. You and I could go together. We could travel to Margate, music playing, Puccini's most famous love duet, and we could sing together – I could be Pinkerton and you could be Madame Butterfly.'

Gwen closed her eyes, hearing the swell of music in her ears: she knew the piece, Pinkerton's smooth voice, Butterfly's beautiful pledge, so sweet, the promise of eternal love, tender and intense. She opened her eyes and Vicente was still there, his eyes hopeful behind the huge frames. He licked his lips nervously. 'What do you say, Gwen?'

'She'll say no.' Mary shook her head. 'Have you had your jab yet? You don't want to be travelling around giving the coronavirus to every poor old person in Margate?'

Vicente proffered an arm. 'I'll get my vaccination soon. I'm only sixty-eight years old.'

Mary huffed. 'Gwen's got a few years on you then, she won't see seventy again. Is it an older woman you're after?' She lifted the hem of her skirt to show a soft round kneecap. 'There's always myself if you're seeking a cougar – there's life in this auld one yet. I'm eighty-one this autumn and I'd be up for a bit of gadding about in the camper van, especially if you throw in some pub meals and a few jars of ale...'

Vicente glanced hopefully at Gwen. 'Might I come in? Just for a moment?'

'I know it's your flat, strictly speaking, but it's my home and...' Gwen's voice became stronger. 'I think it might be better if you didn't.'

'Of course, my lovely Gwen – I understand completely.' Vicente smiled encouragingly. 'I heard on the radio that by the summer this will all be over, and we can all get back to normal again.' His eyes twinkled. 'It will be good to spend time with you then...' He smiled at the thought. 'We could share a duet, something beautiful – you and I, dear Gwen, we could sing a duet from Rossini.'

Gwen momentarily imagined being on stage, miaowing Rossini's 'Cat's Duet' with Vicente. She suppressed the urge to laugh.

Mary took over. 'Well, we'd better shut the door because it's blowing a gale through here, Vicente. The place isn't too warm as it is, and the cold wind plays havoc with my knee joints.'

'I'll come back soon, Gwen, my dear.' Vicente simpered. 'This awful time will be over and then we can all live and breathe and love again.'

'That's if we're not all dead with the Baltic cold coming in...' Mary pushed the door. 'Take care, Vicente, and go get your jab done.' Then it slammed shut.

They heard his voice call Gwen's name from behind the door, full of disappointment. 'You have refused me again. But I will come back soon. I will try anything to win your love.'

Gwen put a hand to her head. 'Poor man. He means no harm. I just don't want a boyfriend...'

Mary turned towards the steps that led to her basement flat. She was about to go down when she noticed Gwen hadn't moved, the flowers hanging down from her hand like a dead bird with beautiful plumage. An idea occurred to Mary.

'Do you like a nice bit of curry, Gwen?'

Gwen shook herself from the daze. 'Curry?'

'A coconut cream and pineapple one with okra and tomatoes and coriander and... basmati rice.' She was suddenly feeling hungry. 'And I have a few bottles of ale.'

'Oh... how wonderful.' Gwen thrust the flowers into Mary's hands, her face flushing with happiness. 'That would cheer me up. Do have these flowers, please – I don't want them.'

'Then that's settled – curry it is,' Mary said emphatically, inhaling the sweet scent of lilies. The front door burst open behind them and Gwen's first thought was that Vicente had returned to check that Gwen hadn't given the bouquet away. She put her hands to her face, feeling suddenly guilty. But there in the doorway stood Vivienne, her blonde hair windswept, shivering inside the woollen coat.

'Hello, Gwen, Mary. Good to see you both. Well, what a day,' she gasped, brandishing a bottle of wine. 'I had to shriek abuse at Joe Pryor twelve times about losing my rent money on the horses. It's ridiculous, performing a marital tiff at twelve paces. It would have been so much better if I could have walked over to him and grabbed him by the throat and yelled in his face.' She sighed. 'I'll be needing this bottle of Chianti, and I've another one in the bottom of my bag.'

Mary's eyes twinkled mischievously. 'So, how about a good curry then, Vivienne?' She waved the bouquet. 'Only Gwen and I are going to dive into one in my flat right now. If you want to bring your bottles of wine and come on downstairs, you're very welcome to join us.'

* * *

The plates were empty, except for smears of curry, but their glasses were full as the three women chattered happily. Gwen's cheeks were flushed; she'd consumed a whole glass of Chianti and she wasn't used to drinking. She was watching Vivienne, how easily she talked, waving a hand, her eyes sparkling, and she felt suddenly awkward and alone.

Mary refilled her own pint glass with beer. 'You're lucky to have any job at your age, Vivienne. I bet it pays well too, being a soap star.'

'As Antony said about Cleopatra, "Age cannot wither her, nor custom stale her infinite variety." No, I can't really complain.' Vivienne pushed a hand through her blonde hair, a practised move of nonchalance. 'It just saddens me that my days of playing glamorous roles have gone.'

'I have to say, the auld boot you play on *The Edge of Edgeware* looks nothing like you in real life at all,' Mary agreed. 'Maggs makes a holy show of herself every week on the telly and yet you're so smart and posh in real life.'

'Not as posh as Robin, who is my co-star.' Vivienne sighed. 'His father was a big deal in the theatre, so he never had a hard time in between jobs like I did, having to wait on tables until a new audition came up.' Vivienne sipped wine. 'But I've been in *The Edge of Edgeware* for almost fifteen years; it's steady work. No, I can't really complain.'

'Nor me.' Mary cradled her glass. 'I loved the nursing in London and I never enjoyed myself more than when I was helping someone else. I lived and breathed it, and when I retired, I stayed on here. Well, there was nowhere to go back to by then – the family had all gone.' She sighed. 'I miss it, though, the craic with the other nurses, the patients, pulling the doctors' legs.'

'I can just imagine you as a nurse, Mary...' Gwen leaned her elbow on the table, nestling her chin in her palm. 'Caring for people every day, making them smile.' She glanced across the table.

'And you, Vivienne, you bring such hope to people's lives during this horrible pandemic.'

Vivienne opened her eyes wide. 'But, Gwen, you're the really talented one. I don't think I've ever heard anyone sing like you can. It's just wonderful.'

'Except for the wailing first thing in the morning,' Mary muttered under her breath. 'And the fecking nymphs and shepherds.'

Gwen shook her head. 'I haven't worked in years, though. I spent my life singing on stage with huge groups of people and now I do nothing, just live by myself.'

'Why don't you talk to someone in Covent Garden, tell them you're available?' Vivienne waved a well-manicured hand. 'There must be lots of openings for someone with your skills and background.'

Gwen sniffed. 'I should, you're right, Vivienne. I used to be so confident. But the work dried up and I just settled for less and less. Now, after all these years, I think I've lost belief...'

Mary snorted. 'But you're in demand in other ways, what with the love-struck landlord after you all the time, with his waxed moustache and handsome face.' She indicated the flowers, stuck upright in a jug on the table. 'He was here again today waving his flowers, all over Gwen like a rash...'

'He's besotted and won't take no for an answer. I feel so sorry for him.' Vivienne banged a fist on the table. 'Right, after the virus has gone away, we'll see what we can do about finding you some work, back in an opera house or...'

'Oh, I don't know if I still have what it takes...' Gwen's voice wavered. She put a hand to her head, momentarily saddened.

Mary reached across the table. 'I'll sort us all out with another round of drinks.'

'Oh yes, please.' Vivienne held out her half-full glass of wine to be topped up.

Gwen was thoughtful. 'Why did you never marry, Mary? Because of your vocation?'

Mary filled her glass to the brim. 'I suppose so, yes. But I've had plenty of love in my time.'

'The patients?' Gwen asked.

'Oh no, I never clambered into bed with a patient in my life...'

Vivienne intervened. 'Gwen meant that you loved your patients – you were a caring nurse.'

'I was.' Mary took a long sup of ale. 'But I had plenty of men who thought the world of me: a doctor, a hospital porter – even an undertaker once. He was a good-looking fella, the undertaker. Jim, he was called. From Birmingham.' Mary laughed. 'We went out together for two years. I never understood a single word he said to me and, do you know what, he never understood a thing I said back at him.'

'How did you communicate?'

'Ah, we had the language of love, Gwen – and it was all about the bedroom action with Jim – he buried the dead by day, and he was a love god by night.' Mary had an expression of pure bliss as she refilled the glasses with wine. 'And how come you never married?'

Gwen stared into the deep red colour of the wine glass and shook her head. 'It was all because of Clifford Edwards.' She heaved a long sigh. 'He was my first sweetheart. We were in love. We were together for years, but it didn't work out. I started to go out with him when I was fifteen. I moved to Swansea at eighteen to sing in the opera, and we were together for a few years after that, into our twenties. He'd come up at weekends, you know, and then I wanted him to move in with me. But he stayed in Llanclawdd and then later on, he fell for someone else. After that, no one else could come close.' She ran a finger around her wine glass. 'Funnily enough, he was tone deaf – he couldn't sing a note.'

'But it's very true, Gwen... once you've had real love, you can't be doing with something synthetic.'

Mary and Gwen glanced at Vivienne and leaned forwards, eager to hear what she would say next.

Vivienne smiled, but her cheerfulness was betrayed by sadness in her eyes. 'I let him go, the love of my life. I'm stubborn, that's the problem. "Cupid is a knavish lad, thus to make the females mad." *A Midsummer Night's Dream.*' She shrugged. 'I've had offers since, but to be honest, I can't see the point.'

All three women lifted their glasses at the same time, sipping drinks at the same moment. Vivienne broke the silence. 'We haven't done this for ages... shared a meal, the three of us, and a good chat.'

'You invited us all on Boxing Day, Vivienne, for wine and canapés. Then we met up in your flat and drank Scotch on Burns Night. Oh, and I had fish and chips round Mary's on New Year's Eve,' Gwen murmured. 'It's just been the odd cuppa here and there since then – I haven't had much fun at all.' She covered her mouth with her fingers, suddenly feeling dependent and awkward.

'We should meet up much more often and enjoy the craic,' Mary suggested. 'I'm always happy to cook a curry.'

'It's my fault that so long has elapsed since we've spent quality time together – I'm usually so busy, rushing everywhere,' Vivienne grumbled.

'And I'm the opposite, I've nothing to do,' Gwen moaned. 'My life is standing still...'

'Right, so there it is.' Mary lifted her glass. 'We need to find new ways to enjoy ourselves. And after this bloody virus is over, we'll get out there, shake a leg and have the best of times.'

'Agreed, Mary.' Vivienne chimed her glass against the other two, lifted into the centre of the table. 'To the three of us and the best of times to come.'

4

Mary sat on the chair in her vest, her coat on her knee, her jumper on top of the coat. Her arm was exposed as the woman in the face mask lifted a syringe.

'I was a nurse back in the day,' Mary muttered, pushing her free hand through her white hair. 'Needles never bothered me at all.'

The woman smiled and Mary was aware of her moving around near her arm and in no time at all, the nurse was done.

'You're all finished now, Mary.' The nurse wiped her arm.

'Ah, I'm done? Well, it's an incredible job that you're all doing.' She frowned. 'Right, well, I'll be off home then.'

'You ought to sit in the next-door room for fifteen minutes, while we monitor you.'

'All right.' Mary realised she'd hardly looked at the slim young woman who had just vaccinated her. 'Thanks, I will.' She began to replace her clothes, the jumper, then the coat, and made her way into the adjacent room and sat on a chair, at a distance from many others sitting on chairs, all looking in front of them.

Twenty minutes later, Mary left the community centre, on her way home. She felt strangely tired, her legs heavy. She muttered to herself that it wasn't the vaccination, she was just getting old. It was late afternoon now so Mary decided that she'd call into Chandra's Convenience Store and buy a few vegetables, make herself some soup. Perhaps she'd offer to share it with Gwen upstairs. She felt sorry for poor Gwen, who was clearly lonely. Last week, when Mary had shared her curry, it had been mostly Vivienne and Mary doing the talking. Gwen was probably a bit depressed, Mary thought, and everyone knows how that feels.

Half an hour later, she turned the corner into Drayton Mews, her bag full of groceries. Her fingers were sore where the handles dug into the flesh. She felt exhausted, her chest ached and she was short of breath. It had been a long walk and Mary couldn't wait until she got into her little basement flat and could collapse in an armchair with a hot cup of tea. As she fiddled with the key in the door, she put a hand to her head. 'Oh, I'm getting a bit old for all of this gadding about.' She struggled down the steps to her flat and went inside. It felt too much trouble to make a cup of tea. She flopped into the armchair and closed her eyes, muttering, 'Ah, that's better now; that's better.'

Vivienne took off her make-up carefully with practised fingers, pulled off the raincoat and the dismal clothing she'd been wearing all day as Maggs Pryor and stood in front of the mirror. She looked tired, her eyes circled with dark rings. Exhaling slowly, Vivienne began to pull on her own clothes. It had been cold on set inside the Pryors' shabby home, and her skin prickled with gooseflesh. She had filmed several scenes with Joe this morning and two with Jared, who played her good-for-nothing nineteen-year-old grandson, Kyle, whom she had discovered had been stealing. Vivienne swallowed; she'd spent most of the day on camera shouting, and a good deal of it being filmed close-up, crying. She'd go home and make herself a salad and have a glass of wine, then tuck up with a good book.

She was conscious that someone was behind her in the dressing room. It was Shreya Mallick, who played Jamuna, the teenage daughter of the Bakshi family who had recently moved in two doors down from the Pryors. Shreya approached the mirror, standing a metre away, adjusting her simple costume of T-shirt and jeans, swishing her waist-length black hair, checking her make-up. She glanced towards Vivienne and murmured, 'You were terrific today. I was watching from off-set when you and Kyle had the argument. I'm learning so much.'

'Thanks.' Vivienne's expression was one of genuine pleasure. 'I worked hard today. All that interaction with Jared wore me out.' She smiled. 'It's amazing how much it takes out of you, full-on emotion, fighting all that testosterone and youthful energy.'

'It's my turn next,' Shreya breathed. 'I have a secret fling with Kyle and that leaves me pregnant. No one finds out until June, but it'll be an emotional rollercoaster.'

'I bet.' Vivienne reached for her coat. Her fingers were becoming stiff and cold from the draught; the door was wide open. 'Apparently we've got some big storylines coming up over the next few months.'

Shreya agreed. 'Have you heard the gossip about the fire?'

Vivienne frowned. 'Oh, we're having a disaster, are we, to boost the ratings?'

'The pub is set on fire.' Shreya winked. 'Someone mentioned it this morning. It's going to be a heart-breaker.'

'Can't wait.' Vivienne belted up her coat. 'Well, I'm off home to put my feet up. I'll see you tomorrow, Shreya.'

'Wish me good luck...' Shreya replied. 'I'm about to do the scene where Kyle and Jamuna share some eye-to-eye non-verbals, and it's where I become besotted with the bad boy for the first time...'

'Good luck,' Vivienne called over her shoulder, buttoning her coat as she turned into the corridor and bumped into Lennie, smart in a dark jacket.

He was pleased to see her. 'Are you off home, Vivi?'

'I am.' She stared into his dark eyes, the colour of melting chocolate. 'I'm exhausted.'

'Come for a drink with me first?' he offered. 'I'll buy you supper?'

Vivienne exhaled. 'One day, you'll be fed up with asking me, Lennie.'

'Sooner than you think, I'm afraid.' He shrugged. 'I have news. I'm leaving the soap.'

'Oh?'

'I have a new job, serious stuff, a big role.' His face was momentarily sad. 'It's what I want to do.'

Vivienne was astonished. 'But you've been in *The Edge of Edgeware* for years.'

'And I'll be forever glad. That's how we met, Vivi.' Lennie sighed. 'But the new role's an opportunity I have to grab – I couldn't turn it down.'

Vivienne nodded slowly. 'I'll miss you.'

'Well, you know I think we should get back together, then you wouldn't have to miss me.'

'We probably should,' Vivienne agreed. 'But then we'd argue and take each other for granted, like we did last time.'

He took her hand. 'I learned my lesson. You're the only one...'

Vivienne wriggled her fingers loose from his grasp and moved back. 'I have my own flat now, my independence.'

Lennie made a mischievous face. 'Where you're alone and sad and you think about me every night.'

Vivienne knew that was true, so she smiled, but replied, 'In your dreams,' and began to walk away.

'You don't have long to change your mind...' Lennie called after her, his voice playful. 'I get killed in the pub fire being heroic. Once I'm gone, you'll have missed the chance of your life, Vivi.'

She carried on walking and called, 'My loss,' over her shoulder.

She heard Lennie reply, 'Mine too.' He sounded sad.

She was still thinking about his words as she arrived at the tube. Vivienne told herself that she was happy alone; she was independent. She missed Lennie sometimes, yes, but she didn't miss his untidiness, the way he was always late for everything, the way he spent money on her without considering the consequences. Besides, she was seventy-one now; too much water had sailed under the bridge. She waved her Oyster card in the direction of the ticket machine and moved towards the steps down to the tube. The thunder of an arriving train met her ears. It was time to go home to her little upstairs flat, and pour herself a glass of red.

It was almost six o'clock, early evening. Gwen had sung an aria from *The Marriage of Figaro* three times and now she launched herself into 'Nymphs and Shepherds'. She stood upright, still in her pyjamas, her spine straight, leaning slightly forward, her hand on her abdomen. Her voice resounded off the walls, clear as a bell. She concentrated on the emotion of the piece, the light and shade, her voice deliberately soft and gentle, then powerful. She finished with a flourish and paused. Her ears were filled with silence. She waited to hear if Mary might respond, if the broom handle would bang against the floor and she'd swear like a demon. Gwen didn't like swearing; the harsh, grating sound of it made her feel intimidated, and blasphemy was wrong. She decided that next time she was in Mary's flat, she'd have a gentle word, explain about her upbringing, that she was strictly chapel, although she wasn't sure what she believed nowadays. Mary was a lovely person – she'd understand.

Gwen began singing 'Nymphs and Shepherds' again, her eyes wide, her face full of the optimism of the words, a pastoral idyll. Then, suddenly, she was conscious of someone banging on the window from outside: the curtains were still drawn – she'd forgotten to open them. She approached the windows tentatively and pulled back the curtains a little, peering through the gap. The cheery face of Vicente de Lorenzo greeted her, waving his fingers. He was wearing a dark overcoat and a red scarf. He motioned to Gwen to come outside, moving his mouth exaggeratedly to enunciate as he shouted, and she motioned back that she would not. Then Vicente gestured at the double glazing; he wanted her to open the window. She pressed the handle and pushed it open, realising that she hadn't let fresh air into her flat since last summer. Vicente was standing on the tiny stretch of gravel that separated the house from the pavement. He indicated the road behind him with his thumb. Parked by the side of the kerb was a huge white motorhome. The top part jutted over the cab with a yellow and green logo proclaiming the brand. Vicente gesticulated wildly. 'Come and meet Venus.'

'Venus?' Gwen shook her head.

Vicente clasped his hands together. 'I thought of you when I bought her. She is a love machine – she will take me and you away for wonderful weekends. We will have a wonderful time. She is insured for us both to drive, you and me.'

'Insured? How did you do that?'

'I am your landlord – I have your details on file, and you gave me a copy of your driving licence as ID when you moved in. I hope you don't mind. I did it as a gesture of my true love, so that we could share good times to come. Oh, it will be delightful, you and me, music, true love and the open roads.'

Gwen looked around the flat. She hadn't been outside in ages. 'I can't imagine...' she muttered.

'Maybe we could go for a ride now? Maybe we should take Venus for a spin?'

Gwen shook her head again. 'I don't really want to ride in a motorhome.'

'I have a wonderful CD player in the cab. We could play music as we drive... Puccini, Vivaldi, Monteverdi, Scarlatti...'

Gwen sighed. She couldn't imagine herself with Vicente driving around the country, singing Tosca and La Bohême in a motorhome.

He was undeterred. 'We could go to the countryside, have picnics on the grass, drink wine, make love beneath the stars.'

'Love?' Gwen put her hands over her ears and the curtain dropped.

'Lunch! I mean we could make lunch...' Vicente sounded desperate. 'We could have lunch in a nice pub by the beach.'

Gwen opened the curtain again and peered through. 'I'm sorry... I don't think so. I'm not really sociable.'

'Maybe we could bring one of the other tenants, to make you feel safer, then when you trust me more...'

'We could take Mary?'

'We could.' Vicente was visibly disappointed. 'As long as I can be with you, Gwen, I will do anything.'

'I'll think about it.' Gwen shrugged, closing the window firmly, letting the drape fall from her fingers. She moved back to her position and began 'Nymphs and Shepherds' again, but she couldn't concentrate beyond the opening lines. The thought of Vicente and his motorhome, Venus, had made her feel unsettled. She didn't want to stay indoors for ever, but she didn't want to go out, and she didn't really want to go out with Vicente. It was the story of her life: she was lonely, but the attentions of her infatu-ated landlord left her feeling cold and just a little guilty. But what other choices did she have? Gwen wondered what to do, then inspiration came to her. She would go downstairs and talk it over with Mary.

Gwen padded down the flight of stairs to the basement flat and rapped on the door marked 104A. She waited and knocked again, but there was no reply. It was well past six, and there were no cooking smells, no sound of Mary moving around inside; there was no television blaring, no Dubliners singing 'Seven Drunken Nights'.

'Mary?' Gwen heard the note of anxiety in her voice. 'Mary? It's Gwen.' She rapped again, this time loudly. 'Mary, can you please open the door?'

Gwen wondered if Vicente was outside, if he hadn't driven Venus away yet he might have a key for Mary's flat. Gwen knocked again, wondering if Mary had fallen, or if she'd fainted, or what if she'd died. Suddenly, Gwen felt a panic seize her: she raised her voice. 'Mary, are you in there? Can you hear me? Mary? Mary? Open the door.'

The door opened and Mary stood, bleary-eyed, her face ashen. 'I'd think all the blessed saints in heaven could hear you. Whatev-er's the matter, Gwen?'

Gwen took in Mary's waxy skin, the thin coating of perspiration on her brow, her lips a strange tinge of blue, and she muttered, 'Are you all right?'

Mary shook her head. 'As the priest said to the bishop, I've not been feeling myself all day. But step in, I'll put the kettle on.' She shook her head as if to clear away the confusion. 'I must have dozed off. I haven't even made myself a spot of soup yet. Come on in, Gwen – we can make it together and you can tell me what that damned fool of a landlord's been doing again.'

'How did you know Vicente just called round? He said he wanted to show me his love machine.'

'Ah, I've heard it called some funny things in my time,' Mary mumbled. 'I could see by the look on your face he'd been round here romancing you again. I've told you – just give in to him. He's a nice enough fella and he's smitten. You could do worse. Well, don't just stand there, come in – I could use the company. I've been asleep – I've been feeling knackered all afternoon, puffed out. Let's make some soup and we can put the Dubliners on.'

5

Vivienne was curled up on the plush, pale pink sofa in her flat, holding a glass of Chianti in one hand; her mobile in the other was pressed hard against her ear.

'Are you sure there's no mistake? No one has mentioned any of this to me.'

The frown between her eyes deepened as she listened to the voice through the speaker. Then she drew a deep breath. 'Well, I'm lost for words, Olivia. After all this time...' She closed her eyes momentarily as the voice spoke again, a quick rush of communication. 'Well, shall I come down to your office in Covent Garden and we can discuss the next move?' Vivienne brought the wine glass to her lips. 'Okay, right, I'll give it some thought, take it all in. I have to admit I'm quite shocked...' She swallowed a gulp of Chianti. 'Yes, thanks, Olivia. Bless you, yes, we'll talk soon... thanks for letting me know.'

Vivienne leaned back into the cushions for support, drained her glass, then sat up frowning, thinking. She reached for the bottle and refilled her glass. Olivia Sheppard's phone call had taken her completely by surprise. At the end of next month, she would be jobless. Her contract in the soap opera was coming to an abrupt end.

Olivia had reassured her that there was other work out there she'd be able to pick up. She'd been Vivienne's agent for years; she'd placed her in the soap opera and, before that, in lots of television programmes and various other projects, stage, film, advertisements, voice-overs. But there was no mistake: the producer of *The Edge of Edgeware* had just phoned to let Olivia know that Vivienne's contract would be coming to an end on the last day of April.

What made it worse, Vivienne thought, pressing cool fingers to her temples, was the manner of her exit. The producer had told Olivia that Maggs Pryor would be leaving in a blaze of glory, literally. Vivienne laughed out loud: it was just that, laughable. Maggs was going to die in the pub fire while furtively trying to return the money her grandson, Kyle, had stolen from the till; she'd break in after hours and inadvertently knock over a candle, left in the bar after an evening session. Lennie's character, Delroy Pickett the window cleaner, would be on his way home from an illicit late-night liaison, he'd notice smoke and flames and be killed trying to save her. It was hilarious: Vivienne spluttered into her wine. They'd die in each other's arms and then they'd both leave the soap forever. She probably wouldn't see Lennie again. Vivienne sighed; that was the least of her problems. She had savings, yes, but she needed to work, not just for the money. It was her life; it was who she was. She'd be lost without it.

Vivienne drained her glass again. Her thoughts were speeding through her mind, crashing into each other. She had been lucky to work through lockdown. Now, it was springtime: other jobs would become available. The country would soon be out of lockdown restrictions; there would be new television programmes, films, lots of fresh opportunities. Vivienne leaped up from the sofa and began to pace around. Who was she kidding? She was seventy-one years old. Most roles would not be open to her.

She strode around the flat. 'Hags, bags, grannies, witches, corpses. That's it now,' she grumbled. 'Maybe the odd comedy role where I'm the butt of the jokes...' She exhaled. 'And I'll just be grateful for anything at all. Anything that gets me off the couch and onto the screen. Ahh, the couch!' She made an exaggerated cringing face, still acting, although the emotion was real enough: she had performed for almost all her life. 'Even those bad old days are over, producers inviting me to stay behind after auditions, asking me to persuade them to give me the role and then I fight them off and become angry and call them sexist pigs. What would I give now for the chance to turn someone down on the casting couch?' She laughed grimly. 'Oh, the irony.'

She sat down again, refilled her glass and realised her cheeks were wet. Then, suddenly, something snapped and she began to blubber. She was sobbing, her chest heaving with the indignity, the humiliation, the unfairness of it all. It was the end of her career and she hadn't seen it coming; she'd had no idea she'd be finished off in a fire in a pub and her career would go the same way, up in smoke. Vivienne put down her glass, rolled onto the couch, wrapped her arms around herself and cried.

* * *

The sun shone, blindingly bright, but the air was still cold. The children had returned to the streets each morning in their various uniforms, on their way back to school. Rains blew in and were whisked away again by bright sunshine as March became April. Some lockdown restrictions had been lifted tentatively, but people still trudged the streets in face masks and moved to one side to allow each other to pass. In all three flats in 104 Drayton Mews, nothing much had changed. Vivienne had been to visit the hairdresser, relieved that her blonde hair was freshly cut and coloured, although by day it was still hidden under Maggs Pryor's grey wig. Every hour she spent on set, she knew, was bringing her closer to the end of her soap career and, strangely, she relished each filming episode like a sip of sweet wine.

Gwen spent even more time with Mary who, clearly, had been under the weather, although she insisted that it was nothing to do with her vaccination. She just felt lethargic. After a week refusing to budge from the armchair in her home, Mary was feeling fit enough to trudge to Chandra's Convenience Store and buy the ingredients for another curry.

Then the end of April was here, and Vivienne arrived at the studio for her last filming session. She breezed in, looking glamorous in sunglasses and a belted coat, offering everyone a charming smile. She was determined that no one would know how difficult it would be to leave the soap that had defined her life for so many years.

Vivienne stood on set, wearing the grey wig, a headscarf and a dark coat. Several cameras followed her movements as she closed the pub door behind her with a soft clunk, the keys in her hand. She slid furtively from the shadows; everywhere around her was in darkness apart from the glimmer of a candle, left on the edge of the wooden bar. She sidled past it, her face pale and nervous. In her other hand she clutched a handful of notes, stolen from the till by her grandson. Vivienne paused, breathing deeply, her face a study of honesty, respectability: Maggs knew what she was doing was the right thing for everyone. She would replace the money, even though it would be enough to pay off the debts that Joe had accrued, a thought that troubled her every moment. Her shaking fingers fiddled with the till, then the money was safely inside.

After a short lunch break, the filming continued. Technicians rushed around, arranging equipment, setting up a green screen, then the cameras shot a close-up of Vivienne, back in her role as Maggs, accidentally knocking the candle with her elbow as she passed, not noticing as it fell into an open box of crisps. Vivienne was on camera again, performing without the benefit of the fire, which would be added later. She stood nervously at the till, replacing the money, then terrifyingly aware that she was surrounded by flames: her exit to the door was barred. Then she bravely tried to extinguish the 'blaze' with her hands, then her coat, as if the inferno was all around her. A shelf of optics fell and Vivienne was instructed that something would crash from the ceiling and catch Maggs across the brow, and she fell heavily. The cameras closed in, Vivienne immobile, her eyes closed, her expression soft and vulnerable.

Vivienne shared a quick cup of coffee with Lennie and then they were back on set. Lennie as Delroy, sauntering past the pub, whistling to himself after a liaison with a married woman, noticed the windows illuminated, then he was rushing into the pub. Delroy braved the imaginary roaring flames, shouting to alert anyone who might be close by, his face a mask of horror as he discovered the unconscious Maggs and tried to revive her, coughing as if smoke was filling his lungs. Delroy looked desperately around him, pulled his mobile phone from his pocket and was about to call the fire services. The director indicated that another beam from the ceiling would crash down, landing a glancing blow on his head. He slumped to the floor, his body falling next to Maggs where she lay.

It was past seven o'clock as Vivienne sat at a table in a little bistro not far from the TV studios, a glass of red wine in her hand. Lennie, opposite, a warm smile on his lips, lifted his own glass in salutation. 'To us, Vivi.'

'To Delroy and Maggs?'

Lennie shook his head. 'To you and me. To the end of an era. We've had good times.'

Vivienne sipped her drink and sighed. 'That's certainly true.'

Lennie leaned forward. 'Thanks for agreeing to one last dinner with me.' He gave a sad smile. 'A last supper.'

The waiter bought dishes of fish, pasta and salad. Vivienne lifted her fork, teasing a piece of penne. She didn't feel hungry. 'So, Lennie, you're off to pastures new.'

'Yes, I may be out of your hair now.' He chewed thoughtfully. 'I'm taking a week off for myself first. I might decorate my flat – you remember the one? It used to be ours...'

'It did.'

'I'll be filming up country this summer. It's a film for TV. I'm one of the major roles.'

Vivienne was genuinely pleased for him. 'You'll be wonderful. You must let me know when it's on TV. I'll be sure to watch.'

'And what about you, Vivi?'

She sipped wine. 'I'll take a break, then go back to find any work I can get. Olivia is looking for new things for me already. There should be more out there once this wretched pandemic is over.'

'You're a household name; it won't be long before the opportunities come knocking.' Lennie was halfway through his food.

Vivienne watched as he munched, seemingly oblivious to how she was feeling. He had moved on and she was still in a daze, a dreamlike state. Her mind was still on the set of *The Edge of Edgeware*, in the pub, lying on the floor surrounded by smoke as he'd cradled her in his arms and shouted for help.

'I think those were the best of times for me.' Vivienne pushed a piece of cod around on her plate.

'It was good to us, the soap.'

'It was, Lennie.'

'We met and fell in love on that set...'

'And broke up there too...' Vivienne felt sad.

Vivienne laid her hand on his, cool fingers against a large warm palm. It was pleasant. Suddenly, it dawned on her that she might not see him again for a long time. She forced a smile. 'We could text each other from time to time? Stay in touch?'

'I'd like that – but it's your call to make...'

Vivienne shook her head, realising that she would probably not contact him, that this was truly the end of the road. She had loved him and it had ended: she was too stubborn to go back. She felt her heart lurch. Hot, unwelcome tears sprang to her eyes and her only option was to flee. She pushed back her chair, lifting the woollen coat with a swirl. Her bag was in her hand as she muttered, 'I'm sorry, Lennie.' She placed several orange-coloured notes from her purse on the table and she was already on her way, out of the restaurant. 'Goodbye – and good luck...'

Then she was outside, her face wet, her chest heaving. Vivienne stifled her sobs, taking a deep breath, pulling herself upright, standing tall. She headed towards the tube, walking briskly. A new phase of her life had begun; the last one was well and truly over and she would go forward and make the best of it.

6

'What's wrong with the man? Why won't you go out with him?' Mary folded her arms across her chest and stared up at Gwen from the battered armchair in her sitting room. 'God knows, the poor fella tries hard enough.'

Gwen sipped the tea Mary had given her, thinking that she could have stood her spoon upright in it: it was almost black and ridiculously strong. Instead, she said, 'I don't fancy him.'

'Ah, he has legs and arms, and I dare say everything else is intact.' Mary grunted. 'And he's got a motorhome.'

Gwen sighed. 'I like to choose my own men for myself.'

Mary snorted. 'When did you last choose a man, Gwen?'

'I've had lots of boyfriends.' Gwen stiffened and placed the mug of strong tea at her feet. 'In my teens and twenties, Clifford Edwards and I were in love. Cliff was lovely. We'd been together for ages; we were about to get engaged.' Her eyes softened, remembering. 'Then it all went wrong, and we split up and I couldn't get over him. So, when the chance came, I left Swansea and went on to London and joined the opera here.'

'Clifford, eh?' Mary rubbed her hands together. 'You should have hung on to him. You obviously still fancy the pants off him.'

'He dumped me.' Gwen sniffed, her nose in the air, piqued. 'Or rather, Siân Roberts came along with her red hair and her wiggly bottom and convinced him that he'd be better off with her. He was weak.' Gwen folded her chin towards her neck. 'I can't abide weakness in a person like that.'

'But he broke your heart into a thousand pieces?'

'Oh, he did, Mary.' Gwen nodded. 'I never really got over Clifford.'

'These bloody men.' Mary drained her cup in one gulp. 'Jaysus, they'll be the death of us, won't they?'

'They will,' Gwen agreed, then she gave a small cough. 'Er, Mary – since we're spending time, you know, as friends...'

'It's good to have another soul to talk to...'

'I wonder if I could ask...'

'Ask away, Gwen – there's no charge for it...'

'Could I ask you, well, I'm a simple sort of woman, from South Wales originally, and strictly chapel. I was brought up to be proper, not to use profanities and...'

'Do you mean will I not swear like a trooper?' Mary nodded. 'Where I come from, blasphemy's a sign of religious fervour. My three brothers had mouths on them. My mammy was the worst of us all, God rest her, but she had every reason to cuss because my father was a useless eejit. But of course, Gwen, I'll try to hold back on the swearing and be less of a gobshite...' Her words trailed off. 'You know, I think I'll go down to the shops. Poor Vivienne's just finished working in the soap opera and she's hardly been out since. She's in her room, moping. We'll invite her down for dinner, perhaps?'

'That's a lovely idea, Mary.' Gwen sighed. 'I thought I heard her crying upstairs the day before yesterday. Funniest thing, she seems such a tough cookie, hard-boiled, but I think losing her job last month has really hit her hard. She's up there now – I heard her shower running earlier.' She shook her head. 'There's no work in the industry though, is there? I've been harbouring thoughts of singing again but you can't have a performance without an audience, and it'll take time to get theatres and opera houses back to the way they used to be.'

'Right then, that's it.' Mary eased herself upright. 'I could make a nice sag aloo tonight. I'll go and see Ravi – I need to buy some bits and bobs anyway. Then when I'm back, you can come and help me cook.'

'Oh, let's not bother cooking. Let's push the boat out – what about a fish and chip supper? We could have it round my place. I haven't entertained in years.' Gwen felt suddenly pleased with herself.

'Oh, chippers would be just the fecking ticket – I'll pop out and get them for us,' Mary retorted. 'And by the way, it's not the same dirty swear word as the English use – "fec" is an old Irish word for shovel or spade. It's not swearing at all in Dublin. But you wouldn't know that, would you, Gwen, what with you being Welsh?'

* * *

Later that afternoon, Gwen watched through the window as Mary stumbled out into the May sunshine, shuffling down the road with her shopping bags. The sunlight overhead was a soft shade of lemon and Gwen recalled a time when Clifford had taken her round to his house and his mother had served up her favourite lemon drizzle cake. He had held her hand in his all afternoon and she'd believed they'd be together for ever. She wandered to the front door and gazed into the road. She closed her eyes, allowing the heat to warm her face, the yellow rays filtering through her eyelashes. Summer was almost here. Gwen breathed deeply; beyond the stale London air was the whiff of new flowers and sweet green grass from a nearby park. She thought briefly about her home outside Swansea, a pretty little village not far from the coast, Llanclawdd. She hadn't been back for a long time; she had no family there now. Her parents, her older brother, her aunts and uncles and three cousins, everyone she'd known had passed away. There would be no point going back, not really. But she wondered how the old house looked, a terrace, red brick, a pretty garden, hills and valleys sweeping into the distance against an azure sky. It would probably be renovated now, with a conservatory at the back, dormer windows in the attic. Gwen thought about her old primary school, Monnow Primary, the singing competitions that were held there, how she'd be in the centre of the choir, her voice clear and resonant as a church bell. Her old head teacher had said as much; he'd written on her school report when Gwen was ten years old: 'Gwen Prichard is an awkward child with not a great deal to commend her until she steps on stage and opens her mouth. Then she sings with the voice of an angel.'

Gwen was about to close the front door when she saw a large white vehicle pull up to the kerb. The top part jutted over the cab with a yellow and green logo and from the open window, music blared. Gwen recognised it at once: it was Pavarotti's rich voice, singing 'O Sole Mio'. And, in the driver's seat, singing along, owning the sunshine and the glorious day, was Vicente de Lorenzo. He skipped from the cab, clicking the door behind him, smart in a bright green shirt and black trousers, his dark hair slicked back, brown eyes hidden behind his huge spectacles, moustache waxed. He raced towards Gwen, grabbing her lightly by the wrist and kissed her hand, flicking the door closed behind him, leading her towards her flat. He whirled her inside eagerly, closing the door, then he smiled broadly. 'I am here, beautiful Gwen.'

Gwen frowned. 'What can I do for you?'

'A cup of black coffee, two sugars, maybe a biscuit would be nice...' Vicente's smile broadened. 'We can discuss our first road trip in Venus, decide where we will go. The sun is shining, the world is ours, just you and me... and today, perhaps you will realise how much I am devoted to you, how much I love you.'

'Oh... I see.' Gwen wasn't sure how she could avoid his request; she rushed into the little kitchen and filled the kettle, rattling two mugs. She wasn't at all happy that Vicente was standing in her living room, begging for coffee and biscuits, begging her to go with him in a motorhome. Vicente, his eyes soft with love, smiling and puffing out his chest, not caring about wearing a face mask and observing social distance. She wished Mary was here, or Vivienne. Both. She wished anyone was here, but not Vicente. Something about his desperate expression, the way his eyes shone as he gazed at her, made her nervous. What made it worse was that she didn't know how to tell him she wasn't interested. She didn't want to break his heart.

Gwen found a packet of bourbon biscuits in the cupboard. Perhaps they wouldn't be to his taste and he wouldn't eat them, then he'd leave soon. She unwrapped the packet and placed five on a plate. She didn't want to eat any herself, so five was too many. She took one biscuit off the plate, another one, then another one. Two bourbons, a sweet black coffee and Vicente would be on his way.

She placed the mug of coffee carefully in the centre of the tray, next to the plate and exhaled slowly. She wouldn't have a coffee with him, or any drink at all; she didn't want to give Vicente the mistaken impression that they were sharing time, conversation, planning a future together, a trip in Venus to picnic in the sunshine. No, Gwen thought determinedly as she picked up the tray, she'd give him five minutes, two gulps of coffee, a quick munch on a bourbon biscuit and then she'd ask Vicente to leave. She'd insist on it, she thought as she gripped the tray. She moved back to the living room with the thought that, this time, she'd tell him once and for all that he was wasting his time wooing her. She'd tell him she wasn't the sociable sort.

Gwen stopped in the doorway and froze. Her eyes bulged as she took in the sight. Vicente was in front of her, down on one knee, all pale pink flesh: he was completely naked. His clothes were on the floor, neatly folded: the green shirt and black trousers on top of his shoes. He was still wearing socks; she could see a blue one that gripped his ankle and made it puffy. Gwen stared. Vicente threw out his arms. 'You see, I told you I love you. Here I am, my darling, as nature intended. I will do anything for you – I am only yours to command.'

Gwen continued to stare at him, at his smiling face, his bulging rosy cheeks, his shining glasses, his wide chest with a few sparse hairs, his rounded belly with a navel thumbprint, his hairy legs and the unmistakable pink thing dangling between them. Gwen gaped again, incredulous, then the tray fell from her hands and she shrieked, the loud piercing scream of a shocked woman with a well-developed pair of lungs.

* * *

Upstairs, wrapped in a dressing gown, a towel on her head and a glass of wine in her hand despite it not being much past three o'clock, Vivienne heard the noise: a loud shriek of horror and then a dull clatter. It was Gwen, clearly, and something dreadful had happened. Vivienne knotted the belt of her dressing gown tightly and bolted down the small flight of stairs. She pushed the door to 104B, which opened easily. Expecting to see blood, or a body, or Gwen in pain, Vivienne charged into the living room and stopped abruptly in her tracks. Gwen was on all fours, picking up bourbon biscuits from the carpet, black coffee soaking into the shagpile from an overturned mug. Vicente de Lorenzo was a few feet away, stark naked, apologising and protesting his well-meaning intentions, waving excitedly. They both froze as Vivienne faced them, hands on her hips.

Her voice was smooth, well-modulated, as if she was on stage performing in a bedroom farce. 'Do excuse me. Am I interrupting something here?'

'No, you're not interrupting anything, Vivienne.' Gwen's body jerked forward, a spasm of embarrassment. 'Mr de Lorenzo is just leaving.'

'Hmm.' Vivienne pointed at the pile of clothes at his feet. 'I think he'll need to put those on first.'

'I am so sorry...' Vicente's face was crimson, an expression of horror. 'I thought... I thought you would see me as I am, a man who loves you, who would give everything for you, who stands here humbly before you without pretence, without his ego, without his clothes... but I was wrong. I have made such a big mistake. I am so sorry... please, please forgive me, Gwen.'

He bent down, swept his clothes into his arms and rushed towards the door. Gwen and Vivienne watched in silence as his pink bottom bobbed out of the room. There was a moment's silence, an intake of breath, and then they heard the front door click open, Vicente gasping in horror in the hallway and Mary, just back from her shopping trip, cackle, 'I haven't seen a man coming at me like that in years. Well, if that hasn't just made my day.'

7

'I haven't seen anything so funny in a long time, Gwen.' Vivienne was still talking about the sight of Vicente's naked body prancing out of the living room, even though four hours had passed since the full-frontal fiasco. She and Gwen sat at Gwen's table in the ground-floor flat, empty plates, full bottles and glasses in front of them, waiting for the fish and chips to arrive. 'The way the poor little man rushed out like a scalded hen – or a plucked one. He hadn't a stitch on.'

'He shouldn't have been there in the first place,' Gwen protested. 'I didn't want him in my home. He asked for a cup of coffee and, well, I thought it was just coffee and a biscuit. Then I came out of the kitchen and he was there, kneeling down in the altogether, not a stitch on his body. I couldn't help it – the tray just slipped from my fingers.'

'Poor Vicente. He hoped you'd fall into his arms at the very sight of his naked flesh.' Vivienne's laughter tinkled. 'But I don't think he planned on showing his fishing tackle to three women in one afternoon.'

'I didn't want to see it,' Gwen insisted. 'I haven't seen one of those in years.' She sighed. 'I suppose he won't come round here for a long time now. He was mortified.'

'Perhaps it's for the best, Gwen.' Vivienne pressed her lips together.

Mary knocked at the door, rushing in and placing the wrapping paper containing fish and chips in the middle of the table. 'I'm here – with our chip supper. There was a dreadful queue,' she gasped as she plonked herself down heavily. The pungent smell of food fried in oil and saturated in vinegar rose from the damp wrapper. Mary was breathless, her face pale. Vivienne poured wine into two glasses.

'Mary, are you all right?' Gwen's face was concerned.

'Ah, I'm grand now.' She reached for a bottle of beer from the table and began to pour it into a sturdy glass. She took a deep breath. 'I'm just a bit knackered – I've been down to the shops twice today.'

'Oh?' Vivienne raised an eyebrow.

'Well, I was tired out this afternoon before I arrived at the convenience store, and when I got there, Ravi wasn't there – his wife's just had two little ones, twin girls. Ravi's auld fella was in the shop, his grandfather. Deepak, his name is, eighty-two years old, a lovely man, so nicely spoken, and he gave me a few free bits and pieces, some fresh ginger, and he told me the secret to a great curry is to add a little sugar at the end as it counteracts the acid in the tomatoes.' She sat back in her seat, panting lightly. The skin on her face was waxy, as if she'd been standing over a steaming pan in the kitchen for too long. 'Then I went back to get the chippers just now, and it was warm outside, and I had to catch my breath because I was so out of puff. I feel out of sorts a bit. It's all the walking, really took it out of me.'

'I wish I'd known,' Vivienne protested. 'I'd have popped down the chip shop myself.'

'I should have offered to go...' Gwen muttered. 'But I've been in shock all afternoon.'

Mary shook her head. 'It's no problem. But wasn't it so much fun to see Vicente all loved up and bollock-naked? Sorry, Gwen. I mean, completely in the altogether. We could all do with a laugh, couldn't we – it's been a tough few weeks for us all.'

'It certainly has.' Vivienne raised her glass. 'So – I propose a toast. To the summer. To better times, to fun times. To a wonderful warm summer full of good things.'

Gwen agreed. 'I'll drink to that. And to no naked men.'

'No naked men,' Vivienne trilled. 'Unless, of course, we want them to be naked.'

Gwen was puzzled, then she held up her glass. 'Oh, right. To naked men – but only if we want them to be naked.'

'And who wouldn't want a nice naked man?' Mary huffed, holding up her brown ale. 'To lots and lots of naked men, the more naked they are the better...' she added with a wide smile, then she collapsed forward into her food in a faint.

* * *

Two hours later, Vivienne and Gwen were huddled together on the sofa in Gwen's flat, their expressions troubled. Vivienne sighed. 'Poor Mary. They are keeping her in. I don't like hospitals, even at the best of times.'

'The ambulance staff were so wonderful, though – so helpful to Mary,' Gwen breathed. 'I don't know how they all do it, doctors and nurses, coping with all this virus as well, twelve-hour shifts and all the risks they take. It must be terrible for them – such a worry.'

'It must be,' Vivienne agreed. 'I was in a hospital drama once. Nurse Jenny Cowan, that was the character I played. I was a young ingénue who was being blinded by the gorgeousness of one of the doctors, David, he was called – he turned out to be a two-timing no-good Lothario: my heart was broken until the scene where I hit him over the head with a defibrillator.' She hugged herself inside the coat. 'It was a fun role. But those days are well and truly over – I'll only get the dying patients now, if anything at all. "With mirth and laughter let old wrinkles come," as Graziano says in *The Merchant of Venice*.'

'I hope Mary's going to be all right...' Gwen's tone was anxious.

'The nurse said over the phone that they were making her comfortable.' She glanced at the clock on the wall; the fingers showed it was half past nine. 'We'll give the hospital a call soon for an update.'

'What a day,' Gwen breathed. 'A naked man in my flat, Mary collapsing...'

'I know.' Vivienne shivered despite the warmth in the room. '"Come, madam wife, sit by my side and let the world slip. We shall ne'er be younger."'

Gwen was puzzled. 'Is that from Shakespeare?'

'Yes, it's *The Taming of the Shrew*. I've played both Kate and Bianca – at different times, of course. It means we should live in the present – it means that right now, this is as young as we're ever going to be.'

'That's a depressing thought,' Gwen murmured.

Vivienne took a breath. 'Well, we won't let it be depressing. We'll use every moment we have to be joyful. We'll make the most of every minute while we can.'

'That's very wise.' Gwen glanced at the clock again. 'Should we ring the hospital for news?'

Vivienne pulled her phone from her pocket, pressing buttons, listening for a moment, then she spoke in her clearest voice. 'Hello, this is Vivienne Goldman. I'm calling for an update on my friend,

Mary Molloy. She was brought in an ambulance a few hours ago. She fainted.'

Vivienne listened for a moment and then she met Gwen's eyes, cupping her hand over the phone. 'Apparently, she's in Primrose Ward. She's had a mild heart attack, but there's no lasting damage done. We can collect her in a couple of days, complete with her new cardiac plan.'

'Oh, that's good news,' Gwen breathed. 'It could have been so much worse.'

Vivienne nodded. 'They said we could talk to her briefly in the ward. Apparently, she's sitting up in bed. I'll put her on speaker.' A voice rattled in Vivienne's ears. 'Mary. How are you?'

Mary's voice boomed back. 'I'm bored already. But I'm not dead yet.'

'I'm glad you're not.' Gwen snuggled closer to Vivienne, listening. 'We were so worried about you, Mary.'

'Well, the doctors and nurses are all very nice and they've explained to me why I was out of puff and dizzy all the time. My ticker's all right but I'll have to take more care of it. To be honest, I ought to make the most of being waited on for a couple of days, and getting light meals served to me and having some rest. It's very strange being in hospital and not being the person in the uniform. I can't say being a patient will be easy for me – I'm not very patient at all.'

'Have you never been in hospital as a patient before, Mary?' Gwen asked loudly.

'Only once, a long time ago.' There was a pause; Mary was easing herself up in the bed. 'I remember the staff being so nice. That was why I wanted to be a nurse – it's what set me off on the training. I wanted to help people like those kind nurses helped me.'

'Were you very ill?' Gwen put her hands to her face.

'Oh, it was just one of those things, but I made a recovery, and all these years later here I am, right as ninepence.' There was the sound of Mary wriggling again. 'But I'm knackered now, so I am. These heart attacks take it right out of you.'

'We'll get off now.' Vivienne's tone was reassuring. 'We'll arrange a taxi when they let you come home – and don't worry about anything. We'll air your flat and stock up the cupboards, anything you need, just ask.'

Gwen agreed. 'Anything at all.'

'The doctor was very nice. It made me laugh when she asked me...' Mary laughed. 'She asked, was there anything that might have caused the attack, you know, tension or a sudden shock to the system, and I had to tell the truth. "Yes, doctor," I said, "I know exactly what set my heart off."'

Gwen leaned forward. 'What was it, Mary?'

Mary laughed louder. 'Seeing Vicente de Lorenzo in the altogether in the hallway, wearing only his glasses and his socks, with his little mickey dangling. I told the doctor, if that doesn't cause me to have the heart attack then I don't know what will.'

'Agreed, absolutely. You rest yourself. Goodnight, Mary,' Vivienne purred before she put the phone down.

Gwen was anxious; she murmured, her voice low. 'Do you think Mary will get better?'

Vivienne winked. 'I think our Mary's going to be all right, Gwen. I think she'll be absolutely fine.'

8

The next day, Gwen was surprised to receive a bouquet of twelve red roses and a brief note from her landlord, apologising profusely for his embarrassing mistake and begging for her forgiveness. Gwen held the roses at arm's length as if they were Vicente himself and proclaimed that she didn't want to encourage him by accepting his flowers, so Vivienne placed them in a vase in the hallway. As she put it, they would mark the place where Mary caught him fleeing from Gwen's flat. The following day, when Mary arrived back from hospital in a taxi, she burst into laughter immediately at the sight of the blooms, claiming they were exactly the same colour as Vicente's cheeks when she bumped into him. 'And,' she added with a wink, 'I don't just mean the ones on his face...'

The next few weeks were quiet. Vivienne had no work, Olivia promising her that many more opportunities would come soon; Mary was convalescing in the basement, listening to the Dubliners, and Gwen was hiding behind her curtains in fear of another visit from the amorous landlord. But the weeks passed and there was no sign of him or his motorhome.

Then the day finally arrived when lockdown restrictions were lifted further. Vivienne and Gwen had received their second vaccinations and were filled with a new optimism: a few cinemas and theatres reopened; advertisements for foreign and local travel were constantly on television; several pubs threw open their doors again. Mary celebrated by taking herself to the parade of shops at the end of the street and calling in to YoJo's, her favourite café, for breakfast, although she declined the offer of a sausage fry-up, asking instead for scrambled eggs because it would be better for her heart.

Then, with her bag containing her purse in her hand and a face mask firmly across her nose and mouth, Mary rushed into Chandra's Convenience Store. She was surprised to see that Ravi was not there; instead, a tall gentleman in his eighties with white hair, a neatly clipped snowy beard and dark-framed glasses was leaning against the counter. He wished her a good morning and she replied with, 'Hello again. So, where's Ravi today?'

The man made a gesture, his palms held upwards. 'Today I gave him the day off. He was awake all night; the babies were screaming. So, I said I'd keep shop today.'

She sanitised her hands, sending liquid shooting across the counter. 'I remember you – you're Deepak, his grandfather?'

'That's right. And you're Mary. Last time we met it was a few weeks ago and we talked about recipes.'

'Well, and here I am again. But I want to make my food as healthy as I can, Deepak. You see, I had a little heart attack.'

'Oh, I'm sorry to hear that.'

'Ah, it was only a tiny one. But I need to make a healthy curry, no sugar and fat, all the best things to keep the heart tip-top. What do you suggest?'

Deepak leaned forward. 'Home-made curries are best, but don't put in any cream. No korma for you now! And not too much oil either.'

'So, what can I put in? Fresh air?' Mary frowned.

He reached under the counter. 'Here – this jar of jalfrezi sauce is good, and it has very low calories. And next time you come in, I will bring you one of my wife's recipes for a chicken or fish curry that is the best you can cook.'

'That's so kind. Does your wife make you a curry every day?'

Deepak shook his head sadly. 'Not any more. But if you're looking for food to keep you healthy, Mary, then perhaps a spoonful of yogurt in the curry is good.'

'Sell me the low-fat yogurt then – and some okra and onions, tomatoes and, ah, I'll take on a cauliflower. That's good for the blood pressure.'

He inclined his head. 'I'm sorry to hear that you haven't been well. I hope you will soon get better. Perhaps your husband will look after you?'

'Oh, there's just me by myself at home. But I have great neighbours, more like friends. The three of us together, it's good craic.' She opened her purse and handed over a ten-pound note, then began to push her shopping into the bag. 'Well, I hope Ravi's new babies stop crying all night long. You know, Deepak – I used to be a nurse, and I know the little ones cry a lot because they're hungry and growing fast. But apparently if you can keep them awake in the day, by the night-time they'll be tired out. And, someone once told me, the sound of a heartbeat sends them off to sleep straight away.'

'A heartbeat?'

'Yes – tell Ravi to buy a CD with just that sound on it. Then they'll sleep like tops.'

Deepak nodded, his face serious. 'Thank you, Mary, I'll be sure to tell Ravi.'

'Good day to you.' Mary marched out of the shops. 'What a nice man,' she murmured to herself as she set off for home. The sun was bright, the sky cloudless, and the walk home didn't make her legs ache at all. Mary felt a lightness in her step, and the joy of it made her smile.

* * *

On the other side of London, Vivienne strolled through a tree-lined street of white Georgian houses where birds twittered from high branches, and arrived punctually at the address Olivia had given her over the phone, a small studio an hour's tube ride from home. She was smartly dressed, her hair freshly styled, her make-up perfect, her silky face mask in place. She pushed open clear glass doors and sashayed towards a desk, where a young receptionist with her hair in one long plait glanced up. 'Hello?'

'Hello. I'm Vivienne Goldman.'

Vivienne expected recognition; the usual response was for someone to greet her warmly and mention how much they enjoyed her role as Maggs in *The Edge of Edgeware*. But the receptionist met her hopeful gaze blankly. 'How can I help you, Ms Goldman?'

Vivienne pushed a practised hand through her hair. 'I'm here to make an advert – my agent, Olivia Sheppard, arranged it.'

'Oh?'

Vivienne tried harder. 'I have to be on a seat and look alluring…'

'Oh, yes, I know the one. Sit down, please.'

Vivienne sat on a hard chair in reception and watched the clock tick. It was exactly two o'clock. She took out her phone and thumbed through, but there were no messages, no missed calls. Then, at twenty-eight minutes past two, a young man in jeans and a pink shirt sauntered out and called, 'Goldman?'

Vivienne stood up, extending herself to her full height. 'Vivienne Goldman.'

'Ah, yes, this way please.' The young man had neatly cropped brown hair and an annoying way of talking to the invisible space beyond Vivienne's shoulder. 'Follow me. We're running late...' He spoke as he led her through more double doors, up some steps, along a corridor and into a large studio where blackout curtains had been drawn and spotlights were on. 'But this shouldn't take long. It's just a quick up and down and out again, if that's all right.'

Vivienne frowned. As she stood in the studio, a woman approached her, neat blonde hair framing a face that wasn't older than twenty-three. 'I'll do your make-up. It's Vivienne, isn't it?'

Then a man appeared behind the woman's shoulder. He was around the same age as the woman. He spoke rapidly. 'Vivienne. I'm Joshua. We'll be ready for you in ten minutes. Candice will show you where your clothes are and so if you can get changed as quickly as possible, that would be nice.'

Vivienne dressed quickly and then her make-up was done. She was dismayed that her costume was so unflattering: she'd expected to be lounging on a plush couch wearing silk or sensuous velvet. But the grey pleated skirt that came to her knees, a twin-set jumper and cardigan in lime green that would have been in fashion in the sixties, along with the string of fake pearls, the white wig and the heavy-framed glasses, made her look shapeless and old. Vivienne thought she looked awful. She walked sadly back to the studio and stepped straight into blinding spotlights.

'Perfect,' Joshua cried without looking at her, then he ushered her towards a camera. 'If you'd just sit down, please.'

Vivienne blinked twice, not believing what she was looking at. The set comprised a makeshift living room, carpeted stairs leading upwards, and an unpleasant chair with armrests at the base that looked exactly like one used in dental surgeries. Vivienne put her hands on her hips. 'Sit where?'

'On the chair, please.' Joshua spoke hurriedly, a tinge of annoyance in his voice. 'You just need to sit still and smile while we take the chair to the top of the stairs on the lift and then back down. You don't need to do anything else except smile a bit. Give us the impression that you're a happy old lady grateful to be enjoying a nice stairlift to your bedroom.' He offered her a brief smile. 'That shouldn't be too difficult.'

Vivienne stood still, wondering whether she should just explain to these very young people that she was an experienced, consummate professional; she'd been on the stage and on screen for most of her life; she'd just finished a lengthy run as a beloved character in a popular soap opera. But they hadn't even recognised her face; they didn't care what she had done before. Right now, she was nothing more than a feeble old lady who needed a stairlift. Vivienne considered telling them in no uncertain terms what they could do with their shoddy little advertisement before walking away with her nose in the air. But she needed the work, any work. Vivienne sighed, then she strolled over to the chair, sat comfortably, adjusted the awful glasses on her nose and offered her most professional smile as the camera followed her gliding upstairs on the stairlift.

* * *

Gwen heard the noise at the front door and held her breath, listening. She wasn't sure if there had been a knock, or if she'd misheard the sound of the letter box. If someone was at the door, they would knock again. She wondered if Vicente was there? She'd allowed him to charge into her home uninvited last time and she imagined him again, sailing past her into the flat, requesting coffee and biscuits, or worse, begging her to go away with him in his motorhome. Venus was the goddess of love: even his motorhome conveyed his dogged romantic intentions.

There was no further sound so Gwen crept from her flat like a fugitive as she approached the front door. Sonia, the young postal worker, had called on her rounds and there were several letters dropped on the carpet. Gwen picked them up; one was to Mary from the NHS, probably a reminder that her second vaccination was due. One was a flyer, promoting a discount on a restaurant that was now open again. The third was a neat handwritten letter, Gwen's name written in beautiful calligraphy on the envelope. She placed the other letters on the shelf and took her own envelope back to her room, opening it carefully.

Inside was a folded letter, dated two days ago. Gwen read the first words, *My dearest Gwen*, and she read them again. She had no idea who it was from. She turned the page over and her eyes searched for the signature at the bottom. *Your adoring Vicente.* Gwen stared, the words blurring. She was puzzled: why was he writing to her? What did he want? She'd had chocolates, flowers, declarations of love from the doorstep, but she'd never had letters from him before.

She scanned the contents quickly and held her breath, suddenly concerned. Vicente wrote that he had been very ill and he was now recovering. He had caught coronavirus and had been extremely unwell; according to his letter, he still could not breathe easily, and he had been afraid for his life. Furthermore, he'd had time to reflect. What he had done, visiting her flat, declaring his love and devotion for her, behaving in a disrespectful way, had been completely due to his spontaneous passion, his impulsive ardour, his love, but now he was full of regrets. He was, the letter said, alone in his huge house. He could barely climb the stairs; he became tired just making himself a cup of tea. He was deeply sorry, but the doctor had told him that it would be weeks, months even, before his strength and good health returned. And of course, he insisted, he was missing Gwen dreadfully; she was in his thoughts day and night, but it would be a long time before they could meet again, before they could go on the romantic journey in Venus that his heart desired more than anything in the world, when he'd sing with her and declare his love beneath the stars.

Gwen was sorry that he was ill, but she was secretly relieved that he wouldn't visit her for a while. She held the letter close to her face while reading his closing words; it smelled of perfume, pansies, violets.

You are forever in my thoughts, my darling. If I can do anything for you from my sick bed, you just have to say the word. And I would be so grateful if you could find the time to write to me while I lie here, alone and miserable...

Gwen shook her head. She didn't really want to write to him. She didn't want to offer him any encouragement whatsoever; the vision of him naked in her living room was still imprinted on her imagination. Perhaps she would send a nice get-well card from herself, Mary and Vivienne, signed 'from your three tenants'. That way Gwen would stay at a safe distance from him; she didn't want to be a recipient of his love or his anything else for that matter.

Gwen held the scented letter between her thumb and finger. She heard the front door click again and breathed out. It was probably Mary back from the shops or Vivienne returning from her work; the anxiety that it could be Vicente at the door had disappeared completely. But one thing was sure, Gwen thought, relieved: however unfortunate it was that Vicente had been so unwell, at least now she felt safe in the knowledge that he wouldn't be calling on her to show her his private parts for a very long time.

9

Two days later, a gloriously warm Sunday towards the end of May, the three residents of 104 Drayton Mews sat in the sunshine on a blanket in the local park sharing a picnic. Vivienne was talking animatedly, holding forth to Gwen and Mary about the advertisement she'd made for stairlifts.

'And if you see it on TV, which undoubtedly the whole world will, I'm afraid, then no one will recognise me. I was a staid white-haired old lady in milk-bottle glasses gliding up and down the stairs with a stupid grin on my face, as if being on a stairlift was the biggest thrill of my life.'

Mary reached for the crisps. 'Well, there's no respect for the old. Wait until you're eighty – there will be nothing left for you but the graveyard...' She shovelled a handful of salt and vinegar crisps into her mouth and began munching.

'Mary...' Gwen seemed anxious. 'You have a heart condition – do you think you ought to eat crisps? All that fat and those empty calories?'

'Ah, it's no feck—' Mary paused, spluttering crumbs of crisps everywhere. 'Sorry, Gwen – you have a point.' She put the crisp packet down and reached for a sandwich. 'Egg rolls, a bit of salad cream. That'll be grand.'

'And what's worse...' Vivienne was still upset. She hadn't eaten a morsel; she was still thinking about the humiliation of the advert. 'I have some new work I've just picked up for next week, voicing a role in a children's cartoon, *Terrible Tales of the Animal Kingdom*. At least I don't have to dress up, but oh, it's just so awful. Do I get the role of the fluffy bunny rabbit? The cute squirrel? Even the strong powerful jaguar. Oh no, not me, not any more.'

'Who are you playing?' Gwen asked, pouring juice into cups from a flask.

'A warthog.'

Mary sprayed egg sandwich from her mouth. 'That's terrible...'

Gwen sipped her juice and looked around. The park was an open green space, dappled sunlight below leafy trees, a small pond filled with gliding ducks chasing each other's tails. Children were enjoying ball games; two youngsters had just whizzed past on roller skates. In the distance, the Sunday joggers were out in full force. She sighed. 'But this is beautiful – to be able to be out again in the fresh air and meet people and not have to worry...'

'We're not back to normal yet,' Mary warned. 'Normal will be after this Tuesday – I'm having the second jab. Then I can do just as I like – throw the mask away... burn it, run naked down the streets.'

'I think we should still be cautious.' Vivienne frowned, reaching for a green olive, holding it between thumb and finger and examining it carefully. 'Who knows what will happen next? People rushing off on foreign holidays...'

'Spain would be nice,' Gwen mused. 'I love everything about Spain. I've been there twice, to Barcelona. They have some wonderful singers. Montserrat Caballé was Spanish. I modelled myself on her. And I love Placido Domingo.'

'Oh, it'd be Julio Iglesias for me.' Mary reached for a cupcake and devoured it in two mouthfuls. 'Lovely set of buns that fella had on him.'

'I always saw myself starring alongside Antonio Banderas. He's Spanish...' Vivienne shook her head. 'But older men still get the good roles, appearing with women co-stars half their age.' She glanced at the olive again. 'It would be so nice to go somewhere, you know, for a break.'

'I deserve a break after the heart attack – the doctor said it would be good for me,' Mary grunted. 'With caution, though, she said – I think she was worried I'd go off on a bender and have a wild old time...'

Gwen was thoughtful. 'The weather is so lovely – perhaps we could go somewhere local. Wales isn't all that far. I haven't been back to Llanclawdd in so many years. I'm sure it will have changed beyond all recognition.'

'I haven't been back to Ireland for sixty years.' Mary reached for another sandwich.

Vivienne was astonished. 'Sixty years? Surely you went home to visit your parents, Mary?'

'No, I settled here, took up nursing, and that was it.' She shook her head. 'Home was a long way away.'

'What happened?' Gwen's eyes were wide. 'Didn't you miss your family?'

'We had a big falling out... I couldn't go back, not in those days.' Mary closed her eyes for a moment. 'It's water under the bridge now.'

'I'd like to visit somewhere I've never been before – somewhere peaceful.' Vivienne's face took on a dreamy expression. 'I'm a city girl, living and working from London. I'd like to explore Cornwall or Dorset, see some of the beautiful coastlines.'

Mary shook her head. 'I heard on the news that everywhere was booked to the hilt. Everywhere. You can't get a room in a B&B for love nor money.'

'So, I'm stuck in London, playing old biddies on stairlifts and fat warthogs?' Vivienne shrugged. 'I need a break more than ever.'

They were silent for a moment, then Gwen piped up. 'The sunrise over Stonehenge.'

'The what?' Mary picked up a slice of fruit cake and took a bite.

'That's what I've always wanted to see, the sun rising between the big stones, like you see on all the photos. You know, the way the bright rays peep through the gaps between the stones and blind you. I'd love to see that.' Gwen closed her eyes. 'While listening to *Turandot*.'

'For me, a real break is feeling the ice-cold bubbling rush of surf over my feet, the grainy sand between my toes, the heat of the sun on my back as I lie on a secluded beach.' Vivienne nibbled the olive tentatively. 'That and a glass of good champagne.'

Mary scratched her head. 'I'd be happy just to sit somewhere quiet, outside a nice pub with a pint of beer, looking at the moorlands and the open sky – you know that big sky when it's everywhere overhead, like a big canopy on a pram and you're the babby inside, looking up.'

'Yes, I could so use a holiday.' Vivienne's hand moved over the olives, considering selecting a second one, then she decided against it. 'Shakespeare says it exactly in *The Winter's Tale* – "To unpathed waters, undreamed shores." Still, we have the sunshine here and we have the rest of the summer to look forward to. This picnic is lovely.'

'It's grand,' Mary agreed. 'So, today's Sunday – how about meeting up this Thursday?'

'It's my turn – I'll order in some nibbles and get a nice bottle of wine or two,' Vivienne enthused. 'I do enjoy our evenings together.'

'Don't you like cooking, Vivienne?' Mary asked, pulling a piece of ham from a roll and pushing it into her mouth.

'Oh, when I was living with Lennie, my last partner, we used to entertain all the time. He was a superb cook. He made the most wonderful dishes, spicy, creamy, all too fattening. Nowadays, though, I just pop into a shop and buy canapés and wine. I don't really entertain enough – and it will be so nice to have you two round.' She was thoughtful, then her face brightened. 'But it needn't be. I ought to make more effort. I should try something new... something retro and delicious – a nice coq au vin, perhaps.'

Mary began to snigger, thinking of something rude to say about coq au vin, then she noticed Gwen, sitting silently, staring into her cup of juice. 'Gwen?' She tapped her hand. 'Gwen? Look at the state of you. You're daydreaming.'

Gwen pulled herself from her thoughts and blinked. 'Sorry?'

'You were away with the fairies.' Mary patted her arm.

'Oh, sorry, I was thinking...' Gwen forced a smile. 'Yes, an evening around Vivienne's will be really nice on Friday.'

'Thursday,' Mary corrected her.

'Oh, of course, Thursday, silly me.' Gwen sat up straight. 'Well, that was delicious. Lunch in the park, after all this time. What a joy it is to be out in the open again. But I think we should be getting back now. I have things to do. Plans to make.'

'Plans?' Vivienne stared. 'Are we keeping you from something, Gwen?'

'Oh, no, no, only...' Gwen protested. 'Just a book I was reading... that I wanted to finish.'

Mary cackled. 'I expect she's got Vicente the randy landlord in the ground-floor flat revving up, with his trousers round his ankles waiting for her in the bedroom...'

'Never you mind what my plans are, Mary,' Gwen retorted, too quickly.

'I think poor Vicente's laid up in his own bed, still convalescing.' Vivienne began to pack the picnic away. 'But Gwen's right – we need to get back. I ought to spend some time practising my reading for *Terrible Tales of the Animal Kingdom*. After all, I have to get Wanda Warthog absolutely word-perfect for tomorrow.'

* * *

It took Gwen two days to summon up the courage to telephone Vicente. She stood in the living room of her flat on Tuesday morning, the phone to her ear. She had rehearsed what she wanted to say. She'd keep her conversation as polite as possible.

'I hope you're feeling a bit better, Vicente... I'd like to come round to see you on Thursday afternoon. I have something to discuss... No, I'm not giving my notice to leave, not at all... No, not a coffee, thank you, I won't come inside the house, not with you having been so ill... Right, so, I'll see you at two thirty on Thursday. That's lovely. Thank you.'

When she put the phone back in her handbag, she wondered if she had done the wrong thing. Vicente wasn't a bad man, in fact he was delightful, devoted and kind. It was just a shame that she didn't share his amorous feelings. He had only ever sought to please her, and he had been so ill; he was still obviously weak. In the letter he had written that it took him a long time to walk to the top of the stairs, so he wouldn't try to engage in any vigorous activities that involved him taking his trousers down. He'd made it clear that he had made a mistake: it had been a desperate act of passion, and Gwen felt sorry for him. Besides, she could say what she was going to say to him from the doorstep.

Gwen imagined herself as Florence Nightingale. She would tend the sick, soothe his turbulent soul, albeit from the doorstep. The poor man was suffering. She needed to build up her own confidence socially and this was her chance: besides, she had an ulterior motive which made her heart knock with excitement. And if she could do it, if she could pull it off, what an incredible triumph that would be.

Gwen sat on her sofa and made a plan. She would take Vicente a token, a card perhaps, a bunch of flowers or a gift that would cheer him up. He was stuck inside his home all day long. Perhaps he'd like a cake, something with fancy icing. Gwen frowned: she didn't want to mislead Vicente. He couldn't perceive her actions as being in any way romantic or flirtatious. She'd settle for giving him a simple card and a cheery houseplant in a pot. And she'd work out what to say in advance, so that he was under no illusion about the fact that she didn't see him as a potential boyfriend; he'd never be anything other than the landlord of 104 Drayton Mews.

But no matter what, she was determined to visit him, to carry out her plan. If she could only manage to achieve her aim, it would be an incredible boost to her self-esteem. She'd have done it alone, and she'd be so proud of herself.

Gwen felt her skin tingle with excitement. For the first time in too long, she was going to do something big, something risky; it was something unlike anything she'd ever done before. Her head swam with images of what she'd do and she closed her eyes and smiled in anticipation of the thrill of it all.

10

The address on Vicente's letter told her he lived at 7 St Anne's Drive. Gwen was standing outside the house at 2:28 on Thursday, holding a potted anthurium in her hands. She stared at the building, an end house three storeys high, the ground-floor exterior in red brick, the two floors above painted white. There was a shiny new blue door, and large bay windows looking out onto the tiny front lawn. A blue car was parked in the small drive and next to it was Venus, the motorhome. To the right, a box hedge separated the house from neighbours. Gwen wondered what it must be like to live alone in such a big house, and to be ill at the same time. She approached the door and rapped the knocker twice. She waited for almost a minute, then the door was opened and Vicente stood in front of her, shrunken and pale inside a grey T-shirt and blue jogging bottoms. His feet were bare and his eyes gleamed, huge behind his spectacles. His moustache drooped as he breathed heavily. 'Gwen. How kind of you to come. Please...' He stood back and took a breath. 'Come in.'

She stuck to her resolve. 'I won't, Vicente. Not with you having been so ill.'

His expression was sad, doleful. 'I cannot apologise enough about what happened at your flat. How could I have been so foolish? I sought only to express my devotion.'

Gwen nodded once. 'I understand. Well, no harm was done, I suppose.'

There was a pause and then Gwen thrust out the plant, her arm straight. Vicente took it, examining the green and red leaves as if it was priceless. 'Thank you – I am deeply grateful.'

'I'm sorry you've been unwell.'

Vicente took another deep breath. 'It has been worse than you can imagine. I am tired all the time, no energy, no appetite.' His eyes shone. 'But it is good to see you, Gwen.'

'I wanted to ask you...'

'Ask anything. I am not just your landlord. I am your friend. I could be so much more, once I am recovered...'

'I'd like to be friends, Vincente, but that's all, please.' Gwen was insistent. 'And that means friends with all three of us, not just me. Mary and Vivienne too.'

He stared at her, then nodded, his face sad. 'Of course. As you wish.'

'The thing is, I wanted to say, since you're not using your motorhome, Venus...'

'Oh, I am far too ill to drive, Gwen. I was hoping this summer we could visit places together, go for lunch, sit beneath the stars – I hoped for so much.'

'Could I hire it from you?'

Vicente shook his head. 'I don't understand. Hire Venus? How?'

'You wouldn't be using the motorhome. And you did say you'd put me on your insurance.'

'Yes...'

'So, do you think I could pay you to borrow it, so that I can take a short holiday?'

'Oh?' Vicente's eyes were moist behind his glasses. 'You have found another man?'

'No, not at all.' Gwen felt suddenly calm and resolute. 'I want to go on holiday with Vivienne and Mary. We all need a break. If I could borrow your motorhome for a week or more, maybe ten days, we could get away...'

'Ah, I see.' Vicente was suddenly smiling. 'Of course – Venus is yours, take her anywhere you wish...'

'I'd pay you, of course.'

'No, no, I won't take money from you, Gwen. It would be a plea-sure to know that you were sitting in the driver's seat where I have sat, sleeping in the bed where I would sleep... It is my way of saying sorry for embarrassing you. It is my gesture of everlasting love.' He paused and shifted his position, then forced a smile. 'One moment.'

He ambled slowly back into the house. Gwen waited. The street was quiet except for the tweeting of birds. Then Vicente returned and held out a key ring, a square plastic fob with a picture of the white statue of Venus de Milo, her face placid, her arms snapped off. Two long keys hung from the fob and Vicente placed them in Gwen's palm. 'Please. Take her where you wish. All I ask is that you think of me from time to time. Maybe – send me a postcard from each place you visit, so I can follow your journey, as if I was there myself.'

Gwen was stunned. 'Are you sure?'

'It would make a sick man very happy to know that you are having a wonderful time. Please – go, and enjoy yourself with your friends.'

'Thank you so much, Vicente. That's really – decent of you.'

'Not at all...' He gave a short bow, then covered his mouth with his fist and coughed, a hard hack. 'I look forward to seeing you when you return with Venus, and I will be well again. Perhaps then you and I can go for a drink together...'

Gwen steeled herself before she spoke: she would make her position clear. 'Perhaps, but only if Vivienne and Mary come too. That's the deal, Vicente. No romance. I'm just not up for it.'

He nodded, his face serious. 'I understand.' He sighed. 'I have made a mistake and it won't happen again. But... I do care for you.' His eyes were tired behind his glasses. 'So, maybe we can continue as good friends now?'

'Why not?' Gwen clutched the keys in her fist. 'After all, we share the same taste in music. Maybe all four of us can go to an opera?'

'Oh, that would be very nice,' Vicente breathed heavily.

Gwen imagined herself with Vicente, Vivienne and Mary at a performance of *La Traviata*, Vicente in a dinner jacket and his tenants in long dresses. The thought made her smile for a moment. Then she met his eyes, her hand jiggling the keys. 'I'm so grateful. And if you're sure you don't want any money?'

Vicente made the face of a tragic hero, his lips pouting. 'Go, my Gwen, enjoy your holiday in Venus. I hope she will bring you smiles and joy. And I hope your friends have a wonderful time. I only wish...' He placed a hand across his feverish brow. 'I only wish I was able to come with you. But no. Go, and have the time of your life.'

'I intend to do just that.' Gwen squeezed the fob in her palm. 'Thank you, Vicente. We'll have a lovely break, the three of us. And when we're back, we will tell you all about it.'

She made her way over to the motorhome, opening the door, clambering up into the high cab and tried the steering wheel. It had been a few years since she had driven anything, but Gwen was sure she'd soon pick it up again. Sitting in a motorhome, so high up, staring through the vast windscreen felt good. She was pleased with herself: Vivienne and Mary would be delighted, especially after their recent conversation in the park. The three of them got on so well together; Gwen valued them as more than neighbours – they were friends: they had become even closer over the last year. Now they all desperately needed a break, and Gwen had organised it herself. She placed the key in the ignition, adjusted the seat and mirrors, and wriggled, nestling comfortably in the seat, before starting the engine. She heard the engine rattle, the steering wheel vibrating in her grip, and she smiled. It felt great.

* * *

Mary waved as she left Chandra's Convenience Store. She had offered Ravi advice about his twin girls, who would sleep better with the heartbeat CD and a single drop of lavender oil in the bath, and he had chatted to her about his grandfather, Deepak, who had left Mary a recipe behind the counter for a syrupy milk powder dessert, gulab jamun, which he knew was high in calories but he hoped she'd enjoy on special occasions.

Then she was on her way home. It was a ten-minute walk but, since the mild heart attack, Mary took it slowly. In truth, she was worried about what would happen if she had another one. She leaned to one side as she carried the bag which felt quite heavy, so she moved it to the other hand. She listened carefully to her breathing; it wasn't laboured as it had been before the attack, and although she felt warm, it was not the heavy debilitating sweating she had endured when she'd been unwell, with the awful dizziness. Mary plodded on; the medication the doctor had given her was doing her good. She'd be all right.

She passed the baker's shop and the café; she could smell sizzling sausages, frying bacon. Then she walked past a red-brick building that had once been a workhouse in the nineteenth century. Mary imagined what it would have been like to work there, helping all the children in threadbare clothes, constantly hungry, their hair matted, their faces scrubbed clean. She was immediately reminded of how much she'd enjoyed her nursing days all those years ago, how pleasant it had felt to care for sick children, to see their faces light up with smiles when she arrived brandishing medication, making a face and a joke.

Then she was conscious of a vehicle behind her, the rumble of a motor slowing down, then idling. Mary clutched the handles of her bag tightly; her purse was in there containing at least twenty pounds. She'd heard of people being robbed by drivers of cars or bags being snatched by young ones passing on fast bikes. Mary increased her pace but the vehicle was still behind her, rattling away, intimidatingly close. Mary turned over her shoulder and looked up into the huge white cab. 'What do you think you're doing, pestering me?' she yelled up towards the driver. 'Why don't you just clear off, you pox bottle, and leave me in peace?'

'Mary...'

Mary was confused as she saw the passenger door being opened and a voice called her name. She was even more puzzled to see Gwen sitting in the driver's seat, waving to her. 'Mary, climb in.'

'Mother of God, Gwen, I thought you were some mad sap trying to rob me...'

Gwen rolled her eyes. 'Get in. It's great up here.'

'Up there?' Mary stared at the step up to the cab. 'Up there? You're codding me. I'll never get up there in a million...' She put her foot on the step, reached up and hauled herself and her shopping into the cab. 'Well, I'm...' She turned to Gwen. 'And where did you steal the caravan?'

'It's a motorhome, and it's ours for a week or so.' Gwen grinned. 'Put your seat belt on, Mary, we're going for a little ride. I need to practise, get the hang of driving it about a bit before we set off.' Gwen moved the gears and the motorhome set off steadily.

Mary's eyes bulged. 'So, what's the story behind all this?'

Gwen's face shone; she was so pleased with herself. She pressed a button and Pavarotti began to croon 'O Sole Mio'. 'I borrowed it, Mary. So, we'll drive round for a bit so I can get used to it, then we'll go home, sit down and decide where we're going for our holidays.'

'Holidays?' Mary rubbed her hands together. 'The three of us are off on our holidays in this thing? Does it have beds in it? What about cooking, washing, and you know – going to the jacks?'

'It's four-berth, Mary, which means it sleeps four people. It has a gas cylinder for cooking, a water tank for the shower, and there is another tank for – the chemical toilet.'

'So, four-berth – that's me, you and Vivienne – we're not taking Vicente, are we?'

'No, we're not – but it's his van and he's kindly lent it to us, so we can explore wherever we like. The whole country is our oyster.'

Mary gazed through the window. From the high vantage point of the passenger seat, she could see the shops, houses, pedestrians. Other cars were lower down and, as she gazed at their roofs below, she felt like a queen. Mary watched Gwen as she skilfully moved the motorhome through traffic and turned into Drayton Mews. She suddenly felt the excitement of an adventure rise like new breath in her lungs.

'Let's get back to the flats and tell Vivienne all about our holiday plan. She's going to be so excited when she sees this big motorhome you've got us, Gwen. And it will cheer her up no end, after a whole day of being a warthog.'

11

In the top floor apartment, the table was crammed with plates smeared with oil and balsamic vinegar; there were hunks of bread in a bowl, half-full wine bottles and glasses. Vivienne pushed everything to one side and sat, legs crossed, with a notepad in front of her, poised with a pen in one hand and a wine glass in the other.

Her tone was businesslike. 'Right, girls, so – where shall we go?'

'Oh, I'll go anywhere in that motorhome. It feels so nice to be high up there in the cab.' Mary licked her fingers. 'I can imagine us all in the countryside, by the coast, the sea, the sand. And I want to go on the moors too, all the fresh air and sheep and ponies.'

'Stonehenge, seeing the sun rise between those huge stones while music plays from the CD player in the cab.' Gwen closed her eyes dreamily. 'And Wales: oh, I'd love to go back to Wales. The coast around Rhossili Bay is stunning. I haven't been there in so many years. It would be lovely.'

Vivienne scribbled something on her notepad. 'Okay, I'm getting a provisional map together here. This is good. We'll start off in Wiltshire and stop somewhere overnight, see the Stonehenge stones at dawn, move down to Devon, Cornwall and then drive all the way up to South Wales via Somerset. I think that gives us at least ten days' worth of fun, don't you?'

'Oh, it will.' Mary's eyes were round. 'Will we be stopping in the van every night, all three of us together, sleeping? Will we be living by the side of the road, like proper Travellers? Ah, that'll be the life, the stars above our heads, the night air.'

'Not exactly, Mary – I found this in the glove compartment.' Gwen waved a shiny-covered brochure with a cartoon picture of a caravan on the front. 'Vicente thought of everything, bless him.'

'An accommodation guide for campers. Excellent.' Vivienne raised her pen.

Mary was disappointed. 'I thought we were staying in the motorhome?'

'We are. It's a booklet of open-air places where you can stop, usually free, all over the country,' Gwen explained. 'You just ring up in advance. If it's a pub car park, sometimes they like you to buy a drink, that sort of thing. Sometimes it's a farmer's field and you buy veggies or a pot of jam.'

'Sounds idyllic.' Vivienne wrote in her notebook. 'I think we're going to have a fabulous time.'

'Right, so when do we go?' Mary asked. 'Only I'm all for packing and going right away.'

'Today's the 27th.' Vivienne scribbled more notes. 'If we have tomorrow to pack and organise everything, buy some groceries, a few provisions, then we'll be ready to go on Saturday 29th. We'll be able to go wherever we please.'

'I can't wait to get into the little kitchen in the back of the motorhome. I'll cook up a storm.' Mary rubbed her hands together. 'We can have curry twice a week, I'll make farls for breakfast, colcannon, soups, stews for any cold nights.'

'I can help,' Gwen enthused. 'I like making pasta and lots of salads.'

'And we can eat out some nights.' Vivienne's eyes gleamed. 'A nice restaurant, a village inn. Oh, we'll have such a lovely time.'

'So, it's all sorted.' Gwen smiled.

'I can't wait,' Mary agreed. 'It's a long time since I've taken myself off on a little holiday.'

'And we get on so well too,' Vivienne added. 'Yes, I think this is exactly the break we all need. I already have your mobile number, Gwen: it'll be easy to keep in touch while we're away if we get separated for any reason. Mary, you don't have a mobile phone, do you?'

'Will you both write your numbers on a scrap of paper, and I'll stick it in my handbag just in case. I can find a telephone box or just borrow some random person's phone if I get lost.'

'Okay – you don't see many phone boxes nowadays, though.' Vivienne searched in her handbag and took out a pen.

'I expect they still have a few in Llanclawdd,' Gwen mused. 'The old red ones.'

'Right.' Mary stood up. 'Well, we should clear all this mess up, Vivienne, and then I'm off downstairs to my bed. Now, if you want to practise for the motorhome trip, all friends together, we can all share the fecking washing up.'

'Mary!' Gwen gasped. 'No swearing on this trip, please. It's not nice.'

'But I've already told you, Gwen – "fec" is an old Irish word for shovel.'

* * *

The afternoon sun gleamed on the white bonnet of the motorhome, illuminating the inside of the cab, warming the fabric covers of the seats. Vivienne was sitting in one of the passenger seats further back wearing huge sunglasses, reading a magazine. Mary was perched in the seat next to the driver's seat, a sunhat over her hair, feeling as important as the queen as she surveyed the surrounding countryside from the vantage point of the M3. Gwen was driving in her distance glasses, her hair tied back, enjoying the sunshine on her face, singing 'O Sole Mio' at the top of her voice. Mary was humming along and, as Gwen finished, she and Vivienne clapped enthusiastically.

'That was so lovely, Gwen,' Vivienne purred from behind.

'Oh, it's one of my favourites to sing,' Gwen chimed. 'It's about the beauty of a sunny day, the air when it is all serene and fresh after a storm.'

'Oh, really?' Vivienne raised an eyebrow. 'I always thought "O Sole Mio" meant oh lonely me.'

'I thought it was a song about an ice cream cornet.' Mary laughed and pointed through the window. 'Look, Gwen, the little sign on the satnav thing is telling you to go left. Go left, Gwen. Go left.'

'Don't worry. It's the exit for the 303. We've passed Basingstoke; we don't go as far as Winchester, just down this slip road towards Andover.'

Gwen drove off the motorway and they were immediately in the middle of rolling countryside, surrounded by stretches of green farmland and swathes of swaying trees. As they drove along, hills undulated as far as the eye could see, the vibrant yellow of rapeseed flashing past, then the muted green of unripe corn, stacked beneath a horizon filled with ruffled white clouds.

Vivienne's voice came from behind the cab. 'Oh, this is more like it. I have missed vistas like this.'

'Look, but will you look?' Mary piped. 'There are cows in that field, and trees and, oh, the sky is so big. Look at the fluffy clouds, just like big sheep. No houses, no shops. Just God's fresh air.'

Gwen suddenly caught her breath in a loud gulp and swung the motorhome to her left, pulling into a petrol station, and immediately switched off the engine.

'Do we need to buy some fuel?' Mary called across. 'I can get out and put it in if you like.'

'No, it's just...' Gwen put her hands across her face and, when she took them away, her cheeks were covered in tears.

'Are you all right, Gwen?' Mary looked over her shoulder. 'Vivienne, she's blubbing.' She turned back, grabbing Gwen's hand. 'Have you hurt yourself? What is it?'

Gwen shook her head and took a deep shuddering breath. 'Oh, it's been so long...' She wiped her cheek with the back of her hand. 'Cooped up in the flat, stuck inside four walls, nothing but lockdown every day, lockdown this, Covid that, people in hospital, washing hands every five minutes, all the worry that if you stepped outside you could catch the virus. So depressing. And now...' She waved a hand. 'Just look – look at all the wide-open space, just for the taking. After all this time, it feels unreal – too good to be true.'

Vivienne was ever practical. 'Shall I pop in the shop and get us a coffee?'

Gwen was shaking as tears slid down her face. 'You've had it easier, Vivienne, working every day in the soap opera, mixing with people just like normal. I don't mean it was easy for you, I know it wasn't. But I've been indoors, by myself, all alone inside four walls, and now... I don't know, I'm not sure I can even walk into a shop and buy a cup of coffee any more.'

'A coffee would be just the ticket, Vivienne,' Mary yelled over her shoulder. 'I like mine sweet with lots of milk.'

Gwen took a breath and called out softly as Vivienne slid out from the side door. 'Thanks, Vivienne. I'm very grateful.'

'And a bag of crisps,' Mary shrieked, making sure she'd be heard as Vivienne strolled towards the service station, her hair and handbag swinging. 'Cheese and onion please, or the prawn.'

Gwen wiped her eyes with a scrunched tissue, pulled from her sleeve. 'I'm being silly, Mary – I'm sorry.'

'It's not at all silly,' Mary sniffed. 'It's normal. What we've all lived through has been very strange. We've had nothing like it before. People have lost lives, livelihoods, loved ones; some of us haven't had a single hug in donkey's years. Of course you feel a little bit shite, Gwen. We've all been through it.'

'But so many people have been worse off than me, by a long way.' Gwen dabbed her face. 'I've just been, well, a bit lonely.'

Mary wrapped an arm around her, giving her small pats with her palm. 'Sure, and we've all felt lonely. I'm just grateful that I've got no one to miss.' Mary thought about her words for a moment. 'And now, this is the first step back to normal times, Gwen. It might not be quick and it might not be easy, but we're lucky – here we are in the beautiful open countryside, and we're off on a little jaunt. We'll have a lovely time.'

Gwen nodded, and smiled weakly. 'You're right, Mary. Thank you. Yes, we'll have a great time. I feel so much better now; I – I'm up for this.'

Vivienne slid back into the motorhome through the side door, passing cardboard cups of coffee to Mary and Gwen, handing over crackling packets of crisps. 'Here you are, dig in. Right, what's the plan now? We have a gas cylinder; the water tank is full; there's flushing fluid in the chemical toilet tank. We can hand-wash clothes and hang them outside to dry on the little line. Is there anything else we need?'

'No, we're all organised for now.' Gwen wrapped her fingers around the cup of coffee, enjoying the burning sensation against her fingers, the strong aroma of roasted beans. 'Well, we're booked into a little farm just outside Larkhill. I thought we'd stop, share some supper and have an early night.'

'You must be tired after the driving, Gwen,' Vivienne agreed.

'So then tomorrow we're up with the lark and off to watch the sun rising,' Mary added.

'I'm so looking forward to that,' Gwen exhaled. 'There's no admission into Stonehenge until nine thirty, but I thought we could get there at dawn, have breakfast, then after we've visited the stones properly, we can drive down to Dorset. We can stop at a nice beach. It's on the map we sketched out, Vivienne.'

'Chesil Beach.' Vivienne already had the notebook open in her hand. 'I wrote it down. Tomorrow, we'll do sunny Dorset.'

'I've never been to Dorset.' Mary closed her eyes. 'It sounds lovely, all pirates and coves and beautiful beaches and gorgeous country pubs.' She smiled. 'I can't wait.'

By 5.30, they were parked in a field in Marston Farm, outside Larkhill. The farmer, a well-spoken woman in a wax coat and green wellingtons, met them outside the enormous white house and told them to drive round the back until they reached the field with the open gate and then they could park wherever they liked. They were the only vehicle in the field, so Gwen parked just inside, facing the exit. Vivienne immediately set to making supper, which involved opening a bottle of red wine and unwrapping some food she'd bought from a delicatessen and placed in the small fridge. Mary was sitting with Gwen at the little plastic table out on the grass. By the time Vivienne joined them, she had already started on a mini quiche, a bread roll in her other hand.

'Well. This is the life.' She munched happily. 'I suppose we'd better sort out sleeping arrangements. It's a four-berth but I can't work out where the four beds are.'

'I suggest two of us share the bed down here and one of us

sleeps above the cab.' Vivienne pointed at the motorhome, towards the narrow space over the driver's seat.

Mary was incredulous. 'Up those steps, in that little space? I thought that was for the luggage...'

'There's a bed up there,' Gwen explained. 'Well, I don't think I'd feel safe so high up. I'd better sleep twos-up with someone else down here.'

'I'll volunteer for the bed in the cab, shall I?' Vivienne offered.

Gwen nodded. 'I think that might be best.' She glanced at Mary anxiously. 'I haven't slept next to anyone else in a very long time.'

'I don't mind.' Mary shrugged. 'When I was a young one, we all slept in one bed, we girls – and the boys had a bed between them in the next room. I'd have my sister, Kathleen, to the one side and Bridget to the other. Kathleen snored like a piglet and Bridget had sharp elbows. But I didn't care, I was warm and dry. I'd sleep like a babby.'

'I don't mind where I sleep or who I sleep with.' Vivienne thought about her words and gave a soft laugh. 'That's often been said of actresses, but it's so untrue.'

Gwen was thoughtful. 'You've been married, haven't you, Vivienne?'

'Twice.' Vivienne hadn't started on her food but her wine glass was almost empty. 'Both total failures, except that when I was with Daniel, I had a son, Dominic. He's in his late thirties and married with children.'

'Where is he now?' Mary asked.

'He's stationed in Germany with the RAF.'

'Don't you ever get lonely, Vivienne?' Gwen sipped red wine. 'Especially after so many men – I mean, you've been used to lots of company, well, what I mean is...'

Vivienne smiled. 'I broke up with my last partner, Lennie, a couple of years ago. He was really my true soulmate.' She nodded once. 'I loved that man.'

'Then why the hell did you let him go?' Mary's voice rose.

'Foolishness, pressure of work, arguments, stubbornness... life.' Vivienne's tone was philosophical as she emptied her glass.

Gwen did the same. 'The thing I think I regret most is not having children. It must be very comforting, to have someone who is your own flesh and blood, who you love unconditionally. Nothing can separate you from your own children.'

Vivienne agreed. 'Dom's always on the other end of the phone, ready for a chat whenever he can, but I do miss him and my grandchildren, of course. It's always wonderful when we catch up. And Lennie has a daughter, Lucia, who I'm very close to. She's like one of my own. We shop together, meet for coffee all the time; she's lovely.'

'I think being a parent's overrated,' Mary grunted, finishing the wine in her glass. 'But then, what you've never had you never miss. All that yelling and changing nappies and then they grow up and there's the backchat and the swearing, and all the worry about them staying out all night and will the police call round, will they get in the family way? No, it wasn't for me, having kids and bringing them up.' Mary refilled her glass. 'Well, I'll just drink this last glass of the plonk and then I'll turn in for the night. If we're after getting up at half four tomorrow, I think we'd better get our heads down.'

Mary inverted the glass, swallowing most of the wine in two gulps, then she wiped her mouth on her hand and disappeared back into the motorhome at speed. Gwen met Vivienne's eyes. 'She has a point, I suppose. Let's pack all this up, shall we, and have an early night? I'm so looking forward to seeing the sun rise over Stonehenge tomorrow.'

12

Vivienne opened her eyes to the sound of drumming on the roof. She rolled over under the warm duvet, tucking in her feet, which had stuck out and become icy cold. The rain pounded on metal above her and, as she twisted round to find her phone, she almost banged her head. It was 4.42. Below, at the other end of the motorhome, a sound like a buzz-saw came from the double bed, the rhythmic sound of someone in deep sleep. Vivienne sighed softly.

Gwen's voice came from the darkness. 'Are you awake, Vivienne?'

'I am. Just listen to that rain.'

Gwen sounded sad. 'So much for seeing the sun rise over the stones.'

Vivienne heard the disappointment in her voice. 'We should go anyway. It's a historic monument. And all those druids must have danced around the stones in the rain all those years ago, so why don't we do the same?'

'It won't be open...'

'No, but you can access it from Willoughby Road, apparently, and go down a little path signed no access – that's just for cars. Even if there's no sunrise, we'll have full view of the monuments and it will be atmospheric in the rain.'

Gwen sounded more cheerful. 'Right then. That would be lovely.' She was quiet for a moment, then she murmured, 'I've hardly slept.'

The sound of the buzz-saw rattled: Mary was clearly still sound asleep.

'You wake her gently, Gwen.' Vivienne slid her feet from the warm duvet reluctantly, reaching for her clothes. 'The sun is up just after five – we should get going.'

'Sun?' Gwen smiled, but she was already in motion in the darkness, searching for her underwear. 'I'm so glad we're doing this. Thanks, Vivienne.'

Fifteen minutes later, the three women had parked the motorhome safely and were trudging along a gravel path, through a wooden gate, towards the stones. The rain thudded on their hoods and ran down their faces onto their coats. Gwen shone a torch on the path ahead and Mary plodded behind, muttering about Holy Mary and the amount of rain, pausing frequently to rest, to complain about her aching feet and to catch her breath.

In front of them, in the hazy darkness, they could see the shape of stones hunched like crowding giants in a field. Their feet crunched on gravel as they approached the looming circle of Stonehenge. They stopped, silently, taking in the mist of grey rain, the rising hulks, thick slabs shaped like enormous uneven teeth.

Gwen spoke softly. 'They've been here a long time, much, much longer than we have, and it's like they know it.'

'There's something about being so solid and sturdy and dependable,' Vivienne mused. 'You know, our lives change all the time and yet these stones are constant, everything stays the same.'

'It's a very odd feeling, being here,' Mary muttered. 'Will you feel the vibrations all around us. The air is just fizzing with it all.

Even in the rain, you can sense the magic, the mystery, the sense of being with the druids all those years ago.'

Vivienne frowned. 'I can feel the cold and the damp, but not much else.'

'Oh, I know what Mary means,' Gwen agreed. 'I can feel it too – the sense of being connected to the past, the strangeness, it's very other-worldly, as if there's something in the history of this place that's much bigger than we are.'

'I'm in the company of witches,' Vivienne joked. 'Like the three hags on the heath in *Macbeth*, emerging from the mist and making spells.' She made her voice deep and throaty, raising her arms as one of Shakespeare's famous witches. '"When shall we three meet again? In thunder, lightning, or in rain?"'

Gwen stared at Vivienne, open-mouthed. 'Maybe we should do just that – you know, chant something. Summon up the magic of the place.'

'Ah, that's a grand idea.' Mary grabbed her arm. 'Go on, will you sing something, Gwen? Sing something we can all join in with. That would be just the ticket.'

Vivienne's eyes grew round. 'Sing? At five thirty in the morning? We'll be arrested for disturbing the peace.'

Gwen gazed upwards towards the grey sky, letting the rain soak her face. Her hood slipped back and her hair was immediately wet. She lifted her arms and belted out three words: 'Oh Happy Day.' Mary raised her arms and began to twirl, responding with 'Oh Happy Day,' her thin cheese-grater voice bursting with enthusiasm. Vivienne joined in, clasping Gwen's hand, threading her fingers through Mary's and they formed a circle, howling out the song joyously, their faces upturned and shining in the rain. The three women leaped and danced and sang, the stones just beyond looming in the mist tall and still, as if listening, as they celebrated the fact that, at daybreak, at a historical site in the middle of Wiltshire, they could stand in the pounding rain and sing their hearts out without a care in the world.

An hour later, they were back in the motorhome. Vivienne was in the shower and Gwen was changing her clothes. Mary, her feet bare, was making toasted sandwiches under the grill, pouring coffee from a metal pot. Gwen took a mug gratefully and sipped the hot liquid.

Mary handed her a sandwich on a plate, gooey cheese oozing from well-toasted white bread. 'There you are, Gwen. The Welsh rarebit for you.'

Gwen closed her eyes and inhaled the aroma of melted cheese. 'What I'm so proud of, Mary, is that I enjoyed this morning so much. You know, normally I'd have been disappointed – there was no sunrise, no light glinting through the cracks in the stones. I've always been someone whose cup was half empty. But not today. No, I felt, you know, uplifted.'

'You should be proud of yourself,' Mary agreed. 'Positive mental attitude is everything in life. Look at me – I had a heart attack a few weeks ago and now I'm in the middle of God knows where in a motorhome with two other women, singing at Stonehenge at the top of my voice.'

'It is wonderful,' Gwen agreed. 'You know, when we sang and danced, I felt really happy that we were all together, enjoying ourselves. It was really special.'

'The connection between women.' Vivienne emerged from the shower, her hair dripping, a white towel around her torso. 'It shouldn't be overlooked, the power of sisterhood. We're strong by ourselves and stronger together.'

'So we are, Vivienne.' Mary thrust a plate into her hand. 'The Welsh rarebit. Get it down you.'

Vivienne frowned in the direction of her breakfast. 'Well, maybe just a bite.'

Gwen was busy munching. 'I have a real appetite this morning – as if visiting the stones has made me full of new energy.'

'So...' Vivienne accepted the mug of coffee Mary passed her. 'Do you think the weather will stay like this, all day? Just incessant cold rain?'

'I'm feeling positive – I don't care if it does.' Gwen thrust out her chin defiantly. 'I'm determined to have the holiday of my life, whatever the weather. I'm going to enjoy everything Dorset has to offer.'

'It offers great pubs, apparently.' Mary's face shone with enthusiasm. 'How about we drive to Chesil Beach, then we'll have a few hours of sleep to catch up, then we'll find a great little country hostelry and treat ourselves to an evening out. Or in. With some home-cooked food and real ale.'

'Oh, that sounds wonderful.' Gwen clapped her hands together.

'Right, we have a plan.' Vivienne sipped her coffee. 'Let's clear up breakfast and drive to Dorset. Chesil Beach, here we come.'

* * *

The satnav took them straight to a little pub overlooking the beach, called the Bay Inn. Mary was the first to roll into bed for her afternoon snooze and Gwen followed soon after, falling asleep almost as soon as her head touched the pillow. Vivienne retreated to the small space above the cabin, lying precariously on her back, attempting to read a book about a woman who lived alone on an island. Vivienne thought she knew how the character felt; Mary and Gwen were very nice, and it was lovely to see them enjoying the holiday, but for her, something was missing. It had been apparent as they'd sung and danced beneath the rain at Stonehenge: it had been spontaneous and glorious, but both Gwen and Mary had talked about vibrations and magic and mystery while Vivienne had just felt cold and a little aloof. She pondered whether that was her lot as an actor: she'd spent most of her life taking on other's characters and identities but sometimes she wondered who she really was.

She picked up her phone and thumbed a quick message to Dominic, her son in Germany, explaining that she was on holiday in a motorhome with two other women and she hoped he, Sylvie and the children were fine. She sent another message to Lucia, Lennie's daughter, promising to catch up at the end of her fortnight. She thought of Lennie, happy with his new job; his exit from the soap opera had led to new and exciting things. Vivienne couldn't help but feel sulky; although she was glad for Lennie, it was unfair that projects weren't rolling her way too. She pressed a button. She'd call Olivia, her agent. The phone rang for a while, then a businesslike voice rattled in her ear. Vivienne was ready.

'Olivia. Vivienne Goldman. I just wondered if there were any new...' Then she paused. Olivia was already talking in her usual efficient style, making suggestions, offering opinions. Vivienne nodded, as if Olivia could see her. Then she said, 'Nothing else? Are you sure?' She listened again: Olivia was insisting that more work would come in soon, but the only thing suitable at the moment was the role of an old lady who is mugged in a police drama, a non-speaking role if Vivienne didn't count the single loud scream of pain.

Vivienne gave a low laugh. 'I think I'll pass on that. I'm away now, taking a short break, but I don't think the role would do my career any good after playing Maggs... what? No, I'm not really thinking of retiring, no, nor scaling it down. I need to work.' Vivienne sighed. 'Thanks, Olivia. Yes, I look forward to hearing from you. Yes, you too, thanks, I will...'

Vivienne rolled over and picked up her book again. Gwen was making light snuffling noises; Mary's buzz-saw had started up. She began reading the next chapter: the woman on the island was welcoming sailors who had moored on her shores and she was going to meet them, wearing her most translucent dress. Vivienne wondered if that was what she should do too, in a manner of speaking: go forward, her most optimistic, her most attractive foot first, and set her sights on achieving what she wanted. The problem was, Vivienne mused as she turned over a page, she wasn't at all sure what that was.

* * *

That evening at 6.30, Mary was ready first, dressed in jeans and a sweatshirt, her hair combed neatly; she sat on the edge of the bed eating a biscuit, watching the others get ready. Gwen wore a smart jacket and a blouse over dark trousers, but Vivienne had, by her own admission, pushed the boat out. Her hair shone and she was dazzling in a cream fitted dress and heels. The three of them locked the motorhome carefully and walked the few yards to the pub. The rain had eased but the ground was wet; Vivienne stepped over the puddles gracefully and led the way to the bar.

The young man behind the bar was probably in his twenties, with a dark ponytail, a cotton face mask and a green T-shirt advertising the Bay Inn. He pointed to a table and suggested they sit down. 'I'll bring your drinks across with the menus. We're not usually very busy this early in the evening.' He offered a breezy smile. 'To be honest, it's great to be back at work again after all this time.'

'Poor little fella,' Mary muttered as she sat down. 'It's been hard for the kids, the lockdown. I'm glad it's all back to normal.'

'I'm not sure it ever will be, not completely normal.'

'I'm hungry,' Mary muttered as the young man arrived with three menus. Vivienne thanked him sweetly and he hovered next to her chair, his speech muffled through the mask.

'Er, do you mind, can I ask – you're not local, are you?'

'No, that's our motorhome parked outside. We're here for the night.' Vivienne offered him a sweet smile.

'It's just – I think I recognise you from somewhere.'

'I'm Vivienne Goldman,' she cooed, as if her name was enough. The young barman frowned, so she added. '*The Edge of Edgeware*. Maggs Pryor.'

He shook his head, as if she was speaking a foreign language. 'No, sorry, I don't watch that – but I've definitely seen you somewhere.'

'I'm an actor – I've been on plenty of things on TV.'

'I can't think what it is...' He scratched his head, his face confused. 'Never mind. I'll be over in a bit to take your orders.'

An hour later, Mary had devoured fish and chips, Gwen had polished off a plate of lasagne and Vivienne pushed away her prawn salad, half finished. Mary was staring into her beer glass. 'Oh look – a horseshoe. That means I'll get good luck.'

Gwen leaned forward. 'What are you doing, Mary?'

'Reading the beer glass. My mammy taught me how to, back in the day. Look – there's a wish, someone is thinking about me, fond thoughts.'

'It's probably us.' Gwen smiled. 'We're all having such a good time. I'll have to buy a small beer and you can read my glass for me.'

'I can do the teacups too,' Mary offered hopefully.

'Oh, that would be lovely,' Gwen breathed. 'I'd love to know my future.'

'Unless it involves more attention from our landlord,' Vivienne quipped, reaching for her second glass of wine.

'Oh, but Vicente lent us the motorhome, bless him.' Gwen was thoughtful. 'I hope he's feeling better – I promised we'd send him a postcard or two.'

Vivienne pressed her lips together. 'I can't say I really believe in fortune-telling and teacup reading, Mary. But if you want to read mine and you can see a good acting job coming up for me soon, I'll be delirious.'

'Oh, I'll do everyone's tomorrow, over breakfast.' Mary folded her arms. 'All that stuff comes natural to me. My mammy could talk to ghosts and I've seen a few in my time.' She glanced around the pub. 'In fact, there's a presence here, in this place, right now.'

Gwen's eyes widened. 'Pirates? Ghosts?'

Vivienne laughed. 'This pub could do with some presence – or at least some more customers. It's so quiet here. The food was lovely and it's a great little pub – let's hope business picks up for them as the summer comes. It's a beautiful setting, just opposite the beach.'

'It is.' Gwen finished her glass of lemonade. 'Well, shall we go back to the motorhome now or shall we order a coffee first?'

'A nightcap would be grand.' Mary rubbed her hands together. 'A small Irish whiskey for me.'

Vivienne nodded. 'Yes, a brandy would be very nice.' She waved her fingers and the young man behind the bar stopped wiping down the surface and rushed across.

'I wonder,' Vivienne asked with a smile. 'Could we have a brandy, an Irish whiskey, and a coffee, please?'

The barman took a pace back. 'Oh, yes – I've got it now.'

Vivienne frowned. 'Got what?'

'Where I've seen you before. Yes, of course I'll bring the drinks across. It was when you smiled. I know exactly where I've seen you.'

'On the TV?' Mary suggested.

The barman nodded, his face flushed with success. 'Yes, it was last night. I was watching an old film with my girlfriend and halfway through, an advert came on. I'm sure it was you. You're the old lady on the stairlift.'

13

The next day, the sky over Chesil Beach was bright blue, low-hanging clouds weaving cotton wool skeins, as Mary picked her way over the pebbles down towards the water. She could feel the sharp, hard stones beneath her trainers as she hugged her jacket around her, the wind blasting in her face, blowing back her white hair, whipping it across her cheeks. 'Holy Mary and Joseph,' she muttered, then she sniggered. 'I'm glad Gwen's not here to listen to me calling on the blessed saints, but it's cold out here.' She picked her way slowly downhill, over the shingle, her head down determinedly, murmuring, 'I should have worn a woollen hat.' Then she reached the position she had been aiming for, just feet away from the surf that rolled in, frothing and spluttering before sucking away back towards the ocean. Mary closed her eyes. 'This is grand.'

She crouched on the pebbles, breathing deeply and taking in the calm blue of the ocean. There was something about the wide expanse of water, rippled waves and the canopy sky that made her feel a part of it all, however small. She sighed. 'This is the life.'

The swelling ocean, the smell of salt water and the cold breeze seeped into her skin, and Mary smiled: the change of scenery was doing her the world of good, making her feel safe, refreshed and strong again. She hadn't been outside of London for years; London was her home now and she loved living there because it had allowed her to find a job that had become a vocation. Working in the hospital had kept her alive. It had rescued her from a certain sense of failure and loneliness that awaited her after she'd come to London and the lovely Callum Duffy had turned out to be not so lovely; he'd abandoned her, left her to fend for herself in the big city. But Mary had discovered nursing, and nursing had taken her under its wing, made her feel important, worthwhile. She could be generous and warm-hearted again; she could give something back to those who needed it. And after she'd retired, yes, she'd missed the nursing, but life had taken on a steady routine. Being sixty-five led to being seventy-five and then eighty, in a repetitive daily tread-mill, the same thing from breakfast to bedtime. It had been exactly that way each day, until the heart attack.

But the sudden fear that her health might fail was like cold water hurled in her face. Mary thought it was just like the breeze from the sea that lifted her hair and slapped her with the strands. It was a wake-up call: she needed to breathe in life like she was breathing in sharp sea air. And she was doing it now, it was making her feel happy, fulfilled. She was alive, really alive.

Voices came from behind her, lifted on the wind, and Mary waved to Vivienne and Gwen who were calling, hobbling across the pebbles. They caught up with her, crouched down and Vivienne wrapped an arm around her shoulders. 'Are you all right, Mary?'

The ocean wind lifted her hair as Mary closed her eyes and said, 'I'm grand.'

'It's only...' Gwen sounded anxious. 'I woke up and you'd gone. It's not eight o'clock yet. Vivienne was awake too and we both wondered where you were.'

'I'm here.' Mary opened her eyes. 'And it's such a lovely place.'

Vivienne agreed, shivering inside her coat. 'Bracing. But I'm making tea and muffins for breakfast. They are ready to go in the toaster.'

'Just look at the sea, the sky,' Mary murmured. 'A week ago, it was all about lockdown in London, and the social distancing, and now we're here, with all this open space everywhere.'

'It's lovely, isn't it?' Gwen whispered. 'Chesil Beach. I'm so glad we found it.'

'It's not quite St Tropez, though,' Vivienne grumbled. 'It's freezing cold and these pebbles hurt my feet.'

'I think it's better than St Tropez,' Gwen protested. 'It's so... real, isn't it? So down to earth, so natural.'

'They say that years ago there were lots of shipwrecks, right here on the beach. You can just imagine it.' Mary waved a hand. 'All the people drowning at night-time in the ice-cold water, the boat rolling on the waves, smashing against rocks, the sailors shouting out in the dark...'

Gwen's voice was low. 'I read that Chesil Beach was named Dead Man's Bay by Thomas Hardy.'

'Tom Hardy, the actor?' Vivienne's face lit up with interest.

'Thomas Hardy, the writer,' Gwen replied. 'He wrote *Tess of the d'Urbervilles*.'

'Oh.' Vivienne was puzzled. 'I think I auditioned for a role in that, a long time ago.'

Mary stood up. 'Muffins, did you say?' She stretched her arms above her head. 'Then it's time for breakfast, and Chesil Beach will still be here after we're done eating it.'

They sat around the portable plastic table outside the motorhome, plates, crumbs and uneaten muffins piled in the centre. Mary was staring into a teacup as Gwen held her breath. 'What can you see, Mary? It's bad news, isn't it? If it is, don't tell me.'

Vivienne snorted softly. 'Can you see a love-struck landlord running around with no clothes on?'

Mary's face was serious. 'I can see a woman here, and she's singing.'

'That's me,' Gwen breathed and Vivienne rolled her eyes.

'She's singing the opera and lots of people are clapping. She's very happy and, oh, oh…'

'What can you see, Mary?'

'A heart. Gwen, there's a big heart, lots of love coming your way.'

'That'll be Vicente,' Vivienne muttered drily.

'Love?' Gwen fanned herself with her hand. 'And singing. What else can you see?'

'That's all.' Mary put the cup down. 'But it's all good.'

Gwen was excitable. 'Do Vivienne's, do Vivienne's. See if there's any new acting work, or any romance.'

Vivienne shrugged. 'Work would be really good. But all you'll see in the cup is me playing old ladies. What I'd give for a tragic heroine.'

Mary was turning Vivienne's cup around and studying the contents. 'There's a woman in a robe…'

'A shroud, no doubt – another corpse?' Vivienne grunted. 'Or maybe I'm a ghost – I haven't done one of those in ages.'

'No…' Mary was serious. 'It's a good role, a big one… maybe it's a queen, no, a nun, oh, maybe a costume drama.'

'Well, that covers just about everything,' Vivienne retorted with a smile.

'And a big romance, Vivienne – someone who loves you more than words can say.'

'My son, probably.' Vivienne clasped her hands. 'Dom's coming home in September. He texted me yesterday. It'll be lovely to see him and the family.'

Mary was disappointed. 'No, no, will you just listen? This is a man, he's handsome, tall, dark, and he is surrounded by hearts.'

'Oh, they aren't going to ask me to compère one of those dating gameshows?' Vivienne laughed. 'Well, Mary, you've certainly cheered me up.'

'Me too.' Gwen's face was serious. 'Two things – love and singing. I'm so excited. When will I find them? On this holiday or back in London?'

Mary shook her head. 'The cup doesn't say. But the leaves don't lie.'

An hour later, they were packed up, sitting in the motorhome, driving along the coast road. Gwen's spirits were high – she was singing 'Chanson d'Amour' softly as Mary stared out of the window of the passenger seat, pointing at the coastline, calling out like a gleeful child. 'Look – oh, how beautiful is this coastline. Look at the sea, Gwen. Look at the sky.'

Vivienne was thumbing through phone messages. 'It's a lovely day for a bit of sunbathing. I think when we reach Lyme Regis, we should have a walk along the Cobb and then hit the beach.'

'Have you been there before?' Gwen was impressed.

'Oh, yes – I was an extra in the film of *The French Lieutenant's Woman* in 1981. I had to play one of the local villagers. It sounds romantic, but all I remember was that it was bitterly cold on set, my costume was too tight and I had to wear a shawl across my face that smelled like a dead skunk.' She pulled a face. 'But at least it was work, and I wasn't playing a hag or an ancient woman on a stairlift.'

'Look at the sea, look – oh, it's so lovely.' Mary pointed, nudging Gwen who gripped the steering wheel for stability.

'I've heard shopping is good in Lyme Regis too,' Gwen added. 'Maybe we could sunbathe, shop, sunbathe again.'

'I tend to burn in the sun – my skin's thin as cheesecloth,' Mary murmured. 'But it'd be nice to sit in the shade with an ice cream and watch the sea roll away and back in again.'

* * *

They arrived in the bustling centre of Lyme Regis around lunchtime, Gwen driving around the same route twice, peering through her driving glasses, looking for somewhere to park. Eventually, she managed to back the motorhome into a space in the corner of a car park not far from the beach, and Vivienne slipped out of the passenger seat to make sure that they'd parked safely between the white lines. Mary, meanwhile, had rushed over to the parking meter with her handbag and was hurrying back, waving a ticket.

'Holy Mother of God, four pounds for three hours' parking,' she huffed. 'Sorry, Gwen, but that was a lot more than I'd thought it would be. But at least we're near the beach and you can have a doze in the sun.'

'It's just like I remember it,' Vivienne enthused as they walked along the prom to the Cobb, an old stone pier forming a long harbour. Beyond were sandy beaches and the blue line of the ocean.

Mary pointed. 'Look, you can walk right to the end of the Cobb and look straight down into the sea. Shall we do that first?'

'Let's just sit in the sun for a bit, shall we? For an hour or so.'

'What about lunch, Vivienne?' Mary asked as she shuffled along.

Gwen noticed a cluster of little shops ahead. 'I'll pop in and get us something to take away, shall I? A coffee and a sandwich? We can eat it on the beach.'

'Great idea – I'll have anything except the tuna,' Mary replied. 'It makes your breath stink for ages after you've eaten it.'

'If you can get me a prawn salad or something...' Vivienne looked hopeful. 'If not, I'll just have a black coffee. That'll do fine.'

'Right then.' Gwen hesitated by the open door of a large shop. Pop music was blasting from the inside. 'I'll get us some lunch. Where shall I meet you?'

Vivienne pointed to a stretch of sand. 'You see the cluster of deckchairs, Gwen? Well, I'm going to put my towel down just beyond there.'

'That's lovely.' Gwen watched as Vivienne and Mary walked towards the beach, one sauntering sedately, swinging her handbag, the other bustling along next to her, chattering away. Gwen smiled, then pulled on her face mask and moved inside the shop. There was a large, well-lit display stand containing warm pies and pasties; beyond, rows of sandwiches and packaged meals filled a refrigerated cabinet. Two women, a very young one and an older one, were busy serving hot and cold drinks at a counter. Gwen gazed at the choices: she could buy a cheese and onion sandwich for Mary. There were no prawn salads, but there was a pasta and seafood salad that Vivienne might like. Gwen wondered about buying a hot pasty for herself, imagining the comforting feeling of eating it from a paper wrapping.

Then she noticed a sign pointing to the toilets and Gwen immediately felt the need to visit: she'd pop to the ladies, spend a penny, then come back and make her purchases. She'd get everyone a hot drink and ask at the counter if she could have a small empty box, so that she could carry it all away.

The ladies' loos were at the back of the shop, behind a shabby door with a silhouette of a person wearing a dress. Inside, the space was cramped; the walls were dingy, with dull white tiles above two old ceramic basins and dripping taps. Gwen rushed to the safety of one of the two cubicles with metal doors, locking it firmly behind her, placing her handbag on the stone floor. She exhaled; the cold sea breeze must have gone straight to her bladder.

Moments later, Gwen stood up inside the cubicle and adjusted her clothing, ready to return to the shop. In her mind, she was already at the sink, washing her hands. But the toilet door wouldn't budge. Gwen's fingers wriggled the lock: it was firmly closed. She looked around; there was a gap, but it would be hard to climb over the top of the cubicle. Gwen took hold of the old metal bolt and pushed it hard. She felt a fingernail break, but the bolt wouldn't move.

Gwen rattled the door, forcing it against its hinge, then she delved into her bag, found the keys to the motorhome and used one to prise the lock apart. But it was jammed tight and nothing would persuade it to move.

Gwen sat down on the toilet lid and pulled out her phone. She'd ring Vivienne – it would be embarrassing, but she'd call for help.

Gwen frowned: there was no phone signal. Then it occurred to her that the shop was a steel-framed building: she'd have no reception. Her hands flew to the lock again and she put all her strength and determination behind heaving it open, but the bolt was stuck fast. Gwen sank down onto the toilet again: she was stuck, and with no means of escape.

14

'I'm as hungry as a starved horse,' Mary announced, sitting on the towel with her bare legs stuck out in front of her, skirt bunched around her thighs. 'Where do you think Gwen's got to?'

'She's been gone a while,' Vivienne agreed, adjusting her sunglasses. 'Perhaps there's a queue.'

'Forty minutes of a fecking queue? Sorry, but it's not swearing...' Mary shook her head. 'You don't think she's got lost?'

'We're only a couple of minutes away.' Vivienne pulled out her phone. 'I'll ring her.'

Mary stared at the wide expanse of sandy beach; beyond, the waves rolled in. Her eyes followed the curve of the Cobb, the foamy splash of water bouncing off the wall.

'That's odd.' Vivienne's mouth turned down. 'It's gone straight to voicemail.'

Mary's eyes blazed. 'Oh, Holy Mother, she's had a heart attack and fallen over. Perhaps the ambulance has her now and they're whisking her off to the hospital.'

'There has to be a logical explanation...'

'Come on, Vivienne.' Mary was on her feet, the folds of her skirt tumbling around her knees as she pushed her feet into sandals. 'Let's go and find her.'

'Or I could stay here with the towels?' Vivienne suggested. 'I expect you'll bump into her just as she's coming out...'

'Yes, maybe you're right.' Mary picked up her handbag and was on her way. 'If I'm not back in forty minutes, send a search party.'

Vivienne watched Mary amble towards the parade of shops and then she leaned back on her towel, stretching her legs, closing her eyes behind the sunglasses, listening to the hypnotic whisper of the waves.

* * *

Gwen wondered what to do: surely someone else must need to use the ladies' toilets soon. She had been stuck inside for over half an hour. But the shop hadn't been busy, people wandering in and out, buying lunch to take away, just as she had wanted to do. She wondered if the facilities were mainly used by the women who worked on the counter. She thought hard: perhaps she could bash the bolt with her hairbrush and force it to open. Gwen rummaged in her bag, found her hard-handled brush with a few dark hairs wrapped around the bristles, and rapped hard on the bolt. It didn't budge; the metal was stuck fast. She whacked it again, harder, and heard something resonate as it hit the floor and rolled away beneath the door. The rounded end of the bolt, the bit she would hold to open and close it, had broken off. Now she was stuck inside the toilet without any means to unlock the door and escape.

Gwen wondered whether to shout for help. She knew her voice was strong. She might be able to yell loudly enough to alert someone, but the facilities were quite a distance from the shop. Then she heard a door open beyond the cubicle, and the shuffle of soft footsteps. Gwen listened for a moment as someone turned on a tap; she heard running water splashing into a basin. Gwen summoned all the power of her lungs and yelled, 'Help, please help. I'm imprisoned in the toilet.'

Gwen frowned anxiously as feet scampered towards the door, then it opened and closed with a bang.

'Please can you help me?' Gwen called, but the silence that followed told her that whoever had come into the toilets had gone away again.

Gwen was desolate and frustrated. In fact, she thought she might cry. Hot tears filled her eyes. She glanced up again to the space at the top of the door, the gap high up at the side leading to the next cubicle. It would be the only way out. Gwen put the lid of the toilet down and clambered on, reaching up to the space at the top. She'd never lever herself up over the top, and the gap wasn't very big – it was completely impossible. She flopped forwards and pressed her hands against the top of the door, rattling it, hoping someone might hear the noise. Then the outside door opened with a hefty bang, a pair of feet marched in and a voice called out, 'Gwen, is that you? Oh, for the love of God, you haven't got yourself stuck in the jacks?'

Gwen pressed her face against the door above the broken lock. 'Mary? Oh, thank goodness.'

'I came into the shop and you weren't there.' Mary's voice came from behind the door. 'Then I asked the young one at the counter if she'd seen you and she said no, but she'd just been in here to soap her hands and she thought she'd heard someone moaning inside the toilet. I knew it was you straight away. So – are you stuck?'

'Yes.'

'Will the lock not pull across?'

'I've broken it...'

'Then you'd better stay there, Gwen. Well, it's not as if you'll be going anywhere else. I'll be back in a minute...'

It took several minutes for anyone to return. Then Gwen heard footsteps and a deep cough that wasn't Mary's: she had no idea what was happening. She called, 'Mary? Is that you? You haven't called the fire brigade, have you?'

Mary's happy reassuring voice came floating back. 'No, but I found this very nice man called Barry and he's a builder. He was just after buying himself a pasty in the shop and I persuaded him to help, and he has his builder's bag with him, so he's going to drill through the screws from the outside and the lock should come off.'

'Oh, thank goodness.' Gwen raised her voice. 'Thank you, Barry.'

A deep voice from outside murmured, 'Hello, Gwen. I'll have you out in a jiffy. Don't you worry.'

'Oh, you're my saviour,' Gwen breathed.

Then there were more footsteps, the clack of high heels, and another voice, a woman's, came from outside the door. 'Hello? Are you in there? I've been telling the manager about these locks for a long time. They need proper replacements.'

'Who are you?' Gwen asked nervously.

'I'm Christine. I work on the counter. I'm so sorry this has happened...'

'Oh...' Gwen was relieved: she'd expected to be chastised for ruining the lock. 'I just want to get out.'

'Well, whatever you want to eat for lunch is on the house today, after all you've been through.' Christine's voice was soothing. 'And I'm so sorry about this...'

Then the door sprang open and Gwen found herself looking at a slim middle-aged man with a tool bag and a wry smile, a serious-looking woman she recognised as the older one at the counter, and Mary, smiling.

'Right, well, that's enough adventure for today. Let's go and get ourselves some free nosh. I'm starved. That is unless you want to use the loo again?'

* * *

On the beach, Mary was tucking into a sandwich. 'She was very nice, the Christine one. Very apologetic. And this free lunch you got us is just the ticket, Gwen.'

'I feel so bad.' Vivienne poked at the pasta salad with a plastic fork. 'I let Mary go back to the shop and I stayed here in the sunshine. I should have been with you, trying to help.'

'No, you were needed here to look after the towels,' Mary insisted. 'Anyway, he wasn't your type, Barry the builder. No, he was more Gwen's.'

Gwen felt her cheeks flush pink. 'I was just grateful to him, that's all.'

'Yes, but he kissed you on the cheek then he said, "Are you all right now, my darling?" I thought he was a very nice man.'

'I was just so embarrassed.' Gwen stared at the pasty on her lap, still wrapped in a paper bag. 'I felt ashamed...'

'You shouldn't worry, Gwen.' Vivienne pushed the salad away. 'The only embarrassing thing was that a man had to rescue you. If I'd have been there, I'd have just borrowed his drill and done it myself.' She cast a glance at Mary and shook her head apologetically. 'No, what I mean is, you did well to find a builder, Mary.'

'It was lucky Barry was in the shop, or I'd have had to call the firefighters...' Mary licked her fingers. 'Come on, Gwen, eat up. You need a breather after all the panic.'

Gwen shook her head. 'I'm not really hungry. Not now.'

'Right,' Vivienne said decisively. 'I know just what we all need. And I know where to get it. We'll go and buy a postcard for Vicente, then I'll treat us all. One thing I can remember about Lyme Regis is the fabulous alternative therapies that are on offer everywhere.'

'Therapies?' Gwen frowned. 'Do you mean we should all take up painting?'

Vivienne laughed, pulling out her phone, searching for a number. 'Do I look like I mean painting, Gwen? No, this is all about balancing, energising – and getting in touch with ourselves again.'

'What on earth is she on about?' Gwen asked Mary.

Mary pulled a face. 'To be absolutely honest, Gwen, I don't have the foggiest.'

But, an hour later, they were sitting on basket chairs in a small waiting room, inside a shop that looked from the outside like a hobbit's home. The sign outside said the place was called 'The Retreat'. Inside, the walls had been painted sea green, with waves in curling patterns on the walls. In front of them were three closed doors, one painted red, one yellow, one blue.

Gwen was nervous. 'So, what are we doing here, Vivienne?'

'I've booked three appointments for us, all different therapies: you can choose which one you'd like, and I'll have the one left over – I don't mind which I have.' Vivienne was pleased with herself. 'There's the oxygen facial, where they spray oxygen into your skin and that plumps it up. There is the relaxing reflexology and the aromatherapy massage.'

'What's reflexology?' Gwen asked. 'I've heard of it – don't they bend your feet about? Does it hurt?'

'Not at all.' Vivienne patted her hand reassuringly. 'It's soothing and relaxing – it's just a light pressure on your feet. It connects to different parts of your body and heals you.'

'I need to relax.' Gwen was warming to the idea. 'Can I choose that one?'

Mary folded her arms. 'I'm not having the oxygen sprayed onto my skin. What's the other one?'

'The aromatherapy Reiki massage is about soothing smells and healing. You'll love that one, Mary.'

'Ah, good. I know a bit about the aroma. I put lavender oil on my pillows to help me sleep. It's very nice. Well, you can take the skin plumping one, Vivienne. Gwen can have her feet flexed and I'll get the massage.'

Then the red door opened and a small woman in a loose brown top and colourful leggings appeared, her face serious beneath scraped-back red hair. 'Hello. Who's for the aromatherapy? This way, please.'

* * *

Mary folded her arms, her face contorted in a frown. 'You want me to take all my clothes off?'

The red-haired woman, who had introduced herself as Phoebe, stared back. 'That's what usually happens. We can't massage aromatherapy oil into your skin unless you take off your clothes.'

Mary was astonished. 'All of them?'

'You can keep your pants on.'

'Pants? Oh, you mean my knickers?' Mary was horrified. 'But I'm eighty years old. And I'll get cold.'

Phoebe tried a placatory smile. 'The couch has a heated blanket on it. And I'll cover you with more blankets. I'll just expose a small bit of skin on your back at a time, so that I can massage the oil in...'

Mary was still dubious. 'And when you rub the oil in, what then? I'll be greasy as a tick...'

'You'll relax,' Phoebe spoke calmly. 'And the Reiki will be gentle and healing.'

'What's the Reiki when it's at home?'

Phoebe was patience personified. 'It's energy healing.' She

noticed Mary's frown deepen and tried again. 'It passes through my palms and you feel better.'

'Like the blessed Jesus healed the leper in the Bible?'

'Not exactly...' Phoebe shrugged.

'And will it be good for the heart attack? I had a very mild one...'

'It'll help you relax.' Phoebe made a final effort. 'I'll leave for a moment, you get undressed and pop onto the couch, cover yourself with blankets, lie on your front.' She scrutinised Mary's untrusting expression. 'Is that all right? You'll enjoy it, I promise.'

'Oh, all right, if you're sure it won't kill me.' Mary wasn't convinced. 'And the lavender is my favourite.'

Phoebe smiled again. 'I'll see you in a few minutes.'

Mary watched her leave, closing the door behind her, and she sighed. Slowly, she took off her clothes, piling them onto a nearby chair, then heaved herself on the treatment couch, swathing herself in two blankets. 'It's like being at the doctor's... pop on the couch... take off your clothes... it won't hurt a bit... then it's agony.'

The door clicked and Mary saw Phoebe slide into the room, moving into the corner of her vision, picking up something in a bottle, and then rubbing her hands together. Some music began to play gently, the whisper of the sea, waves rushing in, then the sound of dolphins, soft whistles and clicks. Mary pressed her lips together; she started to snigger, embarrassment mixed with relief.

Then Phoebe rolled the towel away from her back and Mary squeezed her eyes shut. Her shoulders tensed, rising towards her ears, as she waited for something to happen, something that might involve pain. Then Phoebe's hands rested on her skin, firm and reassuring, and Mary's nostrils were filled with the sweet scent of orange and cinnamon. She breathed out as she felt the hands move in a circle up towards her shoulders, a light pressure becoming firmer, the round motion of massage.

A sigh slipped from Mary's lips; she couldn't help it. Her ears were full of soothing sounds of the seashore; heady scents filtered through her nostrils, the pressure of firm reassuring hands made her muscles relax. Mary smiled; she could get used to this aromatherapy. Her eyelids flickered, she exhaled softly again and then she drifted into a deep, contented sleep.

15

Vivienne, Mary and Gwen parked the motorhome in a farmer's field just outside Lyme Regis and, after a light evening meal, they went to bed early. The various therapies had left them happy and tired, and they slept deeply, blissful and without a care.

The next morning, Vivienne was awake first, snuggled under the duvet in the space over the cab, chattering excitedly into her phone, her voice full of warmth and enthusiasm. 'Well, that's great – really fabulous. Thanks, Berry. Yes, me too. Oh, I know, it's been too long. Yes, love to him too. Later – absolutely. Tons and tons of kisses!'

She slipped from her bed in her skimpy nightgown, padded across the floor and picked up the little coffee pot, filling it with ground beans, sliding it onto the stove. She unwrapped a packet of croissants with fumbling fingers, humming a happy tune as she dropped them onto a metal tray and pushed them into the oven.

Gwen sat up in bed. 'You're cheery, Vivienne.'

'I am.' Vivienne beamed. 'How did you sleep?'

'Oh, like a tot. The reflexology was just heaven.'

A sound came from the pillow next to Gwen. 'Me too. I'm knackered this morning – I can hardly open my eyes. What do they put in those oils? I could do with some every day.'

'Morning, Mary,' Vivienne trilled. 'I've got coffee on, and croissants are warming in the oven.'

Mary sat straight up. 'Oh, I can smell them. I'm starving. Well done, Vivienne.' She wriggled out of bed. 'So, it's breakfast in our pyjamas, is it? Are we letting our standards slip?'

'No, we're letting our hair down.' Gwen pulled the scrunchie from her hair and it tumbled around her shoulders. 'We're on holiday.'

They sat outside in the sunshine in pyjamas and dressing gowns, munching flaky croissants and sipping strong coffee. Gwen stretched her arms over her head luxuriously. 'So – where are we heading today? Devon, isn't it?'

'I have a surprise.' Vivienne was pleased with herself. 'I have a friend in Totnes – we've just been talking on the phone, and we're going to meet her for lunch. She's called Berry. She's a poet.'

'Berry?' Gwen raised an eyebrow. 'Like elderberry and blackberry?'

Vivienne nodded. 'Oh, she's wonderful. We knew each other years ago when I lived in Muswell Hill. We were great friends. Then she moved to Devon and – we're catching up later, after all this time. It will be lovely.'

'For lunch? That's grand.' Mary looked pleased.

'So, where am I driving today?'

'I'll put the address in the satnav.' Vivienne waved a croissant. 'It will be nice having some time in the countryside, before we go on to the coast again.'

'It will.' Gwen lifted a leg. The skin was divided with a pink and white stripe. 'I need to build my tan up slowly – I'm so pale skinned.'

Mary hoisted up her nightdress to reveal a red leg. 'I just burn to a cinder.'

'Well, you're going to love today – a bit of shopping, then lunch and Berry's organising a lovely place for us to stay tonight on the edge of Dartmoor.'

'It sounds idyllic.' Gwen made a dreamy face.

'Oh, it will be,' Vivienne agreed.

Mary folded her arms. 'Well, let's finish off this lovely breakfast and we'll be on the road.' She picked up the map with a flourish and pointed to a small town perched snugly on the River Dart: Totnes looked very inviting.

Gwen drove for an hour, then turned off the A38 and took the narrower road, a river to the right, slowing down behind a line of cars that were crawling along at 25 mph. She was glad to be driving slowly; she peered over her glasses nervously as the road widened, then curved and narrowed. On one side of the road, beyond the trees, the river snaked round bends and splashed over stones.

Mary squealed from the seat next to her. 'Oh, will you look. A waterfall. How lovely.' She was quiet for a moment, craning her neck, then she piped up again. 'An old railway line. Look at that! I wonder if it has any trains on it.'

Then the road leaned to the left; they climbed a hill and suddenly they were at traffic lights, waiting to cross a narrow stone bridge. Mary leaned out of the window and pointed as a shiny black train chugged below, steam billowing in grey clouds from a tall funnel. 'Oh, oh, look, an old-fashioned train. I don't believe it. A proper steam train with a funnel and steam. Look at it go. Oh, I wish I had one of those mobilised phones so I could take a few snaps.'

Vivienne's voice was smooth behind her. 'That's the nineteenth-century steam railway line. They do nice trips, apparently, from here to the coast and back.'

'Oh, can we go? I'd love a railway trip.'

'It would take a whole day, Mary,' Vivienne replied. 'I suppose we could. I'll ask Berry about it, if it's any good.'

'It would be lovely to go on a themed journey,' Gwen mused. 'Dressing up, having dinner.'

'Oh yes – just like the Orient Express.' Vivienne clapped her hands together. 'I was an extra in the film in 1974. I went to France and played a young woman on the train, just a tiny role really – it was wonderful. Albert Finney – he was Poirot – seemed so distinguished.' She sighed. 'Happy times.'

Gwen glanced ahead as the lights turned green. She manoeuvred the motorhome slowly across the narrow bridge behind the line of cars, turning the corner, the engine rumbling as they climbed a steep hill. Then she called over her shoulder. 'Vivienne. Here we are in Totnes now. Where do I park?'

'Berry says it can be a bit tricky...'

'Oh, no...' Gwen was already panicking. 'Where do I go?'

'Okay – just follow the road.'

Gwen squinted through her glasses and leaned forward. 'So – I'm coming off at the second exit of this road island... following the traffic... where shall I go? There's another island... oh, no.'

'What is it?' Mary stared through the huge windscreen. They were climbing slowly up a vertical hill squeezed between ancient buildings and gaudy-fronted shops. Pedestrians were on either side, bustling on pavements and stepping into the road.

'This is so steep...' Gwen murmured. 'Mary – look out for a sign for parking, will you?'

'I will.'

Mary gazed through the side window. There were several shoppers dressed in bright clothes, baggy patchwork trousers, colourful scarves. One woman had long blue dreadlocked hair to her waist. A man in pink dungarees and a cowboy hat strode past with two large wolfhounds. A man stood outside a bank, a wide-brimmed witch's hat on his head, long dark robes, waving a thurible on a long chain, the smoke of incense rising from the metal censer.

'There's a fella doing a spell,' Mary gasped. She blinked hard; a woman with her hair shaved at the sides, wearing leather trousers and a crop top, pushed a pram with two identical babies dressed as pixies, their hair in small plaits. The motorhome engine groaned as the hill became steeper. Mary noticed a woman with rainbow hair dressed in harem pants, purple and gold, and she shook her head. 'It's like Lord of the fecking Rings – sorry, Gwen – it's like Narnia.'

'It's just Totnes; it's a beautiful, unique and unforgettable little town,' Vivienne purred from the passenger seat behind. 'You're going to love it here, Mary.'

It took them a further twenty minutes to park, Gwen driving around becoming more and more anxious as the roads twisted and narrowed, Mary's gasps becoming louder as she offered a running commentary on the various sartorial styles of the shoppers. They finally found a car park just behind the main street, and Vivienne bought a ticket. 'Three hours should be enough. We have until five minutes to three. That should be fine, shouldn't it?'

Mary rubbed her hands. 'So, we're going shopping?'

'Briefly,' Vivienne murmured. 'Then we're meeting Berry and her husband for lunch.'

As they walked around the parade of shops, Mary spotted unusual items in windows and her enthusiasm became even more vocal. 'Look at the funny colours and styles of the shoes. Oh, marvellous, you can buy all the dangly crystals here... and look, you can get the old clothes from the 1900s.'

Vivienne pulled on a face mask and led them into a brightly lit shop where sitar music was playing. She tried on clothes for half an hour, eventually buying a brightly coloured long dress, a tie-dye top and a pair of white cut-off denim shorts that Gwen felt were inappropriate for a woman in her seventies, even though she was an actress. Mary rushed around the shop, pulling garments from rails, yelling, 'Oh, but will you look at this?' every few minutes, then she held up a long dress in a rainbow pattern. 'Well, what do you think?'

'You should try it on,' Vivienne suggested, and Mary spent the next five minutes in a changing room, grunting and puffing, before she emerged in the most spectacularly bright dress which fell to her ankles. 'Well – is it me?'

'It's certainly different,' Gwen muttered. The shop smelled of joss sticks, and the smoke was catching in her throat. She was ready to leave, but Mary's spree had only just begun.

'I'll take it.' Mary pushed the dress under her arms. 'And I'll have this pretty scarf, and these big dangly earrings, and maybe some of the smoky joss sticks for the motorhome.'

'Oh, no...' Gwen groaned.

'Look at this! Hairspray – baby pink, electric blue, purple haze. You spray them on your hair and it livens it up. I can imagine myself with all the bright colours.'

'Which one do you want?' Vivienne offered to help.

Mary's arms were already full of purchases. 'Oh, I'll take the lot – all three of them.'

Gwen stood by the door, breathing in fresh air. 'Can you get a card to post to Vicente too?'

'This one's perfect.' Vivienne waved a multicoloured card of a hippy man on a motorbike and the caption *Born to be Wild*. Mary hauled her choices and dumped them on the counter. She stared at a very slim woman with a heart-shaped tattoo on her cheek. 'What's that smell?'

The woman frowned. 'Pardon?'

'The perfume – it's lovely,' Mary insisted.

'Oh...' The woman thrust out a wrist loaded with leather bangles and a yin-yang tattoo for Mary to sniff. 'It's patchouli oil.'

'Then I'll take one of the patchoulis too,' Mary said, rummaging in her bag. 'I have my debit card. Will that do?'

'Yes, that's absolutely fine,' the woman replied. 'We take all cards and cash. I'm afraid we don't take the Totnes pound any more.'

'Ah, I'm surprised you don't take groats in this place – I've never seen anything like it in my life,' Mary joked. The woman took her card, her face impassive.

Gwen stood by the door, gulping in fresh air. 'Are we ready to go, Vivienne? The smell of those joss sticks is making me queasy.'

'Yes, it's lunchtime.' Vivienne emerged into the street, replacing her sunglasses from her head to her face. 'Apparently, the café is just up the road – it's called Sunshine Grains.'

The path to the café was very steep and Mary lagged behind, puffing, her bags of shopping hanging from her hands. Gwen waited and took one of her bags, then Mary bravely surged forward again. Sunshine Grains café was behind a tiny door: inside, several primitive wooden tables were set out with menus for lunch; there was a counter for serving food at the far end and a board with the specials chalked on it on the wall. As soon as Vivienne stepped into the café, a woman at the nearest table leaped up and threw out her arms. 'Vivienne, darling baby, oh, you look extraordinary.'

'Berry. My lovely. Oh, how marvellous to see you again.'

Gwen and Mary watched as Vivienne hugged a slight woman who was about the same age as her, wearing a long dress, wavy blonde hair cascading to her waist. Next to her, a man was standing, smiling. He wore a small cap on his head, white curls sticking out, snowy bristles on his face, and round glasses.

Vivienne was suddenly effusive. 'Berry, Orlando, meet my wonderful travelling companions, Mary and Gwen.'

Gwen held out a tentative hand. 'Hello.'

Mary shook Orlando's hand with a firm grip. 'So pleased to meet you.'

'Oh, you're Irish, that's so nice,' Orlando enthused.

'Is it?' Mary was puzzled.

'My grandmother was Irish,' Orlando explained, then he kissed Vivienne on both cheeks twice. 'So, Berry, darling, are we drinking wine or sparkling water?'

'It's a weekday, so water,' Berry replied smartly.

They all sat down and Orlando pulled a face. 'But we haven't seen Vivi in ages, darling. Let's push the boat out and have wine.'

'Darling, think of all the toxins – think of your immune system, Orlando.'

'But it's a special celebration, darling.'

'Ah, feck, let's have the wine,' Mary decided, picking up the menu. 'And what's to eat?'

16

Gwen gazed around the table as the others tucked into their lunch, then she frowned at the deep red soup in her bowl and the hunk of black bread on a plate. She muttered, 'Is it nice, the beetroot soup?'

Berry was attacking a similar bowl with a spoon, dunking the bread. 'Oh yes – beetroot does wonders for the blood pressure. It is full of manganese, potassium, iron, and it's great for, you know, one's performance in the bedroom.'

'It certainly is,' Orlando confirmed.

'I wouldn't know,' Gwen murmured to herself.

'It's delicious soup, so creamy,' Vivienne agreed, although her first mouthful was still in the spoon.

Gwen sipped tentatively, nibbled the heavy bread. 'I suppose it's not too bad... it just tastes a bit unusual, you know, a bit like soil.'

Mary was tucking into a plate full of broad bean dip and garlic bread. 'Well, this is very pleasant, but it's a shame they don't put meat in it. It'd be great with chunks of chicken.'

'Sunshine Grains is a vegetarian café,' Orlando explained, finishing a glass of wine. 'Did you know, coronavirus is an anagram of carnivorous. I'm just saying...'

'Meat is so terribly bad for the environment, and it increases the risk of death from heart disease, stroke or diabetes.' Berry dipped her spoon enthusiastically.

'Besides, when you can eat food as delicious as this, who needs meat?' Vivienne agreed.

'I could do with a few sausages on this plate, though,' Mary grunted. 'Still, I've spotted all the cakes they have behind the counter. I'll be starving after I've eaten this little plateful, so I'll have a chocolate brownie or two.'

Berry's eyes bulged, astonished. Vivienne patted her hand affectionately. 'It's so lovely to see you again after all this time. All I did through lockdown was work on the soap opera. It's so nice that we can leave all that awful time behind us and meet our friends again. So, Berry, where have you arranged for us to stay this evening?'

'Well, I'd have loved you to stay with us, Vivi, but my girls are down at the moment.' She sighed. 'Meadow and Ocean are both here until next week with their children, but I phoned some friends who have an organic farm just outside Bovey, and you can camp in their orchard, and they will cook dinner for you too. You'll be right on the edge of the moors and their food is second to none – you really must dine with them while you're here.'

'Do they have the organic meat?' Mary asked between mouthfuls of garlic bread. 'I mean it won't be just plants and rice and stuff, will it?'

Gwen stared despondently at her beetroot soup. 'I think I'll have a cake too, Mary. I'm starving.'

It was half past two when they said their goodbyes. Berry hugged Vivienne as if she wouldn't let go. 'We must see each other more often, darling Vivi. It's been too long.'

'It has, my sweet,' Vivienne muttered into coils of her hair.

'It was really fun meeting you, Gwen and Mary,' Orlando offered, kissing their cheeks.

Gwen pulled away quickly. 'Likewise.'

Vivienne hugged Berry again, then Orlando. 'You must both come up to London, now lockdown is all over.'

'Oh, wasn't it horrendous? I couldn't go through that again, just me and Orlando in the house...' Berry groaned. 'And when you're in Totnes again, Vivi, I must introduce you to my friend, Barnaby – he does the most wonderful colonic irritation with ground-up coffee beans, really good for constipation.'

'I wouldn't think you'd need it – all that beetroot,' Gwen muttered to herself.

Mary picked up the last morsel of Gwen's cake from a plate on the table. 'Well, we should be making tracks.'

Gwen, Mary and Vivienne left Berry and Orlando in Sunshine Grains. Orlando had just ordered a third glass of wine and Berry was chiding him that he didn't need the excessive tannin, it made him grouchy. As they wandered towards the main road that led to the car park clutching their bags, Gwen stopped. 'Oh, listen. Can you hear that?'

Mary shook her head. 'Is it all the hobbits having a conference about Gandalf?'

'I can hear music.' Vivienne pointed to the other side of the road. 'A busker, look.'

Mary and Gwen followed Vivienne's gaze. A young man in khaki clothes, his dreadlocks tied back with a bright scarf, was standing in front of a large shop window, strumming a guitar and singing, his voice reedy and high. Gwen recognised the tune as a Bob Dylan song.

'Let's go over and see.' Gwen tugged Vivienne's sleeve. 'I want to give him some money.'

'Okay – but remember we only have twenty minutes until our parking expires,' Vivienne warned.

'Ah, the motorhome's only a minute's hike away – let's go and listen to the busker,' Mary agreed.

The three women stood huddled together outside the Arc Gallery, a display of paintings behind the shining glass shopfront, as the young man strummed his way through 'Blowin' in the Wind'. He couldn't have been much older than twenty-two. Gwen admired his energy and enthusiasm: he wasn't a particularly strong singer, but he was clearly enjoying himself, his eyes tightly closed, singing from his soul. She reached into her purse and pulled out five pounds. 'Here you are – and thank you.'

The young man's eyes widened. 'A fiver – oh, cool.' He watched Gwen drop the money into his upturned bowler hat. There were a few coins in there but no other notes.

Gwen shook her head. 'You haven't made much money. There can't be more than eight pounds in here.'

'It's been a slow morning,' the young man sighed. 'I've been playing since just after ten o'clock.'

Vivienne was thoughtful. 'How much do you usually make each day?'

'It varies,' the busker replied. 'A good day, twenty-five, thirty pounds...'

'And a bad day?' Gwen asked.

'Once I made three pounds twenty pence and a packet of peanuts,' the young man chortled.

'That's terrible.' Gwen was horrified.

Vivienne suddenly straightened up, businesslike, and thrust out a hand. 'I'm Vivienne Goldman. My friends are Gwen Prichard and Mary Molloy.'

The young man was baffled. 'Pleased to meet you. I'm Wes.'

'Well, Wes – it's your lucky day...' Vivienne patted Gwen's arm. 'So, come on, what do you both know?'

Gwen was confused. 'Me?'

'Gwen's an opera singer,' Vivienne explained. 'She can do a couple of songs with you. She'll attract the crowds.'

Wes stared at Gwen. 'Opera?'

'Oh, yes – she's sung at opera houses – Swansea and London. She's very good.'

'Very, very good,' Mary added.

Wes scratched his locks. 'Do you know "Brown Eyed Girl"? "My Sweet Lord"?'

Gwen nodded. 'Oh, yes, I know both of them.'

Vivienne picked up the bowler hat containing the five-pound note and the loose change. 'Right. You sing, Gwen. Mary and I'll collect the money.'

Wes seemed troubled, but he strummed the opening chords of 'Brown Eyed Girl' and started to sing tentatively. Then Gwen joined in, her voice powerful, controlled, resonant. Vivienne noticed people immediately pause as if hypnotised, turning away from browsing and window shopping to listen. Wes stared at Gwen for a moment: she was in full vocal force, waving an arm as if she was on stage, and then he smiled, joining in with all his might, his voice a quiet rasp beneath hers. People approached, watching Gwen perform, murmuring approval, then even more people arrived, and Vivienne nudged Mary. 'Come on – we'll rake it in.'

Mary bellowed, 'Right, all of youse, get your hands in your pockets and donate your cash.'

Vivienne launched forward, showing her most professional smile, and shook the bowler hat towards everyone she could see, focusing specifically on the men rather than the women. 'Money for the musicians please – thank you so much!'

'Pay up or sod off,' Mary yelled, holding out both hands to everyone.

The money began to flow in. Several men reached into wallets and pulled out notes; many women thrust keen fingers into purses and soon the bowler hat was crammed with money. Gwen had launched into 'My Sweet Lord', her voice soaring with pure devotion and fervour, Wes strumming with all his might, his brow contorted in concentration. One man in the crowd had tears shining in his eyes; a woman with a child in her arms stared, mouth open. Several people were commenting about how beautiful the music was, their faces flushed with approval. Vivienne rattled the hat again. 'Show your appreciation for the musicians, please. Thank you all.'

More money was dropped into the hat. Gwen and Wes finished with a flourish and the crowd clapped and cheered. Wes turned to Gwen. 'Can you come back and sing with me again?'

The crowd started to disperse, and Vivienne hugged Gwen, thrilled. 'We've made so much money. We have at least a hundred pounds in notes here.'

'I collected so much, I had to stash it somewhere.' Mary thrust a hand down her V-necked top and pulled out a handful of notes. 'But we've made a packet.'

Vivienne took the money; the hat was overflowing. Wes's eyes bulged. 'Wow – thank you, thanks so much. This is amazing...' He turned to Gwen. 'Can I share half with you?'

'No, don't be silly – it was my pleasure...' Gwen smiled.

'Are you sure you can't come back again? We'd make a killing on market day.'

Gwen pressed his arm. 'We're on holiday. I'm sorry...'

'Your voice is amazing, Gwen. I'm just gobsmacked: I've never heard anything like it.' Wes hugged the overflowing bowler hat close to his guitar. 'Honestly, I'm really grateful – thank you so much.'

'Oh, my goodness, no,' Vivienne gasped. 'It's three o'clock. We're late for the parking – we'll get a ticket. We have to go.'

Gwen leaned forward, kissing Wes's cheek. 'It was lovely to meet you, Wes. Good luck with the busking. Keep at it. Who knows what it might lead to? All the best.'

'Yeah – yeah, you too, Gwen. Cool. Another time. Bye.'

'Come on, we don't want to get a ticket. Oh, I just love Totnes. I'm so glad we came,' Mary puffed, then they were on their way at full pelt, rushing downhill, their bags held close to their bodies.

The car park was full, but Gwen spied their motorhome parked in the corner next to an old rickety 2CV with yellow flowers painted on the doors. She also spotted the small man in uniform, strutting towards it purposefully, his head thrust forward like a pigeon's. Vivienne gasped. 'Oh, no. It's the car park attendant.'

'Run, Gwen,' Mary commanded. 'Vivienne, you distract him.'

'And what will you do, Mary?' Vivienne gasped. Gwen had already taken off at a pace towards the motorhome, her keys in her hand.

'Ah, I'll just walk slowly – I'm out of puff.'

Vivienne set off towards the attendant, her voice booming. 'Excuse me – excuse me, please.'

The car park attendant paused, turning to her, his body twisting like a snake. He seethed. 'What seems to be the problem, madam?'

Vivienne improvised. 'Can you tell me, is this the only car park in Totnes?'

The man sighed. 'One of many.'

'Only – I think I've lost my Jag.'

'You've lost your what?'

'My Jag.' Vivienne waved her hands, an impression of a confused woman, all hot and bothered. 'Well, it's my husband's Jag really. His Jaguar. His car. I borrowed it to do a bit of shopping earlier and... I've lost it.' She waved her bag of clothes to prove her point. 'Well, I can't remember which car park I parked it in...'

The attendant grunted. 'Well, if you don't know where you left it, I can't help.' He turned to leave.

'Oh, please,' Vivienne begged. 'Can't you phone another car park attendant? The registration number is BUM 123 – or it might be BUT 123, I can't remember.' The attendant was staring. Vivienne was enjoying herself. 'Of course, I'm always doing this. Silly me. My husband, Roddy, he's going to be so cross that I've lost yet another car.' Her laughter tinkled. 'It's a good job he's so rich, he can afford it. He's... a justice of the peace.'

'A JP, you say?' The attendant suddenly gave her his full attention. 'And where did you say you left the car?'

'Oh – in a car park somewhere.' Vivienne waved her hands helplessly. She saw Gwen and Mary clambering into the motorhome; she heard the rumble as the engine started. 'I really don't know. Please don't worry. I can get a taxi. It'll be fine. Roddy can get another car.'

'Where do you live?' the attendant asked, suddenly interested. 'Is it far?'

Vivienne blurted the first place name that came into her head. 'Edinburgh. Ha ha. But please don't worry. Thanks for your help – you've been very kind.'

The motorhome drew level with them as Mary thrust her head out of the window. 'Can we give you a lift somewhere, missus?' she cawed.

Vivienne was still in role. 'Oh, really? Would you? That's so kind. It's such a long way home and I've lost my car.'

Mary winked. 'Where do you live?'

Vivienne climbed up into the seat through the side door. 'Edinburgh.'

Mary burst out laughing as Vivienne pulled on her seat belt and Gwen drove off. The car park attendant watched them go, open-mouthed. Gwen circled the car park twice to find the exit, and was gone, crunching the gears as the motorhome climbed up a winding hill out of Totnes.

17

'Are we there yet?' Mary asked as Gwen manoeuvred the motorhome from the main road into a narrow lane. 'It's all muck and fields around here... I'll get my shoes filthy.'

'We can't be far away now.' Vivienne's voice chimed from behind her. 'It will be lovely. Berry's friends run an organic place, growing vegetables, fruit. They have polytunnels full of tomatoes, peppers, asparagus, strawberries.'

'So, it's a proper farm?'

'Well, it is a farm, Mary, but there are no animals,' Vivienne explained. 'In fact, I think the owners are vegetarian so—'

Mary laughed. 'So there's no chance of a big juicy steak or a bunch of sausages? I suppose it'll be better for my heart, as your friend said, but when I was a kid, my mammy would make us a nice meaty stew and tell us it was good for you – she said it stuck to your ribs.'

'Moderation, that's what I believe in,' Gwen muttered. 'Well, I don't understand it – the satnav says we've arrived but all I can see is fields and a five-bar gate.'

'Just drive on a bit – up the lane.'

Gwen continued slowly along the lane; she was aware of the wild hedges high on both sides, branches rattling against the sides of the motorhome, scraping against the paintwork. The sweet scent of wild roses drifted through the windows and a small bird flung itself from brambles, narrowly missing the windscreen.

'The thing is, Vivienne, we're in a motorhome and it's so difficult to back up or turn round,' Gwen replied anxiously. 'If we get stuck in a ditch, I won't be able to get us out again. And the roads around here are so narrow and winding.'

The motorhome chugged quietly around a narrow bend and Mary pointed at a sign, leading to a dirt track. 'Is that it?'

Gwen peered over her driving glasses. 'It says it's called Pot Belly Farm.'

'That's the one,' Vivienne exclaimed. 'We're here. And the owners are called Toby and Doug.'

'Dug.' Mary began to laugh. 'Perfect name for a farmer, Dug.'

Gwen was still concerned. 'This track is very narrow, Vivienne. If we meet anyone coming the other way...'

'Then they'll just have to go back,' Vivienne said firmly.

'But what if it's a combine harvester?'

'Ah, they'll all be in the fields – a harvester won't come this way, Gwen.' Mary seemed sure of herself. 'Will you look at this place? There are big trees and green fields and it's just so smart. Oh, and look, a big white farmhouse, and there's a little man standing outside and he's waving his hand. Stop, Gwen.'

Gwen slowed down outside the farmhouse, the engine idling, making a low ticking sound. A man approached, them, his face ruddy and smiling. He wore a green cord jacket, jeans tucked into wellingtons; his hair had once been dark but was now greying and smartly combed. He approached Mary's window. 'Hello. Berry said you'd arrive after four o'clock. Perfect timing.'

Mary opened the window and thrust her head towards him. His

face was tanned and weather-beaten; he was probably in his late fifties or early sixties. 'This is a lovely farm. I'm Mary, and Gwen and Vivienne are here with me in the motorhome. Where do you want us to park up?'

'I'm Toby.' He trudged round to Gwen's side of the van as she wound the window down. 'Hello. Would you mind driving on along the track for a few metres? You'll come to a white gate and an open field – there's a sign there that says camping. You can park in the field, anywhere you like. There's no one else staying tonight – you're our only guests.'

'Oh, of course.' Gwen nodded.

Vivienne called from the passenger seat. 'We're dining with you tonight, Toby. What time do you want us?'

Toby raised his voice. 'Is six o'clock all right? It's only a few minutes' walk from the field. Bring a torch though, it might be dark when you return.'

'Fab,' Vivienne's voice tinkled. 'Do we need to bring anything else?'

Toby smiled. 'Just yourselves and a good appetite.'

'Yes, we can do that – and I love vegetables.' Mary was the epitome of positivity. 'Drive on, Gwen – we need to freshen up and get changed for the dinner.'

By six o'clock, the three friends were ready to go. Gwen had showered; she was wearing a dark blouse, trousers, and a light jacket. Her hair was glossy to her shoulders. Vivienne had pinned her hair up, loose tendrils around her face, and she wore the long dress she had bought in Totnes. Mary too was wearing the frock she had found earlier; she held handfuls of it up in her fists as it skimmed the ground. She had asked Gwen and Vivienne to spray her hair, and her once-white locks were now streaked with pink, purple and blue. She was delighted with her appearance. 'What do you think, Vivienne? How do I look?'

Gwen was unsure. 'It's very bright, Mary. Colourful, I mean.'

'It's certainly not dull,' Vivienne agreed. 'You look great, Mary.'

Mary twirled around in one direction and then back in the other. 'I feel like those lovely people shopping in Totnes, so colourful and funky. It's funny, you don't see anything like it in London. But I want to explore the more creative part of me. I've worn sensible uniforms all of my life so tonight I'm going to... what's the phrase?'

'Let it all hang out?' Vivienne suggested.

'Exactly. I'm well up for the organic dinner.'

Gwen seemed anxious. 'As long as we can get to the farmhouse without stepping in anything unpleasant...'

'Oh, you'll be fine,' Vivienne assured her. 'It's a gravel path and it's quite dry.'

'And there won't be any manure,' Mary added. 'Because they've got no animals to eat.'

They arrived at the cottage to be greeted by a tall, white-haired man wearing gold-rimmed spectacles, jeans and an olive-coloured T-shirt with *Pot Belly Farm* inscribed in white. He introduced himself as Doug and kissed everyone's cheek. He was certainly not pot-bellied; he was lean and tanned, and his arms were muscular. Doug spoke to Vivienne. 'We're delighted to meet you. Any friend of Berry and Orlando is welcome here. Toby's still in the kitchen, finishing off the cooking. Can I show you to the table?'

They followed Doug into a vast oak-framed conservatory where several wooden tables and benches were laid out. Mary gasped. 'Is this your dining room?'

Doug smiled. 'We have banquet nights and Sunday lunches here. Toby and I cater for about a dozen people at a time in here, just three days a week, to give them a taste of our organic fare, and they can buy produce too.'

'So, do you sell the vegetables you grow to the public?' Gwen asked, attempting to be polite.

'Oh, yes – people can opt to pick their own, and I run a little shop on the premises as well. We have some quite unusual veg here – we have rainbow beetroot, Romanesco broccoli, we even grow our own artisan tea.'

'Can't you just buy it in the shops?' Mary was astonished.

'It's all about creating something exciting, all by ourselves,' Doug continued. 'Have you ever had a cucamelon?'

'Whatever is one of those?' Gwen asked.

'It's a hybrid, like a melon that tastes of cucumber and lime. We put slices of it in martinis. The guests love it.'

'I'd like to try that,' Vivienne enthused.

'Okay, we'll have vodka martinis now, shall we? Then we'll eat.' Doug waved a hand. 'Take a seat, ladies. I'll bring your apritifs and then we'll make a start. Will you have wine with your meal?'

Mary barked a laugh. 'Is the Pope Catholic?'

Gwen gave a cough. 'Could I just have mineral water?'

'Coming up,' Doug called over his shoulder. 'Make yourselves at home.'

Mary stared around the room; she had never seen anything like it. Flowers in vases in each corner, huge, glazed windows, and beyond, a perfect white path bordered with blooms of all colours and sizes, most of which she couldn't name. She scratched her head, then checked she hadn't picked up any spray colour on her hands. Pot Belly Farm both mystified and thrilled her, the idea of planting and tending seeds and watching them develop, nurturing them like your own flesh and blood until they blossomed or fruited, before cooking them in your own kitchen. She leaned her head against her hands and thought of Chandra's Convenience Store: she'd tell Ravi all about her travels, and Deepak too, if he was tending the shop. She'd have so much to talk about after this holiday. Then she heard Vivienne's voice, almost a sigh, as she thanked Doug for her martini and took a sip. Mary felt a glass placed in her own hands, pale liquid, with something light green floating inside. She took a gulp; it was a sharp, unusual taste.

Gwen shook her head. 'I've never had vodka martini before.' She sipped slowly, as if it was poison on her lips that might kill her instantly, then she tried again. 'Mmm, it's not so bad when you get to the second mouthful.'

Vivienne swallowed a gulp from her glass and closed her eyes. 'Martinis always remind me of the breakfast in bed Lennie bought me once – gin martinis, with cheese, olives, prawns. We didn't get up all day.' For a moment she seemed sad, then she forced a smile. 'Ooh, something smells wonderful.'

Toby and Doug had arrived with plates heaped with food. Mary's mouth fell open as she watched dish after dish being placed in front of her. 'And what do you call all this? I've never seen vegetables like this in all my life.'

Toby put steaming porcelain bowls in front of her with a flourish. 'So, we have roasted asparagus in hollandaise sauce, buttered artichoke hearts, roasted sweetcorn, broad bean salad, glazed carrots with crispy seitan, chargrilled spring veggies, spicy lentil quiche, samphire frittata, feta and radicchio salad, crispy halloumi, flatbreads, various dips, and a selection of other salads and cheeses.'

Mary was astonished. 'Do you make everything by yourself here? All of it?'

'Except the cheese,' Doug nodded proudly. 'A very nice man in Bovey has a great specialist shop. Everything else is grown on the farm and cooked in our own kitchen.'

'How fabulous.' Vivienne clasped her hands together.

Gwen spooned asparagus onto her plate, speared it with her fork and nibbled. 'Oh, my goodness me, this is all just so delicious.'

Mary was chewing frittata. 'I have to say, this is very nice indeed. Sure, and I certainly don't miss the steak at all.'

'That's such a compliment.' Toby was filling her glass with wine. 'We pride ourselves on making every dish as delicious and flavoursome as possible. And it's all nutritious.'

'Is that why you're both skinny?' Mary asked. 'I mean, is it the healthy veggie food or the hard work on the farm that keeps you so slim?'

'Both, and the 80:20 rule,' Doug suggested.

Mary was flabbergasted. 'Is that all the calories you're allowed to eat every day?'

'Not at all.' Toby indicated the food. 'We try to eat nutritious meals 80 per cent of the time and have our favourite treats like wine or cream or chocolate with the other 20 per cent.'

'And we eat mindfully,' Doug added.

'And what on earth does that mean when it's at home?' Mary asked.

Toby smiled. 'We think about every spoonful as we eat, enjoy the taste, the sensations, as if each mouthful is a gift.'

'Oh, what a good idea. I might just try that myself.' Mary was thoughtful as she speared an artichoke heart and tasted soft buttery sweetness, a tang of lemon. She had never eaten anything like it before. She didn't know the names of many of the vegetables in the dishes but, she thought, it might make perfect sense when she returned to London to think more carefully about the food she cooked. She had to look after her heart now: crisps and beer once or twice a week and on the other days, something nutritious like a low-fat curry or a hearty salad made perfect sense. She'd chat to Ravi, or perhaps ask his grandfather for some new recipes. She'd avoid the gulab jamun, though, with all the sugar: it wouldn't do her heart any favours.

Mary was still thinking about the lifestyle on Pot Belly Farm as she walked back to the motorhome in the field, arm in arm with Vivienne and Gwen, who was shining a torch ahead onto the gravel path, a slim beam amid the inky darkness.

'I have to say it,' Gwen's voice was soft. 'That was probably the most sumptuous meal I have ever eaten.'

'It certainly makes you want to come back here again, doesn't it?' Vivienne said. 'Imagine living here and eating like this every day.'

'I was thinking I might ask about an allotment when I'm back in London.' Gwen looked hopeful. 'We could share one. Maybe join a co-operative...?'

Vivienne sighed. 'Oh yes, there's so much I want to do. That's the joy of coming away on holiday. It gives one the opportunity to reset, to think and re-evaluate everything.' She listened to the sound of her heels crunching against the gravel. 'Here's me chasing acting jobs, feeling hopeful and then feeling disappointed when I don't get the ones I'd like most. Maybe I should consider doing something completely different: live in a yurt, take up teaching yoga.'

'Oh, I'd come to your class. I love yoga.' Gwen increased her pace; the motorhome was in sight, lurking in the shadows beyond the white gate. 'You can count me in for that, Vivienne.'

'I've got it,' Mary suddenly shouted and Vivienne and Gwen gave an involuntary jump at the same time as she strode forward between them. 'I've got it. We're getting up early tomorrow. Come on, let's get back to the motorhome. We need our beauty sleep.'

Vivienne frowned dubiously at the smaller woman next to her, hurtling forward. 'Okay, Mary – what's the plan?'

'Why do we need to get up with the lark?' Gwen asked.

'You wanted to see the sunrise at Stonehenge, Gwen, but it was chucking down with rain,' Mary grunted. 'Well, we're going to see it rise over Dartmoor tomorrow. We're only a mile or so away – we'll drive up onto the moors in the dark and we'll watch the dawn break. After a day shopping for joss sticks and singing with buskers in Totnes, then eating all the delicious organic hippy food, it will be just the ticket.'

18

Vivienne woke first, slipping down from the little bed over the cab which she'd said she'd be happy to make her own for the entire holiday, since Gwen had thought she'd bang her head while she was asleep, and Mary protested that she would never be able to get up the ladder. Still in her short nightie, Vivienne padded across to the double bed where two sleeping mounds lay in the darkness, and put out a hand to touch Gwen's arm, which she had flung across the duvet. 'Time to wake up,' she whispered softly.

'Oh, my goodness, is it that time already?' Gwen groaned.

'I'm wide awake.' Mary sat upright. 'Right, so we're off up the moors to greet the sun.' She wriggled out of the bed, almost squashing Gwen. 'I can't see a thing, where are some clean knickers?'

It was twenty to five when they left the motorhome behind them in an eerily deserted car park on the edge of the moors. One other vehicle was stationed there already, an old-fashioned camper van, the metal grimy and peppered with rust, the curtains drawn. Vivienne led the way across a narrow road and up towards Haytor Rock, which crouched above them in the shadows, dark and distant as a sitting giant. She shone a torch ahead; the ground underfoot was soft, and unexpected rocks protruded, cutting through the thin soles of their trainers.

Gwen stubbed her toe and muttered, 'Ouch. That hurt.'

Mary puffed behind them, then she stopped still, grunting. 'I'll never make it. Go on without me.'

Vivienne linked an arm through Mary's, urging her onwards. 'We've got about twenty minutes or so to get to the top. Come on, Mary – we're doing this together.'

'I'm worn out already.' Mary stopped for a moment, wiping her face with her hand. 'Oh, all right, let's carry on. I'll be fine if you get hold of me and tug me along, Vivienne.'

They edged forward slowly, crawling against the steep incline, Mary gasping, stopping then starting off determinedly again, until they were in the shadow of a huge rock. Gwen shook her head. 'We can't climb all the way up there. It's too dangerous.'

Vivienne pointed the torch upwards, making a small area on the dark rock gleam, a little spotlight of rough stone. 'I talked to Toby and Doug last night before we left. It's not as hard as it looks, apparently, although we'll need to be a bit careful in the dark. Toby said there are plenty of handholds and even a few roughly-hewn steps. He said if we take it slowly, we can climb to the top. I'll go first.'

'And I'll go last,' Mary muttered. 'I'm staying here at the bottom. Then I can't fall any further.'

'Aren't you coming with us?' Gwen was disappointed.

'I have a heart condition. I know my limitations.' Mary sat down on a stone and took a deep breath. 'Shout to me when you get to the top. If you fall down, I'll hear you coming.'

'Right.' Vivienne fumbled in her pocket. 'Take my phone, Mary.'

'Why do I need the mobilised phone? Are you going to call me when you get there?'

'No – there's probably no reception here anyway – it has a torch, so you'll be able to see.'

'What will I see? Sheep? Horses? Mad axe-men?'

'The sun will be up in ten minutes. You can watch it from down here.' Vivienne had started to climb. 'Come on, Gwen – it's not as bad as it looks. Step by step and we'll get there.'

Gwen followed behind, too closely, her head next to Vivienne's thigh as she clambered up. 'Is it safe, Vivienne?'

'It's a bit steep in places... just follow me.'

Gwen waited for a few moments while Vivienne clambered ahead, then she gripped the craggy handholds, placed her foot tentatively on a flat surface and hauled herself forward, repeating the action until she arrived at a set of sheer steps. Vivienne called from above. 'I'm nearly there. Just keep going.'

Gwen's voice rose in a panic. 'I can't see anything.' She blinked. Above her the grainy darkness was a sharp rock face of grey stone and dark crevasses. Vivienne had disappeared completely. Gwen hung on, her hands desperate claws; she was all alone on a huge rock and she couldn't see anything. Then the torchlight shone down, and Gwen reached up towards another handhold. She shifted her feet precariously, took several small steps, tugging herself upwards, and heard Vivienne's encouraging whisper. 'I'm at the top. You're nearly there. Keep going. Then I'll give you a hand up.'

Gwen struggled forward, breathing heavily, and reached for a strong hand that pulled her hard. Suddenly, she and Vivienne were standing on the flat top of Haytor Rock in complete darkness, gazing around at shadows of undulating hills and jagged rocks.

Vivienne bellowed. 'We're here, Mary. And the sun will be coming up at any moment. I hope you can hear us.'

There was a low sound from below, a single hoot of confirmation.

Gwen waited, staring into darkness, feeling her heart thud. Then, before she knew it, she was pointing a hand towards a speck of red gold in the distance, a smudge of light in the sky. It happened too quickly: an explosion of crimson against indigo, then the sun, a white disc, suddenly visible, lightening the sky to turquoise, trailing blotches of bleeding red and orange. Gwen stared at Vivienne, who had her arms in the air, her eyes closed. She muttered, 'This is glorious. It's better than I thought it would be.'

Vivienne threw her head back and started to recite.

> *I'll tell you how the Sun rose –*
> *A Ribbon at a time –*
> *The Steeples swam in Amethyst –*
> *The news, like Squirrels, ran –*
> *The Hills untied their Bonnets –*
> *The Bobolinks – begun –*
> *Then I said softly to myself –*
> *'That must have been the Sun!'*

Goosebumps rose on Gwen's skin, and she began to softly sing 'Here Comes the Sun'. Both women stood together, shoulder to shoulder; as Gwen's soft voice lifted in pure reverence, the darkness dissolved and the sky became an oil canvas, heavy with blue and pink brushstrokes. Vivienne's smile widened. 'That was truly spectacular.'

'What was the poem you recited, Vivienne?'

'Emily Dickinson – "I'll Tell You How the Sun Rose".'

Gwen's voice was hushed, full of admiration. 'It was lovely. Really beautiful.'

Vivienne threw an arm around Gwen's shoulder. 'We make a great team, reciting poems and singing songs. I wish Mary could have been with us to see it from up here.'

'I'll remember that sunrise for ever,' Gwen breathed. 'I'm in my seventies – I shouldn't be climbing rocks at my age, but I'm so glad I did.'

'Never say never.' Vivienne's face was determined. 'The sunrise from up here should be on everyone's bucket list.'

Gwen's face shone, half of it illuminated by the glowing sunshine. 'I'm so glad I got to share it with you.'

'Me too.' Vivienne threw out her arms and whirled round in a circle. 'What a view. What a beautiful place. I could stay here for another hour. We should have bought champagne and toasted the new day.'

'We should have. But I suppose we'd better climb down and see how Mary is.'

'Yes, we ought to,' Vivienne agreed. 'It'll be much easier going down than climbing up, but you still have to watch your footing.'

'Oh, I'm not worried about descending,' Gwen said. 'At least we can see where we're going now – or where we've just been. That helps.'

At the bottom, Mary was sitting in a dishevelled heap on a rock, smiling. 'Well, I don't know what it looked like from up where you were, but from down here, it was just remarkable. I've never seen a sunrise like it.'

Gwen caught her breath as she placed her feet on more solid ground. 'It was wonderful. Did you hear me singing? And Vivienne recited a poem.'

'I think all of Dartmoor heard the pair of youse.' Mary beamed. 'It was beautiful, the glowing sun and the booming voices. I loved it.'

'So.' Vivienne folded her arms. 'Shall we walk back to the motorhome and make some breakfast?'

'Then we could drive to a nearby little village I noticed on the map and perhaps I'll buy another postcard for Vicente.'

'I've got an idea.' Mary shook her head. 'I don't know about you two young ones, but this old lady needs a rest. While I sat here by myself, I came up with a plan.' She struggled to her feet, brushing her coat, standing up straight. 'We go back to the motorhome and we have a doze for a couple of hours. Then, when we wake up, we'll drive to the little village Gwen has found, and I'll buy us all a healthy breakfast. How does that sound?'

'It sounds fantastic,' Vivienne said, linking her arms through Gwen's on one side and Mary's on the other. 'Right, shall we amble back to our residence and get our heads down for a bit more beauty sleep?'

'Oh, I'm not sure I'll be able to doze off, not after that wonderful experience on the rock,' Gwen gasped. 'But I'll certainly try.'

The climb to the top of Haytor must have tired them out more than they'd thought. It was past one when they woke, and at two o'clock Gwen drove the motorhome steadily into a car park in a small picturesque village called Widecombe. She gazed at a stately church with four high turreted towers, a perfectly neat village green surrounded by white-painted stones and leafy trees, and a row of quaint shops and cafés. Gwen braked suddenly as a dappled horse strolled across the road, taking its time, oblivious. Mary was beside herself with excitement. 'Did you see the little horse, Gwen? Vivienne, this place is full of ponies, everywhere, on the grass, nibbling away, standing by the side of the road. All over.'

Gwen switched off the engine. 'That's why they have the signs up everywhere, "Drive with Moor Care", Mary. There are Dartmoor ponies and sheep and all sorts of animals running wild around here.'

Vivienne was ecstatic. 'But this little village is so charming. Free roaming ponies and all the little shops and cafés. I'm going to buy souvenirs, things I can take home. It's just so sweet.'

'I'll buy us a late brunch,' Mary offered. 'Unless you fancy a Devonshire cream tea instead?'

'Cream tea for brunch? That sounds very daring,' Vivienne quipped.

Gwen licked her lips. 'I'm up for a cream tea, Mary – but what happened to your 80:20 regime?'

'I'm still doing the 20,' Mary retorted. 'No, no, but I'm serious. When I get back to London, I'm definitely going to do the 80:20. But at the minute, I'm on my holidays, so I can stretch the 20 out a bit.' She considered her words. 'And the waistband.'

It took an hour before they arrived at the café and sat down: Vivienne was determined to traipse into several shops first, buying postcards and bags full of souvenirs: a ceramic Toby jug depicting Tom Cobley, Devon cream fudge, a silver spoon, a fridge magnet and an expensive painting of the sun rising over Haytor Rock, which Vivienne said 'called to her and demanded that she buy it, whatever the price'.

Mary led the way into the tea rooms and installed herself at a pretty table covered with a white lace cloth. A waitress in a black dress with a white hat and apron approached her with a menu, as Vivienne and Gwen sat down. Mary screwed up her face. 'It says selection of sandwiches and selection of cakes. But what ones are they?'

The waitress was in her fifties with pale hair. Her accent was a soft burr. 'The selection is salmon, cheese and tomato, cucumber and egg mayonnaise today.'

'On one sandwich?' Mary leaned forward. 'It sounds lovely.'

The waitress smiled. 'It's a selection, all different ones. And the cakes are over there.' She pointed to a cabinet filled with a variety of sponge cakes, chocolate, cream, Swiss rolls, eclairs. 'You can choose whichever one takes your fancy.'

Mary groaned. 'The 80:20 has just become 100:0.'

Vivienne raised an eyebrow. 'I'll just have a toasted muffin and a pot of Lady Grey, please.'

'A cream tea for me, scones and jam.' Gwen handed the menu to Mary. 'It's indulgent, but I can't remember the last time I had a cream tea.'

'I hope it was a proper Devon one.' A mock-serious voice came from the next table, a dark-haired woman in her seventies, who wore an anorak and sipped tea from a china cup. 'Not a Cornish one.'

The woman in the anorak had made a joke; her companion, a man of a similar age in spectacles and a dark coat, was amused, his jovial face creased in a pleasant smile.

Gwen was suddenly nervous. 'Is there a difference?'

The woman leaned forward. 'Oh, goodness me, yes. You don't want to get it wrong, not when you're in Devon.' She opened her eyes wide. 'We locals might not let you leave.'

Gwen felt uncomfortable. 'Oh, dear.'

'I'll have the sandwiches and cake – and a cup of peppermint tea.' Mary sat up straight, placing the napkin on her knee. 'Peppermint is probably good for the heart. I'm sure Toby and Doug drink peppermint tea.'

Gwen gazed around the room; the couple at the next table were still sipping from delicate cups. The woman spoke loudly to her companion. 'Would you care for a refill, Henry? There's tea left in the pot.'

The man agreed, then he addressed Gwen. 'This is the first time we've been out for afternoon tea since lockdown. Isn't it nice to be out again?'

Vivienne answered for Gwen. 'Oh, yes – we're on holiday. We decided we'd escape from London, now we can travel again.'

'And Devon's so lovely,' Mary added. 'We've all been climbing Haytor Rock and watching the rising sun.'

The woman was impressed. 'You climbed up Haytor Rock? That must have been quite challenging for women your age?'

Vivienne shook her head firmly. 'Not at all – we just flew up there.'

The man laughed. 'It would be much harder after one of the cream teas you get here – they are quite substantial.'

On cue, the waitress appeared with a tray, laying sandwiches and cakes and teapots on the table. Gwen stared at the plate in front of her: two scones had been split in half; next to them were little pats of butter and small pots of jam and clotted cream. She picked up her spoon and was about to ladle strawberry jam on to the scone.

'Oh no – stop!' The woman in the anorak gasped. 'That's sacrilege.'

Gwen was alarmed. 'What did I do wrong?'

The woman's tone was calm but firm. 'You don't start with the jam. That's a Cornish cream tea. Here you sit the cream on the scone first, then the jam on top of it. Otherwise, it's wrong.'

The man laughed softly. 'You still get the death penalty in Devon if you eat a cream tea the wrong way round.'

Gwen was momentarily alarmed; she piled cream on the scone and looked up for approval, but the woman was drinking tea again. She gazed at Vivienne, who was pouring pale tea into a china cup. She moved her eyes to Mary, whose expression was ecstatic as she bit into a salmon roll. Gwen picked up her scone and noticed the woman in the anorak and her companion smiling with approval.

Gwen exhaled. 'I had no idea it was so dangerous, eating a cream tea. Next time I'll order the crumpets.'

But an hour later, as they set off towards Tavistock, Gwen's nerves were even more frayed. The roads had become very narrow, and she was terrified that traffic approaching from the other direction might demand that she reversed. Vivienne coaxed soothingly from behind and, on one occasion, Mary yelled that a four-by-four was hurtling towards them and Gwen should brake: she managed to pull into a makeshift lay-by and let it pass.

Gwen's heart was pulsating in her throat for fear that she'd scratch Vicente's motorhome again on the overhanging branches. As she drove, the road was dappled with sunlight, then blotched with shade, then too bright again, then the sharp light was filtered by overhanging leaves again. Mary's repeated excitable exclamations about how pretty Dartmeet was, or how lovely the little babbling brook was below the bridge and did they have time to go paddling, made Gwen even more nervous. But finally, the road to Tavistock widened and she managed to guide the motorhome into a field next to a farm near Peter Tavy. It was only five o'clock, but she was exhausted.

19

Mary took the pile of breakfast plates back into the motorhome and deposited them in the sink. Then she changed her clothes, swapping the voluminous nightdress for a thin top and three-quarter-length trousers. She placed a straw hat on her head, stood on the steps and gazed upwards. 'It's going to be the hottest day yet. Look at the sky. It's clear blue.'

Gwen and Vivienne were seated at the plastic table, mugs of coffee next to them, poring over a map. 'So, where do you think this lovely beach is, Vivienne?'

Vivienne adjusted her large sunglasses and traced a road on the map with her fingertip. 'I think it's around here, just outside Bude. We stayed in a caravan park, the three of us.'

Mary barked a laugh. 'So, how long ago was this?'

'Sixty-three years ago. I was seven and my brother, Pete, was nine.'

'Things might have changed a bit since 1958, Vivienne.' Gwen's expression showed that she was dubious. 'And you can't even remember what the place was called?'

Vivienne frowned, staring at the map again. 'I do recall the names of some of the places, Sandymouth, Northcott Mouth... they sound very familiar. Dad took us all over the place in an old Ford Zephyr.'

'So where was your mother?' Mary asked.

'She left us when I was four years old.' Vivienne sipped from her mug. 'She went off with someone else, a man called Bill. Dad took care of us, bless him. He promised us we wouldn't go without anything, hence the car he bought, working all hours to pay it off, and the caravan holidays near Bude.'

'I bet they were the loveliest times.' Gwen sighed. 'Memories of childhood are so sweet, so innocent. They were my best years, being a youngster.'

Vivienne pulled a face. 'At first, we were all right, yes, but Pete and I used to fight like cats and then my dad married a woman called Shirley who loathed me, and I loathed her. My teenage years were quite tough.'

'Was it your dad who encouraged you to go on stage, Vivienne?'

'He never said much at all really, Gwen.' Vivienne rested her chin in her palm. 'And Shirley told me in no uncertain terms that actresses, as she called them, were no better than prostitutes, so that made me determined to leave Leicester, move to London and go on the stage, and that's what I did. I got a place at the Central School of Speech and Drama when I was eighteen and I never looked back.'

'But those were happy times, just you, your dad and your brother in the caravan in Bude?' Gwen stared at the map.

'I suppose so. I just wanted to see the area again, after all these – oh, look. Duckpool Bay. I remember we went to the beach – there were little rock pools everywhere.' Vivienne's eyes shone. 'Can we set the satnav to take us there?'

Mary sat down, picking up her abandoned coffee mug and draining the last dregs. 'Yes, the seaside on a hot day would be grand. But will we sit on the beach all day, because if we do, I'll need to buy sun cream for my legs. They're peeling something shocking after the day in Lyme Regis.'

'Sun cream is a must,' Vivienne agreed.

'Looking at the map,' Gwen pointed with her finger, 'the beach would be a lovely place to relax. And the coastline might be great for a little walk. Since we went for the climb up Haytor Rock yesterday, I've been keen to stretch my legs each day if we can.'

'Splendid,' Vivienne agreed. 'Sunbathe, a stroll and then I'll book us into a pub not too far away for the evening.' She moved away, talking animatedly into her phone.

Mary raised her eyebrows. 'It's hot already. I'll fry like a prawn on the beach.'

Gwen nodded. 'I burn so easily too – we'll have to take care, Mary. Vivienne already has a tan to die for.'

Vivienne rushed back, pushing her phone into her pocket. 'Right, I've called the pub. The landlord is called Pip – I spoke to him on the phone and he's charming. He was fine with us parking there overnight. They have a huge car park to the rear of the pub. So, I booked us in for an evening meal for seven o'clock. I thought it might be nice not to cook again after the beans on toast I made for us last night.'

'If we skip lunch and go for a hike, then maybe we'll all be ready for a pub dinner.' Mary rubbed her hands together. 'And we've not far to stagger home afterwards.'

'As long as I don't have to try a Cornish cream tea.' Gwen smiled. 'I'd be scared to get it wrong after the one I had yesterday – I was so nervous; I still don't know what to put on the scone first.'

'Okay.' Vivienne stood up, still in her short pyjamas. 'Let's get dressed and put our faces on, and then we'll head off to North Cornwall. I'm looking forward to a stroll down memory lane.'

* * *

The sun was high in the sky and meltingly hot, as Vivienne, Gwen
and Mary picked their way down the cliff path and over the rough
pebbles towards the sandy beach of Duckpool Bay. The cove was
picture-postcard-perfect, the sea stretching towards an infinite blue
line on the horizon, merging with a cloudless sky. The beach was
almost deserted, except for a family who sat in the distance, sharing
a picnic, and two surfers who were standing at the water's edge with
their boards held vertically, talking. Vivienne shook out her beach
mat, placing it on damp sand, then peeled off her dress and
stretched out in a white swimsuit.

Mary couldn't help herself. 'You look like one of those French
film stars, Vivienne – all tan and swimsuit and sunglasses.' She
plonked herself on a straw mat. 'I'll roast to death in all these heavy
clothes. I wish I had a swimsuit.'

Vivienne's eyes were closed behind the shades. 'You should buy
one, Mary. You too, Gwen.'

Gwen was horrified. 'I don't own one, Vivienne. I'm seventy-
four. Women of my age cover it all up, we don't show it to anyone
who wants to look.'

Vivienne laughed softly. 'I don't care about anyone looking. I
wear what I want, and to hell with what anyone thinks.'

'But you're lovely and slim.' Gwen looked despondently at her
own legs, sticking out from beneath a bunched-up skirt. 'I can
remember my mother telling me, "You've perfect legs for trousers,
Gwen." So, I keep it all hidden.'

'I'm always told I'm too thin.' Vivienne assumed a mocking
voice. 'My stepmother always said, "You need more meat on you,
Vivienne."' She laughed. 'I've long ceased caring what anyone says.
It's my body.'

'Well, you're right,' Mary said determinedly. 'In this weather, we should all wear swimsuits. But I'd look the beached whale in a bikini.'

'Rubbish.' Vivienne stretched out long legs. 'There are some swimsuits and tankinis in really flattering designs. I tell you what.' She rolled onto her front. 'Later on, we'll go shopping and buy swimwear.'

'Oh, I'm not sure.' Gwen was doubtful. 'It might be embarrassing.'

'Or it might be glorious,' Vivienne suggested.

'I'm all for the glorious.' Mary lay back, closed her eyes, and allowed the sun to filter through her eyelashes. 'So, this is Duckpool. Is it how you remember it as a young one, Vivienne?'

Vivienne thought for a moment. The image of herself, reed-slim in a blue swimming costume, fair hair tousled in the wind, splashing through the surf, lifted high onto her father's shoulders, came rushing back to her. She murmured, 'Nothing's changed much, except me.'

'I know what you mean.' Gwen gave a low sound, a sad snuffle. 'When I was a child, singing was everything in my life. And my career happened without me really doing anything much to make it occur. In my twenties, thirties, forties even, I just sang and sang. Then the opportunities seemed to come less often. By the time I was sixty, I was asking people to let me sing. Now, look at me – I'm like Echo.'

'Echo?' Mary wriggled on her mat.

'She ended up in a cave, nothing left, just a voice. I'm the same. The rest of me has vanished away.'

'Then that has to change,' Vivienne murmured, her chin on her arms.

'It was in your teacup, Gwen, the singing and a new love, both together, both at the same time. I saw it.'

Gwen shook her head. 'I wish you were right, Mary. But my

chances of love disappeared when Clifford Edwards dumped me for Siân Roberts. I never got over him.'

'So, there was no one else after Clifford?' Vivienne asked.

'Oh, yes, a few men here and there in London – but they'd do the chasing, and I'd give in, then I'd realise a bit further down the line that they weren't Clifford, and I didn't love them.' Gwen felt her skin tingle in the sunlight. 'I'd have liked a simple life, being a mother, then a grandmother, you know, a big family. But it didn't work out. I lived all over London, with friends, performing in the opera, then teaching singing, then two years ago when Vicente advertised this flat was available, I moved in.'

'I did the same, not long after you, Gwen. You've been at Drayton Mews for years, though, Mary.'

'I have. It was owned by a lovely couple and they rented out the basement to me when I retired from the nursing. Then Vicente bought it and converted the other two floors into flats.'

Vivienne sat up and delved into a bag. 'Right. Sun cream. Come on, girls – you need to slap it on all over.'

'Thanks, I will.' Gwen sat up and began to cover herself with sunscreen. Mary stayed where she was, thinking. Gwen handed her the bottle and wriggled onto her front. 'So, Mary, what about your own teacup? Did you see any love for yourself in the leaves?' She wiped the residual cream from her hands onto her nose and face. 'I know you had plenty of boyfriends when you were a nurse. But didn't you want to marry any of them or start a family?'

Vivienne laughed. 'Or was it – what was his name – the lovely Callum Duffy, who didn't turn out to be so lovely? Was he the one?'

Mary slopped cream on her arms and legs, then flopped back, squeezing her eyes closed. 'Perhaps. I don't know.'

'So why wasn't he so lovely?' Vivienne asked. 'What did he do?'

'Well...' Mary wasn't sure what to say. She recalled a freckle-faced young man, wisecracking, full of himself, with dark curls, dancing blue eyes, a ready laugh. She remembered how they had come to London on the boat, then the bus; he had promised her that their new life together would be wonderful and she, at twenty, had defied her mother's angry words, the fierce warning that it would all come to no good. She had ignored her father's sad expression, the single tear on his cheek, and she'd boldly announced that she and Callum would be fine, they'd go to London and they'd want for nothing.

She remembered how it happened, how the lovely Callum had stopped being so lovely. They were sharing a flat with another couple, a bedroom each and a tiny kitchen. Callum had gone to work on the building site as he usually did, early in the morning, but he had left his sandwich box behind on the kitchen worktop. Mary recalled how awkward and out of place she felt walking through London in her floral A-line dress, her hair in a ponytail. She arrived at the building site and she could still hear the laughter of the other builders, a raucous, grating, mocking bark, as they looked down from the scaffolding and saw a naïve girl with a rounded belly holding a lunch box.

As Mary lay on the sand, her eyes shut, she could still feel the shame; she remembered that her cheeks burned as she stood alone on the building site clutching the box. One bulky man in dirty trousers, his chest bare, had snarled, 'You girls get yourselves knocked up and come crying after a man. Do yourself a favour – go back home to your mother.'

Another man was more kind. He came down from the scaffolding and walked over to Mary. 'Callum Duffy, darlin'? He doesn't work here now. I think he's moved to another site, over on North Road. But I wouldn't go chasing after him there if I were you. Like Tommy says, go home, forget him. He's not your type.'

Mary recalled the tears pricking in her eyes, her hands flying to her belly. 'I need to see Callum.' She held out the sandwich box as if it was proof.

Then the kindly man said, 'Let it go, love, and go back home. We know him well – Callum chases everything in skirts. When he worked here, he used to see a bird most lunch times from the shop over the road. I think he probably had another one on the go too. Walk away, darlin'. He won't be any use to you.'

Mary remembered how she'd turned around, clutching the plastic box of jam-on-white-bread sandwiches to her belly, remembering the many nights that Callum had popped out for a drink down the pub by himself, or how he'd insisted he wanted to take a walk alone, and he'd come home very late, the faint smell of perfume on his skin, and how she'd ignored it. How she'd been determined to believe that everything would somehow be all right.

It had been a long walk back to the flat, and a longer wait for the lovely Callum to come home. Then, when she'd asked him about other women, he had laughed: he hadn't tried to deny it. She had trapped him; he needed his freedom; he was twenty-one and he didn't want a girl and a baby tying him down. Then he had left her, and that was that. He hadn't been lovely at all and she suddenly found herself alone, in London, penniless and eight months pregnant.

Mary closed her eyes and realised her cheeks were damp. A sigh escaped from her lips.

'Well, the lovely Callum is just water under the bridge, Vivienne, and it was a long time ago,' she muttered. 'But I got over it, I survived, and here I am now lying in the sunshine on Duckpool Beach. No, I'm grand now.'

20

They stayed on the beach until late afternoon, dozing, chattering, slathering on more sun cream. Then Vivienne leaped up, brushed sand from her swimsuit, announced that she'd love a swim in the sea but she wasn't going by herself, and led Gwen and Mary back to the motorhome, which was in the car park at the top of the cliff. Then she declared that they were going into Bude to shop for new swimwear.

An hour later, at a quarter to five, they were huddled around a display stand of brightly coloured bathing costumes in a small shop in Bude. Vivienne was pulling out hangers and the others were laughing.

'I'm not joking, Gwen – you'd look great in this.'

'What is it? What's the tie bit here?'

'That's the shorts. It's a tankini.'

Gwen put a hand to her mouth. 'But it's red. I normally wear black because it's supposed to be slimming.'

'Of course that's not true – it was just made up by skinny people who wanted to make women with figures look dull.' Vivienne's voice was firm, almost bossy. 'You're an attractive woman with dark hair. The red will look lovely. You don't need boring black. And this is only twenty pounds. Go and try it on.'

'But what if it doesn't fit me?'

Vivienne's eyes were warm with good humour. 'Then we'll try another one in another size, Gwen.'

Gwen disappeared dutifully towards the changing room. Mary patted Vivienne's arm. 'I don't suppose anything here will fit me. I'm too old now for a swimsuit.'

'Mary, can you swim?'

'Oh, I haven't been in the water in ages, but I used to swim like a fish.'

'Then you need a swimsuit.' Vivienne hoisted hangers apart and plucked out a multicoloured costume, thick stripes in a tie-dye effect. 'Here – it will match your hair with the lovely pink and blue in it.'

Mary put a hand to her hair, which still contained strands of pink, purple and blue spray dye. 'But it has stripes – stripes make you look fat. And my backside is fat enough...'

'This, Mary, is a flattering V-necked swim dress in a batik print. Go on, try it on.'

'And will it fit me?'

'There's only one way to find out. Meanwhile, I'm going to try this one...' She held up a tangerine swimsuit. 'Strapless, plunge neckline – this has my name written all over it.' Vivienne smiled. 'Come on, Mary – by the time we've decked ourselves out in this little lot, they'll be signing us up to be the next Bond girls.'

Mary pulled a face. 'It depends on who the Bond is... if it's that nice young fella with the twinkly blue eyes and the smart dinner jacket, I might just say yes.'

By seven o'clock, Gwen parked the motorhome at the back of the Smugglers Arms, a white-painted seventeenth century pub with a thatched roof, where Vivienne had arranged for them to stay overnight in the car park. The landlord, a man in his thirties who introduced himself as Pip, ushered them to a quiet part of the pub which was laid out as a restaurant. All three of them were hungry: they'd skipped lunch and, as they ate dinner, they talked excitedly about the new swimsuits they'd bought and how they couldn't wait to test them out in the sea. Mary downed a pint of the local ale, Old Sheepface, which she declared was delicious, and Gwen sipped sparkling water. Vivienne picked at her salad but managed to consume two glasses of red wine. When they had finished their meal, Vivienne announced that she was not ready to turn in for the night, so she led them through the pub, finding a comfortable table in the brightly lit lounge bar.

Pip was busy serving drinks, but a friendly barmaid brought over more wine, ale and sparkling water. The three friends glanced around; several beer drinkers were hunched over a table, talking and laughing. Two younger men were playing darts, their faces composed and serious. The lounge bar had a smell of stale beer, a mustiness that stuck in Gwen's throat. Mary had been quieter than usual through dinner, but Vivienne was still holding court about her opinions on the injustices experienced by older women.

Gwen frowned. 'But you can't deny, Vivienne – when you get older, your body changes. Things start to crumble and sag. You're not the same woman you used to be, not so attractive.'

'I don't agree.' Vivienne waved her wine glass. 'I think older shouldn't mean worse, even if it does mean different. Older women are still attractive, desirable.'

'Are they?' Gwen was doubtful. 'I mean, would you rather be Julia Roberts or Jane Fonda? They both look nice, but one is really old.'

Vivienne's laugh was triumphant and a little loud. 'Julia Roberts is in her fifties.'

'Oh?' Gwen waved a hand. 'I don't know the names of any of the young female actors.'

'My point is,' Vivienne's voice had risen to tannoy level, 'older women are knowledgeable, wise and they still have so much to offer. Any man in his right mind would be mad not to be interested in someone in their, let's say, sixties, seventies.'

'Eighties,' Mary added, taking a gulp of beer.

Gwen noticed the men sitting at the table nearby stop talking and glance across. One of them, a portly man in his fifties or sixties, seemed to be taking an interest in Vivienne. He nudged the man sitting next to him, and both men leaned forward, listening.

'Of course, with me it's all about landing the best acting roles,' Vivienne hooted. 'I used to have the stereotypical stuff, you know, femme fatale, or the victim, or the little wife. Thank goodness I don't get stuff like that any more.'

'But you don't get anything at all,' Mary murmured.

'It's awful,' Vivienne complained, draining her glass. 'Look at older male actors, Hopkins, De Niro, Pacino. They have wonderful roles. All those meaty roles for older men – Brando in the Godfather, or Hopkins as Hannibal Lecter. Al Pacino played the devil. Imagine if I had a role like that, instead of the ancient woman in the stairlift. I mean, it's ludicrous.'

The stocky man, his black hair gleaming, had wandered over to loiter at Vivienne's elbow. 'Excuse me...' His accent was a soft Cornish burr. 'I just wanted to say – I'd come and see you in a film if you were the playing the devil.'

The other men at the table, three locals in threadbare jackets huddled over pints of beer, cackled together. Vivienne didn't miss a beat. She thrust out a delicate hand. 'Vivienne Goldman.'

The man at her elbow was momentarily lost for words, then he grunted, 'Ian Hodges.'

Vivienne raised her glass. 'I'm an actor. We're on holiday. What a lovely part of the world this is.'

'Have I seen you acting in anything on TV, Vivienne?' Ian asked.

'The last big thing I was in was *The Edge of Edgeware*.' Vivienne wriggled in her seat.

The two younger men who were playing darts had just finished their game and they stopped to listen to the conversation. One of Ian's friends leaned over. 'My daughter watches *The Edge of Edgeware*. She's never missed an episode.' He screwed up his eyes and studied Vivienne carefully. 'Oh, are you the one who plays the old bat, Maggs Pryor? The one who died in the pub when it caught ablaze?'

'That's me,' Vivienne declared proudly. 'The old bat.'

Ian was anxious. 'That's not very nice, Stan.' He turned to Vivienne. 'I don't think you're an old bat at all. I think you're very glamorous.'

Stan agreed. 'She was an old bat in the soap, but she's gorgeous in real life.'

One of the young darts players had lost interest. The other called out, 'Dad, come and play darts. We're about to start a new game.'

The one called Stan leaned towards Vivienne. 'I never met a real actress before.' He pushed a hand through thick white hair. 'Can we buy you all a drink?'

'Are you all actresses?' Ian asked, adjusting his jacket, pushing a hand through oily hair.

'Actors,' Vivienne corrected him. 'And no, Gwen's an opera singer and Mary's – Mary's retired.'

Stan raised an eyebrow towards Gwen. 'Opera, eh? Can you sing us a song, Gwen?'

Gwen shook her head. 'Not in here – the air's a bit musty.'

'Maybe after a drink?' Ian reached for his wallet. 'What will you have, ladies?'

'I'll have a pint of best ale.' Mary lifted her empty glass.

'Red wine, please,' Vivienne said sweetly.

'Dad!' The young darts player insisted. 'Come on – I need a game.'

'I'm busy.' Stan turned his attention to Gwen. 'So, opera singer, eh?'

Gwen surveyed the scene, her mind in overdrive: the enthusiastic attentions of Stan, who was lurching from his seat, moving towards her, his eyes twinkling, made her anxious. He was about to ask her to sing again. There was only one thing for it. She stood up sharply. 'I'll play darts.'

Ian was at the bar. 'What are you drinking, Gwen?'

'Sparkling water, please.'

She moved towards the young man, who held out the darts and asked, 'Can you play?'

His friend laughed. 'Do you even know which end to throw?'

Gwen shrugged. 'I've played once or twice. I'll give you a game.'

The young man was surprised. 'I'm very good, you know.'

Gwen examined his face, the spattering of livid spots on his chin, the dark curl of his hair. He couldn't be older than twenty-one. She found her distance glasses in her handbag and settled them on her face, then she held up the darts. 'So, I'm Gwen.'

'Craig.' He glanced towards Stan, then back to Gwen. 'So, the purpose of the game is that you start with a score of 501 and we take turns to throw three darts and subtract the total until we end up with zero. First person to zero wins.'

'Right,' Gwen murmured. 'I think I get it.'

He winked at his friend, a blond-haired young man who had positioned himself at a scoreboard on the wall, chalk in his hand.

Stan and Ian had taken up residence at the table with Vivienne and Mary. 'Go easy on her, Craig,' Stan joked.

Craig stood behind the oche and threw three darts. His blond-haired friend cheered 'Sixty, twenty, twenty. That's a hundred. Good start, mate.'

Gwen took up position, holding a dart pinched between her fingers and thumb. She muttered under her breath. 'Wish me luck.'

Vivienne was halfway through the glass of wine, chatting loudly as Stan and Ian listened. 'My best role, apart from Maggie in *Cat on a Hot Tin Roof*, was probably Mother Courage. Of course, I've done a few Brechts – I was Grusha in *The Caucasian Chalk Circle*. But I've done a lot of TV, dramas, serials.'

'Have you ever played a nurse?' Ian asked, his eyes glowing.

'Countless times. Oh, the number of medi-dramas I've been cast in.'

'I was a nurse, in real life,' Mary mumbled into her glass. 'In a real hospital.'

'Have you ever acted in the nude?' Stan leaned forward, his face serious.

'One has to, really. I mean, it's required in some scenes.'

'Like when?' Stan urged Vivienne to continue.

Behind him a voice called out, 'One hundred and eighty.'

'Oh, so often. I played a topless dancer in a play about the roaring twenties; I was completely naked in a Sarah Kane play, and I've been a prostitute so many times I can't remember.' Vivienne shrugged and held her glass out for a refill. Stan scraped his chair, stood up and padded over to the bar.

'Mine's best ale,' Mary called after him.

Another shout came from the darts players, 'A hundred and eighty.'

'So, have you ever been in a big screen film, like Hollywood?'

Ian gazed at Vivienne in pure admiration. 'What are you doing now?'

'I'm sitting in a lovely pub in North Cornwall with two great guys I've never met before who are buying me wine,' Vivienne quipped.

'He means your next role,' Mary explained.

Vivienne found her comment hilarious. 'I know, Mary. Oh, my agent is in touch with me daily while I'm away. I'd like something I could get my teeth into though, really. A film, perhaps, a serious role.'

A cheer came from near the darts board. Mary bared her teeth. 'Poor Gwen's getting murdered at the darts.'

Stan returned with another round of drinks. He rooted in his pocket for a pen and handed it to Vivienne. 'I don't suppose you'd sign a beer mat for me, make it out to Carol, that's my daughter. She won't believe I met a real actress in the pub. And you being Maggs Pryor too.'

'Of course.' Vivienne gave her most beatific smile. 'It's always a pleasure to sign something for a fan.'

She scribbled her signature on a beer mat, almost knocking over her glass of wine in the process. Another howl came from near the darts board, then a voice shouted. 'Ten. Double twenty. That's it. We're all done.'

Stan gazed over his shoulder. 'That didn't take long.'

Mary rolled her eyes as she swigged beer. 'Ah, well, never mind, Gwen.'

Then Gwen appeared at the table, sat down sedately and picked up her glass of sparkling water.

Stan met her eyes. 'He's a very good darts player, my son Craig.'

'He is.' Gwen arched an eyebrow.

'He's won competitions, so I shouldn't feel too bad about it if I were you, love.'

'Oh, I don't.' Gwen crossed her legs smartly and sipped water.

Then Craig appeared at her shoulder. 'Well, I'm buying. What do you want to drink, Gwen?'

Stan stared. 'The loser usually buys the drinks, Craig.'

Craig shrugged. 'She beat me fair and square. She's just phenomenal, Dad. I've never seen anyone like it.'

Gwen smiled. 'All those quiet nights living in a little village in Wales. We needed to do something to pass the time.' She pressed Mary's arm. 'I used to sing arias as a teenager while I beat everyone at darts at the youth club in the village hall.'

Vivienne downed the last of her wine. 'Well, now it's time for my beauty sleep. Come on, ladies. It's time we were getting back to our... hotel.' She met Mary's eyes meaningfully. 'It was so lovely to meet you, Stan, Ian. Absolutely. Oh, and, Craig – why don't you buy us a bottle of bubbly to take away? That should serve as a round of drinks. Goodnight, gentlemen, it was a pleasure...'

The men shuffled to their feet, their faces humble. 'Oh, the pleasure was all ours, Vivienne,' Ian murmured.

'Imagine my daughter's face when I show her the signed beer mat. Thanks, Vivienne,' Stan called as Mary and Gwen guided Vivienne to the doorway.

Outside, Vivienne leaned against Mary, flopping to one side. A cold breeze had blown in her face and the sharp blast of the gust made her realise that she had drunk too much wine. 'I need to get back to the motorhome... I need to lie down.'

'Ah, you're grand, Vivienne,' Mary whispered. 'Come on now, one foot in front of another.' She turned to Gwen. 'And you showed them, Gwen. A smart woman can beat a man at the darts any day of the week.'

Gwen's face shone. 'I did, didn't I? They had no idea I was village champion in Llanclawdd during my teens.'

Vivienne staggered on her heels. 'I showed them too. I still have what it takes. I might be seventy-one, but I still have that *je se nais quoi*.' She tried again. '*Je ne sais quoi*.' Vivienne sighed, 'Oh, damn it,' then she burst into tears.

Mary and Gwen supported her, one on each side, and led her towards the motorhome in the distant darkness of the car park.

21

Mary and Gwen sat quietly outside the motorhome in the car park behind the pub as the morning sun shone on their faces. They'd placed three seats around the little plastic table, but one was currently empty. As they drank coffee and nibbled toast, Mary stared at a map and Gwen scribbled notes on a paper pad.

Mary chewed a fingernail. 'So, you've been on a vernacular railway before, Gwen?'

'Funicular. I've been up the one in the Great Orme, oh, years and years ago; it was like a tram or a cable car. That's why it's funicular. But the one in Lynmouth is a bit different because it's operated by water.'

'I think I'd like a go on it. A cable car, you say? And the view'd be fantastic too from high up.'

'I think so, Mary, yes. So, right, we go to Lynmouth and then we can pick up some nibbles and travel on towards Minehead, maybe we can stop by a beach for a picnic lunch.' She scrawled more notes on her pad. 'Where looks good?'

'Oh, it's a doddle to sort it all out.' Mary's face was too close to the map. 'We go down this little hill and then there's a perfect beach before we get to Minehead itself. Will I find us somewhere to park the van for the night on the moors here?'

'That's a great idea.' Gwen passed her a small glossy book. 'There's Vicente's camping guide. Just look up places near Minehead to camp and ring one of them on my phone so we can book ahead.'

'Right.' Mary began to thumb through the book purposefully. 'Oh, this is interesting. Dulverton... and we don't need to ring, we just turn up – hand me your pen, Gwen, and I'll write down the postcode for the satnav...'

'Ohhhhh, never again.' Vivienne propped herself up in the doorway of the motorhome, leaning her head against her arm. She was wearing a short dressing gown, sunglasses on her face. 'I feel awful this morning.'

'What a lightweight.' Mary laughed. 'You only had four wines...'

'You're so right, Mary,' Vivienne gasped. 'Once upon a time, I'd meet friends in a wine bar, we'd drink all night then head off back to someone's flat and start on the brandy... I can't do that now.'

Gwen offered a kindly arm. 'Come and sit down, Vivienne. Mary and I have sorted out the whole of today, where we're going, what we're doing. You just rest. I'll get you a coffee and some toast.'

'Just black coffee, please,' Vivienne protested. 'I couldn't eat a thing. And I'll never have another drink, as long as I live. As Othello said, "O thou invisible spirit of wine! If thou hast no name to be known by, let me call thee devil!" I'm on the sparkling water now, like you, Gwen.'

'Oh?' Mary teased gently. 'So, you didn't see the bottle of champagne Gwen has in the sink in the motorhome?'

'I did notice it,' Vivienne muttered.

'Craig bought it in the pub for us last night because I won at the darts.' Gwen was pleased with herself. 'I brought it back in my bag.'

'We thought we'd save it for a special occasion, you know, the end of the holiday or something else,' Mary added. 'But you won't be wanting any, Vivienne, what with you giving up the drink and all...'

'Oh, I'm sure I'll feel much better by then,' Vivienne began and then burst out laughing. 'What am I like?'

'You're a lush.' Gwen patted her arm affectionately. 'Here's a strong black coffee.'

'Oh, thanks Gwen, lovey.' Vivienne lifted the mug to her lips.

'And this is what we have organised for the whole day,' Mary explained. 'We're going up a water-propelled cable car, so I hope your stomach's going to be up to it, Vivienne.'

'I hope so, too.' Vivienne sipped quietly and mumbled to herself. 'After last night, I'm not really sure I'm up to anything any more.'

* * *

The drive to Lynmouth took over two hours; there was a lot of traffic on the A39, which weaved through farmland and tall hedges, slowing to a crawl on bends. Vivienne sat behind Gwen, complaining constantly that the swaying motion of the motorhome was making her feel nauseous. 'Every time the gears crunch – it's not your fault, Gwen, it's these twisting roads, but I feel a bit woozy. And it's so hot in here, even with the windows open.'

Mary was sympathetic. 'When we get there, we'll maybe get you an iced water, or a cup of the peppermint tea.' She sniffed mischievously. 'I've always found a big greasy bacon sandwich with a runny egg in it to be the best cure for a hangover.'

Vivienne clutched her stomach. 'It's my own fault. I don't suppose it would be okay if, when we get there, I pass on the cable car ride and have a sleep for a bit instead?'

'That's probably a good idea,' Gwen agreed. 'You rest, and Mary and I will gad about in the funicular carriage.'

'Then hopefully you'll feel better by the afternoon.' Mary turned and offered a friendly wink. 'I've planned for us to get a late lunch on a beach not far away. You'll feel grand by then.'

Gwen was surprised to find a parking space in Lynmouth close to the pavement and wide enough for her to install the motorhome. As Vivienne relaxed on the couch reading a magazine, Gwen and Mary set off by themselves, promising to be back before the two-hour parking limit expired. Vivienne appeared to be a little better. 'If you're a bit late, don't worry – I'm a dab hand at taking care of grouchy car park attendants.'

Lynmouth was charming, a small romantic village reminiscent of times gone by, with tiny fishermen's cottages clustered around a pretty harbour, boats bobbing in the sunlit water. Above, the village of Lynton perched high on the clifftop. Gwen and Mary reached the cliff railway quite quickly and stood at the bottom, watching twin cable cars rise and descend, the carriages meeting in the middle of their journey. Mary couldn't wait to get on board. 'Can we go? Let's go!'

Gwen studied the admission prices. 'We can buy a return – travel up, then wander about in Lynton, then come back. How does that sound?'

'It sounds grand.'

They bought tickets and clambered into the green cable car, Mary squeezing her way to the front, despite Gwen's protestations that they'd be moving backwards. Mary was insistent. 'I want to see everything.'

She and Gwen stood gazing over the bay as the ropes hauled the cable car towards the top. The ground fell away and Mary found herself in mid-air, staring down at the shimmering bowl of the sea as the rocky green coastline became smaller. She caught her breath. 'It's like being in a spaceship, hurtling away from the earth. And look at it all down there, the ocean, the bay. Still and placid and shiny as a new plate. Gwen, this is wonderful.'

Gwen had to agree. Next to her elbow, an older man was taking photos. He smiled. 'I used to come here with my wife at weekends. She always loved it. Now I come by myself.'

Gwen wasn't sure how to reply, so she simply said, 'Oh, it's lovely, isn't it?'

When they reached the top, Mary hugged Gwen's arm as they clambered from the carriage. 'My legs are failing me, Gwen.'

'Are you all right, Mary? Do you want to sit down?'

'Oh, not at all. It's just the excitement making my legs wobble.'

They walked on into Lynton for five minutes or so. Gwen spotted a supermarket and decided that, on the way back, they'd pop in and buy some groceries for the picnic. Then they arrived at a grey-fronted church, and Mary stopped. A few people were leaving, drifting from the wooden doorway, talking softly.

'Can we go in, Gwen? I know it doesn't look much but I like to go into a church sometimes, when I can.'

Gwen followed Mary inside, gazing at the huge expanse of the church, the high roof, the walls that echoed with the soft ring of voices. Mary slid into a pew, sat down and clasped her hands, resting her forehead on top of them. Gwen decided she needed solitude, some quiet time to reflect, so she stood silently at the back of the church, taking in the white walls, the rounded arches, the high window with a tall cross. At the altar, a priest in long robes was talking quietly with a woman in a brown coat and Gwen thought she heard the word 'peace'. She was suddenly seized with the inclination to take a deep breath and sing 'Ave Maria'; the acoustics would make her voice resonate with purity. Churches were perfect places to sing, and Gwen imagined how angelic and reverent her rendition could be. But that would be a performance, not an act of devotion. She pulled out her phone to glance at the time: they ought to be getting back to Vivienne soon.

Mary was muttering to herself, as she always did in church, moving her fingers as if she had rosary beads in her hands. She always said the same prayer in the same order: 'O God of goodness and mercy, to Thy fatherly guidance we commend our family...' then she'd name her mother, her father, her sisters and brothers, the young sister who died as a baby, then she'd mention her own child. She'd always pause after the mention of the name she'd given her daughter at birth on the certificate, wondering where she might be, what she might be called now. Then Mary would ask for a blessing for friends and finally, for herself, in humility. She uttered the last few respectful words under her breath, her lips moving: 'O Mary, Mother of grace and of mercy, defend us against the wicked spirit, reconcile us with Thy Son, commit us to His keeping, that so we may be made worthy of His promises.' Mary paused for a moment to reflect, then opened her eyes. 'I'm done now, Gwen,' she whispered over her shoulder. 'We should be going back.'

Gwen and Mary's journey in the cable car to Lynmouth was a quiet one; both women were still lost in their separate thoughts as they trudged along the hot pavements. But back at the motorhome, Vivienne was unable to sleep. The air was humid; black knots of flies buzzed against the open windows. She thought about phoning her agent, Olivia, but she didn't want to appear desperate, so Vivienne rang Dom in Germany and chatted about her holiday instead. She laughed, telling him she had escaped from London and was having a fabulous time at the seaside, then she had phoned Lennie's daughter, Lucia, and told her the same thing. Lucia had replied that her father was having a great time by the sea too, but he was at the other end of the country, filming. He had been there for two weeks already. Apparently, he had phoned Lucia last night, joked that it had taken almost an hour for the artist to do his make-up for the role, and then he'd asked after Vivienne. Lucia knew that he was missing her, and she urged Vivienne to contact him, but Vivienne had changed the subject.

And now, after the call, Vivienne's head was throbbing. She'd taken two painkillers, but she knew the ache wasn't due to the effects of alcohol or the heat. It was Lennie, again: she was examining her feelings as she had done so many times since their split. Yes, she admitted to herself, she still loved him. So what was the problem? They'd bickered many times, their relationship had been tempestuous. But maybe passionate was a better word. They'd had ups and downs but, Vivienne realised, the real issue was something much more troubling. He was a successful actor, he was popular, attractive to women and men; people readily warmed to his humour and he was versatile – he could play almost any role. And yet all Vivienne was offered nowadays was – what had been her phrase? Grannies, corpses or witches.

Despite the heat, Vivienne shivered: as if iced water had been thrown in her face, she realised that she was probably a little jealous. She'd never stopped to unpack her feelings before; she'd never given herself time, but she was sure that her envy of Lennie's easy acquisition of new and exciting roles was a factor. She would never have thought of herself as a grudging person: she was always proud of his talent and his successes, but fundamentally, she had to acknowledge that she'd been a little indignant that Lennie was still finding satisfying roles and she wasn't.

Vivienne shook her head and decided she'd reach for the two things she usually resorted to, other than wine, when she was troubled: black coffee and dramatic quotations. She lifted the kettle, filled it with water and spooned ground coffee beans into a carafe, then she murmured a favourite Shakespeare line which she knew only too well: she had played Viola in *Twelfth Night*, forty years ago.

"'O time, thou must untangle this, not I. It is too hard a knot for me t'untie.'"

22

Vivienne was all smiles when Gwen and Mary returned carrying bags of shopping for the late lunch they would have when they arrived on the beach, which Mary insisted wasn't very far away. Gwen typed the postcode into the satnav and they began the journey out of Lynmouth with the air conditioning on full and Gwen's CD of Thomas Tallis's *Spem in Alium* blaring. Mary was still thinking about being inside the church, her quiet prayers and her time of reflection, so she muttered, 'Ah, anyone outside would think we were a vanload of blessed monks.'

Gwen smiled. 'I love Thomas Tallis.'

'It's very restful and uplifting, the harmonies and the choral singing.' Vivienne closed her eyes and let the music drift over her. She exhaled slowly; she had come to a decision. She'd enjoy the holiday with Gwen and Mary and then, when she was back in London, she'd go and see Lennie, talk things through with him, show some humility and kindness. She'd play it by ear: he might ask her if they could try again, and she'd consider it seriously now. But perhaps he'd already met a co-star on set while he was filming in the north. Perhaps he'd fallen in love with someone else. If that happened, Vivienne would wish him the best, with no feelings of jealousy. She'd stop acting like a spoilt prima donna from this moment forth. She'd make amends.

Gwen peered over her glasses as she drove along the main road. Mary and Vivienne were unusually quiet, so she concentrated on the bending roads and driving carefully. There was a great deal of traffic and it was quite humid inside the cab. From the lofty position of her seat, Gwen could see the expanse of blue ocean stretching like a turquoise ribbon below to the left, glistening in the sunlight. Beside her, Mary was silent: Gwen expected her to chortle about the view of the sea and wave her arms like an excited child, but her eyes were closed, shaded by sunglasses. Vivienne in the passenger seat behind was sleepy too. Gwen assumed it was still the effects of the wine she'd drunk last night. Gwen was glad of the sweet choral music that filled the cab and made her spirits soar; she sang along, her voice trilling on the high notes. After twenty minutes or so, she realised she felt quite hungry and was looking forward to sharing a picnic lunch on the pretty beach Mary had found.

Gwen peered in the driver's mirror; behind her, Vivienne had fallen asleep, her head lolling to one side, a magazine perched on the edge of her on her lap. Mary, next to Gwen, had her mouth open and was making little snorting sounds. Gwen smiled. The road sign on the bend in front of her announced that she was approaching Porlock Hill, and that it was steep. Gwen paid little attention: she would be all right going downhill; she had good brakes. In front of her, an old Transit van was chugging slowly, belching out black smoke. Then Gwen felt a sudden vibrating, a juddering accompanied by a loud rattle sound as the motorhome jolted across a cattle grid.

Mary sat uptight. 'Holy Mother... sorry, Gwen. What was that?'

'Just a cattle grid. Don't worry – we're just going down a little hill now.'

'Aren't we there yet? Where are we?'

A road sign warned that Porlock Hill was a 13 per cent slope, and a low gear was needed. The battered Transit in front showed its flickering red brake lights and Gwen pressed her foot down steadily to slow the motorhome. They turned a sharp corner and the incline of the road became suddenly perpendicular. Gwen leaned forwards, catching her breath. 'Oh, my goodness gracious me.'

To the left and right, the road fell away, a vertical gradient. The Transit stopped in front, forcing Gwen to slam her foot on the brakes, and the motorhome jolted forwards. Vivienne woke up, murmuring, 'Have we crashed?'

Gwen eased the motorhome into the lowest gear and braked hard again as they hurtled forwards. In front, the Transit was crawling along, black smoke billowing from the exhaust. There was a strong smell of something acrid, the stench of rubber burning.

Mary's eyes bulged behind the glasses. 'Is something on fire?'

'It's brake pads, I think...' Gwen peered forwards. 'I hope it's the van in front, and not us.'

They turned a corner and the gradient became even sharper. On either side, the grassy banks and houses leaned away. Gwen's foot forced against the brake pedal so hard that the bones in her ankle ached. The motorhome crept around a corner, then a bend, the gradient harsher than ever, the Transit in front of them slowing to a crawl. Gwen shook her head anxiously. 'There must be an easier road to the seaside than this one. It's horrendous.'

'You're doing very well, Gwen.' Mary gazed out of the window, then her mouth opened wide. 'Oh, blessed Saint Joseph, the road has just disappeared.'

Vivienne leaned forward. 'It's a one in four, the road sign says. This hill is ridiculous. How do they expect ordinary cars to—'

'Look, there's a bunch of bikers coming up the hill the other way,' Mary howled, pointing her finger as a line of cyclists in bright

Lycra clothes rounded the bend on the other side of the road, pedalling easily. 'And they're expecting to climb up this mountain – on bicycles? Their legs must be made of metal springs.'

Gwen's nerves were on edge. 'And the Transit driver keeps slowing down all of a sudden in front with his smelly diesel and his boot flat on the brake pedal all the time – this is just horrible. Oh, thank goodness. The satnav tells me I can turn off here. We're going to Bossington beach, isn't that right, Mary?'

'It is.' Mary nodded. 'It's nearly two o'clock. I'm starving. We'll get ourselves a picnic lunch on the beach.'

Gwen breathed out with relief and indicated left, guiding the motorhome into a narrow lane. She felt the tension set hard into her back muscles, which were now stiff as steel: if she encountered another vehicle, she wouldn't be able to reverse.

She sighed. 'Well, the beach is just down a track here. It's very beautiful, but I've no idea how I'm ever going to turn round and get us out of here again.'

'Ah, never mind,' Mary retorted. 'We're away on holiday. It's all part of the craic.'

Gwen shook her head and exhaled, one hard breath. 'I'd have enjoyed the craic, as you say, Mary, a lot more if I wasn't the only driver in this damned motorhome and someone other than me could have driven it down that bloody hill.'

It was a ten-minute trudge from the car park in Bossington down to the beach, and Mary was soon puffing due to the hot sun overhead and the heavy bag of bread and cheese she was carrying. Vivienne had changed into skimpy shorts and a vest; her bag was bulging with beach mats and sun cream. They arrived on the shore, a wide stretch of sharp-edged stones, mound after mound of huge piled pebbles. They stepped precariously over rocks of various sizes and, not far from the sea, a long band of deepest blue, Vivienne threw her bag down. 'We'll sit here, shall we? It's not flat, but then – nowhere is.'

'I'm putting a towel on top of my mat,' Mary grunted. 'These pointed stones will bruise my backside.'

Gwen flopped down on a mat and began to unpack food. She gazed towards the rolling waves, a light breeze brushing her cheek. 'But isn't it beautiful? And there's no one else here but us, and it's so sunny. What a lovely find, Mary.'

Mary was delighted. 'Our own personal plot of beach.'

Vivienne tugged a bottle of water from her bag and took a sip. 'It certainly blows away the cobwebs, being this close to the sea. I suggest we have a bite to eat and then we soak up some rays.'

'I might even have a sleep after we've had lunch.' Gwen fanned her face. 'I'm exhausted.'

An hour later, as they were packing lunch away into bags, Mary sat bolt upright. 'Can we swim in the sea here?'

Vivienne shook her head. 'No, the current is too strong.'

'We could have a paddle, though,' Gwen suggested. 'Dip our feet in the ocean.'

Mary kicked off her sandals. 'Right. Come on. I'll race you to the water's edge.'

Vivienne was already on her feet, nimble in shorts, skipping across the stones. 'You're on.'

Gwen struggled to stand, tugging off her trainers, tucking up her skirt. 'Wait for me.'

The three women ran, hopped and stumbled towards the sea, shouting in pain and laughing as the jagged rocks pressed against the bare soles of their feet. Then they leaped into the frothing waves, kicking water towards each other, foam dribbling from their toes.

Mary lifted a foot, whisking a dripping arc towards Vivienne.

'This is so much better than being stuck in a basement flat in London.'

'It certainly is refreshing,' Vivienne screamed, a cold splash filling her mouth, then she brayed with laughter and began to hurl as much water as she could over Gwen. Gwen, in turn, swished an armful of sea towards Mary and the three of them laughed, splashing in the rolling waves and drenching each other's hair and clothes until they were exhausted.

Gwen was the first to tire, pushing back drenched hair, bending over with laughter. 'I'm bushed. We should go back to the motorhome.'

'You're right, we should,' Vivienne gasped, noticing her drenched top for the first time. 'Oh, but that was such good fun. And just the therapy I needed.'

'Yes, we should get off now, before we all catch cold.' Mary gazed in dismay at her soaked trousers. 'But there's nothing like the seaside to bring out the big kiddie in you.'

'I agree – I feel so much better now.' Gwen smiled. 'We'll drive to the place we're staying tonight, shall we, and just chill out.'

'I can't wait – we're spending the night on Exmoor,' Mary beamed.

'How beautiful.' Vivienne shook wet hair, her eyes shining.

They walked together back to the beach mats, arm in arm, their hair and clothes dripping wet, their feet pricked by hard pebbles, their faces glowing with happiness.

23

The three friends clambered out of their wet clothes and into warm, dry ones before resuming their journey, teeth chattering. The postcode in the satnav led them through the pretty coastal town of Minehead before Gwen turned the motorhome into a narrow lane and drove up a hill for several miles until they arrived at the top of a rugged cliff that overlooked the vast ocean. The terrain was wild, untamed: the patchwork of moorlands formed a bright quilt of sharp colours leading to craggy rocks, a steep drop then, below, a wide strip of white sand and the breaking waves.

Mary was ecstatic. 'Here we are, here we are.'

'Yes, but where are we?'

'This is Exmoor, Gwen.' Mary waved her hands in triumph. 'And we can stay here all night. We don't have to pay anyone; it's nobody's land or car park or farm. In the brochure, it said it was an ideal place to stop in a camper van overnight.'

'Well, we'll park up here then,' Vivienne said decisively, unclipping her seat belt and slipping out through the passenger door. 'I think it's fabulous, Mary. Just look at this place.'

Gwen followed her, dropping from the driver's seat to stare at the view, her arms folded. 'Do you think it's safe to be up here by ourselves?'

'Ah, we're grand. There's no one around for miles.' Mary's cheeks were flushed pink with success. 'What do you think?'

Vivienne breathed out slowly. 'It's beautiful.' They were standing on heather that stretched into the distance, a rolling carpet of purple, spattered with green grass and yellow gorse. Below, the cliff came to an abrupt edge and dropped down to patchwork fields in the distance. Just beyond, the shining arc of ocean curved around a ribbon of yellow sand. The sun had slipped behind clouds, dripping soft orange light that reflected in the sea.

'It is idyllic,' Gwen admitted. 'Very tranquil, restful. So, what shall we do now?'

Vivienne gave an involuntary shiver. 'I think a shower is in order. We need to rinse our clothes through and find a tree so that we can put up the washing line.'

'We'll need to refill the water tank again tomorrow if you're washing clothes and having another shower, Vivienne,' Gwen observed.

'I vote we get everything cleaned up and get into our pyjamas, then I'll make us a nice hot chocolate.' Mary rubbed her hands together. 'All we've had is a couple of sandwiches at the picnic – so we're probably allowed a bit of indulgence, you know, the 80:20.'

It was after nine o'clock as the three women in pyjamas and dressing gowns stood in silence, watching the sun disappear behind the sea. Mary pushed her hands deep into her pockets. 'What a lovely day this has been. I love the way the sun drops down into the water. It's like pictures by that painter who chucked oils all over the canvas and painted burning ships and steam trains.'

'Turner,' Vivienne murmured. 'He'd have painted this sunset so vividly.'

The white-hot disc of sun was visible on the horizon, cushioned between vermilion clouds, reflecting a narrow golden path across the ocean. Mary's face was illuminated by reflected light as she murmured, 'From where the sun rises to where it sets, the name of the Lord is praised.'

'What's that from?' Gwen asked.

'Psalm 113.' Mary closed her eyes. 'It's one of my favourites.'

Vivienne glanced in her direction. 'Are you a believer, Mary?'

'For sure, I am,' she whispered. 'The good Lord gave me life and love and hope.'

Gwen frowned. 'I don't know what I believe, after all these years. I suppose I'm a bit of a doubting Thomas, really. I went to chapel every Sunday as a child, but I don't know what to think nowadays.'

'I believe whatever makes people happy and filled with love is a good thing.' Vivienne was thoughtful. 'There needs to be more love in the world. And more fun.' An idea came to her. 'Who's up for a glass of brandy?'

'I thought you'd given up drinking?' Gwen was astonished.

'That was then. This is now,' Vivienne quipped. 'And I've got a nice bottle of Armagnac tucked away somewhere inside the motorhome.'

'Oh, that's grand.' Mary licked her lips.

Gwen was momentarily worried. 'I've never had Armagnac before.'

'So, now's a good time to try it.' Vivienne turned abruptly and hurried back into the motorhome, followed by an enthusiastic Mary in pyjamas and dressing gown. Gwen glanced at the sunset. The sky was almost dark overhead, a turbulent rolling expanse of pink and blue, like a spreading bruise. She shrugged her shoulders and moved slowly towards the passenger door. She didn't really feel like drinking brandy.

An hour later, Gwen had only taken a single sip. She was holding the small glass of Armagnac in her fingers. It tasted sharp, a little surprising, leaving a burning sensation on her lips. She thought briefly that the tingling taste of brandy was not unlike a first kiss, then her mind floated to Clifford Edwards, his tender embraces, the soft words he'd whispered, then she tugged her thoughts back to Vivienne, who was speaking animatedly, her second refill of brandy almost finished.

'So, what do you think? A few days in one place would be just perfect.'

Mary nodded. 'I think it might be very nice indeed. What do you say, Gwen?'

Gwen blinked. 'What do I say?'

Vivienne filled her small glass up, then reached for Mary's, took it from her fingers and repeated the action. 'We were talking about Swansea Bay. We could spend a few days there, so that we stay in one place for a while.' She chewed her lip, thinking. 'So, how about we spend the rest of our time in Swansea Bay, one location, and put some roots down? That way we can get to know the place a bit.'

Gwen nodded. 'We should go to Rhossili, on the Gower peninsular.' Memories were flooding back, times when she was young and full of hope, and she smiled. 'It's just so beautiful there.'

She was thinking of him again, handsome Clifford Edwards, as she'd clung to him on the back of his motorbike, as they'd driven to Rhossili one evening in August. They had watched the orange sun sinking, strolled on the beach hand in hand as the light became dusk – it had been so perfect, so innocent, and as the stars filled the sky, he'd promised to love her forever. She'd believed him, every word. Then he had let her down. Gwen became aware that Mary was laughing.

'Ah, Gwen – you're away with the fairies tonight.'

'Sorry?'

'I asked if you grew up near there,' Vivienne explained. 'Near Rhossili.'

'I was born not too far away, several miles inland. A small village. Llanclawdd.'

Mary sipped from her glass. 'I'm not sure I've been to Wales. Oh, no, I might have been to the north of it, just once. I went to Llandudno with a young man I was dating when I was in my late twenties. He was a hospital porter called Harry. We went for a dirty weekend up the Great Orme and we didn't get out of the hotel room much. Harry Pike, he was called. Dark hair, a little goatee beard. I thought I was in love with him.'

'So, what happened to Harry Pike, Mary?'

'I didn't love him at all, as it turned out, Vivienne. We drifted apart. I left him for a radiographer called Roger – or was it Robert?'

Gwen's face was serious. 'You've had a lot of boyfriends.'

'Not in the last twenty years, sadly. They've all dried up a bit.'

Gwen sighed. 'I think I've dried up a bit. I was just wondering what it would be like to go back to Llanclawdd again.'

'When were you last there?'

'Many, many years ago, Vivienne.' Gwen clutched her glass. 'I went home after my mother died. I sang at her funeral. That was in 1994. I sang "Myfanwy". That wasn't her name. My mother was called Grace Prichard.'

Mary's voice was quiet. 'Sing it for us, Gwen.'

'All right, I will.' Gwen closed her eyes, thought about her mother, the image she'd always had of her bent over, sewing in dim light, her hair grey, pinned severely, then she recalled the dark wooden coffin in the vast church, and she began to sing slowly, each note mournful.

> *Paham mae dicter, O Myfanwy,*
> *Yn llenwi'th lygaid duon di?*
> *A'th ruddiau tirion, O Myfanwy,*
> *Heb wrido wrth fy ngweled.*

Mary's cheeks were damp with tears. 'You sang that for your mammy? Oh, that's so nice, Gwen – may she rest in peace.'

'You have such a beautiful voice.' Vivienne knocked back more Armagnac.

'You were lucky in a way, Gwen, to be able to give that song to your mother as a gift and send her on her way. It's very respectful. I didn't see my family at all, any of them, not since 1960.' Mary sighed. 'But they probably didn't miss me. We were a lot of mouths to feed. There were six of us, three girls and three boys. Well, there were four girls at first but the little one, Nora, she didn't live long.'

'What happened to her?' Gwen leaned forward. 'Wasn't she well?'

'No, she wasn't well at all.' Mary's voice was low. 'She had tuberculosis. I was seven years old – I remember my mammy holding her tight in her arms because she had the night sweats, and she was coughing, poor little thing, a little high-up cough, like a wheeze. She could hardly catch her breath. My da sent me running for the doctor, who lived half a mile away. I was scared stiff – it was pitch black outside, it was gone ten o'clock and I had to run past the pub. I was only a little scrap of a thing then.'

'What happened?' Gwen's face was serious. 'Did you get to the doctor's?'

'No, I never got there.'

'Why not?'

'I saw a ghost.'

Gwen's mouth dropped open. 'A ghost?'

Mary nodded. 'Just as I drew level with the pub, there wasn't a soul about and I looked up at the wall, a dirty old brick wall, and I stopped dead in my tracks. At first, I thought it was an angel, like a face painted on the bricks, pure gold and smiling. But then I stared at it and it didn't go away, and it wasn't an angel. It was little Nora, smiling. She had her eyes closed and so I knew she was dead. Then I just took myself off home again.'

'And was she? Dead?' Gwen whispered.

'She was. I got back and she'd just passed. If I'd brought the doctor, there was nothing he could have done. And that was it, little Nora was no more. My mammy was crying, saying she was the loveliest one of us all, the sweetest natured one, and how it shouldn't have been her who was taken, and I thought then that she'd have preferred it to be me instead.' Mary shrugged. 'I was always the one who let her down.'

'I'm sure you didn't let her down.' Vivienne drained her glass. 'You were a nurse, Mary. She must have been so proud of your achievements.'

'Ah, I don't think so.' Mary held up her glass, gazing at the amber liquid. Sometimes it was better to say nothing at all.

'But you saw a ghost – you must have been so terrified. I know I would have been.'

'Not really. I just took it as a sign. Besides, lots of us little ones were unwell from time to time. You sort of expected it to happen eventually. I had diphtheria myself. Kathleen had scarlet fever, so did Patrick, my brother. Those ailments were very common then.' Mary thrust out her glass. 'I'll just have a small one for the road, Vivienne. Then I think I'll turn in for the night.'

'Me too.' Gwen stretched her arms above her head. 'It was a tough day today; I spent so much time at the wheel, and if we're off to South Wales tomorrow, I'll need to have my wits about me. It'll be a long drive – about four hours, and we'll need to stop for fuel and to refill the water tank.'

'We're on holiday, Gwen,' Vivienne insisted. 'It's your holiday too. We'll go at your pace, stop somewhere for lunch, take a break. I'll treat us. After all, you're not a taxi service. We really appreciate you doing all the driving. I know today has been tough.'

'Especially the big hill, the Porlock one,' Mary suggested. 'And the narrow bumpy ride to Bossington beach. And the journey back again. And the little track up to the top of this cliff.' Mary finished her drink. 'Ah, you're a gem, Gwen.'

Gwen smiled gratefully, closing her eyes. She was tired, her limbs felt heavy, and she hoped that as soon as she curled up in the space next to Mary, she'd drift into a peaceful sleep.

But then, she thought anxiously, Mary had been talking about ghosts, and the notion of ghosts troubled Gwen deeply. Besides, the possibility of going back to visit Wales after such a long time away had stirred memories of her childhood, her family and of Clifford Edwards. Now she'd probably never get a wink of sleep all night.

24

Gwen had been deep in slumber, but suddenly she was wide awake, sitting upright. Something was hitting the roof, hard thudding like the banging of many fists. She exhaled slowly: it was just rain, a heavy downpour. She could hear it beating against the window behind the little velvet curtain. Mary was asleep next to her, the regular chainsaw rattle escaping through her nose. Gwen glanced at her phone; it was 5.20. She sighed; the sun would be up, almost, but she doubted she'd see much through the window except grey rain. She rolled over and Vivienne's voice whispered from the cab, 'Gwen? Are you awake?'

Gwen nodded, and realised that Vivienne wouldn't be able to see her in the gloom. 'I am.'

'Oh, what are we doing, wide awake at this hour?' Vivienne's tone of resignation suggested that she hadn't slept for a while.

'The rain woke me.'

'It's been pelting down for hours.' Vivienne sighed. There was a pause, then she added, 'You must be looking forward to going back to Wales, Gwen. How long is it since you've been?'

'Too long, I suppose. But then, I've had nothing to be going back for.'

Vivienne gave a dry laugh. 'What are we like? I haven't been back to Leicester for years – my brother, Pete, lives in Loughborough now. I see him occasionally, Christmases, birthdays. You don't go back to Wales any more, and Mary hasn't been back to Ireland in years.'

There was silence, the darkness momentarily oppressive, then Mary's voice piped up, 'I've nobody in Ireland now. It's like we're all three orphans.' She snorted. 'Ah, who cares? Not me. Home is here, now, in this motorhome, tucked up with warm feet under a duvet.'

Vivienne gave a small cough. 'But what about the people in your village in Wales, Gwen? Will you know any of them?'

'Rhossili's just going to be a seaside stay...'

'In the rain...' Mary grunted.

'But when we travel on to Llanclawdd, well, I'm not sure. I left over fifty years ago. Everyone I knew will probably be dead.'

'Not everyone.' Vivienne was quiet, thinking. 'What about the old boyfriend, Cliff...?'

'Oh...' Gwen scratched her head, an audible scraping of nails against scalp. 'I'm not sure I want to bump into him ever again.'

'No?' Vivienne persisted. 'It might be good, you know, to put the past to rest.'

'Not if he's still with Siân Roberts.' Gwen couldn't help the words that burst from her lips. 'Do you know, I've wanted to punch her in the face for fifty years.'

Mary laughed, a wild hooting that continued for almost ten seconds, ending in a hiccup. 'I'd pay money to see that, Gwen. You at the wedding standing at the back of the church in your best bib and tucker, Siân and Cliff all serious, taking their vows at the altar with the priest in his robe, and in you rush to the front and slap her one right in the face. That would be a scream...' Mary stopped, sniffed once and said, 'No, but it must be a bad memory. Perhaps it's best if you don't bump into her. She'll be old and fat now, anyway...' Mary could see that she wasn't helping Gwen; that she wasn't cheering her up as she'd intended. 'Don't pay any mind to me, I'm making a holy show of myself.' She waited for an answer and then added, 'Just listen to that rain? It's bucketing down.'

Gwen wiped a tear from her cheek with the back of her hand and took a breath. 'Oh, bother Clifford. He's best forgotten.' She made her voice cheerful. 'So, what are we all doing awake? It's not even six o'clock.'

There was a dull thud; Vivienne had slid from the bed in the cab and was standing in the grey light in her shortie pyjamas. 'It's time for coffee. I could murder a proper double espresso. We'll have one of those later in a café, perhaps? I'll just put the kettle on and fill the carafe and...' She heaved the door open. 'Oh, wow – just look at the view.'

Gwen was beside her in seconds and Mary padded to stand behind them. The rain was heavy, soaking the soft ground, puddles filling with mud in spaces between the heather. In the distance, several ponies stood in the downpour, their heads bent, munching grass. A brown foal huddled next to a mare, who nuzzled it with her nose. A grey mist hung over the sea, the sand and ocean grainy and blurred. The air was cool, scented with the fresh sweetness of grass and the tang of salt from the ocean.

Vivienne moved to the cooker and opened the curtains; globes of rain had settled on the windows like pearls. She poured coffee. 'Well, it's decision time. Shall we make breakfast now, or go for a walk, or go back to bed and sleep for a bit longer?'

'I'd love a walk.' Gwen shrugged. 'But we don't have wellingtons and our anoraks are only light.'

'And you've all that driving to do, Gwen. You'll tire yourself out,' Mary suggested.

'So, breakfast it is,' Vivienne said, her voice conveying too much enthusiasm. She'd been keen to go for a walk no matter how wet her clothes became. 'Perhaps the rain will ease off soon and then we can just walk along the path not far from the cliff edge and look at the view, or see if we can persuade the ponies to let us give them a hug.'

'That would be lovely,' Gwen replied.

'What do we have left for breakfast?' Mary licked her lips.

'Toast and marmalade.' Vivienne indicated the half-eaten loaf, wrapped in waxy paper. 'Or we might have a leftover muffin or two?'

'Is that all?' Gwen pulled a face. 'Never mind – tomorrow we'll be in Wales and we'll be eating proper breakfasts.'

'Welsh rarebit?' Mary looked hopeful.

'Oh no, proper laver bread and cockles, eggs, bacon, sausages…'

'Oh, that would be grand – I vote we get off to Wales right now.' Mary rubbed her hands together.

'Cockles?' Vivienne pulled a face. 'For breakfast?'

'Oh, they are lovely.' Gwen had perked up. 'And I haven't had proper laver bread in ages.'

'What's that when it's at home?'

'Laver bread, Mary, is to die for – we Welsh call it *bara law* and it's like a purée made from seaweed, served on hot buttered toast with seafood.'

'I'd give it a go, definitely,' Mary said heartily.

Vivienne was waving Vicente's accommodation guide with the glossy cartoon picture of a caravan on the front. 'Right, I'll ring this place I've just found. It's a farm overlooking the sea, owned by a Mr David Gwilym, and they offer free accommodation for motorhomes in the field, plus they'll do breakfast and evening meal for a reasonable price. I think we deserve a treat. I'm going to ring them and sign up for everything. If we're going to Wales, we may as well enjoy the full shebang.'

* * *

Hours later, the rain was still spattering the windscreen in fat droplets. Above, the clouds hung low, grey and brooding. Gwen drove along the motorway, muttering to herself about typical English summer weather, then she realised they were only a few miles from Wales. The wipers swished rhythmically, as the CD blared at full volume, a male baritone singing a song about guardian angels, his voice slow and serious. Gwen's lips twitched in a small smile: after so many years she was going home to the land she loved, to the valleys, the welcoming people, the sweet lilting voices not dissimilar to her own. Mary frowned from the seat next to her.

'Don't you have any music by Abba?' She leaned forward. 'Or better still, the Dubliners?'

Gwen kept her eyes on the road beyond the hypnotic windscreen wipers. 'It's Sir Bryn Terfel. He's Welsh. We're just about to cross the border into Wales. We're coming up to the Severn Bridge.'

'What about some Tom Jones?' Vivienne chimed from the seat behind. 'He used to be so sexy. And he's Welsh.'

Gwen smiled and turned the CD up two notches; Sir Bryn was singing 'Amazing Grace' and it reminded her of her mother.

Mary rubbed her ears. 'It's past one. Shouldn't we stop for lunch? I can't exist all day on a scrap of brown bread and jam.'

'A nice espresso would be good,' Vivienne murmured. 'Where can we stop close to Wales, Gwen? It's my treat today – I'm buying lunch.'

'We could stop at the services at Aust – we're almost there. There's a nice view of the Severn estuary from the café, I've heard.'

Gwen stared at the road absorbed beneath them as the motorhome surged forwards. 'Decision time – the services are just ahead. Are we going for lunch there or not?'

'Yes,' Mary and Vivienne chorused.

'I need coffee,' Vivienne added. 'Let's stop now.'

Mary rubbed her brow. 'And I need a break from Brian Teflon's bellowing. Fair play, he has a lovely voice on him, but all that belly aching is making my head bang.'

'Right.' Gwen flicked the indicator. 'Lunch it is, and some peace and quiet – unless they are playing Abba in the café.'

Back on the M4 towards Swansea an hour later, the rain had started to ease. A white sign with a red dragon welcomed visitors to Wales with a cheerful *Croeso i Cymru!* The scenery was becoming more dramatic, green hills rising around the grey motorway crammed with traffic. Gwen had slowed the motorhome to a crawl as they passed through an area of road-works, then she accelerated away. Mary was asleep, her cheeks pink from the warmth inside the cab. Gwen glanced into the driver's mirror and noticed Vivienne was on her phone. She called over her shoulder, 'Anything exciting on the job front, Vivienne?'

Vivienne replied without looking up. 'I'm texting Olivia now, just a quick check-in. She knows I'm away now, so I don't suppose she'll be looking very hard for work for me until I'm back in London.'

'What would be the perfect role for you now? Seriously, if you could have any role at all, you know, a proper one?'

Vivienne leaned back in her seat and closed her eyes. 'I'm deter-mined to be positive. I've had a long talk with myself, and there's no point me moping any more. I'll take what I'm given.'

Gwen kept her eyes on the traffic, watching the looming hills grow ever closer. 'You remind me of Helen Mirren to look at, Vivienne. And you're younger than she is, but she gets glamorous roles, you know, detectives, calendar girls – the queen.'

'Oh, Helen Mirren is a phenomenon. I'm just Vivienne Goldman.' She was thoughtful. 'I'd be happy to play Margaret in *Richard the Third*, even though she's about a hundred years old and one-dimensional. Just to let all that rage go on stage. "Poor painted queen, vain flourish of my fortune!" It would be so cathartic. Or I'd gladly play something light and fun, you know, Wilde's Lady Brack-nell, Shaw's Mrs Warren.' She waved a thought away with her hand. 'I'd take anything now – mistress, dumped wife, anything as long as it wasn't the bloody woman on the stairlift. But of course, I'd give my eye teeth for a good juicy film role. Oh, how nice that would be, something that would give my career a kickstart again.'

'You're very famous, Vivienne – everyone knows your name, and they loved your character from that soap you were in for all those years.'

'Maggs was burned to a crisp in the pub. She's in the past now.'

Gwen was aware that the line of traffic in front was crossing the River Neath, and suddenly a strange feeling crept onto her shoulders, the odd sense of a homecoming, a mixture of trepidation, excitement and nervousness. The satnav told her that junction 42 was ahead and that she would need to turn off the motorway at the next exit. She glanced in the mirror and noticed Vivienne studying her phone still.

'I'd love to sing again, you know – just in a chorus, I wouldn't mind what part I had. But, if I could pick anything for myself, it would be Prince Orlofsky in *Die Fledermaus*.'

Vivienne was suddenly interested. 'Do women play men's roles in opera?'

'Well, they can, although the best parts are usually kept for the young and attractive singers unless they are big names, you know, Lesley Garrett and the like, but sometimes we ladies get a nice male role – it's called a *travesti*, but some people call them trouser or breeches roles. It's ideal for an older woman who is a mezzo soprano like me.'

'Oh, I'd love that.' Vivienne clapped her hands. 'What a brilliant thing it would be if I could play men's roles. The list of what I'd do is endless – Hamlet, King Lear, Iago. Or I'd be Quasimodo, Jekyll and Hyde, God.'

'Oh no, you shouldn't play God. I don't think that's right, not really.'

'Morgan Freeman did, Gwen. And Groucho Marx. Why not a woman?'

Gwen changed the subject. 'Only an hour and we'll be at Rhossili. We'll be there by four, I think.'

'Great,' Vivienne murmured, closing her eyes. She was imagining herself on stage as King Lear, her hair unkempt, her eyes wild, bulging as she raged and wailed and spat her lines. She'd be perfect for the role, arrogant, foolish, broken, throwing all her energy into becoming an object of pathos. She imagined the dramatic photos of herself in the newspapers, wearing royal rags, a crown askew on her head. She could see the headlines, the rave reviews: *Goldman was born to play Lear*. It would be so wonderful.

The rhythmic humming of the engine, the whirring wheels on tarmac and the warmth inside the motorhome had made her feel soft and relaxed; images of herself performing on stage and before cameras filled her imagination and lifted her into a dream. Vivienne was deep in slumber, her mind filled with happy thoughts, when Gwen's voice came from the front.

'Well, wakey wakey, everyone. Here we are in Rhossili. We're at our destination, just outside the farm. It's called *Maes-Y-Wawr*, and there's someone by the front door coming to meet us.'

25

Gwen wound down her window and thrust out a hand. 'Hello. I'm Gwen Prichard. Pleased to meet you.'

'Oh, you're Welsh.' The small dark-haired woman in her sixties, wearing a floral dress, large boots and a thick hooded jacket, beamed as she shook her hand. 'I'm Olwen Gwilym. *Braf cwrdd a chi.*' She glanced into the cab. 'It's a pleasure to meet you.'

Mary waved a hand. 'I'm Mary and this is Vivienne in the back.'

'It was Vivienne I spoke to this morning on the phone.' Olwen's tanned skin and ruddy cheeks gave her the look of a healthy woman who worked outside a lot. 'David's up in the fields with the sheep. The camping field is just down there, if you drive along the track a little way you can't miss it.'

'Thank you,' Gwen replied.

Olwen glanced inside the cab again. 'Well, why don't you go down and settle in? Dinner will be around eight o'clock, if that's all right. That gives David time to get back and have a shower.'

'It's very beautiful here,' Gwen breathed.

'Oh, the view from the field is incredible – you can see the ocean. And there's a water tap by the gate to fill up your tank, everything you need.' Olwen pushed her hands into her pockets. 'So, dinner at eight. I hope nobody's vegetarian.'

'Not at all,' Mary said enthusiastically.

'Right then, I'll see you later.' Olwen turned to go. 'No airs and graces here, wear what you like, but don't worry about dressing up.' She peered into the cab again. 'People take us as they find us, but we'll make sure you eat well. Well, it's lovely to meet you. Now I've a chicken to kill, so I'll be getting on.'

Olwen waved and disappeared inside the large red-brick farm-house. Gwen started the engine. 'Right, shall we find the field and settle in?'

'Coffee, strong and black, for me,' Vivienne exclaimed.

'I'll second that,' Mary yelled.

Gwen closed her eyes for a second. 'A good sleep, that's what I need, after all that driving.'

'Right, Gwen – you have a rest and Mary and I will put the kettle on.'

It was almost five as Mary and Vivienne plonked themselves at the plastic table and sipped coffee from large mugs, gazing across the sweeping field, the arc of honey-coloured beach and the clear azure line of the sea below. The sunshine warmed the air and a striped bee hovered and buzzed in the grass, sipping on purple clusters of clover. Gwen was still inside the motorhome, stretched on the double bed, her shoes off and her eyes closed.

Mary indicated the view. 'So, this is Wales? It's very lovely here.'

'Rhossili is gorgeous,' Vivienne agreed. 'I'm looking forward to spending a few days here. We can kick back, relax, lie in the sunshine and forget about the world.'

'Just what the doctor ordered,' Mary quipped. 'Well, mine did. And I have to say, what with the medication and the holiday, I'm starting to feel much healthier.'

'You look great.' Vivienne reached out and touched the soft white hair, still streaked with baby blue and pink. Mary's face was tanned now, her arms and legs a golden brown, and her eyes twinkled.

'Oh, I'm feeling much better. But it's done us all the world of good. London's a lovely place, but the routine was getting to me, shopping and cooking and not doing much else.'

Mary sipped her coffee and then pointed in the direction of the gate, towards the farmhouse. 'So who are those people coming towards us looking like they'll fight us or chase us away?'

Vivienne twisted round, adjusting her sunglasses. 'It looks like a welcome party.'

Three women were hurrying towards them, all identically dressed in blue sweatshirts and navy jeans. One was blonde, one red-haired and one had short white cropped hair. They appeared to be in their sixties. They smiled broadly as they approached. Each had an identical crest on her sweatshirt; the blonde one also sported a brooch of a huge yellow daffodil. She spoke first. 'Hello. Olwen said you'd be here.'

Vivienne opened her mouth, but Mary was there first. 'We're here because we're camping in her field.'

The blonde one smiled eagerly at Vivienne. 'I'm Annie Parry.' She thrust a hand towards Vivienne. 'You're Vivienne Goldman, the actress. I've seen you on TV in *The Edge of Edgeware.*'

The red-haired woman edged forward. 'We are great fans of the show. I'm Ceri Lloyd.'

'Gaynor James.' The woman with cropped white hair smiled warmly as if she'd known Vivienne all her life. 'We loved Maggs Pryor. She was such good fun.'

'It's a pity she died in the pub fire,' Annie muttered morosely.

'She should come back – it could all have been a mistake,' Ceri added, running a hand through her red hair.

Gaynor agreed. 'Yes, perhaps she was hiding in a cupboard all the time, and when the fire was put out, she was fine.'

'This is Mary Molloy.' Vivienne waved a hand.

'Are you an actress, Mary?' Annie asked.

'No, I'm on holiday,' Mary replied, staring at the identical jumpers, wondering what the women wanted. She decided to ask. 'Well, what was it you all wanted? I can get you a cup of coffee. And if you like, you can all sit down and admire the view.'

'Oh, it was Vivienne we wanted to see,' blonde Annie blurted.

'Well, we sort of wanted to ask for a favour,' Ceri tried.

'Or at least ask your opinion,' Gaynor muttered.

'Oh?' Vivienne raised an eyebrow.

'Well, we're all members of the same WI.' Annie smiled.

'Ah, that explains the matching jumpers,' Mary observed.

Annie's smile broadened. 'Well, we're arranging a fashion show in the village tomorrow night. We have managed to find three local clothes shops to sponsor us, and the idea is, people will buy tickets, then there's a raffle, and refreshments, and we show off the clothes and people can buy them from the shops by ordering them on the night.'

'I see.' Vivienne nodded.

'Well, it's in aid of our last secretary of the committee, Dora Morgan. She died a year ago tomorrow, Alzheimer's it was. She was ninety-seven. That's why we're having the fashion show – to raise money for Alzheimer's,' Annie continued.

'Of course, Dora wasn't the secretary when she died. Annie has been our secretary for seven years now,' Gaynor enthused.

'She's our lynchpin,' Ceri agreed.

Vivienne frowned. 'So, how can I help you?'

'Well,' Annie began, and the three women moved closer to Vivienne. 'With you being an actress and famous, I wondered if you'd come to the show.'

'Or even be in it?' Gaynor suggested.

Ceri agreed. 'People might attend if you were there, Vivienne.'

Vivienne looked dubious but Mary was pin-sharp. 'So, how many tickets have you sold up until now?'

Annie's expression was sheepish. 'Ten. Mostly all Women's Institute members.'

'Well, you need to sell some more,' Mary stated, matter-of-factly.

'We do,' Ceri moaned. 'But we just can't get any interest.'

'Say you'll be a model for us, Vivienne,' Annie pleaded.

Vivienne was thoughtful, then she asked, 'How many tickets have you sold to men?'

'Men? At a fashion show?' Ceri was aghast.

'There must be some husbands, brothers, sons…?' Vivienne took off her sunglasses. 'Won't they support the event?'

'Oh, the men mightn't want to come,' Gaynor was thoughtful. 'They're probably not interested. We didn't ask them, to tell the truth. They haven't been able to meet down the pub in ages, bless them, so I just assumed they'd rather be doing that.'

Vivienne stood up and put her hands on her hips. 'No, you need to ask them to support you and to double the numbers. It's a great cause.'

'Oh, it is, Vivienne,' Annie agreed. 'But I just thought, well, they mightn't get much from it.'

'You need all the support you can get,' Vivienne demanded. 'Where are they all now?'

Ceri sighed. 'Probably in the Pig and Whistle.'

'It's my fault.' Annie sighed. 'I didn't think it was their sort of thing. Now I wish I'd asked them to come. We so need to fill the room.'

'It's too late now.' Gaynor shook her head. 'They think we don't need them there – and you're right, we do.'

Vivienne raised a finger. '"All the world's a stage and all the men and women merely players." Leave this to me – I've got this.' She folded her arms. 'Right. I need to find a suitable frock and put my face on. Mary, go and wake up Gwen and tell her to get ready. Dinner isn't until eight. We're going down the pub.'

* * *

The bar in the Pig and Whistle was gloomy, a few dim amber lights glowing in each corner. The air was stale and the stone floor was damp. As Vivienne sauntered in wearing a tight-fitting black minidress and red heels, she noticed the dozen or so older men seated round two tables, pots of beer clutched in their hands, glance up and then go back to playing cards and dominoes. In the far corner there was a pool table and a dartboard, where five younger men were playing, oblivious.

Vivienne sashayed to the bar. Mary was at her elbow, wearing the Totnes rainbow maxi dress, and Gwen was in jeans and a neat blouse. Vivienne leaned over the bar and spoke too loudly. 'Do you think it's too early for champagne, girls?'

'It's never too early for bubbles,' Mary boomed in retort.

Gwen's voice was softer. 'What about some nice cocktails?'

'Oh, cocktails, what a marvellous idea,' Vivienne hooted. She was aware without turning round that most of the drinkers in the bar were now watching her. The barman approached cautiously, a middle-aged man with hairy sideburns and a rounded belly.

She played her trump card. 'Hello. I'd like a Buttery Nipple please.'

Mary hid the snigger on her face with her hand as Gwen gaped in shock.

'I beg your pardon?' The barman's eyebrows shot up.

Vivienne raised her voice. 'I'd like a Buttery Nipple. Three, if you have them. I assume you know how to make a Buttery Nipple?' The barman stared, amazed, so Vivienne continued. 'That's thirty millilitres of Butterscotch Schnapps and fifteen millilitres of Irish Cream liqueur, please.'

'I'll have a Kahlua, Irish Cream and a whisky cocktail,' Mary piped up. 'Otherwise known as a Duck's Fart.'

The barman stood completely still, shocked and baffled. He had never seen three women at the bar ordering cocktails before, let alone three brightly dressed peacocks demanding unusual drinks. He coughed. 'I'm sorry, ladies, but we don't have...'

'Three orange juices then, please,' Vivienne purred on cue. Mary pulled a face: she'd have preferred a cocktail. Vivienne whirled round and addressed the entire bar. 'Well, this is a beautiful little pub.'

The drinkers had abandoned their dominoes and cards now and were openly staring at her. A lean man hunched inside a dark jacket muttered, 'It's our local. It's a quiet place.'

A second drinker, a muscular square-shaped man, agreed. 'We're here for a nice drink.'

'That's so sweet,' Vivienne brayed. 'But I'm here for the fashion show tomorrow night.' She gazed over the drinkers' heads towards the window. Outside, three small women in blue sweatshirts had poked their heads above the sill, a blonde one was pointing energetically towards the lean man and then back at herself and nodding, then they dived down in unison, out of view.

Vivienne was aware that all eyes were still on her, even the young men in the corner. They were astonished: a poised, sophisticated woman like Vivienne seldom visited the Pig and Whistle. One of them muttered, 'What fashion show? Oh, the one my wife is involved in. She did say something... but I don't think they want us there.'

'Yes, the one that's on tomorrow night,' Vivienne murmured,

lowering her voice to a soft drawl. 'And they very much want you all there. I'm Vivienne Goldman, the...' She chose her word. 'The actress. You must have seen me in *The Edge of Edgeware*. I'm the special guest at the fashion show tomorrow.'

The slim man spoke to himself. 'My missus likes that soap. Annie watches it all the time.'

'Gaynor watches it too,' the bearded man nodded.

'I'm featuring in the fashion show tomorrow.' Vivienne smiled. She picked up her orange juice and strutted towards the men's table. 'Who knows what we'll be wearing? I expect we're modelling nightdresses, leisure wear, stunning ball gowns, sportswear and lingerie.'

'Lingerie?' the bearded man repeated and a voice from the pool table said, 'That's underwear, Dad.'

'So, you'll all be there, won't you? It's for charity, after all.' She dipped her hand into her bag and produced tickets, magically shaped in a wide fan. 'Twenty pounds each. Come on, boys, out with your money.'

The bearded man scratched his hairy face. 'Well, I don't know. I didn't think we'd be needed there.'

'Of course you are – it's a community event.' Vivienne slipped a ticket into his hand, lodging another in the slim man's top pocket. 'Come on, boys – it's for charity. Your wives need the support – they are relying on you. And we'll all be so fabulous in our best dresses. It'll be fun.'

Six pairs of hands reached for wallets. The bearded man said, 'It's for charity, I suppose, isn't it?'

'And I'll be supporting my Annie.' The slim man handed over two ten-pound notes.

Vivienne gazed towards the window where three smiling heads above blue sweatshirts were giving the thumbs up.

As money was handed over, swapped for tickets clutched in

sweaty palms, a sullen youthful voice from the pool table said, 'I thought the WI ladies would be doing their own thing. They said so, didn't they, boys?'

Another young man mumbled. 'I can't see what use I'd be at a fashion show.'

'You should buy a ticket and come with us, Marc,' the bearded man suggested. 'I have to admit, I'm looking forward to it. I wish Gaynor had told me she wanted us all to come. It'll be good to have a community village event, all of us together, after the year we've had.'

'I don't know so much,' the young voice grunted from the gloom.

Vivienne whirled round and stared hard at the speaker, a young man with long curly hair and thick eyebrows. She smiled. 'Are you a darts player, young man?'

'The best in South Wales,' he replied, his eyes shining.

'And are you a betting man?'

'I don't mind a bet.' The young man thrust out his chin with a slow smile.

'What's your name?' Vivienne scrutinised his face: he couldn't be more than twenty years old.

'Marc.' He gazed around the bar for support.

'Right, Marc.' Vivienne threw back her head. 'Meet my friend, Gwen. She'll play you at darts. If you win, I'll give you fifty pounds. If she wins, you and your friends will all buy tickets and come to the fashion show.'

Marc nudged his friends, who nudged him back and snickered. Then he chuckled. 'All right. You're on. I'll play against your friend, Gwen.'

Gwen winked at Vivienne, strolled over towards the dartboard and quietly picked up three darts.

26

That evening at dinner, Vivienne, Gwen and Mary had changed into casual, comfortable clothes and were sipping water across the table from Olwen and her husband, David, a giant of a man with broad shoulders and an easy smile. Olwen was carving a roasted chicken as Mary piled potatoes onto her plate.

Olwen served David with slices of meat first, ruffling his pale hair fondly as she passed him. 'You know, Annie rang me and told me all about what you did in the Pig and Whistle, Vivienne. I was so impressed. You sold twenty-two tickets and then you went back and sold another dozen for their friends. How did you do it?'

Vivienne pushed a hand through her newly washed mane. 'I act. I'm used to it. That's what I do. But I must admit it was fun, especially ordering the cocktails. And the darts match was such a laugh.'

'Vivienne was incredible.' Mary had resprayed her tresses, a bright fluffy candyfloss of baby pink and blue. 'And so was Gwen.'

'Oh?' David lifted an eyebrow. 'Are you an actor then, Gwen?'

'She's an opera singer,' Olwen said proudly.

'And she can play darts like an expert,' Mary added. 'She beat that young man, Marc, into a cocked hat. You should have seen the gob on him when he had to pay up.'

'Vivienne made all his friends buy tickets.' Gwen lifted her fork. 'It was very funny.'

'We're going to the fashion show tomorrow, David, so you'll have to finish work a bit earlier,' Olwen reminded him as she passed a ceramic bowl full of cooked broccoli, peas, beans and carrots. 'I'm helping with refreshments.'

'It'll be a five o'clock finish for me then.' David helped himself to vegetables. 'That's lovely.'

'It'll be such fun.' Vivienne smiled. 'Gwen and Mary and I'll just sit on the beach all day tomorrow soaking up the sunshine, and then we'll be fresh for the fashion show in the evening. We're all taking part. I've arranged it with Annie.'

'I know, Annie's delighted – you three have saved the day.' Olwen passed gravy to her husband. 'I have to say, without you, Vivienne, it would have flopped miserably.'

Vivienne raised her glass and frowned at the water. 'It will be a great evening; we'll make sure of that and Annie will make lots of money.'

'Will you sing tomorrow, Gwen?' Olwen asked.

Gwen felt immediately bashful. 'Well, I love singing. It's the time I feel happiest.'

'Gwen's from Llanclawdd, David,' Olwen explained. 'She's a local girl.'

'Oh, Llanclawdd's only half an hour away.' David stopped eating, his fork in the air. 'Are you planning on going there in the next few days?'

'I'm hoping to pop in just for a visit later...'

'Only, I think they have an event on at the moment – I read something about it in the paper. I'll see if I can dig it out for you.'

'Oh, I don't know anyone there now, David, so I won't be

attending any events.' Gwen lowered her lids. 'By the way, Olwen, the food is lovely.'

David wrapped an arm around his wife proudly. 'My Olwen is a wonderful cook. I tell you, she's the best cook in Wales. You wait until breakfast tomorrow when you sample the cockles and the laver bread.'

Mary had finished every scrap of food on her plate. 'That sounds just the ticket, David. I can't wait.'

The next morning, three women in bright swimsuits lay on straw mats and soft towels on the beach at Rhossili. Mary was in the centre, wearing a V-necked swim dress in a batik print and a large straw hat. Gwen felt a little uncomfortable in the red tankini, although Mary assured her that she looked 'the business', before turning to Vivienne and commenting, 'That new swimsuit of yours is very skimpy, Vivienne. You look like you're wearing orange dental floss.'

Vivienne smiled, adjusted her sunglasses and lay back, her skin gleaming with sun oil; Mary's words were a compliment. At seventy-one years old, she knew she could still get away with looking good in swimwear. She decided that the reason she was slim was because she chose between food and alcohol – you couldn't have both. She was pleased that she'd passed her helping of laver bread and cockles to Mary who, delighted by a second delicious helping of Olwen's breakfast, had wolfed it down.

Gwen rolled onto her front and opened the pages of a book, pushing her hair over her shoulder. Mary closed her eyes; the sun was strong overhead and she could feel her flesh start to sizzle. She reached for Vivienne's sun cream. Gwen put her book down and sighed. 'So, tonight at the fashion show – what happens?'

Vivienne shrugged, nonchalant. 'We turn up at the village hall half an hour before it starts, put on some glamorous evening wear, strut our stuff on the stage and let the WI do the rest and make money for charity.'

'But I won't have to be one of the models, will I?' Gwen was anxious. 'I can't strut my stuff. I'll just feel silly.'

Vivienne raised her eyebrows over her sunglasses. 'You'll be great, Gwen. Just follow me – we'll be fabulous. Most of the women are modelling – Gaynor, Ceri – and I have a trick or two up my sleeve. It will be such a great night.'

'Annie – she's the blonde one in the blue jumper?' Mary mumbled.

'That's right.' Vivienne stretched her legs.

'Only, I think that's herself rushing towards us from the path over there. Look, she's hurrying across the sand, waving her hands.' Mary waved back. 'Yoo-hoo, Annie.'

'Oh, no.' Gwen looked up. 'You don't suppose the whole fashion show has been cancelled? Perhaps the men have asked for their money back?'

'Well, they won't get it,' Vivienne said emphatically. 'The deal was well and truly done last night.'

'Hello, hello, hello.' Annie greeted each of them in turn and plonked herself hotly on the edge of Vivienne's towel. Her face was red and damp; the sweatshirt was heavy, and she pulled it over her head, revealing a white polo shirt with the same WI logo. 'Olwen said I'd find you all down here, on the beach. Lovely, isn't it? Best beach in Europe. Only, I wanted to go through the final arrangements for tonight.' She glanced at Vivienne. 'I'm not ruining your holiday or taking up too much of your time, I hope?'

Vivienne smiled. 'We're glad to help. It'll be fine. We'll turn up at the village hall as planned...'

'You've done a lovely job,' Annie enthused. 'We've sold even more tickets now word has got around that our men are coming along. And do you know, my husband said they were glad to be asked – they are really looking forward to being there. Lots of other people from the other villages want to come now they've heard you're in the show, Vivienne.'

'That's great news.' Vivienne was delighted. 'So how can we help?'

'Well, the thing is – I was going to compère tonight, because we had no one else who'd do it, but I'd rather flounce on the stage in my best bib and tucker, you know, be one of the models with the others.' Annie looked hopefully at Mary. 'I don't suppose you'd introduce us all one by one, over the microphone?'

'I'll certainly do that,' Mary offered. 'I'll enjoy it – I'm much better off doing the patter than I am strutting my stuff wearing fancy pants.'

'Oh, that's wonderful,' Annie breathed. 'And we've got background music that will play while we're walking up and down the little wooden stage. I thought Max Boyce might be lovely.'

'Mmm.' Vivienne raised an eyebrow. 'He's very good, but don't we need something a bit more racy, up-tempo?'

'What about the Dubliners? "Seven Drunken Nights"?'

'I was thinking more Madonna, Taylor Swift, Kate Bush...' Vivienne waved a hand. 'There will be something in the glovebox – we all brought CDs – leave it with me, Annie. I'll find something that will allow us to make our entrance.'

Mary muttered. 'Anything, as long as it's not Sir Brian Teflon.'

'There's nothing wrong with Bryn Terfel,' Gwen muttered. 'But it's not really fashion show music, not even in Wales.'

Annie clapped her hands. 'Then we're all organised. I have the clothes hung up backstage and ready to go, the tickets are all sold and we've made so much money already. Gaynor is doing a raffle – oh, I can't wait. This is the first opportunity the parish has had to come together in the hall for ages. It will be lovely. Oh, and one more thing...'

Mary looked hopeful. 'Cockles and laver bread?'

'No, but we're really so grateful for everything you've done. So, is there anything I could do for you in return?'

Vivienne beamed a smile as bright as the sunshine. 'There is. Can you mind our clothes and bags while we go for a dip in the water?'

'Oh, it would be my pleasure.'

'Thanks, Annie.' Vivienne was on her feet, waving a hand towards Mary and Gwen. 'Come on, we have wanted to swim in the sea all holiday and now's the perfect chance.' She glanced towards the glittering waves, sunlight dazzling on the water, then she breathed in the tangy salt air and murmured, 'I'm going to take my tangerine dental floss costume for its first dip in the ocean.'

* * *

The sunshine was still warm at ten minutes to seven, as Vivienne, Gwen and Mary arrived at the WI. David had dropped them off, then returned to the farm to help Olwen, who was preparing a late supper for after the show. Inside the little white-fronted village hall, several women were rushing around, laying out chairs and organising food and raffle prizes. Red-haired Ceri rushed up to Vivienne immediately. 'Right, you're guests of honour. You can just relax backstage – we'll do all the running about.'

They were joined by Gaynor, her white cropped hair gleaming and freshly washed. 'Are we all ready and raring to go, girls?'

'We certainly are.' Vivienne noticed Annie at the door with her husband, the slim man in the dark jacket. 'Ah, here's my man.' She held out her hand. 'Annie – and this must be your husband.'

Annie's face shone as she looked at her husband, who puffed

out his chest proudly. 'This is Gareth. I believe he's helping you
tonight.'

'I am...' Gareth chimed. 'I'm looking forward to it.'

Vivienne smiled. 'It's good to have you with us, Gareth – and
young Marc is helping too, Gaynor's son.'

'He'll be along shortly,' Gaynor called over from the long table
where she was arranging raffle prizes. 'He's had his orders from me
and since he lost the darts match fair and square, he's not getting
away with missing out on tonight. Huw, my husband, is bringing
him here any minute now. Apparently, he has quite a following. All
the local girls have heard what he's doing, and they've all bought
tickets...'

On cue, the bearded man arrived with his son, who appeared
nervous and sheepish. Vivienne strolled over to him and spoke
warmly. 'Marc, you're here – that's brilliant. Right, now everyone's
here...' She waved a hand. 'And the music is ready to go. We'd better
go backstage and get our skates on.'

Mary was seated on the edge of the stage, muttering into the
microphone. 'One two. One two.' She tapped it several times, gazed
around and tried again. 'Pop pop popsicle, ice ice icicle, test test,
testing one two three.' She grinned and met the gaze of Gaynor's
husband, Huw, who winked. Everyone else was far too busy, oblivious to her joke.

The hall had started to fill up, people sitting down on wooden
chairs, chattering in low voices, an expectant hum, then the primitive stage was lit with two floodlights, the houselights were switched
off and music began to blare through the speakers. Kate Bush,
singing 'Wuthering Heights', was abruptly muted and Mary took
advantage of the sudden silence. Her accent was more strongly
Irish than ever before.

'Ah, well, welcome to the fashion show and it's top of the
evening to y'all. We are all here tonight to make money for charity –

the Alzheimer's Society is a wonderful, wonderful cause, so get digging deep into those pockets. And as you all know, there are refreshments and raffle tickets, so get digging even deeper. For those of you who don't know me, and I don't suppose you will, I'm Mary Molloy, your compère for the evening. So, to start off proceedings, we have someone you all know from the screen and the stage, it's our one and only Vivienne Goldman in evening dress...'

Kate Bush started up again, a loud wail as Vivienne sauntered onto the middle of the stage in a long shimmering silver dress, her hair swept up, her chin lifted, her lips crimson. She held the audience's gaze with a practised pose, turned, glancing along the line of her nose, then slowly twirled around. The audience clapped and cheered.

'And here's our lovely Welsh rarebit, Gwen Prichard, in a frock to stun you all.'

Gwen walked in nervously, her dark hair shining, wearing a green ballgown. She strolled halfway to the centre of the stage, whirled around, holding both arms out from her body, twizzled in the other direction and rushed off quickly.

'Wuthering Heights' became 'Vogue' by Madonna. Mary was enjoying herself.

'Right, now...' She consulted the list Annie had given her. 'Let's not forget the fellas. Just take a gander at your man Gareth Parry in his fancy pants.'

There was a sudden roar of laughter then warm applause from the audience as Gareth marched on, slim in a tuxedo and red cummerbund. He stood in the middle of the stage, flexed the muscles in his arms once, strode around the stage in a circle like a prowling rooster, then strutted offstage. The cheers were deafening.

Mary laughed. 'And here's one for all you youngsters. Wearing the latest get-up and looking the total business, here's young Marc James.'

There was a pause, then Marc walked on hesitantly, waddling like an awkward penguin, wearing a white silk suit. A deep male voice called out, 'I'd have paid double to see this.' Marc blushed, edging forward. Then he noticed all eyes were on him; in the front row several teenage girls, their faces flushed, watched his every move with awe, mouths open, and his confidence blossomed. He stood tall, extending broad shoulders, looking down his nose and thrusting out his chin. The applause increased; Marc turned, sauntered off stage gazing back over his shoulder at his adoring new fans and cannoned straight into Annie who was walking on, her head high, wearing a long floral frock. She shoved him out of the way and sashayed into the centre of the floodlit stage, smiling sweetly.

Mary improvised. 'And our Annie is looking gorgeous in a flowery little number...' The audience applauded, cheered and roared approval.

* * *

It had been a wonderful night. As Annie explained in her final speech, surrounded by a peacock array of smiling models, the community had come together to raise money, to remember Dora Morgan. It had been an incredible evening, Annie said: the whole village had come together as one and the success of it was all due to the famous actress, Vivienne Goldman, and her friends. It was half past nine, so Annie wished everyone a pleasant evening and a safe journey home. A chair scraped as someone stood to leave, but Mary was on her feet, centre stage, speaking into the mic.

'Hang on – we've not finished yet.'

All eyes were on her, everyone statue-still, so Mary pointed in Annie's direction. 'A huge round of applause please for the organiser, Annie Parry.' The audience obliged with loud cheers.

'But we're not done quite yet – so get your wallets out again,' Mary yelled. 'Because there's one final thing left, and you've all got to give me some more lovely charity money. Gwen Prichard is going to sing.'

Backstage, Gwen's eyes grew huge, and she placed her hands on her face. 'Oh no – she didn't tell me she was going to do this.'

'Well done, Mary. What a great idea.' Vivienne patted her shoulder. 'Go on, Gwen. Get out there and do what you love best.'

Mary was shouting, 'Come on – let's see the colour of your money,' and people were pushing notes towards Annie as Gwen took her place on the stage. There was silence. Gwen noticed Olwen and David in the audience, their faces lifted in anticipation.

She spoke quietly. 'Well, it's only proper that I sing this song for Dora Morgan, because it's Dora we are honouring this evening. It is her night and we're raising money for her charity, so here's a song you'll all know. It's called "All Through the Night".'

With no accompaniment, Gwen began to sing, her voice strong and pure, the hymn of an angel, the sound drifting from her lips upwards to heaven. There was a shuffling of feet as everyone stood up in unison, a sniff from someone sobbing into a handkerchief, then silence as Gwen sang:

> *Holl amrantau'r sêr ddywedant*
> *Ar hyd y nos*
> *Dyma'r ffordd i fro gogoniant,*
> *Ar hyd y nos.*
> *Golau arall yw tywyllwch*
> *I arddangos gwir brydferthwch*
> *Teulu'r nefoedd mewn tawelwch*
> *Ar hyd y nos.*

27

It was past nine the next day when Gwen opened her eyes, blinking in the blinding sunlight that flooded through the window. She stretched her limbs luxuriously and realised that there was a space next to her in the bed. Mary was not there; Gwen could hear her in the shower singing, the water running like a downpour, and she called out, 'We'll need to remember to refill the water tank again today.'

Vivienne was standing by the open door, enjoying the warmth, wearing her dressing gown, her hair rolled in huge curlers. She smiled. 'We've all slept in this morning.'

'We have.' Gwen eased herself to the edge of the bed. 'We must be properly relaxed – this holiday is doing us all so much good.'

'Gwen...' Vivienne sat down next to her. 'I have to say, you were truly wonderful last night – what a professional you are. Everyone loved it so much when you sang "All Through the Night" for Dora, so spontaneously. I had goosebumps.'

'It's what I do, Vivienne. When I sing, I'm just – in the zone, I suppose. It's second nature.' Gwen clutched her arm. 'It must be the same for you when you perform. I mean, when you walked on stage last night, so sure of yourself and so slick, it was obvious that you're a professional. You just have this air of confidence and, you know, beauty.'

'It comes from a lifetime of training.' Vivienne's hand floated to the curlers. 'But acting has left its mark. There are times when I'm not sure who I am – if I'm performing or if I'm me. It's quite a tough life, not knowing where your next job is coming from. I can be guilty of defining myself by my own success, I suppose, if you know what I mean. As if I'm only as good as my latest role. But that's what I've learned from being on this holiday – there's more to me than the role I'm playing.'

'It's been just lovely, being away, hasn't it?' Gwen sighed. 'It's been so good for us all. It's a pity we've only a few days left. That reminds me, we need to send Vicente another postcard. I'm so glad he lent us his motorhome... I wonder if he's still unwell.'

Just then, Mary emerged from the shower, swathed in a white fluffy towel, her hair plastered to her scalp. 'I hope Olwen's got the laver bread and cockles on the go again today.'

'Mary.' Gwen clapped her hands. 'You were magnificent as the compère last night. Such a presence, such banter and humour. You were brilliant.'

'You reminded me of Bob Geldof on *Live Aid*, the way you goaded everyone to pay more money...' Vivienne leaped up and hugged her. 'You were totally fantastic.'

Gwen joined them and the three women were united in a warm hug.

'It's the mutual appreciation society.' Mary grinned. 'But you have to admit it, we do make the best team.'

When they arrived in the big farmhouse kitchen, the table was laid and Olwen was ready with breakfast. David, apparently, had been out since six o'clock tending the lambs, and Olwen had been busy since then making fresh bread rolls, one of which she placed on a plate for Vivienne with a pat of farmhouse butter, salad leaves and dressed prawns. 'Because I know you're not a big eater, Vivienne, and I heard you like your seafood. But as for you two...' Olwen piled laver bread and cockles on hot buttered toast for Gwen and then she took a dish of sausages, bacon and eggs from the Aga and laid it in front of Mary with a flourish. 'It's a proper Welsh breakfast for you both.'

Mary was delighted, but she protested weakly, 'I'm recovering from a heart attack.' However, she dug into the sausages with gusto. 'So, when I'm back in London, I'm starting the 80:20 diet – well, it's not a diet, it's more of a way of life.'

Vivienne winked in Gwen's direction. 'So, you eat and drink everything you want 80 per cent of the time, Mary, and for 20 per cent of the time you eat more frugally.'

Mary was puzzled. 'I thought it was the other way round,' then she realised Vivienne was joking and she burst out laughing. 'I want to keep up the supper-sharing nights round each other's flats when we get home, though. Will we do that?'

'Certainly,' Gwen agreed. 'I don't think I could manage without them.' She was quiet for a moment. 'It will be funny, won't it, being back in London? But at least things are getting better there for everyone – and I might even find some opera work. It's been such fun being able to sing here.'

Olwen placed a hand on her shoulder. 'You have such an incredible voice, Gwen. When you sang "Ar hyd y nos" last night, I was moved. I was so glad David and I rushed over to see it once we'd finished here. It was so beautiful.'

'I haven't sung in Welsh for years, and I realise how much I miss it.'

'You must sing in Welsh more often then,' Olwen said. 'So, where are you off to today?'

Vivienne sat up straight. 'Right. Plans for today. We'll have a drive around, see the scenery, have a picnic on the cliffs, maybe spend more time on a beach, then we'll organise somewhere to stay overnight just outside Llanclawdd, so that Gwen can see the old place again.'

'It's a very nice, pretty little village, Llanclawdd. Very traditional.' Olwen picked up Vivienne's empty plate with a smile, noting that all the food had been polished off. 'You must be looking forward to seeing it, Gwen. I doubt it's changed much over the last fifty years. Maybe some buildings have been updated, but you'll find it very traditional. Did your parents live there?'

Gwen nodded, distracted, playing with her food. 'They lived there all their lives; they are buried in St Pabo's church.'

'And do you know anyone there still? Do you have any old friends there?'

'No,' Gwen spoke quickly. Mary and Vivienne exchanged glances. 'No, I don't know anyone.'

'You'll enjoy seeing the old places, though – maybe the house where you lived as a child.'

'I'm a bit worried about it, to be honest. I've no idea how I'll feel. It's going to be interesting, though.'

Vivienne patted her arm. 'You don't have to go back there if you don't want to, Gwen.'

Mary patted the other arm. 'But it might, you know, lay a few of the old ghosts to rest.'

'If I don't go back there once more, I'll wish I had.' Gwen sighed.

Vivienne scraped her chair back. 'We should be making a move.' She gazed up at Olwen. 'It's been really gorgeous meeting you and David.'

Olwen opened her arms for an embrace. 'It's been lovely having you here. Don't forget us. There will always be a welcome in the hillside for you all at *Maes-Y-Wawr*.'

Gwen, Mary and Vivienne wrapped their arms around Olwen. 'It's been grand,' Mary murmured.

'Oh, and I have something for you. Annie came round earlier this morning. She'd have given it to you herself, but she had to get off somewhere.' Olwen wandered into the pantry and came out clutching a bouquet of flowers and a bottle of champagne. 'She wanted to say thank you from the WI for everything you did to make the fashion show so memorable.'

Vivienne took the flowers like a ballerina, her lips curved in a graceful smile. 'These will make the motorhome smell beautiful.'

Mary clutched the champagne to her chest. 'And this will make me feel beautiful too. After a glass or two of this, I'll think I'm Angelina Jolie.'

* * *

The noon day sun filtered through the window, warming her face as Gwen drove along the twisting roads. Ten minutes later, she turned the motorhome into a narrow lane and pulled into a car park.

'I'm just going to stop here for a moment. I want to show you something. We're going on a little walk.'

Vivienne and Mary slipped from the side doors and hauled out bags and towels. Mary was baffled. 'Is it far, where we're going? What was it we were going to see?'

'I can't say, just in case you're disappointed, but I just wanted you to look. Apparently, in the summer, they are often around here...' Gwen locked the motorhome and pushed the keys in her pocket, her face glowing with enthusiasm. 'Just down here there should be a little path and we can walk to the headland...'

Gwen led the way, the sea breeze whipping her hair across her face. They walked one behind the other along a narrow dirt track, the sea far below them. Mary waved a thumb towards the vast craggy drop and muttered, 'I hope a big wind doesn't blow us all off over the top.'

'By the way,' Vivienne began. 'I booked somewhere for us to stay tonight while you two were packing up before we left. It's a ten-minute walk from Llanclawdd, a watermill owned by a woman called Rhian White. We can park up right by the stream. She sounds lovely. She said it's a perfect time to visit Llanclawdd. There's so much going on there right now. She said we'd have a wonderful time.'

The path began to descend, taking them towards a headland that dwindled to a small outcrop of rock. Gwen put her bag down and spread out her towel. 'We're here.'

Mary was puzzled. 'I thought we were going to sunbathe on the beach.'

'This is much better.' Gwen delved into her bag and pulled out her driving glasses, replacing her sunshades. 'I just want to stop here for a few minutes because of the view. I've been here before, years ago, and I just thought we might... ah, there, look, look.'

They gazed down on a stretch of beach, white grains of sparkling sand as far as the eye could see banded by the bluest sea surging forward, each wave spluttering cascading foam before ebbing back. Bright light winked on the waves, diamond sharp.

Mary screwed her eyes into tiny bullet holes. 'And what am I supposed to be looking at?'

'There,' Gwen yelled excitedly, pointing towards the water. 'There, look, in the ocean.'

'Oh, yes. How marvellous.' Vivienne sat down next to Gwen, tugging out her phone. 'I must get a photo.'

'Of the water?' Mary was confused. 'What on earth can you see there?'

Vivienne held up her phone as Gwen waved an arm. 'Can't you see them, Mary? The dark blobs moving around?'

Mary leaned forward. 'What blobs? I'm blind as a bat half the time. What can you see? Is it a diver?'

'It's dolphins, Mary.' Gwen pointed with her finger. 'Basking in the sunlight in the ocean – look, three, four of them, gliding along.'

Vivienne clutched her phone, delighted. 'I have such wonderful snaps of them. Oh, I'm so glad we saw them. Well done, Gwen.'

Gwen's voice was full of excitement as she watched the dolphins leap and play, the sea glittering around them as they frolicked and splashed. 'I used to see them here all the time – there are so many dolphins in the summer, and white fluffy seal pups in autumn. Oh, I used to love seeing them as a teenager. And once I went on a boat trip – we should have done that today, gone on a wildlife trip. But how lucky we are to see them. I think dolphins are so beautiful, so romantic. I have a CD of them singing at home – it's so relaxing. I haven't listened to it in ages.'

Vivienne pointed upwards, towards the cloudless sky. 'And look up there – that's a buzzard, isn't it?'

Above them, a huge brown cross-shaped bird spread its wings, flying in a spiralling circle, then it paused, hanging on the wind.

Gwen shielded her eyes from the sun with her hand. 'You're right, Vivienne, it's a buzzard. It's so majestic, isn't it, the way it just stays there, hovering?'

Mary gazed up at the sky, her eyes squeezed myopically. Vivienne sat completely still. She lowered her voice. 'It's probably looking for prey.' She watched as it flicked its wings once and rose high again. 'It's such a privilege to sit here and watch some of the beautiful things nature can offer... dolphins, buzzards.'

'It is,' Gwen murmured, thinking that the last time she had sat quietly on the headland gazing at dolphins splashing in the water, Clifford Edwards' arm had been resting on her shoulders.

28

Gwen woke before everyone else and pulled on a warm top, jeans and trainers. It was just after seven in the morning; Mary and Vivienne were breathing softly, sound asleep, so Gwen closed the door of the motorhome behind her with a click and stepped outside onto damp grass into early weak sunshine. She was back in Llanclawdd and she wasn't sure how she felt about it. They had stopped on a gravel square at the end of the garden; a second car, a small Fiesta, had been parked next to them. The little stream bubbled a few feet away; Gwen felt it pulling her like a magnet as she approached the edge and crouched down. She knew the river and the watermill so well: memories were rushing back, the years plummeting away. She'd paddled in the stream on so many occasions as a child. Behind her, the building stood as it always had, quiet and solid, the wheel unmoving, no longer in use.

But something about it was different: the garden was bright with flowers; there were chintz curtains at the kitchen window. It had been so very different when Gwen was a mischievous eight-year-old. She and Wyndham Lewis and Beth Siddons had often crept into the garden after dark to see if they could spot old

Virginia Thomas. All the local children had called her Ginny Green Teeth, and believed she was a witch. The three of them, led by Beth, who was the pluckiest, most mischievous and forthright girl in the village, used to hide beneath the windowsill and pop their heads up every so often, leering, laughing, watching Virginia Thomas pottering in her kitchen behind rag curtains. And, of course, often Ginny Green Teeth would spot them and shriek a spell, and Beth would stick out her tongue and run away, followed by Gwen and then Wyndham, who had a bad leg and could only limp. Gwen smiled, remembering: Beth grew into a clever, ambitious girl and became an air hostess. Gwen thought she'd married a pilot. She had no idea what happened to Wyndham.

A loud noise tugged Gwen from her thoughts, a lively barking followed by a bounding dog who threw himself at Gwen, leaping up at her legs. She stood up slowly and ruffled the soft furry ears of a black spaniel. Then she became aware that a woman was watching her. She was in her twenties, visibly pregnant, wearing black-rimmed spectacles, her dark hair tied back. She smiled. 'Hello. I'm Rhian. We haven't met, but I spoke to Vivienne last night when you arrived. I hope Jakey isn't bothering you.'

'Who?' Gwen glanced down at the spaniel, who was sitting on his haunches, his tongue hanging out. 'Oh, no, he's lovely. Pleased to meet you – I'm Gwen.' She indicated the watermill. 'This is a beautiful house, gorgeous setting. Have you been living here long?'

'Seven years. My partner and I have done loads of work renovating it. We both come from Swansea.' Rhian rubbed her bump with a gentle palm. 'The little one's active this morning.'

'Oh.' Gwen smiled, unsure what to say; she had no knowledge of babies. Instead, she said, 'So, what do you think of life in Llanclawdd?'

'Oh, it's lovely. We want to settle here and bring up a family. It's such a peaceful place and the people are lovely. Also, the primary school here is supposed to be really good.'

'Monnow Primary?' Gwen replied without thinking.

'Do you know it?' Rhian's eyes shone with interest behind her glasses.

'Not really, no.' Gwen shook her head. 'We're off into the village later today. I expect we'll find plenty to do.'

'Oh, you will – there's a lot going on now, as I'm sure you know.'

Gwen nodded; in fact, she didn't know anything. Last night they had approached the watermill from the other direction; she hadn't been into Llanclawdd yet.

Rhian extended fingers towards the spaniel. 'Come on then, Jakey – let's get your breakfast.' She grinned cheerily. 'Enjoy your day, Gwen. If there's anything you need, just call me at the back door. If I don't hear you, bang on the kitchen window.'

Rhian pointed to the building. Gwen wanted to tell her she knew which window led to the kitchen; she had watched Ginny Green Teeth there many times as she leaned against the sink.

Gwen gazed up at the sky; it was going to be a hot day, but she felt herself shiver. She'd go back to the motorhome and open the packet of croissants they had bought yesterday when they'd filled up with petrol, then she'd make coffee. But it troubled her that the freedom of being away from the flat in London was starting to feel normal, and she almost wished she could do this each day. Gwen felt a strange emotion stirring, one that was akin to disappointment or sadness. She didn't want the holiday to end. She was having fun with Vivienne and Mary: they'd become close. And, of course, once they were back at 104 Drayton Mews, they'd slip back into their old ways: Vivienne would find work, Mary would be cooking in her kitchen all the time, listening to the Dubliners, and Gwen would be back in the ground-floor flat fending off an amorous Vincente or staring at the same four walls, practising her arias for no one.

After breakfast, as they approached Llanclawdd, an increasing number of flags, balloons and banners could be seen with words mostly in Welsh, some in English. Gwen was suddenly interested. 'Oh, of course – it's the eisteddfod. We're here for the last few days of it. That's nice.'

'Eisteddfod?' Mary muttered. 'That's the women in the tall hats, singing and playing the harp?'

'There's lots of singing and performing.' Gwen turned to Vivienne. 'Poetry reciting and the Chairing of the Bard; there will be lots of competitions.'

'That sounds exciting.' Vivienne adjusted her sunglasses. 'Can we enter?'

'Oh, no, it's not for us – this one's just a small local thing – there are eisteddfodau all over Wales throughout the summer.' Gwen's face flushed pink. 'There is a wonderful competition, singing, improvising over the harp. It's called the *cerdd dant* or *penillion*. Oh, I have such lovely memories of singing here in eisteddfodau.'

'So, did you ever win, Gwen?' Vivienne asked.

Gwen's blush deepened. 'I won it for nine years running, from being nine to eighteen, when I left home. It was one of those things – I just sang every year and people rolled their eyes and said, 'Gwen Prichard's gone and won the *cerdd dant* again.' No one else ever got a look in; it was a bit embarrassing, really.'

'It's because you were such a good singer,' Vivienne answered simply.

'You still are.' Mary pointed to the array of flags on lamp posts and posters in windows as they approached the village. 'Ah, but the eisteddfod is a really big deal here, for sure.'

'It is.' Gwen agreed. 'It's important to the local people, especially if you win anything.'

'Your parents must have been so proud of you, winning nine times in a row,' Vivienne exclaimed.

'Oh, they were proud in their own way, especially my father. My mother used to say, "Don't fuss over Gwen, Clive, she'll get too big for her boots," and my dad would always sit quietly in his chair, but I knew he was really pleased, then when my mother was out of the room, he'd slip me a fiver and say, "Well done, Gwenny, you remind me so much of my sister – singing runs in our family." He was really so thrilled.'

They turned onto the main street of the village, a cluster of shops either side, bright banners advertising the eisteddfod and the *cerdd dant* in the window. The narrow road was flanked by pretty terraced cottages, each window displaying a Welsh flag emblazoned with a red dragon. In the distance, they could see the village green, a mass of colour, tall flagpoles and fluttering bunting, people in costume bustling, busy with their preparations. Vivienne stopped to look around her, putting her hand on her hips. 'Well, Gwen, has it changed much?'

'Oh, yes, it has.' Gwen's hands flew to her mouth. 'When I was little, there was a grocer's, a baker's shop, a butcher's, a couple of pubs, the school, and that was it, really. Now look – there's a mini supermarket where Janet Baxter's grocery used to be, and see the baker's shop? It's all changed – it was small and really old-fashioned. It's so huge and impersonal now.'

Gwen stared, dismayed. She recognised the houses on either side of the village green, stacked together like shuffled cards, but they all had large glazed windows as opposed to the rickety thin ones that used to rattle in the wind, and the fronts were painted in clean colours, magnolia, yellow, blue. Edwards' Bakery was now called Bake 'n' Take. Next to it, a vibrantly painted café had been opened; it was once a large brick house, but now there was a wide window, twinkling lights, smart chairs and tables and a shiny counter inside. The sign over the door read Happy Beans. Vivienne inhaled the aroma of coffee and said, 'Shall we go in? We can have an espresso and ask about the eisteddfod.'

Gwen nodded, and Vivienne led the way in, sitting at a small table near the window, picking up the plastic-coated menu. Mary plonked herself down.

'Oh, I'd love a proper cup of tea. It always cools you down in this heat, a cup of tea.'

'Oh, yes, a nice cuppa.' Gwen exhaled in anticipation. 'Tea, that's what I'll have.'

Vivienne pulled on a brightly coloured face mask and approached the counter where a young woman with dark red hair and freckles, whose name badge said she was called Tina, promised to bring it over.

Mary was gazing out of the window: it was an ordinary Wednesday, shoppers going about their business, an old gentleman sitting on a bench next to a huge display of flowers watching the world go by. 'So, tell me all about the eisteddfod, Gwen.'

'It has always been quite modest and low-key in Llanclawdd, Mary – in some places it's really big, but the villagers here love everything about it, the competitions, the celebrations, the tradition.'

'So, can we go and watch? I like a bit of the harp and the singing myself, although I prefer the traditional Irish singing.'

'We'd better find out...' Gwen watched as Tina, in a yellow apron and little cap, placed cups of tea and coffee on the table.

Vivienne piped up. 'Excuse me, can you tell us about the eisteddfod, please?'

Tina smiled, tucking the empty tray under her arm. 'Oh, yes, you'll love it. Visitors are very welcome. The *cerdd dant* is happening this evening and tomorrow in the village hall across the road from Monnow Primary. Do you know where that is?'

'Yes, I think so.' Gwen nodded.

'Oh, you're from round here?' Tina exclaimed. 'Have you been to eisteddfodau in Llanclawdd before?'

Gwen tried to keep her face impassive. 'Years ago...' A thought was worrying her. 'This café wasn't here then.'

Tina laughed with disbelief. 'This place has been here since 1992 – before I was born.'

'Oh.' Gwen framed her next question carefully. 'When I was here the last time, I remember an old baker's shop next door, it sold all sorts of delicious things, Welsh cakes, *bara brith*. Lovely, it was.'

'You mean Edwards' Bakery. The owner retired about ten years ago and sold it. Bake 'n' Take make delicious Welsh cakes, though. You should try some.'

'So...' Gwen asked tentatively. 'What happened to the family, the Edwards?'

Tina shrugged. 'I don't know where Mr Edwards is now. But Mrs Edwards lives a couple of doors away, in the old house where she's always lived.'

'Mrs Edwards?' Gwen caught her breath. She was thinking of Siân Roberts, now Siân Edwards, who must be around seventy-five years old now. If she lived there alone, perhaps Clifford was dead. She felt her legs tremble beneath the table.

'Old Mrs Edwards must be well into her nineties now. I know she's still there. We were furloughed during lockdown, but I used to come in sometimes and check the café over, and she'd be standing in the street at her door in the cold February wind, looking very baffled and lonely, poor soul.' Tina turned to go. 'It's great that we're back to normal now. That's why the eisteddfod is so special this year. It's a proper celebration. Pop over to the village hall – someone will give you a leaflet about what's happening and then you can join in. It'll be great fun.'

'Thanks.' Gwen watched Tina walk away, reached for her tea

and took a sip, then noticed Mary and Vivienne scrutinising her carefully. She frowned. 'What's the matter?'

Mary's face was a picture of innocence. 'Oh, nothing. Just that – this Welsh tea is very nice. Very tasty.'

Vivienne raised an eyebrow. 'So, your old flame Clifford Edwards used to own the baker's shop, then? And the old lady who lives just down the road is probably his mother. Gwen, the plot thickens.'

'No, Vivienne, the plot doesn't thicken. I'm not interested in Clifford Edwards, not at all.' Gwen reached for her tea, her cheeks glowing. 'I just wanted to get up to date with how things have changed around here, that's it. Nothing more. Nothing, do you hear me?'

29

Gwen stood in front of Monnow Primary, staring at the building, and Vivienne watched her carefully, scrutinising her face for any sign of emotion. Mary placed a hand on her shoulder, her voice soft. 'I think the old school might have altered a little over the years, Gwen.'

'It has, it's changed.' Gwen recognised the main building, all red brick, gabled roof and huge windows, but the school had been extended to encompass two grey and white extensions with flat roofs. Compared to the old original block with its two arched entrances, one for boys and one for girls, this new school was tall and modern. On the upper floor of the extension, there was a room almost completely composed of glass windows. Above the door, a sign, black letters on a white background, welcomed the world to Monnow Primary, with a logo, a standing dragon clutching a book, and the motto, *Dysgu Gydol Oes*, which Gwen knew meant 'learning for life'.

Gwen held her breath; she was whisked back to her childhood. She recalled standing up straight in the main hall in her uniform, aged eight or nine, singing her heart out, sandwiched between

Wyndham Lewis, who was picking his nose, and Beth Siddons, who was bored, playing with her hair. Miss Drew was moving her fingers lightly over the old piano, her eyes closed, her expression blissful, while the head teacher, Mr Parsons, conducted the choir, frowning furiously. Gwen had loved singing in the echoing hall that smelled of steamed cabbage and spilled gravy from lunchtime, the tall radiators that belted out no heat at all until she curled up happily against one during story time on a Friday afternoon listening to the teacher read *Wind in the Willows* in a sonorous voice, while the heat burned her flesh through the thin cloth of a school jumper.

Gwen remembered the polished wooden parquet floors, the raised stage where Mr Parsons stood at a wooden lectern with an open Bible on it, yelling about 'family values', 'morality' and 'being proper', while the children huddled together, nervous and unmoving, waiting for him to finish. Images formed in her mind: herself as a child, standing upright, examining the children in the row in front, the boys' short haircuts, shaved behind protruding ears, the girls' tight plaits, white ankle socks and pinafore dresses. She'd smell warm urine and sweat from some of the children hunched in front of her, the ones with dirty necks and scruffy uniforms. Gwen's mother had always instilled in her the importance of cleanliness and godliness, and to this day she found it difficult to stop being routinely fastidious.

The sound of light voices chanting in unison wafted from an open window, children learning Welsh. From another window, folk music drifted out, the sound of a harp and pipes, and Gwen imagined the small children dancing in costume, practising for the eisteddfod performance on the village green tomorrow.

She felt the light pressure of Mary's fingers on her arm. 'Are you feeling all right?'

'Oh, I'm fine.' Gwen shook her head, dispelling memories.

'Shall we go into the village hall? We'll be able to watch the singing practice.'

Vivienne smiled, her eyes kind. 'Come on then, Gwen. It must be very strange, being back here after all this time. Are you up to listing to the songs? Not too many unsettling memories?'

'No,' Gwen protested. 'I want to hear the youngsters practise for the *cerdd dant*. It will be really lovely.'

Despite the warm sunshine outside, it was dark and shadowy inside the village hall and it took the three women a while to get used to the gloom. Blinking, they moved to find seats halfway along the hall. A few other people were sitting in clusters, adults with girls of various ages, presumably contestants with their parents or singing coaches. On stage, an old man with yellowing hair was seated playing the harp, his nimble fingers plucking the strings, and a girl of twelve or thirteen was singing, her voice clear as a bell. As she sang, she moved her face expressively, her eyes wide, as if each word filled her with a new passion. Vivienne and Mary exchanged glances, impressed by the purity of the singing. Gwen leaned forward: the girl was good, but she'd heard better. The standard was expected to be extremely high.

Then the girl finished abruptly, and from somewhere an efficient male voice called out another name. A tall slim teenage girl walked on the stage, her head bent modestly, then she stood and waited. The harpist began to play, the notes from the strings bubbling, fresh water in a brook, and she began to sing, her voice rising, crystal clear. Gwen closed her eyes and imagined herself walking on stage as a child, so nervous that her legs wobbled, then she'd take a breath, compose herself and, as soon as the first notes were out from her lips and floating on the air, she was in a different world.

The second singer's voice rose and fell and she finished her song, bowed her head and walked back to her seat, no other sound in the hall except the dull echo of her feet tapping on the wooden stage.

The authoritative voice called out 'Elinor...' and a girl, wearing the same uniform as the first two, pushed back a seat where she had been sitting alone and shuffled hesitantly to the front, ascending the steps to the stage as if she was walking to the gallows. Gwen noticed her pink cheeks, the red hair that hung down to her waist: she couldn't be older than eleven. Elinor took her place and the harpist began to strum, touching the strings lightly. The girl's mouth opened, but no sound came out. The harpist stopped playing and there were some quiet words and Elinor tensed visibly, her body taut, before the music began again. This time, she sang a note, launched into a tune, too fast, her voice weak, straining for the high notes. She continued for a few minutes, awkward, out of tune, and stopped abruptly. A few more unclear words were spoken on stage, a deep irritated tone, Elinor's staccato squeak in reply, then she rushed back to her seat. She scraped back her chair and hunched over as if scolded.

Mary raised her eyebrows and whispered, 'She won't be winning anything, for sure.'

Vivienne shook her head. 'Poor kid.'

The authoritative voice announced there would be an hour's lunch break and they would resume at one o'clock. Gwen was thoughtful for a moment, then she slipped from her seat and moved towards the small red-haired girl. She squatted next to Elinor, who lifted a flushed face. She had been crying.

'I'm Gwen. I heard you sing.'

Elinor sniffed and her head dropped down to her chest. She muttered, 'I'm sorry.'

'You've nothing to be sorry about.' Gwen waited until Elinor met her eyes. 'I'm a singer and I used to be scared too, a long time ago.'

'But I'm so rubbish.'

'Do you have a singing teacher?'

Elinor shut her eyes. 'My mam says it's a waste of money. She doesn't like me singing. But I want to.'

'Why?' Gwen asked softly.

'I sing at home in my bedroom, and it makes me happy. I sing all sorts of songs, pop songs, folk songs, hymns. But when I go on stage, somehow I can't seem to do it the same...'

'You're Elinor, aren't you?' The girl nodded and Gwen continued. 'What are you doing for lunch?'

Elinor indicated her bag. 'I have sandwiches.'

'Good. Let's stay here and practise then, while there's no one about, shall we?'

Elinor frowned. 'Why?'

'Because I think I can help you find the best voice you've got.' Gwen smiled.

Vivienne and Mary were watching from their seats.

Mary grunted, 'She'll never get a sound out of that kiddie. If you just can't sing, then you can't, and no one can get you to do it.'

Vivienne shrugged, reaching in her handbag for her sunglasses, then raised her voice. 'Gwen, are you staying here?'

Gwen glanced over her shoulder. 'Yes – Elinor and I are going to have a session on the *cerdd dant*.'

'Right.' Vivienne stood up. 'Mary and I are going to take a little walk around the village.'

'Fine.'

Vivienne caught Mary's eye. 'We'll go and buy some Welsh cakes – we'll bring you one back.'

'Oh, lovely.' Gwen wasn't listening properly; all her attention was on Elinor, whose little face had closed down in a sulk. Teaching her to sing the *cerdd dant* would be a challenge.

Mary winked, her eyes sparkling with mischief and lowered her voice. 'So, we're playing Miss Marple now, are we, Vivienne? And where do you suggest we start? The bakery?'

Vivienne smiled. 'Where else? Let's see what we can find out about a certain Clifford Edwards...'

Twenty minutes later, they stood behind two middle-aged women in a queue in Bake 'n' Take, listening to their conversation. The larger woman said she was looking forward to watching the dancing on the village green the following afternoon, then they began discussing the *cerdd dant* competition in the evening. According to the shorter woman, young Ruth Morris was bound to win: she was head and shoulders better than any of her competitors. Vivienne cleared her throat.

'Excuse me – I couldn't help overhearing...'

The larger woman stared at Vivienne, her expression surprised. 'Oh?'

Vivienne's smile was charming. 'I'm just fascinated by the eisteddfod – my friend here and I are reporters for *Saga* magazine; we're down to watch it.'

'Oh, we are,' Mary agreed. 'We're writing a big article.'

'And someone in the village told us that no one has ever won the *cerdd dant* girls' competition more than five times in a row. We want to get our facts straight, so that we can give the village a really big splash. Is that true?'

'We want the whole world to know about...' Mary couldn't remember the name of the village.

'Llanclawdd,' Vivienne finished her sentence. 'We'll put it where it belongs, on the eisteddfod map.'

The larger woman faced Vivienne. 'I'm not sure anyone has won it more than twice in a row. Competition is very fierce and our singers in Llanclawdd have such a good reputation.'

'Oh, but what about that girl years ago, in the sixties – Gwen something – she won it several times. She went on to become a professional.' The smaller woman placed a loaf of bread in a basket.

'That would make such a good story,' Vivienne enthused. 'A professional singer rises to stardom from the competition she won as a child...'

'It would,' Mary added. 'The story told by two local people, pillocks... pillars of the community.'

The large woman frowned. 'Who was it, Helen? Do I remember her?'

'She moved away.'

Vivienne addressed the smaller woman. 'And your name is...' She thrust her phone in front of the woman as if it was recording. 'So that I can put you on the front page.'

'I'm Helen Ringgold,' the small woman enunciated.

'And I'm Susan Cadwallader.' The larger one spoke clearly and loudly.

Vivienne offered them her most impressed face. 'So, how can I find out about this Gwen, Llanclawdd's famous opera singer? Who would know about her?'

'I've no idea – I don't think she has any family here.' Susan shrugged. 'She's probably dead now...'

'What about an older member of the community, someone who's lived here all their life, who'd remember Gwen – whatever? Do you know anyone like that, with local knowledge?' Mary asked with a toothy smile.

'Oh, I know who'd know – Elizabeth Edwards. She's ninety-seven. She knows everything about Llanclawdd,' Helen suggested.

'Wonderful.' Vivienne glanced at Mary. 'And where might we find her?'

'Ah, that's easy,' Susan replied. 'She used to own this bakery, then her son did. She lives two doors away, the brown door. You can tell which house is hers.'

'It's a very old person's house,' Helen added. 'It looks like it needs a bit of work doing, if you know what I mean.'

Both women turned to go. 'What paper did you say we'd be in?' Susan asked.

'*Saga* magazine,' Vivienne replied without missing a beat. 'Next month.'

'Or the month after,' Mary added.

'That's lovely,' Susan said to Helen as they strolled out together.

'Nice to meet you,' Mary hollered after them.

The shop assistant, a young man with a white overall and cap and a fresh face met Vivienne's eyes. 'Hello? And what would you like today?'

'Welsh cakes – six, please.' Vivienne smiled sweetly. 'And I wonder if you could tell me what cake Mrs Elizabeth Edwards, the old lady who lives two doors away, likes best? You see, we're about to call on her and we'd like to take her something really nice...'

30

Gwen shook her head. 'It's about confidence, Elinor. If you believe you can sing, then you'll discover that you have a unique, personal voice. That's why you sing so much better in your bedroom than on the stage – you feel safe in your own space. But there are also a few tricks you can learn that will help you no end.'

'Tricks?' Elinor's eyes were round, trusting. 'Are there really tricks to make me sing better?'

'There are, certainly. It's all about breathing, using the right muscles.'

Elinor frowned. 'My mam shouts at me to shut up when I sing in my room at home. She yells, "What's wrong with the cat? Is it sick again?" I shouldn't have entered the *cerdd dant*. Everyone will laugh at me.'

Gwen shook her head. 'What song do you like to sing best at home?'

'"Mercy", by Duffy. She's my favourite. She's Welsh.'

'Okay, go on.'

Elinor frowned. 'What?'

'Sing me the first line of "Mercy".'

Elinor hesitated and Gwen coaxed her again. 'The harp player has gone to lunch – there's only us here, me and you. Just sing the first line.'

Elinor shook her head twice, then gazed away. There was a moments silence, then she suddenly belted a few words out, her voice strained.

Gwen smiled. 'That was okay. But – what do you think the song is really about?'

'It's about mercy.'

Gwen nodded, encouraging. 'What mercy? From whom? Why does the singer want mercy?'

'It's because she's got feelings, she cares about someone and it hurts, so she doesn't want to feel like that any more.'

'So – we all know about wanting to shout out about injustice. Someone we care about is hurting us, and it's wrong. Oh, I know how that feels. Elinor...' Gwen was suddenly excited. 'Do you ever feel like that?'

'All the time.'

'Give me an example.'

'My mam lives with her boyfriend and I hate it when they gang up on me: they laugh at my singing. It makes me feel rubbish.'

'Right, so, sing the first line for them, your mam and her boyfriend, *at* them. As if you want them to stop hurting you.'

Elinor closed her eyes and sang the first line, her expression concentrating, frowning.

'Again.'

Elinor sang, louder, angrier.

'Again.'

Elinor roared out the lines, then opened her eyes, surprised at the power of her own voice.

'Good. You do have a voice.' Gwen smiled. 'Now listen to me

sing it.' She inhaled, then sang the line of the song herself, powerfully and slowly, each note vibrating.

Elinor was amazed. 'How did you do that? It was incredible.'

'By controlling your emotions, and therefore using your voice properly, you can sing strongly. That way, you can move the audience – they are suddenly in your power.' Gwen lifted a finger. 'Right – we're going to learn four important things: how to warm your voice up and how to use your diaphragm. Then we'll learn how to breathe properly and how to make your voice powerful without straining it. Once we've mastered that, you'll hear and feel the difference.'

'Can you teach me all that in an hour?'

'I can make a start.' Gwen put a hand on Elinor's shoulder. 'You'll improve dramatically. Then when you sing again this afternoon in the practice, you'll sound really good.'

'And what about how scared I feel when I'm standing on stage?'

'I'm always scared too. Being scared makes you a better singer if you learn to channel it. That is what makes me good. I use all the fear to push myself into a place where I'm stronger. You can do that too.'

Elinor's eyes shone. 'Can you make me sing like you do?'

Gwen inclined her head. 'If your mam and her boyfriend don't like you singing, who do you sing for? Yourself?'

'Yes, and I sing for my dad who works away on the oil rigs, and my granddad who loves the *cerdd dant*.'

'Then we'll practise singing for them. That way, it's a special gift you're giving them. Okay, Elinor – we have forty minutes. First, let's talk about breathing. You need to imagine a rubber ring around your waist. Right? That's your diaphragm. Now breathe in and try to push the ring outwards...'

* * *

Mary and Vivienne stood outside a brown door, staring at flaking paint. Vivienne knocked and they waited, Mary hugging a lemon drizzle cake wrapped in brown paper and a bag of Welsh cakes. Vivienne rapped the door again, her ringed fingers circling the knocker.

'Perhaps she's asleep?' Mary suggested. 'Or perhaps she's just died. Oh, that would be typical, wouldn't it – we just get here to talk to her and she chooses the exact moment to pop her clogs.'

Vivienne was about to reach for the knocker again, when the door opened and a small woman in a floral apron, her thin white hair curled tightly on her head, pulled the door ajar. She studied Mary for a moment, her eyes small, then she turned her gaze on Vivienne and leaned forward. She showed a few sparse teeth. 'I know who you are.'

Vivienne was momentarily surprised. 'Me?'

'You're Maggs Pryor, from *The Edge of Edgeware*, the one who was burned in the fire and died in the pub.'

Vivienne said simply, 'Yes, that's me. I've brought you a lemon drizzle cake, Mrs Edwards. This is Mary. Can we come in?' She took the cake from Mary and held it up.

'My favourite, it is, lemon drizzle.' Elizabeth's voice was husky, like the dust of dried leaves. 'Well, there it is. You'd better come on in, Maggs. It's very nice to meet you, though I have to say, it's a bit of a surprise to see you at my door. I don't get many visitors.'

She led them through a chilly hallway into a small, gloomy room. The heavy curtains were almost closed and in the corner a lamp gleamed, illuminating an old mahogany sideboard with a row of ancient photos in frames. Elizabeth moved to a wingback armchair, eased herself into the seat, then said, 'Sit on the sofa, will you? It's comfy.'

Vivienne and Mary sat down, Vivienne still clutching the cake. 'So, Elizabeth, it's nice that we're out of lockdown now.'

'Oh, I thought it would never end,' Elizabeth complained. 'Every day was the same, on my own most of the time. Terrible, it was.' She leaned back and closed her eyes. 'I thought we'd never be out of it. It was like being in the war, only there was no one to have any camaraderie with. But at least I have the telly. I always watch *The Edge of Edgeware* – I love it so much. It keeps me going.'

'I'm so glad...' Vivienne began.

Elizabeth opened her eyes. 'Of course, I know you're not really Maggs Prior. I'm not stupid. I might be old but I haven't lost all my marbles.' She frowned. 'But that was my whole world for a year, the telly. It still is now, really. And I loved the way you were such a strong woman in *The Edge of Edgeware*. You wouldn't take any rubbish from your husband, or anyone else. I like that, strong old women who say what's what, who speak their mind and don't take any prisoners. It's how I wish I had been, to be honest. You kept me smiling, Maggs Pryor.'

'Thanks,' Vivienne murmured. 'The thing is, Elizabeth, I wanted to ask you about someone I know, who used to live here in Llanclawdd.'

'Who might that be?' Elizabeth leaned forward.

'Do you remember Gwen Prichard?'

'Who?' Elizabeth frowned, thinking. 'Oh, Gwen Prichard? Yes, I do remember her – pretty girl, dark hair, beautiful voice, a singer. My Cliff was sweet on her for a while. She used to come round – lovely manners, very polite, she was. Is she dead?'

'No.' Vivienne exchanged glances with Mary, a complicit agreement to say nothing about Gwen being in Llanclawdd: Gwen might not want Elizabeth to know. Besides, Vivienne wanted to find out about Clifford Edwards: that was the main purpose of the visit. Vivienne proffered the brown paper bag. 'Can I make you a cuppa, Elizabeth? And a nice slice of this drizzle cake?'

'Oh yes, lovely.'

Vivienne's nose led her to the kitchen, a tiny, damp, cramped room with a sink, a kettle, a fridge and an oven. The floor was covered in grey patterned linoleum, something Vivienne hadn't seen for sixty years. She busied herself with filling the kettle and searching in the badly hinged cupboards for teabags.

Elizabeth noticed Mary huddled on the sofa. 'Are you an actress? I haven't seen you before.'

'No, I'm Mary. I'm a nurse,' Mary replied.

'Oh, a nurse, is it? Well, I don't think I've had my tablets today – the three bottles on the dresser. I don't suppose you'd get them for me, would you, Mary love?'

'Of course.' Mary moved towards the dresser, picking up bottles and examining them. They were anti-inflammatories. She checked the instructions, measured out the doses and handed them to Elizabeth with a glass of water from the table. Elizabeth took her medication dutifully and, as she handed the glass back, Mary noticed that the skin on her hands was chilled.

'Can I make you more comfortable, Elizabeth? You're icy cold and that old chair could have a few more cushions on it, to stop you slipping down so badly.'

'Oh, that's lovely.' Elizabeth gazed up. 'I wish you were my nurse. The one who calls round every day, she's very nice, but you're older and you do things properly.'

Mary plumped up the cushions, found a woollen throw and wrapped it over Elizabeth's knees and stomach, tucking the corners in firmly, then she lifted a stool, gently placing Elizabeth's feet on it just as Vivienne arrived with a tray of tea and cake.

'It's nice to be fussed over.' Elizabeth smiled, gap-toothed. 'My son, Cliff, fusses over me when he visits. He's a good boy.'

Vivienne smiled; her son must be in his seventies, the same age as Gwen. Mary was quick to reply. 'Does he live in the village?'

Elizabeth nodded. 'It's a fifteen-minute walk from here – not that I can walk for fifteen minutes now. Dylwyn Street, it is. Very pricey houses they have up there, with nice conservatories and gardens.'

Vivienne nodded. 'I expect he visits you all the time.' She met Mary's glance. 'And his wife.'

Elizabeth's face clouded. 'Don't talk to me about her.'

'Oh?' Mary leaned forward. 'His wife?'

'She makes my blood boil, that one.'

'I can see that.' Mary nodded, encouragingly. 'Ah, not all wives make the best daughters-in-law.' She had no idea what she was talking about, but Mary nodded her head as if Elizabeth had a problem she needed to share.

'She's a no-good hussy,' Elizabeth spat.

'That's often said about actresses,' Vivienne replied.

'Oh, you're all right.' Elizabeth wrung her twisted hands. 'Siân Roberts, though. She was never any good. I told Cliff before he married her, I said she'll bring you nothing but heartache, and I was right.'

'So, he's not with her now?' Mary asked.

'No, he lives alone. She went off with an estate agent. She wanted a bigger house.' Elizabeth's eyes widened. 'In Swansea. She got one too, with a swimming pool, I heard.'

Mary patted her hand. 'Did she and Cliff have any children?'

'My grandson, Daniel. His wife was no good either. Like father, like son, he married a floozy.'

Vivienne suppressed a smile. 'Did she leave him too?'

'Oh yes, she pretended it was his working away that did it. She said she needed a man in her life all the time. She went off with a painter and decorator and moved to a house in Skinner Road, not far from Cliff. I thought that was terrible, on his doorstep, too. It's the children I always feel sorry for. But never mind, it's all done now.'

'So Cliff is single?' Mary suggested hopefully.

'He's all alone, like me. But he's happier living by himself in that big house. He likes it. The view's lovely – the hills, and you can see the river too.' Elizabeth nibbled her cake. 'My favourite. Lemon drizzle cake.' She gazed at Vivienne and her eyes glittered. 'It's so nice to have company again. And it's lovely to meet you, Maggs Pryor, and your friend Mary, the nurse. Thank you for visiting me.'

'It's been a pleasure,' Vivienne replied.

'And it's good to know that Gwen Prichard is still alive. Is she still singing?' Elizabeth supped her tea noisily. 'Cliff should have married her instead, Gwen Prichard. I think they might even have been engaged at one time. Yes, I liked her. She was a proper girl, nice manners.'

'Well, Gwen's very much alive, and she's still singing.' Mary lifted her cup, a smile spreading across her face. 'Your son, Cliff, should have held on to her while he had the chance. But he's available now, isn't he? And so is she...'

31

Mary, Vivienne and Gwen sat on the soft grass outside the motorhome, the watermill behind them, their feet dangling in the cool stream that bubbled around their ankles. They each held a glass of white wine in their hand; Vivienne had insisted that they needed liquid refreshment after the delicious salad they'd just eaten for supper.

Gwen was still talking about Elinor, and how she had performed on stage that afternoon with so much more self-belief. 'She's improved far more than I thought she possibly could. When she practised with the harpist this afternoon, before you came back from the bakers, she was really quite good.'

'Ah, it must make you feel so great, Gwen,' Mary said. 'Knowing you can make such a difference to the young one's confidence with just one single lesson.'

'It does. I was so thrilled for her. Can we go and watch her sing in the competition tomorrow evening?'

'We must,' Vivienne agreed. 'I love the idea of seeing the children folk dancing tomorrow afternoon, then the Crowning of the

Bard, and the singing competition is in the evening – what's it called again?'

'*Cerdd dant*,' Gwen smiled.

'Then, after that, we're going back home?' Mary sighed. 'It's a shame, for sure.'

A silence followed, as the three women sipped wine, watching the sunlight illuminate the yellow liquid in the glass, each lost in her own thoughts.

Then Gwen said, 'I've enjoyed myself so much during this holiday.'

Vivienne nodded. 'Oh, I have too – I've found two best friends for life.'

'I agree,' Mary muttered. 'But I'm not ready to go back yet. Can't we stay on for a bit longer?' An idea came to her and she brightened. 'What if we stole Vicente's motorhome and took off for a month. We could go anywhere – we could go to Ireland.'

'We could see more of Wales,' Gwen mused. 'Or we could just take our time going back to London, stop over somewhere, have another day or two?'

'It's a lovely thought.' Vivienne closed her eyes. 'But I need to go back. I have to find work soon. I hope Olivia will have something new for me before too long. I'll take anything.'

'Except stairlifts,' Mary offered.

Vivienne's expression was wistful. 'Do you know, I think I'm ready to accept whatever I can get now – chairlifts, Zimmer frames, funerals. Whatever I get is work, and it all proves I'm not completely done yet.'

'You have a point there.' Mary raised her glass, barking a small laugh. 'To not being completely done yet.'

Gwen and Vivienne lifted their wine glasses, smiling. 'To not being completely done.'

'This is so nice, so relaxing, just being here, no stress, no worries.' Gwen gazed at her bare feet in the stream, ripples of water swirling around her ankles.

Vivienne finished her wine with a flourish. 'Right, ladies. I vote we get an early night. Tomorrow, we're going to go and see the house where Gwen lived.'

'Oh, that'll be fun.' Mary patted Gwen's arm. 'Then there's the dancing in the afternoon and the music competition later. It'll be grand. So, where did you used to live, Gwen? What was the old Prichard house like?'

'It was humble, but it was cosy – it was home.' Gwen's eyes shone, reminiscing. 'It was a Victorian terrace on Hewson Street, which was on a steep incline. We lived halfway up – even as a healthy kid, you'd puff and pant climbing to the top. But the view is spectacular, the hills rising high in the distance, right up to the sky. Even when it was rainy, it looked beautiful, all misty. When the snow came, it was to die for – we'd steal our mams' trays from the kitchen and use them as toboggans. I had a wonderful childhood in many ways. Times were tough but I remember it so fondly. It'll be interesting to see if everything's still the same.'

Gwen recalled Hewson Street as a line of brick-fronted terraced houses facing each other in two identical rows, each with red sash windows, brick chimneys and a door that led straight onto the pavement, apart from a grey stone step, which Gwen's mother would scrub clean every Friday. Now the houses, probably all privately owned, were very different: the windows were double glazed; the front doors an array of wood or uPVC with opaque glass in a range of designs. Gwen remembered the houses being uniform and identical back in the sixties but now the slanting street full of terraced houses was a contrast of bright colours; the brick fronts had been painted, window surrounds here a garish blue, there a bright yellow, elsewhere a deep red. Gwen shook her head sadly. 'That house over there, number ninety. It used to belong to an old gentleman, Cedric Gladstone, not a hair on his head. He was grumpy and all the children were frightened of him. Apparently, he'd been a war hero. Now look at his home – the brickwork has been painted mauve. And those floral curtains, and the stained-glass flowers in the plastic door. He'd never have believed it.'

'I think it's a lovely setting here, Gwen.' Mary pointed down the street. 'The way the road curves away and in the distance, the rising hills keeping everyone safe and sheltered. It's so peaceful and calm.'

Vivienne placed a hand on Gwen's shoulder. 'How do you feel, being back?'

Gwen exhaled. 'It's a bit like – everyone else has moved on, and I've stayed the same. As if I belong in the past when all these houses were red brick, and my mother was at the stove at night making lamb stew while my dad sat in his chair reading the paper and watching the black-and-white TV...'

'No, you've done so much with your life since then.' Vivienne pulled her in a hug. 'You're an opera singer. What an incredible achievement.'

Gwen's mouth turned down. 'I suppose you're right. But sometimes I think that all I really wanted was to be a wife and a mother.'

'Ah, perhaps that's not all it's cracked up to be. Being a parent works for some people and for others, it just doesn't. Why not be happy you have your health and good friends?'

'Yes, you're right, Mary, I should count my blessings.' Gwen put a finger to the corner of her eye, wiping a tear that had lodged there. 'Hewson Street is in the past, along with my childhood. Those were good days, but now I have my life in London and, do you know, when we get back there, I'm going to get into singing again properly. I'm determined to do something with the rest of my life. I've stagnated for too long.'

Mary tucked an arm through Gwen's. 'So, how long is it since you've been on the stage?'

'Too long.' Gwen's face was determined. 'Before I came to Drayton Mews, I lived in various places across London, coaching singers, doing some private teaching. I loved that. Then, a few years ago, I thought I ought to retire but, do you know, it's been boring. I miss it. It occurred to me again yesterday when I was helping young Elinor, I would like to start to coaching singing again.'

Vivienne took her other arm. 'That's the spirit. You can do anything you want. Singing is in your blood, so it makes sense that you should carry on doing the thing that keeps you alive. It's the same with me and acting.'

Mary looked around at the quiet street, the distant hills beyond. 'Right. Now, we have a downhill walk back to the village, so it won't take too long. Then how about stopping for a lovely cup of Welsh tea in that nice café before we go to watch the dancers on the green?'

* * *

People crowded around the village green for the folk dancing, Mary pushing to the front to see better, muttering, 'I'm an old lady – let me through.' Vivienne and Gwen joined her, clapping their hands as music from flutes and pipes played and youngsters dressed in black and white twirled and skipped sedately through carefully practised moves. Behind them, the flag of Wales had been hoisted high on a pole, a fiery dragon proudly lifting a claw. Bunting shivered in the breeze from other tall posts as the dancers moved, heads held high. The boys wore red socks and the girls had long red aprons, and little white caps on their heads. Vivienne murmured, 'This is so enchanting.'

'The dance is called *Ty Coch Caerdydd*: The Red House in Cardiff,' Gwen replied. 'I know every step.'

The dancers whirled, circled, whirled again, bowed and curtsied, then they scurried away and suddenly there was a hush. The crowd stood expectantly waiting as three men walked on carrying a carved wooden chair, then several serious-faced young men in purple robes formed a line. Mary frowned. 'Is this the King of Wales?'

'In a manner of speaking.' Gwen winked. 'It's the *Coroni'r Bardd*, the Crowning of the Bard. He'll be announced in a minute, the winner of the *pryddest*, the free verse poetry writing competition, and one of the people about to crown him will have won it last year.'

'Is he going to perform?' Vivienne whispered.

'Watch.'

Gwen pointed as a man stepped in front of the crowd dressed in a flowing purple robe, lifting a silver heraldic trumpet to his lips and blowing a long, majestic sound. Another man made a purposeful entrance as if he was in charge, lifting a hand, poised in purple robes and cap. Mary joked, 'It's the Welsh Pope.'

He uttered several words in Welsh and paused meaningfully, then the audience clapped heartily as a young blond-haired man walked out of the audience, his expression a little stunned, and was immediately flanked by two other men in white, with matching headdresses.

Mary was puzzled. 'It's the shepherds. Is this a play about the blessed nativity? Are we in the wrong place?'

Vivienne arched an eyebrow. 'And don't any women ever take part?'

Gwen held a finger to her lips as the chief man began to utter more resonating important-sounding words, then the blond poet was ceremoniously dressed in a lavish gold and indigo robe. He sat on the carved wooden chair and a silver crown was placed on his head. There was more clapping, a heraldic trumpet note, then the blond poet stood tall, intoning something beautiful in Welsh.

Mary shrugged. 'It's all Welsh to me.'

But Gwen had tears in her eyes. 'No, it's magnificent. He's so talented.'

The crowd clapped again. The blond poet lifted his hand in a ceremonious wave and everyone cheered. Behind him, more flags and colourful buntings on tall poles flapped in the breeze as if applauding too. Someone blew another trumpet, a long, languid note. Mary was restless, ready to leave. 'What time is the singing competition in the village hall?'

'Very soon.' Gwen watched as the crowd dispersed around her. 'It will last for about an hour, then we can go back to the motorhome and have a bite to eat. How does that sound?'

'With a glass of wine? It sounds fabulous,' Vivienne agreed.

'Right,' said Mary. 'So we have a plan. Let's go and see how your latest new pupil gets on with the singing.'

Gwen felt a familiar clawing sensation in her stomach, the beginning of nervousness. 'Oh yes, the competition. I do hope Elinor will be all right.'

32

Gwen felt nervous as she took her place on one of the wooden seats in the village hall. Gazing at the empty stage, the harp and microphone already in place, she was anxious for Elinor. People were taking their places, muttering in hushed voices, and a few of the contestants and their families had moved to the reserved seats in the front row. She turned to Mary.

'Oh, I hope she doesn't dry up on stage or make too many mistakes. Poor little thing. I felt so sorry for her.'

'Will her family come along and support her?' Mary asked.

'She lives with her mother and the boyfriend who don't seem very bothered – Elinor told me they have a two-year-old toddler who seems to be their main priority. Elinor's all by herself, unsupported, that's why I was so happy to help her.'

'It must be tough for the little mite.' Mary shook her head. 'You have to admire her pluck, doing it alone. I hope she wins.'

'Oh, she's unlikely to win – the competition's so tough in these events. I just want her to get through it and be able to hold her head in the air.' Gwen suddenly paused. 'Look she's here – there she is.' She pointed to a small, smartly dressed girl in the front row who was waving furiously, her red hair hanging to her waist. Gwen waved back and called, '*Pob lwc*, Elinor – good luck.'

Vivienne, on the other side of Gwen, squeezed her arm gently. 'In my experience, having no support from home makes us tougher and even more likely to succeed. I know the wicked step-parent scenario. It spurred me on – I was determined I'd do well. Elinor will be okay.'

Gwen sighed. 'My dad was so supportive about my singing. My mother, too, although she was very strict and I felt like I was never good enough. She'd have tears in her eyes when I sang though, my mam. And they both supported me when I moved to Swansea at eighteen to sing opera. My dad would take me there in the car and bring me home at weekends; my mam would have the meals ready, my favourites. They were very good, my parents.'

Mary closed her eyes, dispelling all memories of family. She took a breath. 'Gwen, Vivienne and I have something we probably ought to tell you.'

'Ah, yes,' Vivienne said meaningfully. 'We ought to mention what we've done.'

'What's happened?' Gwen's face was suddenly alarmed. 'What have you done?'

'Oh, it's nothing to worry about,' Vivienne began.

'Well, not much. We met someone yesterday who remembers you – well, what we did was, we called on her in her house. A woman called Elizabeth Edwards.'

'Clifford's mother?' Gwen paled. 'Why ever would you visit her?'

'We wanted to find out all about your Clifford Edwards,' Mary admitted.

'He's not *my* Cliff—'

'He's still alive, Gwen – and he's single,' Vivienne interrupted.

'Just in case you were still interested...'

'Well, I'm not interested, Mary.' Gwen folded her arms. Her

cheeks had flushed red. 'In fact, as far as I'm concerned, Clifford Edwards can go to—'

A man in a dark suit had taken his place on stage and was speaking clearly into the microphone, the harpist was at his seat and there was a hearty round of applause. The man continued to speak in Welsh; there was more clapping and the first contestant was called to the stage to sing.

Gwen found it hard to concentrate as each singer took her turn: seven, maybe eight contestants had already performed, and she'd hardly noticed them. One singer in particular, Ruth Morris, was extremely talented and Gwen was sure that she would win. But her mind kept floating back to Vivienne's words – *he's still alive – and he's single*. Clifford Edwards was in her thoughts again and she couldn't keep him out. Gwen wasn't sure how she felt about the news of his single status, other than that her nerves were wriggling like spiders beneath her skin. She was pleased that Clifford was alive, but she certainly didn't want to meet him. And if he was single, what had happened to Siân Roberts? Gwen knew they'd married: her mother had kept her informed about his life during her home visits, although she hadn't wanted to know: it had been too painful to imagine him happy with Siân. She knew they'd had a son, Daniel, and she'd seen Clifford and Siân and a child in a pushchair once during a visit, while she'd been shopping in the village, which had been horribly embarrassing, but she'd heard no news of him since her mother had died. She hadn't wanted to.

A girl called Beth was currently singing on stage; she had a clear voice, but Gwen was sure she could be so much better if she was properly coached. Gwen knew she could improve the girl's diction easily and make sure she hit the higher notes well. Gwen pulled her thoughts back to the present: she'd go back to London, create a sparkling website, and start to coach singing again. She'd enjoy that, it would be more than a hobby; it would fill her days and build her confidence again. Then thoughts of Clifford slunk back into her mind and she imagined meeting him again. He was single, he was available. Gwen pushed the thoughts from her mind with a mighty effort and glued her attention to Beth's singing. Then the girl finished, inclined her head in receipt of the applause and moved away from the microphone. The man in the suit returned, lifted a hand and called out, 'Elinor Megan Edwards,' and Elinor walked smartly to the microphone and stood still, fiddling with her fingers while the harpist began to play. Vivienne shot Gwen a sharp look. 'Edwards? As in Clifford Edwards?'

'Or perhaps not...' Mary hissed from the other side. 'Isn't it a common name? Are there lots of them in Llanclawdd?'

Vivienne shrugged, a slight nervous movement, and fixed her attention on Elinor, who had already started to sing. The girl's voice was strong and more determined; she had remembered everything Gwen had taught her yesterday. She was using her diaphragm properly, unafraid of the high notes, creating light, shade and meaning. Gwen listened carefully to every note of the song, concentrating on every syllable, willing the girl to succeed. Elinor sang boldly, her face expressing every moment emphatically, and she reached the end of her song almost faultlessly. Gwen clapped as hard as she could as she watched Elinor return smartly to her seat and take her place next to a tall broad-shouldered man in a brown tweed jacket who turned to whisper something in her ear, Elinor beaming back excitedly.

Gwen froze. She recognised the shoulders. She had clung to them, been hugged against them; she had ridden on them on Rhossili beach over fifty years ago. He might be older, but she knew the man in the brown jacket, despite his thick hair being snow white now. She'd know him anywhere. It was him, Clifford Edwards – he was Elinor's grandfather. Gwen wanted to dash from the village hall immediately, but her legs wouldn't lift her. She was stuck.

Vivienne glanced at Gwen, raising an eyebrow dramatically, then she leaned over and hissed, 'That's him, isn't it? Mr Brown Jacket?'

Gwen gulped, and she felt Vivienne clasp her hand on one side and Mary reach for the other one at the same time.

'Don't worry. It will lay the ghosts to rest, Gwen,' Mary muttered. 'You mark my words – and they do need laying to rest, your ghosts.'

Three more contestants sang and were applauded, then there was a pause for adjudication. Elinor waved nervously at Gwen and she replied with a cheery thumbs up. Then the man next to Elinor turned round and Gwen recognised him, the soft expression, the searching eyes. Gwen saw him mutter something to Elinor, then she looked away quickly, pretending she had no idea who he was.

The room was immediately hushed as the results were announced. As Gwen had thought, Ruth Erin Morris was the clear winner. After so long in the profession, she had a judge's ear for ability when it came to anything to do with singing. Then the man's voice announced that Elinor Megan Edwards was awarded third place, and the girl rushed on stage to receive her award. Applause resounded; Vivienne squeezed Gwen's knee and whispered, 'Well done. You're such a good teacher.' But Gwen hardly heard her; Elinor's grandfather turned round and met her eyes; he had smiled at her and now he was standing up with his granddaughter; they were leaving their seats; they were making their way over towards them.

Gwen thought her heart was going to knock a hole in her chest; her legs had lost all ability to hold her up. Mary took her hand and squeezed it too hard. Vivienne insisted, 'You're up to this, Gwen. Go on. Talk to him.'

Then the man and the girl were standing next to her, smiling; he was holding out a hand, Clifford Edwards, just as she remembered him. Although he was older, his sweet smile, his gorgeous eyes were just the same. He took her fingers in his hand as if they were fragile porcelain.

'I can't thank you enough for what you did for Elinor today.'

Gwen's heart pounded; the same lilting voice melting her heart over again. She managed a few words. 'I was glad to help.'

'Congratulations, Elinor,' Vivienne hooted.

'You sang like an angel from heaven,' Mary added as both women attempted to occupy Elinor's attention, manoeuvring her away from Gwen.

Clifford was standing too close to her. 'Gwen. It's you. I knew it had to be when Elinor said she'd met an opera singer called Gwen who'd spent lunchtime teaching her.'

Gwen said simply, 'Yes.'

Clifford's eyes twinkled. 'So, are you living here again? Are you back in Llanclawdd?'

'No, I'm just passing through.'

'So, are you still in London?'

Gwen thought her legs would give way. The room was spinning too fast. She nodded. 'London, yes.'

'It's been a long time, Gwen.'

'It has, Cliff.'

He tried harder. 'Are you staying here for a while? I'd love it if we could catch up, maybe have dinner together.'

'No.' Gwen didn't know what else to say. Words came out by accident, from sheer nervousness. 'I'm going back tomorrow.'

'Then we can meet up tonight.' He still held her hand. 'We have this evening. Oh, I have so much to say to you, things I've wanted to say for fifty years.'

Gwen shook her head. 'I don't want to hear them, Cliff.'

'You might,' he said hopefully. 'Just give me the chance, eh? The chance to speak my mind, to say what's in my heart. Just a few hours? An hour?'

Gwen felt her resolve weakening. The only word in her mouth was yes: he had that way with him, Cliff; she'd agree, she'd bend like a willow just to please him. She took a breath. No, that had all been fifty years ago. She was different now: she was someone else.

'No, I can't do it,' she blurted. 'No more, no, no.'

Then she grabbed her handbag, turned abruptly and rushed from the village hall, her heels pounding hard on the floorboards.

Cliff Edwards looked stunned. His granddaughter was by his side, her expression concerned. 'Are you all right, Granddad?'

'I don't know...' he muttered, his eyes still staring towards the door, where Gwen had disappeared.

Vivienne took a sharp breath. 'Well done on achieving third place, Elinor. You were simply fabulous. Keep up the singing, sweetie, and don't let your mum's wicked boyfriend put you off.' She glanced at Clifford, the corner of her upper lip lifted in a slight sneer. 'Well, you tried, I suppose, Cliff, but you missed your chance years ago. And, in all fairness, you are fifty-something years too late. So, if you'll excuse me, I'm going to find Gwen.'

Mary watched Vivienne trip smartly towards the door, then she winked at Elinor, giving her full attention to her grandfather. 'Ah, so, you're the famous Clifford Edwards, then?' She gave a soft laugh. 'Well, if you don't mind me saying, you've been a right eejit. You made a proper bags of it all where Gwen is concerned.'

His face was sad beneath white brows. 'I have.'

'I'm Mary.' She took his hand and squeezed it hard. 'We're staying in a motorhome. It's parked outside on the grass, by the old watermill, just ten minutes from the village.'

'I know it.'

'Right. Well. We'll be leaving tomorrow, I suppose, around ten, once we've had breakfast and tidied away a bit.' She met his eyes.

'Just in case that information is useful to you.' She watched as he breathed in slowly and nodded his head. He seemed a little dazed. Mary was about to follow Vivienne, but she turned on her heel and added, 'In your place, Clifford, I'd leave her alone for tonight. Gwen has fifty years of rejection to get out of her system. But by tomorrow, who knows? She might be feeling a little more like listening to your pathetic excuses.'

33

The next day, Vivienne was rushing around inside the motorhome, packing away underwear, searching frantically for her hairbrush. Mary was sitting on the bed with her feet up; she had packed her case already and was gazing through the little window under the pretence of looking at the sunlight dancing on the water in the stream. Gwen was still jittery; she had hardly eaten breakfast and last night, after they had returned from the singing competition, she hadn't been able to manage a single bite of supper, her stomach had been so unsettled. Vivienne was throwing cushions around, upending the plastic table. 'I've lost my brush and a heated roller. Has anyone seen it? It's pink.'

'Ah, it's so pretty, the way the sunlight reflects off the stream. It's such a nice watermill. I do love it here,' Mary observed.

Gwen groaned. 'Perhaps I should have talked to him. Perhaps I should have let him say his piece. After all, I owe him that much.'

'You don't owe him anything,' Vivienne replied. 'Here's the hairbrush. Now I've lost my phone. Whatever is wrong with me this morning?'

Mary pointed through the window. 'Look how the stream's so

relaxing in the bright sunshine. And the grass smells so sweet.' She glanced up and down the path nervously; it was ten minutes to ten. She was sure Clifford would arrive at any minute; he had seemed so devastated, so disappointed after Gwen had left. She sighed. 'It's such a shame we have to go back so soon. Can't we stay on for a few hours, maybe have lunch here, or just – I don't know – paddle outside a bit in the stream?'

Gwen's head rested in her hands, distraught. 'Should I have gone to dinner with him? I mean, what if I'd gone – what if I'd talked to him?'

'Ah, here it is – one heated roller, now I have the full set.' Vivienne grasped at something that was hidden under the bed and lifted it up with a flourish. 'Now where's the damn phone?'

'I don't think I can ever forgive him for Siân Roberts though...'

'Oh, that's wonderful.' Mary's hand twitched the curtain. A white-haired man in his seventies wearing a brown tweed jacket was rushing down the path. 'Ah, yes, it's definitely going to be a lovely day today.'

'My phone was in my pocket all the time,' Vivienne yelled.

'Right,' Gwen said sadly. 'Then we should go back to London and before it's late.'

'There's no hurry, we've all day.' Mary smiled. 'Just step outside, Gwen, and say your goodbyes to the old village one more time.'

Gwen nodded. 'Yes, all right, Mary, I will, just once. After all, I'll probably never be back again.'

Gwen moved towards the passenger door and flung it wide, standing on the step, just as Clifford Edwards was about to knock. She gasped at his fist raised in mid-air. 'Oh.'

'Gwen, can we talk?'

Inside the motorhome, Vivienne rolled her eyes. Mary clamped a triumphant hand over her smile. Gwen stepped outside the van and took several paces towards the stream as Clifford followed her.

'I won't ask you how you knew I was staying here, Cliff.'

'It's a small village,' he muttered tactfully as Mary and Vivienne loitered near the small window, listening intently. 'So...'

'So?' Gwen put her hands on her hips. 'Why are you here?'

'I owe you an explanation.'

'Oh?'

'About Siân.'

'Your wife, Siân, you mean.'

'We split up a long time ago.'

'But you married her. She was the one you chose, not me.'

'I made a mistake. When you were in Swansea, I should have moved up with you properly, instead of staying home and just coming up to visit at weekends. We might have still been together.'

'I know.'

'There was never anyone else I loved. Only you, Gwen.'

They faced each other, Clifford's eyes on Gwen as she looked away uncomfortably. 'It's too late now.'

'No, it's not. You could stay here. We could start again. You could meet Elinor, give her singing lessons, and my son, Dan, is coming home from the oil rigs soon, and we could visit my mam. You could come back to live in the village.'

Gwen frowned. 'You mean we could pick up after all these years and start again?'

'Yes – that's what I want. You are what I want.'

Two faces peered around the side of the door, leaning out of the motorhome, desperate to hear every word.

'I don't know.' Gwen looked at her shoes.

'Why not?' Clifford took her hand. 'We love each other still. It's meant to be.'

Mary hung out of the motorhome, her thumb up, nodding her head in encouragement. Vivienne poked her gently with her elbow, frowning in disagreement. Mary mouthed, 'He loves her.'

Vivienne shook her head and mouthed back, '"Hell hath no fury like a woman scorned..."'

'You could... you could live with me.'

'Here, with you? In your house?'

'Yes.' Clifford was breathless. (Mary was ready to leap out and cheer.)

Gwen took a breath. 'In the house where you lived with Siân Roberts?' (Vivienne shook her fist in agreement.)

'It could be our house, yours and mine, for ever and ever,' Clifford urged.

'Amen.' Mary couldn't help herself.

Gwen's face flushed pink. 'How dare you? How dare you, after all this time, after everything you put me through? How could you imagine that I'd come back to you and live in the same house where you made your home with that woman?'

'We could move somewhere else...'

Mary was standing on the steps, arms folded, unable to drag herself away. Somewhere inside the motorhome a phone rang, and Gwen could hear Vivienne projecting loudly, talking excitedly to someone on the other end of the line. She gazed at Clifford.

'No, it's over. I've changed. I'm an opera singer now. I have my own life in London; I have friends.' She turned away. 'Sorry, but it's finished. Well... it never really started again, did it?'

Clifford rested a hand on her arm. 'Please, Gwen.'

'No. I have nothing to say to you, not now, not ever.' Gwen lifted her shoulder dramatically, shrugging him away. 'Goodbye, Cliff.'

She strode back to the motorhome, climbing into the cab, slamming the door behind her. Clifford stayed where he was for a moment, his head bent, then the passenger door opened. Mary slithered down the steps and rushed over to him, placing a torn piece of paper in his hand. 'Here – it's her phone number – just in case she changes her mind. I had it in my bag. Don't tell her I've given it to you.'

'Well, how will I explain...?'

But Mary was gone. Gwen was already inside the cab, starting the engine, revving it too loudly as Mary climbed in beside her and buckled her seat belt. Vivienne called from the passenger seat behind. 'Just like Hermia in *A Midsummer Night's Dream*, eh, Gwen? "Though she be but little, she is fierce,"' and she shot Gwen a glance of pure admiration. Then the motorhome chugged away, down the gravel path and out onto the road, leaving Clifford standing in a fog of fumes in its wake, shaking his head.

Gwen drove frantically, her foot on the accelerator, as the motorhome headed along the main road towards Rhossili.

Mary murmured, 'I think we're going the wrong way.'

'I just had to drive, I had to get away from him.' Gwen was flustered. 'Just let me get to a place where I can stop, and I'll set the satnav. We can take the scenic route back to London and take our time. I thought we might go via Herefordshire, maybe stop over somewhere.'

'The thing is, there have been developments,' Vivienne piped up from the passenger seat behind her. 'That was my agent on the phone, just a while ago. I have work.' Her voice was suddenly excited. 'I have a role in a TV film about Dracula. I'll have to rush back to London today and get a train to Yorkshire or wherever it is tomorrow – I need to be there in two days' time for the morning shoot. I have a great role.'

'Oh.' Mary was fascinated. 'Who are you playing?'

'A nun.'

Mary brayed with laughter. 'Are you sure they know what you're like? What sort of nun will you be? One that wears lipstick and suspenders and drinks like a fish?'

'I can do a nun, Mary.' Vivienne smiled. 'Olivia says it's a great role – she's emailing me the script to read this morning. She says it's perfect for me, and could lead to so many other things. The director's really busy right now, he has lots of projects lined up, so if he likes my work – and I'll make sure he will – I'm in.'

'Great.' Gwen's voice was soft. 'I'll pull into this lay-by and we'll set the satnav. Oh well, it's time to go back home.'

'It is,' Mary agreed, her face downhearted as she watched Gwen's fingers on the touchscreen.

'So, it's five hours to London at a steady pace.' Gwen adjusted her driving glasses on her nose. 'Six, if we stop for lunch.'

'That's great.' Vivienne stretched out her legs, a satisfied smile on her face. 'So, we'll be home by this evening, and I can get myself organised to buy a train ticket to Whitby.'

'Oh, Whitby?' Mary sounded fascinated.

'Have you been there?'

'Never, Vivienne. I've no idea where it is. Have you been there?'

'No, but I think it's very pretty.' She leaned forward. 'I can hardly believe my luck. Do you know, the woman who was playing the role I've got now had to drop out because someone in her close family became ill. She's quite a big name too. Anyway, they needed a quick replacement and Olivia mentioned me and the director jumped at it. Which is quite surprising as the woman who was given the role first is only in her forties.' She clapped her hands excitedly. 'A nun. That's just so funny.'

Mary was thoughtful. 'I've always wanted to go to Whitby.'

Gwen sighed. 'Maybe you can go up with Vivienne to watch the filming?'

'Why don't we all go?' Mary wriggled in her seat. 'Let's all go to Whitby with Vivienne. We don't need to go back to London. We can just all drive north now.'

'Oh, we can't do that.' Gwen was astonished.

'Why not?'

'Because it's not our motorhome, Mary. It's Vicente's. He lent it to us in good faith.'

'Ah, he won't be going anywhere in it. He's too poorly.'

'But we can't take his motorhome up to Whitby – it's...'

'Ring him.' Vivienne's voice was commanding from the passenger seat. 'Ring him, ask, see what he says. If he'll lend us the motorhome, let's all go to Whitby.'

'But we can't.'

'We can.' Mary was insistent. 'It'd be great craic. I don't want to go back to London yet.'

Vivienne took a breath. 'Gwen, can we get from here to Whitby in two days?'

'Oh yes. It's not difficult – we could find places to stay on the way, one overnight stopover should do it...'

'Then ring Vicente. It would be a hoot if you could both come with me and watch me film, or just explore the area. Go on...'

'Go on, Gwen,' Mary urged. 'I'd love to explore Yorkshire. I've heard it's lovely there.'

Gwen hunched over her phone, pressing buttons, listening to it ring. Then her voice was tentative as she muttered into the speaker. 'Hello, Vicente, it's Gwen Prichard. How are you?'

She listened for a while as a voice wheezed at the other end. 'Oh, well. We're so happy you could lend it to us. We've had such a wonderful time driving around in it. In fact, I was thinking...'

Vicente's voice crackled at the other end, Gwen nodding, smiling. 'So, me and the girls, we wondered, well, if we could borrow it for... just a few more days.'

Vivienne nodded, mouthing, 'We'd probably not keep it for more than a week,' and Mary held up her thumb hopefully.

'Oh, all right, yes, I see...' Gwen raised her eyebrows as she listened. 'Oh, that's not very nice... oh, well, that's good, I'm pleased to hear it. Well, yes, it's ideal, isn't it?'

Gwen listened again, moving her head. 'Oh, I'm so glad you got the postcards. No, well, I suppose being a bit jealous is a sign – a sign she likes you. Yes, yes, thank you so much. Well, we'll be back in a week's time, hopefully, I mean, we'll definitely be back before then, and we'll be sure to send you another postcard from Whitby. Yes, get well soon, all the best, and thank you.' She replaced the phone and breathed out slowly. 'Well, that's a turn up for the books.' She met Mary's eyes. 'Vicente says we can borrow the motorhome for another week.'

'That's grand.'

'So, what was a turn up for the books? What did he say?' Vivienne asked.

'Well,' Gwen leaned back in her seat, 'you know he's been really poorly. It seems he's got himself a carer, a lady who comes round to visit every day now. And – guess what? They've become an item.'

'What sort of an item?' Mary pulled a face.

'A romantic one.' Gwen pressed a hand over her smile. 'She's called Cherilyn. And she's been quite jealous about his postcards from other women – us. So, he wants me to send him another one – to keep her on her toes. He says he likes Cherilyn being jealous – she's very passionate, apparently, and won't let him out of her sight. Anyway, we can have the motorhome for as long as we like, he says. So – it's all arranged.'

'Perfect,' Mary cheered, waving an arm.

'Yes...' Gwen seemed stunned. 'So, it seems that we're going to Whitby.'

'We are indeed,' Vivienne boomed. 'Reset the satnav, Gwen. We're off up north. This holiday isn't over yet.'

34

'I know where we are on the satnav, but...' Gwen's voice was nervous as she gazed around at the endless road flanked by hedgerows, and an occasional farm building. She seemed to have been driving along it for hours. 'We could be anywhere. Whose idea was it to take the scenic route? Perhaps the motorway might have been better.'

The sun streamed hotly into the cab and, despite the windows being open, Gwen's face was red and perspiring behind the lenses of her driving spectacles. Mary gazed out at the lush scenery, sweeping valleys and swelling hills. Beyond the hedges, grass rolled away as far as the eye could see; in the fields, fleecy sheep grazed and dappled cows stood in groups, immobile as a painting. The sweet scent of honeysuckle drifted into the cab.

'Ah, but it's lovely here in the North of Wales, I didn't see much of it the one time I was here because of all the sex. I stayed in the hotel all the time with Harry Pike, the hospital porter, sweet as you like with his little goatee beard. Lovely fella, he was. So let's be glad we came this way, Gwen, and not on the stuffy motorway with all the roadworks and slow down signs. Here, we can just go along slowly. It makes all the difference.'

Vivienne agreed. 'And it'll be lovely to stay at the farm tonight. The woman I spoke to on the phone was so nice. She's allocated us a prime spot in her field, she said. And we can't be too far away from it now – what's the place called, Gwen?'

'Nantyglas, thirty minutes away.' Gwen was concentrating on negotiating a severe twist in the road. 'It's between Mold and Ruthin. I suppose you're right – it'll be nice to stay in Wales tonight, rather than parking up in a motorway service station.'

'Oh, I think there's a fine if you do that anyway,' Vivienne called. 'No, our plan is wonderful. We do the longer drive today, the slightly shorter one tomorrow through Cheshire then Yorkshire, and we'll be in Whitby after breakfast the following day. I'm just so thrilled to have a part in a film and even more thrilled you two are coming with me.'

'I'm shattered, to tell you the truth.' Gwen put a hand to her damp brow. 'It's been a long drive.'

'You aren't to do a single thing when we stop, Gwen,' Vivienne insisted. 'Mary and I will make supper. You just put your feet up and sip wine.'

'Thanks, Vivienne – I will. I might have a shower and an early night. I've been feeling tired.' Gwen knew why she was weary; concentrating on the roads had been hard enough, but driving away all thoughts of Clifford Edwards, his sweet smile, the affection in his eyes, had made her wonder if she had made a mistake. But Gwen reminded herself, it was done now, it was in the past. She braked hard to avoid a sheep that was loitering by the side of the road, evidence that she needed to keep her wits about her as she drove.

'Ha, we just missed out on the meat for tonight's stew,' Mary quipped. 'Well done, Gwen.' She called over her shoulder to Vivienne. 'Did you book the place we're staying in tomorrow night while you were organising tonight?'

'I did.' Vivienne was thumbing through emails on her phone. 'It's all sorted, Mary.'

'Grand. I can't wait to tell everyone I spent a night on Robin Hood's Butt.'

'Butts, plural.'

'He had more than one butt, Vivienne?'

Vivienne smiled. 'It's a little place on the Yorkshire moorland, very atmospheric. The farmer says they have lots of space and it's not far from Whitby.'

Another sheep hurled itself across the road and Gwen braked suddenly, causing Mary to lurch forward. 'Blessed Joseph – sorry, Gwen. I thought I was getting better at not cussing.'

'You're doing so well, Mary.' Gwen smiled kindly. 'I'll be glad when we get to the farm at Nantyglas. I'll take you up on that glass of wine, Vivienne. A nice red, that's what I'll have. I think I deserve it.' Gwen set her chin firmly. She was on holiday; she was going to Whitby and she was going to have such fun. Clifford was in the past now. She could do it – she could move on.

'My script has just come in by email,' Vivienne exclaimed excitedly, studying her phone. 'Oh, I love it. My character is called Sister Camella. She has some great lines and – would you believe it, it's a revamp of the original. Revamp, ha ha, hilarious. And I meet a sticky end, oh, this is such a great scene to get my teeth into. Oh, I'm so going to enjoy this.'

'Will you want to practise your lines in the motorhome after supper, and keep us all amused?' Mary asked.

'I might,' Vivienne muttered coyly. 'But then you might not get any sleep all night – it's such a scary storyline.'

'And sleep is what I need,' Gwen murmured as she noticed a white sign indicating the turning to Nantyglas. 'And food. I didn't eat properly last night. Well, it's three miles to Hafoty Farm. I'll be so glad when we get there.'

The owner of Hafoty Farm was a young woman in her twenties. She wore a lacy floral dress and a leather jacket over wellingtons and a scarf tied back her long brown hair. She waved as Gwen approached in the motorhome.

'Hi, you're the first to arrive.' She scrutinised Gwen's face. 'We don't usually get, you know, people over thirty. Anyway, you're very welcome – just drive on and you'll come to the field – the gate's already open. Help yourselves, enjoy, it's all free. I'm Gina, by the way.'

'Hello, Gina, I'm Gwen.'

Gina was already on her way back to the farmhouse, hurrying along a path spattered with colourful flowers. Mary frowned. 'She was dressed strangely for a farmer. I wouldn't have thought a dress was any good for driving a tractor.'

'She's not local either,' Vivienne added. 'That was a broad Lancashire accent.'

Gwen was steering the motorhome along a bumpy track towards an open gate. She drove into the field and parked by a tall hedge. 'Well, this is home for the night. I think I'll take a nice shower and help myself to something cool to drink.'

'It's past five, so it's gin o'clock,' Vivienne agreed.

'It's nearly six, and that makes it dinner o'clock. Dinner and gin are a good combination.' Mary unbuckled her seat belt, then pointed over her shoulder. 'Oh, look – someone else is stopping the night. We've got fellow guests.'

A yellow and green camper van rolled into the field and accelerated past them, horns blaring, a young man waving through the window. Mary sighed. 'Ah to be twenty-one again.' She was opening the fridge, organising ingredients. 'How about I make us a nice curry? We haven't had one in ages.'

'I'm going to learn my lines.' Vivienne made herself comfortable at the back of the motorhome. 'Oh, look – another camper van has arrived – they must be friends with the boys in the yellow one.'

'I'll have a shower if you don't mind – I'm shattered,' Gwen breathed.

'You go and knock yourself out, Gwen.' Mary smiled. 'Vivienne can check the water tank and sort out the wine, and I'll make us a lovely madras.'

* * *

Two hours later, the motorhome was filled with the rich aroma of Mary's cooking, sweet aromatic spices, delicate herbs, and pungent flavours. The empty curry dishes were stacked by the sink. Vivienne continued to practise her script, staring at her phone, a full glass in one hand. Gwen sipped her wine, eyes closed. 'We've had some good times in this motorhome. I've really enjoyed myself.'

'Whitby's going to be fun too.' Vivienne still didn't take her eyes from the screen.

'Do you remember that, at the beginning, Vicente called the motorhome Venus? He thought it was his little love machine.' Mary burst out laughing. 'We should call it Cupid instead. We should find ourselves a few fellas and bring them back here.' She moved the curtain back and peered through the Perspex window. 'Oh, look, there are three, no, four little camper vans here now. One has a big peace sign painted on it. I wonder if there are any nice older men...'

'It annoys me a bit that men name cars and boats after women, as if they are playthings, you know, things they own and control.' Vivienne was still reading.

'You mean like the *QE2* and the *Marie Celeste*?' Mary asked.

'Perhaps we should rename Venus, then?' Gwen was feeling relaxed, calmer, her feet up on the bed. 'What about something manly, like Hercules or Achilles?'

'Or after someone big and brainless because the motorhome is huge and goes where we tell it.' Vivienne was still reading. 'Colossus, Atlas.'

'I've had plenty of big brainless boyfriends. Maybe we should name the motorhome after one of our exes.' Mary gulped wine, thinking: in some ways, Callum Duffy fitted the description perfectly. He had been tall, muscular: he'd worked on building sites since leaving school, and the way he'd treated her had been incredibly heartless.

'I don't think that's a good idea,' Gwen grunted, shaking her head. Vivienne lifted her eyes from her script and thought of Lennie. A newspaper had once described him as the older woman's crumpet. Vivienne sighed. She missed him.

Then, suddenly, the music started. It was loud, a rattling of drums, a thumping repetitive beat, hypnotic notes bubbling, rising and falling, then a lower heavy bumping noise. Vivienne tried to carry on reading her script for a few minutes and then she heard a booming voice, distorted and echoing, repeating the words 'core' and 'hardcore'. She threw her phone on the bed. 'We've come to Hades.'

Gwen's eyes were wide. 'That's not music. That's torture.'

Mary tugged the curtain back. 'Oh, it's all the young ones. They're having a little dance in the field around a fire. It looks grand.'

'It's awful,' Gwen protested. 'And I was ready for bed. How will I get to sleep?'

Vivienne frowned. 'I'm going to tell them to turn it off.'

'You can't do that.' Mary was aghast. 'They're just having fun.

They aren't hurting anyone. It's just a bit of techno music and dancing and chat and the recreational drugs.'

'Drugs?' Gwen was horrified. 'But what if the police come? We're in the same field with them. We'll all be arrested.'

'Ah, they're doing no harm – there's no one about to hear them for miles,' Mary shook her head.

'I'm here and it's making my head thump,' Vivienne grumbled. 'No wonder the farmer woman said we looked a bit old. She was expecting a party tonight, obviously.'

'It's just a little rave-up. Leave it to me, Vivienne. I'll sort it out.' Mary reached for her jacket, then found a half-full bottle of brandy in the cupboard. 'I'll have to take this, though. A bit of a peace offering.'

Vivienne ground her teeth. 'You can hit them over the head with it, Mary, for all I care. Just get them to be quiet.'

'Trust me, I know I can,' Mary murmured, and disappeared through the passenger door.

Twenty minutes later, the music was a soft rhythmic hum in the distance. Vivienne was in bed above the cab, still avidly reading her script on the phone. Gwen was tucked up in the double bed, stretching her legs out luxuriously: she had all the space to herself for once. She was warm, cosy, and she could feel sleep settling around her like a soft fleecy rug. She exhaled softly, wondering how it would feel if Cliff was there, his arms around her, and she was snuggled against his broad shoulder. There was something reassuring about the idea of another person being next to her, warm and breathing softly; someone who she could nestle close to, resting her cold feet on warm ones and feel the heat spreading to her own flesh. It was a pleasant thought, and Gwen fell asleep imagining the sensation of slumbering in someone's arms.

Then, probably much later, she was aware of Mary crawling across the bed and flopping down next to her, her breath smelling sharply of alcohol. She heard an expletive as Mary stubbed her toe and then cold feet touched her warm calves. Mary grunted and collapsed again. Gwen sighed, stared into the darkness for a moment, and then rolled over and allowed herself to be tugged back to sleep.

35

The next day, Mary was unusually quiet, sunglasses covering her eyes as she slumped in the seat next to Gwen. Vivienne was behind them, muttering over and over to herself, practising her lines. Gwen was feeling refreshed, the driver's window wide open, a breeze in her face and Puccini's *La Bohême* playing as she drove along the M56, M6 and M62, flying past Manchester, Leeds and Castleford. The roads were busy, but it was calm inside the cab, Vivienne's clear voice repeating a phrase in a character voice from time to time, and Mary sighing occasionally, then turning to gaze out of the window at juddering lorries and the lines of cars that whizzed past as they overtook.

They reached the small farm on the edge of the moors around 3.30 and followed a sign with an arrow that pointed the way for camping. Gwen brought the motorhome to a standstill in a field of close-cropped grass and overhanging trees. 'Well, here we are, Robin Hood's Butts.'

Beyond the field, the grassland stretched into the distance, faded gorse and craggy rocks leading to a cluster of trees stretching spindly branches. Beyond, the sky hung low, iron grey and flecked with mottled clouds. Vivienne leaned forward. 'It looks very beautiful, a little bleak – quiet, deserted and kind of eerie. Just the sort of place I need to be to get in the zone for the role of Sister Camella.'

'So, what shall we do for the rest of the afternoon?' Gwen studied her friends' faces. Vivienne was still engrossed in her script. Mary was hardly moving, her face pallid and a little clammy. Gwen recalled the mild heart attack she'd suffered a few months ago and became suddenly concerned. 'Mary, are you feeling all right?'

'Well, I drank far too much last night.' Mary sighed deeply. 'I was all right while I stayed on the brandy. Then a lovely fella called Mouse passed me bottles of barley wine and that was the straw that broke the camel's back.' She brightened for a moment. 'Oh, but they were such lovely kids. And when I told them I'd been a nurse, they were very keen for me to join them. We had some grand discussions about life and parents and politics. It was a good craic.'

Gwen stared at Mary in pure admiration. Then Mary took off her sunglasses and rubbed bleary eyes. 'I think I'll go and take in a bit of the fresh air. A walk will do me good.'

'Does anyone mind if I have a bit more time preparing my script for tomorrow?' Vivienne asked.

'Right then,' Gwen beamed; she had a plan. 'I'm going to lie down for an hour and rest my eyes, then I'm going to make us all dinner. Does anyone fancy a nice pesto pasta tonight?'

'Sounds just the ticket,' Mary agreed. 'I'll be back from my little stroll by then and I'll give you a hand.'

'We'll all cook together,' Vivienne suggested. 'It's about time I stopped being so selfish and engrossed in this thing. Yes, let's spend quality time together this evening and cook the most delicious pasta ever – and have a nice bottle of wine.'

Mary left the field and the motorhome behind her, feeling the fresh air on her face, the breeze blowing away the heaviness inside her head. She wandered across Brow Moor, her feet sinking into soft earth beneath prickly gorse. She was following a narrow path that led up a slight rise; from the top, she could see the grassland fall away, then climb again, a patchwork of fields and hedgerows. The sky was vast, low-hanging silver clouds masking blotches of blue. Despite her jacket, Mary felt quite cold; a hollow wind was howling softly, in a low whine, and it curled around her ankles and huffed sharply against her cheeks.

She puffed to the edge of another mound of gorse and stopped. The view on every side was wide, stretching as far as the eye could see, hotchpotch shades of greens and greys and yellows. She loved the wildness of it, the way everything was natural and haphazard. Little flowers sprang up anywhere, as they wished; there was no order or planning, just nature's whim. Rocks and tufts of heather lined the path and Mary saw another hill in the distance, a green peak that seemed to be formed of soft velvet. She decided she'd walk a bit further.

Mary's skin was warmer now, despite the chilly wind. Her hair blew around her face and her head cleared. As she wandered along, she breathed in the fresh moorland air, a pure icy coldness that made her lungs feel clean. Her legs were beginning to tire, the muscles in her thighs aching, but she trudged on, enjoying the way her thoughts shifted and fell into place clearly. She thought about her childhood, her teenage years, the turbulence at home over her staying out until the early hours with Callum, how she had been so foolishly optimistic when she'd first arrived in London. Then her life took another direction: as a nurse, she had been popular, she had felt important and needed; she'd given so much to so many people and she'd been good at her job. Now she was eighty and she was not sure where her life was leading. In truth, it was only leading to one place, the final place. Mary had spent her life being positive, happy, buoyant, but the truth of it was, time had passed her by in a flash and now she was alone.

She turned back to look at the path she had just walked and blinked, a little confused. The terrain suddenly looked different from where she stood. She had shifted course from one route, taken another, wandered in a different direction. Around her were fields, mounds, heather, gorse. They all looked the same. Mary suddenly realised she didn't know the way back to the motorhome. She couldn't recognise the path she had taken. She was lost.

* * *

Gwen was singing to herself as she chopped onions. It had been too long since she'd sung a whole aria and now she was bouncing her vocal cords around Mozart's 'Non so più' from *The Marriage of Figaro*. Vivienne was still holding her phone, but she looked up from learning her lines and was staring in admiration, mouth open.

When Gwen had finished, Vivienne applauded, her voice mock envious. 'You are just so brilliant, Gwen.'

'I love singing. It really lifts my mood.' Gwen waved a bulb of garlic. 'I find it improves my cooking, too. I'm no cook really, but I can do pesto, especially if I'm singing opera.'

'Gwen.' Vivienne's gaze was direct. 'I just want you to know how much I appreciate everything you've done to make this holiday great. It was you who organised to borrow the motorhome, you've driven us everywhere, you took us around the Gower peninsula. It's been just tremendous. And now you've brought us up to Yorkshire.'

Gwen shrugged, bashful. 'That's not bad for a Welsh girl who, three months ago, stared at the same four walls every day for months and lived in fear of the landlord calling round.' She smiled. 'I think I've surprised myself a bit. Perhaps there's more to Gwen Prichard than I thought.'

'You've been totally brilliant.'

Gwen stared. 'And yet half the time I have no confidence.' She laughed drily. 'And the other half of the time, I'm singing.'

'That tells you something, then – you need to sing all the time. You should find some work when you're back in London.'

'I will – I'm going to start teaching again. One-to-one coaching, opera, competitions, that sort of thing.'

'Working keeps me sane,' Vivienne agreed. 'Gwen – do you think I'm selfish?'

Gwen frowned. 'No. Well, I suppose you can be a bit – focused, at times.'

'Focused.' Vivienne laughed. 'I can be self-obsessed. I've been learning my lines all day, getting into the character, and I sometimes lose myself in what I'm doing and take people for granted. I'm sorry if I've been a bit of a cow today, thinking of nothing but this film.'

'I think you're lovely, both you and Mary.' Gwen was puzzled. 'Which reminds me. Where do you think Mary's got to? She's been out walking for ages. She should be back by now. It's nearly six. She said she'd be back by dinner time.'

Vivienne approached the little work surface and picked up a sharp knife, then began chopping a red pepper. 'We'll just finish here, then we'll go out and look for her.'

'You don't think she's fallen over somewhere and hurt herself? Or had another heart attack?'

'I hope not.' Vivienne's face was concerned. 'Should we go now?'

'Perhaps we ought – oh, it's my phone buzzing.' Gwen reached into her jeans pocket and tugged out her phone. 'Hello?' Her face changed suddenly, from warm and hopeful to horrified. 'How did you get my number? No, no. I don't want to talk to you.'

Vivienne placed a hand on her shoulder. 'Are you all right, Gwen?'

Gwen met her gaze and hissed, 'It's Clifford. He wants to meet with me.' She pushed the phone hard against her ear. 'No, I'm not in London. No, nor Wales. I'm heading to Whitby actually.' She listened, his soft tones, his persuasive words, and her frown deepened. 'Vivienne's working on a film and we've come up here with her to watch. No, you can't come up, Cliff. I don't want to talk things through. I told you before...' She breathed in sharply. 'Well, I'm sorry you feel that way. No, I won't, not just for a day, or half a day... No, please don't keep asking me... I won't change my mind. I'm sorry, Cliff, but there it is.'

She pressed a button and turned away. Vivienne's gaze was sympathetic. 'Is he giving you a hard time?'

Gwen nodded. 'I've no idea how he got my number...' She closed her eyes. 'It was Mary, I suppose, being the matchmaker.'

'Do you still have feelings for him?'

Gwen sighed. 'The truth is, I don't know. Sometimes I think I do. Sometimes, I think I've always loved him and that will never change. But then, I'm thinking of him as he was years ago, young, my sweetheart. I don't know him any more, he's just a memory in my past. I'm different now and so is he. No, I don't think I want to try again. It's not the same, is it?'

'You know best.' Vivienne wrapped her arms around Gwen. 'Your heart will tell you what to do. Sometimes a relationship's over and you can't ever go back. But sometimes there's still an ember smouldering and...' She thought of Lennie again and the expression on her face softened. 'And it might just be worth fanning that ember and waiting to see what happens. It might ignite into something really warm and wonderful.'

Gwen shook her head. 'Do you think so, Vivienne? I'm not so sure...'

'What will be will be.' Vivienne threw her hands wide, a dramatic gesture. 'You hold all the cards. Oh, why am I talking in clichés?'

'Listen...' Gwen's eyes widened. 'Can you hear that? The chugging sound...'

'It's an engine,' Vivienne muttered. 'A motorbike, perhaps.'

'You don't think...' Gwen was suddenly anxious. 'It could be the police with news of Mary? Perhaps she's been found on the moor, airlifted to hospital?'

They rushed down the steps of the motorhome and outside into the field, fearing the worst. A quad bike had bounced through the gate and was hurtling forward, two figures astride the saddle. It drew level and the quad bike came to a standstill. Mary was sitting behind a young man in his thirties, a woollen hat on his head, his denim shirt rolled up at the sleeves to reveal inky tattoos. Behind him, Mary clutched his waist enthusiastically with both arms, a curving smile on her lips. He slithered from the saddle and helped her down from the bike.

Mary was exhilarated, either by the quad bike ride or by its owner. She gave a breezy laugh. 'Sorry I'm so late. I got a taxi home. Meet Jason. He's a farmer.'

Jason shoved his hands into jeans pockets. ''Ow do. I found her on t'moors, lost.' His accent was a soft drawl, long vowels, warm sounds. 'I was out checking t'sheep. She war wandering round, so I brung her back, safe-like. I knew which farm she war on – t'other's mine.' He pulled off his woollen hat and ruffled his dark hair. 'I think she likes t'quad bike, Mary. She war laughing so hard all t'way back, I nearly went deaf.'

Mary stood on her toes and kissed his cheek. 'I'd still be there now if it wasn't for you, Jason. And the quad bike ride was grand. Every bump we went over made my bottom jiggle and I laughed so hard I nearly cried. So – thanks.'

Vivienne held out a hand. 'We're making pasta – do you want to stay to supper?'

'That's right nice of you, but t'missus has a rabbit in t'pot. I'd best get home.'

'Well, lovely to meet you,' Gwen called as Jason straddled his quad bike, the engine throbbed loudly and he took off, roaring back towards the gate.

Mary put her hands on her hips. 'Oh, he was very nice, Jason. Such a helpful man. I was completely lost on the moors. I'd still be there now if it wasn't for him finding me. And the quad bike ride was lovely, so it was. In fact, I was thinking.' She met Vivienne's eyes and her own crinkled with mischief. 'If we wanted to rename the motorhome and call it after someone who was a big hero, then perhaps we should call it Jason.'

36

The motorhome rolled into a windy Whitby on Sunday morning, at ten o'clock. The previous evening, after Gwen's delicious meal of home-cooked pasta and wine, Mary had drawn a rough cartoon on a piece of cardboard of a man astride a badly drawn quad bike wearing a woollen hat, with exaggerated biceps and bright tattoos, his shirt open to the navel revealing a hairy chest. She had labelled the drawing with the words THIS MOTORHOME IS CALLED JASON. The picture had now been sellotaped to the back window of the motorhome and Mary was delighted with her new choice of name. She hadn't stopped talking about the escapade on the quad bike since she was safely delivered home.

But now they were driving through the quaint town of Whitby, past the little harbour and rows of quaint little cottages. In the distance, a vast green hill loomed, a skeletal church perched on top, stark against a cloud-stippled sky. Mary wanted to see the town and buy ice cream and Vivienne said it was vital to know the area before she arrived on set the following day, which she said was on the site of a seventh-century abbey which overlooked the town and the sea.

Gwen was suddenly interested. 'So, what's the film actually about, Vivienne?'

'I would have thought it was obvious – it's a gothic horror. Sister Camella is one of a group of nuns in the abbey, but there's a dark force at work amongst them and one by one they get killed.' She clapped her hands together. 'It's a remake of the old Dracula story. My agent says the director wants to form a team to do more gothic films. This TV film's not a one-off. Ştefan wants to do a series of them filmed across the UK. I hope he likes my performance, and I can charm him into asking me to be in the others.'

'What's he like, this director?' Mary's nose was pressed against the window, looking for ice cream parlours that were open on a Sunday morning. 'Is he young?'

'Fifties, probably. He has a lot of experience steeped in the gothic genre. Ştefan Davidescu – he's very serious and exacting. Apparently, he's a great director to work with, a perfectionist, fab reputation.' Vivienne's eyes shone, then she exhaled sharply. 'Oh, who am I kidding? No one wants aged actresses now, not when there are so many talented young ones. I have no chance of being in his next film. He's hardly going to pick me for a lead when there's a bevy of sweet young things.'

'Vivienne!' Gwen was surprised at the energy in her own voice. 'Stop doing this to yourself. You're talking yourself out of a role. You have plenty of self-belief – so use it. You have talent. You remind me of Joanna Lumley, so attractive and versatile, and you bring warmth and glamour to every role you do, whether it's serious or comedy. You can do this. Now pull yourself together and have faith.'

'Thanks, Gwen.' Vivienne nodded sagely. 'You're absolutely right. We shouldn't undervalue ourselves, whatever our age. "Self-love, my liege, is not so vile a sin as self-neglecting." *Henry V.* Let that be a lesson to all of us.'

'Amen,' Mary added. 'Oh, and look – there's a little place over

there with the sign of a cornet with a flake in it. Will we stop there
and get a mint chocolate chip ice each?'

* * *

It was past nine in the evening and the sun was melting behind the
bay, the water mottled indigo blue and rosebud pink, as the three
friends huddled inside the motorhome on a campsite overlooking
the sea. Vivienne had insisted on the site, as it was a short drive
from where she would be filming on Monday morning, and she
intended to make an entrance first thing. Many of the cast and the
director Ştefan Davidescu had booked accommodation locally; they
had been filming for several weeks already. Vivienne announced
that although she was only the second-choice stand-in for the role
of Sister Camella, she would arrive at the filming location looking a
million dollars and wow everyone. She would need to be up at six
to prepare.

So, to mark the occasion, she had bought everyone their
favourite takeaway meal. Mary had chosen a madras curry, Gwen a
chow mein, and Vivienne had surprised them all by buying herself
fish and chips. And, as had become the habit of the holiday, they
were sharing a bottle of wine. Mary laughed as she scooped up a
forkful of food. 'So, the 80:20 way of life starts when I'm back in
London. By that time, I'll be the size of half a house.'

'While Vivienne's filming, you and I will go and see all the local
sites, Mary. We'll do lots of walking around to discover new places,
and we'll get plenty of exercise,' Gwen suggested. 'And we've been
skipping lunches most days, so we deserve a special treat for supper
occasionally.'

Vivienne snorted softly. 'I'm dreadful – I always starve myself. I
tell myself that actors need to be reed-slim. My usual reason for

refusing food is that you can't have both wine and a meal, so I usually just go for the wine.'

Mary waved a hand. 'Those chips look good, though.'

'Yorkshire chips. I don't think you can beat them.' Vivienne thought for a moment. 'Or is it Lancashire where they do the best chips? I think I've just restarted the Wars of the Roses. I'm sure both types of chips are wonderful. These are completely delicious but I'm full, and I've only eaten a handful of them and a few bites of the fish. I haven't allowed myself chips very often since I was a child. And the sea air makes them feel even more authentic. I'm treating myself – you know, as if it's the last supper – ha ha.'

Gwen studied Vivienne for a moment, her shaking hands, the erratic movements of her shoulders. She was unusually jittery, skittish, a nervous colt before a race. 'Vivienne, are you worried about the filming tomorrow?'

'Terrified.' Vivienne waved a chip. 'I'm always like this before filming on location. It was different with the soap – I was on set all day, and then there was a short break and a banter, then I'd be back on again.'

'How is this type of filming different?' Mary asked.

'There will be lots of waiting around, then lots of doing everything a hundred times over to get it absolutely right, everything is out of sequence, it's just – camera, action and you have to be there immediately, in the zone.'

'I'm sure you can do that just fine, Vivienne.'

'I can, Mary – but strangely, only if I go through the nerves beforehand. They kickstart something in me as an actor.' Vivienne waved the same chip. 'I won't sleep a wink tonight.'

'Gwen and I will buy you something with lavender in it tomorrow – you'll sleep like a tot.'

'It's not even as if it's a big role,' Vivienne fretted. 'I get killed off fairly quickly by the baddie. But there's lots of tension before that – he has me in his sights, pursues me, lures me, then there's a big face-off before he makes his final move. It's a small but meaty role.' She glanced at the chip again which was now cold. 'Oh, I do hope the director likes me.'

'And what about the rest of the cast? You'll get on well with them too, I hope.'

'I worry about that as well, Gwen.' Vivienne rolled her eyes. 'I haven't had time to do a chemistry test.'

'What's one of those?' Mary laughed. 'Will you have to answer questions about the periodic table?'

'No, it's the chemistry with the other actors – I can usually switch it on, even if I hate my co-star.' Vivienne made a soft self-deprecating sound. 'What am I like, thinking I have a co-star? The main actor kills me off – I'll be done filming by Friday. Oh, but I so hope this opens doors for me...'

'It will.' Gwen gazed through the plastic window towards the sea. The sky was indigo now, slashed with a few streaks of livid red that reflected like blood in the ocean. 'So, it's a scary film then?'

'I love a good horror.' Mary collected her aluminium containers into a pile. 'This beats washing up,' she joked as she shoved the rubbish into the bin.

Vivienne sighed, a ragged sound of frayed nerves. 'I'll look a horror tomorrow if I don't at least try to get some sleep.' She screwed the chips and paper into a hard ball and hurled it in the bin. 'I vote we all get an early night. I have to say, I'm starting to feel my age.'

'Nonsense,' Gwen said. 'You'll knock 'em dead tomorrow.'

'I completely agree, but I won't say no to a good night's sleep tonight,' Mary groaned. 'I was drunk as a skunk last night and this afternoon I got myself lost and found on the moors. I think it's time we got our heads down and slept the sleep of the innocent, don't you?' She indicated the cartoon drawing of the hunk on a quad bike stuck to the window and added in a mischievous voice, 'And don't worry about a thing, Vivienne – our motorhome's called Jason now – we'll sleep like we're covered in golden fleece.'

Vivienne was up early, wrapping her hair around heated rollers, smearing a slime-coloured face mask over her cheeks. Gwen muttered, 'We'll need to refill the water tank again if you're having another shower, Vivienne.'

Mary brewed a pot of tea and was keen to read everyone's leaves again, 'Just to make sure that we'll all be having a good day.'

Gwen sat next to her, peering nervously over her shoulder into the teacup. Mary was making low growling sounds, dissatisfaction or foreboding, Gwen couldn't tell.

Gwen's voice was anxious 'What's happening. Mary? Is it all terrible news?'

'No... not terrible.' Mary bunched her mouth into a shape that showed she was thinking hard. 'There are two big things here, very big. I'm just trying to interpret the signs; will you hang on? I can see a set of scales. That means a big decision coming up. You have to weigh up a problem, it's time to make up your mind.'

Gwen stared ahead. 'Oh, that's Clifford, I suppose. I wish you hadn't given him my phone number. Well, I just won't pick up his call again. There you are – decision made. Is that all?'

'No, that's what I can't work out, Gwen. I've seen this before, a woman surrounded by musical notes. It's you singing opera and there are hearts, love, lots of love. I saw it last time.'

'I just love singing – that's not difficult to predict.'

'But there's someone attracted to the singing, a man, who finds you irresistible – and there's love. I can see a letter of his name, it's a... a letter C.'

'Oh, not Clifford Edwards again, please.' Gwen was dismayed. 'I think you should probably leave my teacup alone and read Vivienne's instead.'

Vivienne was staring in a mirror, applying make-up. 'Yes, do mine please, Mary. I could do with cheering up.'

'I told you before that I could see a woman in a robe – a queen or a nun. I think it's you on film, Vivienne.'

Gwen was impressed. 'I remember you mentioning the nun before. She was right, Vivienne – she predicted you'd get that role.'

'And love, too. I said there would be love on the film set.' Mary stared into the cup. 'Yes, it's here, definitely, true love.'

'Well, I am playing Sister Camella who is loved so much that I am pursued and devoured by the lustful leading man...' Vivienne gave a short laugh. 'I suppose that's love of sorts.'

'Oh no – this is the real thing, love for ever and ever,' Mary murmured. 'It will change your life, this film, being a nun. You'll meet someone new and you'll never look back.'

'I hope you're right. That would give me something positive to look forward to. At the moment, my knees are shaking like jelly. I'm absolutely terrified.' Vivienne checked her hair in the mirror, then reached for her jacket. 'But I'll do.'

'You might fall in love with the director?'

'That's very unlikely, Gwen – he's fifty years old and gay. But Ştefan is a genius – perhaps he'll fall in love with my work. Now that would be really good.' Vivienne caught her breath. 'Oh, look at the time. We should be going. Drop me off at the set, please, and then I'll message you later about what time to pick me up.'

'Right, we're ready to go.' Gwen moved towards the cab. 'By the way, what's the film called?'

'*The Shadow on the Shore*.' Vivienne grimaced. 'And this week, the shadow's latest victim is me. Wish me luck.'

37

Vivienne slipped from the motorhome and moved towards the film set, where many people were rushing around, busy making preparations. There were vans and trucks parked haphazardly; people were setting up all types of cameras, some hoisted high on cherry pickers, some on stands, and organising a great deal of equipment: booms, tripods, light reflectors, portable digital audio recorders. Gwen and Mary stared as Vivienne marched towards a woman with a clipboard and started speaking to her, so self-assured and purposeful.

Gwen exhaled. 'You wouldn't believe she was so nervous a minute ago.'

Mary pointed a finger. 'Look at the little fella up there, putting up that big camera on a stand. He's half the size of the pole he's had to climb up. Let's just see if he falls off. I hope he won't.'

'These people know what they are doing, Mary.' Gwen glanced over her shoulder. A yellow and black lorry was behind her, the engine idling. 'We'd better be going, I think, we're in the way.'

'Ah, right – Robin Hood's Bay it is, Gwen. We've seen his butts – now we'd better go and look at the rest.'

Vivienne was unaware that the motorhome had pulled out of the parking area and was moving towards the main road. She was too busy talking to a young woman whose name badge said she was called Lola. She held a clipboard and ticked off a name. 'Vivienne Goldman.' Lola's voice had a nasal quality. 'Right, let's get you into make-up and costume, then we can pair you up with Tam and you're both ready to go. You'll be filming outside the abbey and the church of St Mary on East Cliff, looking over the sea, so it'll get very cold. Do you know Tam Downey?'

'No...' Vivienne began.

'Oh, she's lovely – she's playing Sister Angelica, the young nun who comes to you for advice. I'm surprised you don't know her – she was at the Theatre Royal just before lockdown. It's been so difficult, hasn't it, all that time with no theatre or film work.' She raised her eyebrows. 'I suppose you were out of work for the year too?'

'No, I was lucky – I was in a TV show,' Vivienne replied.

'Oh.' Lola suddenly waved a hand. 'Here's Tam now, and the team you'll be working with today. I'll just introduce you...'

Two hours later, Vivienne was standing in the biting wind dressed in a nun's thin habit, her face made up to look pale and strained. She decided that the headdress did her no favours; it covered her hair completely and made her expression severe and old. Next to her, Tam Downey wore a similar costume, but it suited her much better. Despite her dark hair being covered, her skin was smooth and her face cherubic. Vivienne thought her robes made her look like a tent pole whereas Tam's habit fitted her well and showed off her curves. Vivienne folded her arms and gazed at the river to one side and the sea below. 'It's very beautiful from up here, but it's so chilly.'

Tam nodded. 'And I'm dying for a ciggie.'

'So.' Vivienne recalled her lines. 'We're filming the bit where I spot the ship and then we cut to you and me talking about catching sight of the stranger.'

'Yes – you have a real sense of him being, you know, bad news, but I'm all innocent and like, he seems really nice, so kind and friendly and we should trust him.' Tam glanced at her fingernails, then started to chew the end of her thumb. 'I filmed the scene where he kills me last Thursday. It was great. He kills you too, doesn't he? You'll love doing that bit this week. It took me a dozen takes to get the moment right where I fall onto the ground and he leaps over me then blood leaks from my neck... Hilarious.' She winked. 'I'm so glad to be working again.'

Vivienne felt the wind lift the hem of her habit and chill her ankles. Her calves were freezing and she wished she'd worn trousers or leggings underneath. Then she noticed a man approaching at a brisk pace, flanked by two men and two women who all seemed to be talking to him at the same time. By his gait and his mannerisms, he seemed to be important: there was an aloofness, a self-assuredness in the way he stared ahead, not paying attention to anyone else. He wore sunglasses, jeans and a dark donkey jacket, and a black cap covered his longish grey hair. His face was lean and rugged. Tam caught her breath. 'It's Ştefan.'

Vivienne raised an eyebrow, feeling the material of her head-dress tighten across her forehead. 'What's he like?'

'How can I put it?' Tam rolled her eyes. 'Exacting, bossy, moody, changeable. But everyone loves him because he's just so damned talented.'

Ştefan Davidescu drew level with them and raised a hand in greeting. 'Nuns are here, good,' he growled. His voice was deep, a guttural eastern European accent. 'Right, ready to go now. Vivienne?' He indicated her with a sharp movement of his thumb. 'I want you standing over there, overlooking the water. I want to see the moment you notice the boat and then you see him in there, *Dracul*, the evil one, the lonely one, the dragon. Then, Tam, we'll do the scene with the nuns together. Okay, you got it?'

'Right.' Vivienne was ready.

Ştefan raised a hand. 'Then, if we have time left after I make those scenes, and the light is right, I want something with you and *Dracul* together, the first time you face him, the meeting of eyes that promises your fate.' He met Vivienne's gaze, his expression mocking. 'Of course, I know about that moment – it will be special. I'm looking forward to that powerful meeting, to capture it on film. I'm sure you are too.'

'Of course.' Vivienne shrugged. 'Why wouldn't I be?'

Ştefan gave a smile that was a sort of sneer. 'I believe you both know each other very well. I was happy that you are free to take this role when the other actor left. It will be nice, better, the chemistry, I think?'

Vivienne leaned towards Tam. 'What's he talking about?'

Tam shrugged. 'I don't know – do you think he'll let me have a cigarette break before our scene?'

'So, we start now, please. Lennie is ready to come here if I call him, if we have time for his scene today – maybe we do, maybe we don't.' Ştefan raised his hand. 'Now, we begin.'

'Lennie?'

Vivienne found it difficult to move for a moment, while her thoughts fell into place. She should have known – Lennie had told her he was filming up north; he had a lead role. It had to be Lennie who was playing the 'shadow on the shore' and soon they'd share a scene in which he'd hold her in his arms, kiss her neck and drain her life away. She smiled: the idea had suddenly started to feel very appealing.

'Right,' she called. 'Yes, I'm certainly looking forward to it. Ready when you are, Ştefan – bring it on.'

* * *

It was past nine when an exhausted Vivienne dragged herself up the steps of the motorhome, flopping into the passenger seat and closing her eyes, exhaling hard.

'Well, how did it go?' Mary asked.

'I need wine,' Vivienne gasped, her voice a whimper of agony. 'Just lots of wine and lots of sleep. And to feel warm. My skin is so chilled I'd ice up a freezer.'

Gwen started the engine. 'Mary and I already made supper. Let's get you back to the campsite and into the shower, shall we?' She smiled over her shoulder. 'Just tell us in one word – how did it go?'

'Nightmare,' Vivienne gasped histrionically and put her head in her hands. 'But tomorrow will be very different.'

An hour later, she had warmed up and was pushing chilli, beans and rice around a plate with a fork, sipping wine and laughing. 'I just stood there for hours with my face all screwed up, staring out at the sea, and my eyes were watering because the wind was so cold, and my fingers were freezing. Tam must have smoked a whole packet of cigarettes while she was waiting to do her scene with me and I have to say it's funny seeing a young nun chain-smoking. And Ştefan kept yelling that the light was wrong and that he wanted to do it all over again because he knew he could make it even better.'

'So, what's he like, the director?' Gwen asked.

'Creative, imaginative, a perfectionist – I like him.' Vivienne drained her glass. 'This week's going to be exhausting but it's going to be fun. And guess who plays *Dracul*, the "Shadow on the Shore"?'

Mary's expression was hopeful. 'Is it Brad Pitt?'

'It's Lennie Lindo, who played Delroy Pickett in *The Edge of Edgeware*.' Vivienne made her voice casual as she held out her glass for a refill. 'It'll be nice to see him again.'

'Isn't he an ex of yours?' Gwen asked. 'The older woman's crumpet?'

'That's the romance I told you about this morning.' Mary was suddenly very interested. 'The teacup. It was all in the teacup.'

Vivienne deliberately kept her face impassive and her voice casual. 'Oh, we go back a long way, Lennie and me. Yes, we have some history, but this is acting, darling – almost everyone has crossed paths with each other at some point.'

Gwen was insistent. 'But you lived with him for years, Vivienne. You told us you'd had gin martinis in bed, with cheese, olives, prawns, and you didn't get up all day.'

'Did I say that? Then it must be true.' Vivienne waved a hand, dismissing the past. 'Well, that was then and tomorrow I'll meet him again and we'll do the scene where we lock eyes and he kills me, then it will be Friday and I'll go back home again and that will be that.'

'But do you still love him, Vivienne?'

'I'll find out tomorrow, Mary.' Vivienne stared into the deep red liquid as she swirled the red wine in her glass, and she thought of being in Lennie's passionate embrace, falling into his arms as he climbed across her body, his pointed teeth bared. She smiled: seeing him again would be interesting and playing the scene in his arms might tell her what she needed to know, if she and he still shared the spark that had always ignited their relationship. She stretched her arms in the air. 'Well, I need an early night tonight. What are you two doing tomorrow?'

'I want to go on the steam train at some point.' Mary rubbed her hands together. 'The North York Moors Railway has some beautiful scenery and so I want to get a ticket and go to Pickering and then come back. It'll be just grand to see those views out over the moors.'

'And Pickering is a wonderful little market town – tea rooms and antique shops, and it has an old church and a castle,' Gwen added.

'But we might go there the day after tomorrow,' Mary suggested. 'Tomorrow we were thinking of doing Whitby harbour and the museum. There's a microbrewery too...'

'Mary and I thought we'd keep it local tomorrow, have a touristy day out. It'll be lovely on the beach in Whitby if the sun shines.'

'The weather forecast for tomorrow is sunny, bright and cold,' Vivienne said happily. 'Perfect for filming a gothic horror on top of a freezing clifftop overlooking the North Sea. I'll be wearing leggings and thermals under my habit this time – I'm not getting caught out again.'

Mary snorted mischievously. 'You'll be wearing passion-killers? Is that a good idea, what with handsome crumpet Lennie being on the scene tomorrow?'

Vivienne laughed. 'Sometimes passion happens despite excessive underwear.'

'Not to me,' Gwen muttered grimly. 'Clifford rang me again today and asked me how long I was in Whitby and when I was in London again and was I going back to Llanclawdd soon, and could we meet for a chat.'

Vivienne was alarmed. 'What did you say?'

'I told him no to everything. I don't want to see him again. I'm not interested...'

Vivienne caught Mary's eye. 'What did Gertrude say in *Hamlet*? "The lady doth protest too much, methinks."'

Mary agreed. 'It was in your teacup – Clifford starts with the letter C. I'm sure you still have feelings for him, Gwen.'

'And I'm sure I don't, and there's no more to be said about it.' Gwen folded her arms stubbornly. 'So, if you'll excuse me, I'll tidy the supper things up and get myself off to bed. And I'd advise you both to do the same – you have a busy day tomorrow, Vivienne, and we have some serious tourism to enjoy.' She wagged a finger. 'Which I intend to make the most of, Mary. So, I don't want to hear

any more mention of the name Clifford Edwards, do you hear?
Never again.'

38

Vivienne had taken extra trouble to look her best, arriving at the location in a plush warm coat, her hair glossy and her make-up perfect. But Lennie was not to be seen anywhere amongst all the people frantically setting up for the shoot. She was greeted by the costume and make-up artists and prepared quickly, then she rushed to the film set outside St Mary's church and graveyard. Vivienne stood waiting in the cold weather in her thin habit and head-dress, blinking in the icy wind. All around, cameras had been set up on different levels, trucks were parked and equipment unloaded as people rushed around, yelling out instructions to each other. Ştefan had appeared, wearing sunglasses and the same donkey jacket, flanked by his entourage, and was waving his arms, deep in conversation with a man in overalls. Vivienne moved over towards the cliff to stare at the North Sea below, gazing at the crinkled grey waves, then up at the blank sky overhead, the colour of concrete. She muttered to herself, 'Whoever suggested this was a glamorous profession?'

Then she felt a pair of arms circle her waist and she knew who it was immediately. Lennie's voice whispered in her ear, 'Today is the day the silent shadow seduces the reluctant nun.' She whirled round and he smiled. 'Hello, Vivi.'

'Lennie.' She put a hand to her face. 'Oh, I must look awful.'

'Beautiful as ever.' Lennie was dressed in tight black clothes, a loosely laced doublet revealing his chest, his hair twisted into small dreadlocks extending to his shoulders. He placed a hand on her arm. 'I heard you'd taken on the role of Camella. I'm so glad you're here.'

She heard low mocking laughter from a few metres away; Ştefan strode over, smiling his strange sneer. 'Are we ready to roll?'

'Absolutely ready,' Lennie replied, and Vivienne nodded.

There was more activity, people rushing around, cameras and sound equipment being moved and adjusted, then Ştefan lifted a finger and the scene began. Vivienne, as Sister Camella, walked forward through the graveyard, her habit sweeping around her heels, her eyes anxious. She sensed something was amiss. She paused, listening hard, then her fingers fumbled at her throat, an unintentional foreshadowing of her fate, and she walked forwards again. Suddenly, unexpectedly, Lennie stepped out from behind a tall grey hewn stone inscribed with the name Swales, and the date 8th August 1890. Vivienne met his eyes and stood still, frozen in fear. Lennie gave a little bow, a half-smile. 'Sister Camella.'

'You?' Vivienne's eyes were wide. 'What have you done to Sister Angelique?'

Lennie stepped back, innocent. 'Forgive me, Sister: you have fear in your eyes. Perhaps I startled you? But there is nothing to be afraid of.'

Vivienne turned away, another camera picking up the tension around her mouth. 'Please, go away and leave me alone.'

'You know I cannot do that, Sister Camella. You know the

reason. People like us...' He stared into her eyes, the same melting chocolate gaze she had always loved so much. 'We can't escape what will happen. We can't stop fate, the power of what will be. There can be no denial, no refusal. All you have to do is... say yes.'

Vivienne held her breath, a small gasp of fear, as she tried in vain to pull her gaze from his magnetic stare, then she uttered the word, soft as cotton on the wind. 'Yes.'

'Cut.'

Ştefan rushed over. 'Well, the chemistry between you is very strong. I like this very much. And in this setting, everything is magnificent, just what I need – the real gothic moment when the evil shadow of a man becomes more powerful again, he comes back to life. The church is perfect, the lighting, the shade. Everything is as it should be.'

Vivienne's eyes lit up. An idea had just popped into her head. 'Ah, but is it all perfect? Isn't there something missing?'

Lennie reached for Vivienne's hand, squeezing it, a gentle warning: people rarely challenged Ştefan. The director whirled round, his face pinched. 'What did you just say?'

Vivienne shrugged. 'Just a suggestion – but I think something really important is missing, and I know exactly what it is.'

'Really?'

Vivienne nodded, her face calm. 'Yes, of course. It's quite obvious.'

'And so, Vivienne, please tell me, as I am director, what is so obvious that I don't know it.'

Lennie was staring at her, his expression suggesting that she had just made a huge mistake, that she had challenged Ştefan's indisputable authority.

'Well?' Ştefan whirled around, his body coiled like a snake, waiting for her to reply.

She offered him a sweet smile. 'We're a convent of nuns. This is a church. We're in a graveyard. So, to complete the scene, you need a voice, a single nun, singing a beautiful hymn, "Ave Maria", from inside the building, signifying the sense of purity and goodness and safety in the church while *Dracul* is outside having his wicked way.'

Ştefan was thoughtful. He took off his black cap, rubbed his head and replaced it. 'A singing nun?'

'Exactly.'

'It could work, yes. I like the idea. A nun in silhouette, a voice pure as an angel, then cut to *Dracul* with each victim. A coda, an ongoing symbol. Very good. But...'

'But?' Vivienne raised an eyebrow.

'But where...?' Ştefan's voice rose, frustrated. 'Where do we find this singing nun on a freezing cold cliff in the middle of Whitby?'

Vivienne beamed. 'Oh, I know just the person. She'd be absolutely perfect. And she's only a phone call away.'

* * *

Gwen was sipping tea, staring through the wide window of a pretty tea shop in Whitby, overlooking the harbour, listening to Mary chat about Dennis Mulhern, a paramedic she'd met at a hospital Christmas party when she was in her forties. Dennis had seemed like the perfect match until she discovered that he had a wife and five children. Mary seemed to find it extremely funny, although she added that she hadn't been very impressed at the time. Then Gwen's phone rang; she sat upright, opening her handbag and delving inside.

'Oh, no, please don't let this be Clifford again. I don't want to talk to him ever—' Gwen's expression changed to a smile. 'Oh, hello, Vivienne. Is everything all right?'

Gwen listened carefully, her eyebrows rising slowly in surprise, and Mary leaned across the table, pushing the teapot to one side so that she might catch the odd word that was being spoken at the other end of the phone. When Gwen finished the call, her serious eyes met Mary's.

'Well, I never. They want me to sing.'

'Who wants you to sing what, Gwen?'

'The film people want me to dress up as a nun and sing "Ave Maria".'

'Holy mother of – I mean, that's very nice, Gwen. When do you start?'

'Now, right now. They want us to drive up to the film set and then, that's it. I'm on set in costume, singing in a church.'

Mary grabbed her bag, leaped up and headed to the counter to pay. Over her shoulder she called, 'Well, what are you waiting for, Gwen? I'll sort this out and we'll be off in the motorhome. For sure, every gothic film needs a singing nun.'

Gwen, dressed in long tunic, scapular and cowl, stood tall on the steps at the altar in the church, her hands clasped, her eyes piously raised to heaven. Ştefan scuttled around, talking to camera operators, sound technicians, lighting experts, then he took up his position. Vivienne and Lennie were holding hands, and Mary, her arms folded and a wide smile on her face, watched from behind him, waiting. Then Ştefan raised a hand, the signal to start, and Gwen began to sing a capella, her voice drifting through the gallery to the top of the roof. Every person in the church was hushed, holding their breath, listening to the simple notes laden with reverence and beauty. Gwen finished her song, and there was stillness. Then Ştefan rushed forwards.

'Perfect. Perfect. Now I have the new idea that I want more of this. Every time the shadow of *Dracul* kills a beautiful woman, we have your voice – or maybe the close-up of the mouth, the lips moving as they sing each word, and then we can cut to the scene of tragedy, of death. Yes, this is what I want.' He grasped Gwen's hand. 'What else can you sing? What else, in the same style?'

'Oh, whatever you like. I can do Thomas Tallis, 'Spem in Alium' – I mean, it's for a choir, but I can make it sound all right by itself. Or I can do Mozart's "Lachrymosa" from the *Requiem Mass*.'

'Requiem?' Ştefan squeezed her hand. 'Yes, sing that. Sing it now.'

'All right, I will.' Gwen inhaled and composed her breathing, her face smooth, professional, then she began to sing in minor key, her voice steeped in grief, excess of tragedy, the pain of mourning and too much sorrow.

> *Lacrimosa dies illa*
> *Qua resurget ex favilla*
> *Judicandus homo reus*
> *Lacrimosa dies illa...*

The sound echoed around the high walls, bouncing off the ceiling, and the listeners breathed in slowly, as if surrounded by an angelic presence. Several people wiped tears from their eyes as Gwen's pure voice soared higher, ending with the simple final two notes, 'Amen.'

Ştefan was ecstatic. 'This is perfect, perfect.' He seized both of Gwen's hands. 'Can you come back tomorrow, Thursday? I want more of you, much more.' He called to one of his entourage, a young blond man in a polo necked jumper and jeans. 'Please can you sort all of this out, so that we agree how much to pay, we give her a contract.' He turned back to Gwen. 'Do you have an agent?' Gwen shook her head. 'Where are you based? In London? Oh, for me this is just... what is the expression? – a game changer.' Ştefan smiled. 'Vivienne – you were so right, so right. This is wonderful.'

* * *

Later that evening, back in the cosy warmth of the motorhome, Vivienne brandished a bottle of champagne that had been chilling in the fridge. 'Remember when we got this?'

'Is it the one I won when I beat young Craig at darts?' Gwen asked.

'Or the other one that the WI gave us for doing the fashion show?' Mary frowned. 'To be honest, Vivienne, I don't mind which one it is. Let's crack it open and celebrate.'

The cork popped from the bottle, champagne frothed into three mugs and the three women hooted and cheered. Mary put the mug to her lips, feeling bubbles explode on her tongue. 'So, what exactly are we celebrating?'

'Success. Gwen was just incredible today.' Vivienne lifted the bottle. 'Oh, did you see Ştefan's face when he realised that Gwen could actually sing? Up to that moment he thought I'd been making it all up and then suddenly, whoosh.'

'Whoosh!' Gwen raised her mug. 'And there I was, dressed as a nun, singing my heart out in the church. Oh, I loved it, Vivienne, every moment.'

'And I got to see a real film set.' Mary was delighted. 'It was fascinating to watch how it all happens. I mean, you see a film on the telly and it's just the people acting on the screen – I never thought there would be so many other things going on in the background, people just running around with wires and cables and furry sticks.'

Vivienne cleared her throat. 'There's something else, too.'

'What?' Mary asked.

'Something else to celebrate. I think Ştefan Davidescu really likes my work. He has invited me and Lennie to have dinner with him tomorrow at the hotel where he's staying. He says he has a project he'd like to discuss with us.' She brought a clenched fist to her mouth. 'I'm so excited.'

'That's wonderful news, Vivienne.'

'And he loves your singing too, Gwen. I mean, this must kick-start your career again. Isn't that just what you wanted?'

'It is.' Gwen's eyes shone. 'I want to sing properly again and to help others to do it. I can't stay at home and sing arias to the walls any more. I've realised that.'

'Oh, and there's something else.' Vivienne's tone was hushed.

'There's more?' Mary laughed, gulping from her mug.

Vivienne nodded. 'Lennie and I are getting back together. He asked me today and I said yes, I want to try again.' She smiled. 'I think we might get it right this time.'

'That's just perfect,' Gwen exclaimed.

Mary was excited. 'I told you, I told you. It was in your teacups.' She grasped Gwen's arm. 'Now it's your turn. The singing, and all the hearts around it – you're bound to meet someone on the set tomorrow.'

'But what about you, Mary?' Gwen was momentarily saddened. 'Vivienne and I will be busy all day with the film. What will you do? Do you want to come and watch? I feel awful – I don't want you left out, by yourself.'

'You can be the guest of honour...' Vivienne suggested.

'Not at all. I've tomorrow all planned out, if you don't mind.' Mary's voice was firm. 'I'll take myself down to the steam train with a picnic lunch and I'll go for a little ride to Pickering and back. Then maybe Gwen and I can have a quiet evening in with Jason the motorhome; she can tell me all about the film while you go out for a swanky dinner with your director, Vivienne.'

'That would be lovely,' Gwen agreed.

'Perfect.' Vivienne held up the bottle. 'It's all coming together, isn't it? Everything is starting to be just how it should be. So – I propose a toast.' She poured more fizz into mugs. 'To the three of us. To wonderful things to come. And to good times.'

Three hands were raised, three mugs held high. 'To good times.'

39

After leaving Mary, complete with lunch in a bag and a flask, at Whitby station, Gwen and Vivienne drove into the car park and walked arm in arm down towards the film set, which was a hive of activity as ever.

Vivienne glanced at Gwen. 'Are you nervous about today?'

'Not really, not now,' she replied. 'I'm singing and I'm never nervous once I start to sing.'

Vivienne shivered. 'I'm cold, but that might just be nerves. I'm a complete neurotic. But I'm really looking forward to filming today – it's the day Lennie bites my neck.'

'I wish I'd done this sort of thing years ago, Vivienne – it's so interesting.' A moment's anxiety flickered across Gwen's face. 'I hope Mary will be all right on her own though.'

'She'll have a lovely time on the train,' Vivienne said. 'She has a picnic, and the weather's bright; she'll be warm in the carriage and the views are spectacular. I checked online and we'll be finished in time to pick her up.'

'She's so tough on the outside and so feisty, but she's fragile too.'

Gwen bit her lip. 'I worry about her. Especially since she had the heart attack.'

'Gwen, I've been giving something a lot of thought.' Vivienne's voice was strong, determined. 'During this holiday, the three of us have become close. We have a bond. We just used to co-exist, three flats, three separate lives. We did our own thing too often, and our paths didn't cross enough...'

'I know – and I was too depressed to make much of an effort.'

'So, all that has changed. We look after each other now. All for one and one for all. I know Lennie and I are together, and I might move in with him, back to our old place, but nothing will change. We're friends, and you and I'll be there for Mary. We'll go shopping together, days out, we'll help her stick to the 80:20 plan, we'll have dinner once a week, we'll go out for films and we'll even borrow the motorhome again—'

'Jason?'

'We'll persuade Vicente to lend it to us and we'll go off again. I was thinking it might be lovely to take Mary to Ireland one day.'

Gwen nodded. 'She doesn't say much about her past. And she was so young when she came to London.'

Vivienne made a low, cynical sound. 'I think she was quite badly let down. The lovely Callum Duffy who turned out not to be so lovely.'

'I bet Mary was a wonderful nurse, so caring, so patient.'

'We'll look after her. That's what friends are for.' Vivienne noticed Lennie and Ştefan approaching her. 'Well, we have the personal touch this morning. We must be very special.'

Lennie hugged Vivienne briefly and Ştefan kissed both her cheeks, then he repeated the action with Gwen. He seemed very cheerful, touching her arm affectionately, and as Lennie led Vivienne off to one side he murmured, 'Please – I want a word or two.'

'Oh?' Gwen waited.

'I like the music you make for me yesterday. It changes the film so much, just as I want it. So last night, I speak on the phone to an old friend from New York and he tells me he wants to meet you. He is a singer, a baritone, and he has singing schools in the USA. He wants to open one in London, and I say to him, you must meet Gwen and he asks me for your phone number. So, is it all right?'

Gwen was confused. 'Is what all right?'

'I give your phone details to him and when he comes to London, he can talk to you about the singing school?'

'Oh… yes, of course.'

'Then that is very good. Come, Gwen – it is a busy day, and we need to make much more of the opera music. Today, your friend, Vivienne, will meet a gruesome end. I am looking forward to all of this. Come, we go.' Ştefan took her arm and led her away, Gwen feeling baffled but somehow quite special. 'And I too will keep your details on my file, if I may. I have never worked with a professional singer. I want we work together in films, many, many times.'

'Oh.' Gwen strolled along, her arm tucked through the director's. 'All right. Yes, I suppose that would be all right.' She was thoughtful for a moment. 'A few weeks ago, I was all alone in my living room in London and now I'm singing for the whole world. Not bad for a shy girl from Llanclawdd who was told as a child that she hadn't a great deal to commend her until she opened her mouth. I think I've come a long way.'

* * *

It was late afternoon as Mary stood on the draughty platform at the railway station in Pickering, watching the approaching steam train shunt to a stop. She was looking forward to being back in Whitby: her legs ached and her bag was heavy. She dragged herself into a carriage and flopped into a soft seat. A lot of people were settling down, chattering noisily. Mary closed her eyes to shut them out and felt the lurch of the train pulling away.

She'd spent most of the day in Pickering and somehow she'd missed the castle altogether. The uphill drag to the shops had almost finished her off, then she'd stumbled on to the flea market at the end of a back alley and spent far too long buying little knick-knacks to take home. Then she'd stayed in a tea shop for two hours, eating cakes and talking to a local woman about how Yorkshire tea was the best brew you could find because Yorkshire was God's own county. Mary gazed out of the window as the steam train rattled along: she couldn't disagree. The scenery was stunning. The railway track followed a little winding stream, open farmland and opulent valleys on both sides, and Mary's eyes roamed over rising pine trees and yellow gorse. She would be back in London soon and, although she loved the bustling roads, the welcoming shops and cafés near Drayton Mews, she intended to remember the views from the train window for a long time. This holiday had been one of her best and she felt a little sad that she'd return to the normality of her old everyday life soon.

The train journey was less than two hours: she'd be in Whitby before six, when she'd meet Gwen and Vivienne. Inside the carriage, sitting with her head against the glass, Mary felt the streaming honey sunshine settle on her face and shoulders. The train's roll and shuffle rocked her in a lullaby, the repetitive rhythm of wheels against the track in her ears, and her eyelids were heavy. Mary's aching body relaxed, and she slipped into the warmth of a doze.

The train lurched to a sudden standstill and people were bustling, noisy, moving around. Mary blinked her eyes open and pressed her nose against the glass: the train had stopped at a pretty station called Grosmont, and more passengers were clambering on and off. She felt like she had stepped back in time as she gazed beyond the platform at a row of old cottages nestling among leafy trees and rising fields, smoke seeping from their stone chimneys. A young woman was struggling into the carriage with a baby in her arms while she was hauling several bags of shopping; she flopped down in the seat opposite Mary and they exchanged polite smiles as the train pulled away. Mary noticed the baby was dressed in pink and white; it had a rosebud mouth and a shock of black hair, and couldn't be more than six months old. She heard the mother breathe out, an exhausted sigh, as she settled into the comfortable softness of the seat. Mary took in her tired eyes, the hair that fell in a dark tumble over her face, the crumpled denim jacket, then she stared out of the window again and into the distance. She heard the guard amble past, checking tickets. The train rattled over an old bridge, the drop falling away to a river below. Mary stared at undulating hills and gorse land of the deepest purple that stretched for miles. She wished she had a camera: it would be hard to explain to Gwen and Vivienne just how breathtaking the view was. She decided she'd buy a few postcards at Whitby station, one for Vicente and several to take back.

Opposite, the baby had started to whimper; she was making small snuffling sounds and the young mother replied with a reassuring, 'Shhh-shhh.' Mary glanced across, offering a sympathetic smile. The mother shrugged awkwardly. 'I fed her before we got on the train. She can't be hungry again.'

Mary nodded. 'Ah, babies will always let you know when they want something, that's for sure.'

'They will that,' the young mum replied. She heaved the baby onto her shoulder and the child began to whine, a soft grumble of unhappiness now. The mother offered Mary an apologetic smile. 'No one warns you how hard it's going to be, looking after a baby.'

'You're right there,' Mary agreed. 'They can be a handful.'

'I live with my mum, she helps.' The young woman shifted the child to her other shoulder. 'I've split up with the baby's dad. I'm on my own.'

Mary nodded, her face sympathetic. 'It's hard by yourself.'

'She's called Bella.' The mother was jiggling the baby energetically. The child had started to cry now, wriggling irritably. The mother frowned and muttered, 'Bella, stop it, please.'

'Ah, but she's a sweet little thing,' Mary muttered.

Bella squirmed, arching her back, and she let out a bellowing wail. The young mother blushed. 'Bella...' She glanced pleadingly at Mary. 'I'm so sorry.'

'Not at all.' Mary held her hands out. 'Shall I have her for a little minute?'

The mother's brow creased, hesitant, unsure. Mary added, 'I'm Mary. I know about babies. Let me give you a break from little Bella.'

The young mum handed the writhing child over and Mary lifted her easily, placing her face down across her knee. She rubbed the baby's back with her open palm, making smooth, circular movements. Bella wriggled for a moment, beginning to relax, then she lay still. 'Shhh, there, there. Go on with you. Just a bit of wind. I thought so.'

The young mother watched, her mouth open. 'Oh, however did you do that?'

Mary picked the baby up in her arms and held her closely, touching the soft petal cheek tenderly with her finger. She breathed in the sweet smell, feeling the warm bundle nestle contentedly in her arms. 'Ah, it's second nature now.'

'Thanks, Mary.' The young mother's smile was pure gratitude as she held out her arms, keen to be reunited with her child. Mary reluctantly passed the soft bundle back and watched as the mum hugged her close. 'I'm Courtney.'

'Pleased to meet you.' Mary was still staring at the baby, the eyes closed in sleep, the tiny, bunched fists. 'And it's nice to meet Bella too. So – are you away off home now? Will your mother be making the tea?'

'Oh, she's been great, my mum. I don't know how I'd have managed without her. She was even there for the birth last February.'

Mary closed her eyes for a moment, recalling herself at the same age, alone in a hospital ward with a new baby, a long way from home. She realised that Courtney was speaking to her. 'What was that?'

'I asked if you have any kiddies, grandchildren.'

Mary took a breath. 'Yes, I have a daughter, Orla. She'd be sixty now. Can you believe that?'

Courtney's expression was blank, as if it was easy to imagine Mary with an old lady for a daughter. Then she said, 'Orla's a nice name. Did you pick it or did your husband choose it?'

'It was my favourite name. She was Orla Rose.' Mary sighed, imagining the baby she'd held in her arms for such a brief time. Orla had been the image of Callum: she had his eyes, his freckles. Mary wondered what Orla Rose was called now: the people who took her would have certainly changed the name. Mary pondered, as she often did, if Orla had children, grandchildren, where she was living, what she was like. Courtney interrupted her thoughts again.

'So, were you always so good with babies?'

'Ah, yes – I was a paediatric nurse for years at Great Ormond Street,' Mary replied. 'I know a case of the wind when I see it.'

The steam train rattled and started to slow down. People were gathering belongings and rising from their seats. Courtney heaved Bella onto her shoulder and began to collect her bags. 'Well, it was nice to meet you, Mary. Thanks again – I'll try Bella on her tummy next time she cries. It worked like magic.'

Mary watched as Courtney twisted from the seat, the baby and her bags of shopping filling her arms. She called after her, 'Good luck with little Bella. And take care of yourself.' Then she stretched out the muscles in her legs and gazed down with a smile. On her knee there was a round wet patch, baby dribble, the badge of parenthood. Mary sighed and reached for her heavy bag.

40

Mary had been quiet all the way from Whitby station, where Gwen picked her up, throughout the drive back to the camping site. She clutched her packet of postcards and listened intently as Vivienne chattered about her scene with Lennie, how they had several takes of him hurling her onto the damp grass and nuzzling her throat. Vivienne thought it was hilarious: she had suggested to Ştefan that the violent interaction between herself and Lennie's sinister creature would be poignant if it was more tender. She wanted to be hypnotised by his presence, not dragged roughly to her death, and Ştefan had agreed straight away. Lennie had whispered to her that she could twist both him and the director around her finger. She recounted the story, laughing as they sat in the motorhome, each with a cup of tea.

Then it was Gwen's turn. She had sung her heart out and she had felt deliriously happy. Furthermore, Ştefan had said that she would be paid handsomely for her trouble and there would be more work for her in the future. He had spoken to his American friend, a man called Sorokin, who was travelling to London to organise his new singing venture and had been delighted to hear about Gwen and to receive her mobile number.

Mary hadn't touched her tea. She was still thinking about baby Bella and how it had been so nice to hold the warm bundle against her chest. Of course, Mary had held so many babies and children throughout her career as a nurse. She had held them to comfort them, to lift them up, to help them get better and, once or twice, she had held them at the end as they breathed out and didn't breathe in again. She had held them professionally so that she could forget how sweet it felt to hold her own baby, Orla, but having Bella in her arms had brought that feeling back, the feeling of pure love followed by the immediate painful sensation of emptiness, of nothing to hold. It was a feeling that was familiar to Mary every day, an emotion that had stayed with her, whispered in her ear and had never really gone away. It never would. She glanced up at Vivienne.

'Aren't you getting ready to go out? I thought you and Lennie were up for the big meal tonight with your man, the director?'

Vivienne laughed. 'Weren't you listening. Mary? You're not with us. I just said, I postponed it. I told Ștefan that I wanted to spend my last night of our holiday with my two best friends and he suggested Lennie and I have dinner with him tomorrow night instead. So, tonight, Mary, you, Gwen and I are going to share that final bottle of champagne and have a wild night out somewhere. I thought we could book a restaurant in Whitby, let our hair down, go a bit crazy.'

Gwen agreed. 'We deserve it, and it would be a lovely way to end the holiday.'

'No, it's not for me.' Mary wrinkled her nose. 'I'm not feeling like myself this evening. Just the two of youse go. I'll stop here and have an early night.'

'Oh, you will not.' Vivienne was insistent. 'All good friendships come in threes. The Three Degrees, the Three Stooges, the Three Amigos.'

'The Three Musketeers.' Gwen smiled. 'Charlie's Angels.'

Vivienne crouched next to Mary and hugged her. 'Come on, Mary, get your glad rags on and let's hit the town.' She offered a pleading expression. 'My treat?'

'I'm not feeling in the mood...'

Gwen wrapped her arms round Mary. 'Oh, please. It will be a great evening. Vivienne suggested a swanky restaurant in Whitby. We could get a taxi there and back and share a few drinks, but if you prefer...' She squeezed Mary closer. 'We could go for a curry instead.'

'I'm not hungry, to tell the truth. You go, Gwen, Vivienne. I'll only make the pair of youse miserable. Just go on. I'll be fine here myself.'

'We are simply not leaving you behind,' Vivienne exclaimed.

Gwen was concerned. 'Are you feeling unwell, Mary? It's not your heart, is it?'

'No, it isn't.'

'Then what is it?' Vivienne persisted. 'You need cheering up.'

'No, I just want to be by myself.'

'Oh, we won't let you away with this Garbo act of—' Vivienne stopped speaking. Mary's face was wet with tears. She hugged her again. 'Mary, what's the matter?'

'You've been unhappy since you got off the train at Whitby station. Did something happen?' Gwen asked. 'Oh, Mary, love, what is it?'

Mary felt herself compressed between two sets of protective arms, two warm bodies. Someone was stroking her hair and she felt herself falling apart. The sobs came quickly, then more sobs, and she was shaking with the heartbreak of it all. Her head was full to aching, keeping everything secret, silent for so long, her lips pressed hard together. Then suddenly her mouth sprang open and words began to bubble out. 'I helped a girl on the train – her babby had a bit of wind – and it took me back to my own... my own little one, all those years ago.'

'Little one?' Gwen frowned. 'A baby?'

Vivienne was still hugging Mary, stroking her hair. 'You had a baby?'

'Me and Callum. That's why we came to London – I was pregnant, and my parents told me to go, to leave the house. I'd brought shame on them. So, we came away together, me and Callum. I trusted him. But he let me down. He left me by myself.'

Mary felt a soft kiss against her ear and Vivienne's voice. 'What happened to the baby?'

'Orla Rose.' Mary wiped her face and her hand came away wet. 'I gave her up.'

'For adoption?' Gwen urged.

'To a lovely couple, apparently. They couldn't have children. I never met them.'

'Couldn't you keep her yourself, Mary?'

'It was 1961, Vivienne. I was by myself. What could I do? A woman came to see me just after I'd given birth and she told me the best thing to do was to let her find Orla a good home. Of course, she's not called Orla now.' Mary sniffed. 'I don't know what she's called.'

'That makes me so cross,' Vivienne snapped. 'You had no support, no one to help you, and they took your baby...'

'I agreed to it.' Mary snuffled. 'I couldn't give her a good home. And the woman said the couple were well off, they'd give her everything she needed.' She sighed. 'But I'd have given her all my love.'

Gwen took Mary's hand and squeezed it. 'And you've been carrying this memory around all this time?'

'I've never told a soul.' Mary's brow puckered. 'Then today I told the young one on the train, Courtney, that I'd had a baby, but I didn't say I gave her away. It made me feel a bit – unclean, like I'd let Orla down all over again.'

'There are ways of getting in contact, even years later – you could find out where she is,' Vivienne suggested. 'I'd help if you wanted…'

'No, it's best left alone now,' Mary murmured. 'She has her own life. It's best if I don't rock the boat. But…' She gazed up at Gwen and forced a smile. 'At least I've told someone now. It feels like a stone's been taken out of my chest. I feel a bit – lighter.'

'I'm glad you told us, Mary,' Gwen said. 'You've been very brave.'

'I think you're marvellous,' Vivienne agreed.

'All those years of nursing in the hospital, all those children on the wards that I worked with, and I never told a soul about Orla.'

'But now you have, maybe you can start to heal,' Gwen suggested.

'And I still stand by what I said before,' Vivienne insisted. 'Let's get our glad rags on, a bit of lippy and let's go out on the town, move forward together.'

Mary shook her head. 'I'll never forget her.'

'No, you won't,' Vivienne agreed. 'She'll be in your heart, safely locked there. She's your treasure, your memory to keep. And I'm sure she looks in the mirror now, and knows she had one of the best birth mums she could have had.'

Gwen patted Mary's shoulder. 'I'm so proud of you, Mary.'

Mary tried a smile, and it suddenly felt a little bit better. 'Ah, well. You're right. She has her own place in my heart and no one can take that away from me. So…' She heaved a deep breath, then her smile broadened. 'So, will we go out on the town for some fun tonight? What's the swankiest place in Whitby – since you're paying, Vivienne?'

* * *

They sang in the taxi on the way back to the campsite, Vivienne leading the Madonna song 'Like a Virgin' at the top of her lungs but still not able to drown out Gwen's resonant voice. Mary had her own version of the song, which was quite rude in places but, fortunately, inaudible beneath Gwen's rich booming rendition. The taxi driver raised an eyebrow: the three women behind him were clearly in their senior years, although one of them was wearing a short skirt and thigh-high boots and another had pink and blue hair. The third seemed to think she was an opera singer although, given the power of her lungs, she might actually be. The taxi driver decided to pay no mind: he'd had worse passengers.

They had drunk a bottle of wine and a bottle of champagne, although Gwen hadn't had more than a small glass of each. Vivienne, who had protested throughout the meal that she'd look a sight the following day if she drank any more, was clearly not in control of her wrists: she kept reaching for the bottle, pouring more and then drinking continuously while she chattered. Mary kept up with her, declaring that she'd start the 50:50 diet when she returned to London, much to Gwen's amusement: Mary had no idea that she'd changed the numbers. Then suddenly, Vivienne began to sob.

'I wish we could do it all over again.'

Gwen was alarmed. 'What's the matter, Vivienne?'

'Oh, I must look hideous.' Vivienne's eyes streamed tears. She pulled huge sunglasses from her handbag and pushed them on her face. 'I've just had such a lovely holiday and made such wonderful friends for life. The whole thing was wonderful. I wish we could go back to the beginning and do it all again.'

'Well, we should,' Mary agreed. 'Let's steal Jason for ever and take off somewhere.'

'Mary...' Gwen said gently. 'You know Vivienne's not coming back with us tomorrow?'

'No, I didn't know... When did you say that, Vivienne? Was I there?'

'I told you earlier, but I'm not sure you were able to take much in. I'm staying on with Lennie – he has more filming to do and so I'm staying at his hotel. Then when we're back, I've decided to move in with him.' She sniffed loudly and rooted in her bag for a tissue. 'But we'll meet up all the time, promise me we will.'

'Ah, we will,' Mary agreed. 'I hope we'll get a nice handsome fella coming to live in your flat, Vivienne.' She eyed the taxi driver hopefully. 'One with nice legs on him and a hairy chest.'

'We had such a lovely time. Do you remember when I got myself locked in the toilet in Lyme Regis?' Gwen murmured, her voice full of emotion.

'And I had a lovely aromatherapy massage,' Mary added. 'And you beat the young one at the darts in the pub and we did the fashion show for the WI?'

'And it rained at Stonehenge, but we climbed Haytor and watched the sun rise...' Vivienne murmured dreamily.

'And we all bought ourselves new swimsuits,' Mary piped up.

'And what about the lovely food at Totnes and the wonderful people we met there, and we helped the busker,' Gwen chimed in.

'Oh, and the eisteddfod was wonderful,' Vivienne sighed.

'And I had a ride on the quad bike with Jason,' Mary shouted gleefully.

'And I've told Clifford Edwards six times now that I won't talk to him.' Gwen laughed. 'I've washed that man right out of my hair. He's out of my life for good.'

The taxi driver's voice came from the front. 'Here we are, girls.'

They had arrived at the camping site and he had driven his car next to the motorhome and pulled up, the engine idling. Gwen thrust some money into his hand. 'Thanks so much, it's been lovely.'

The three women slithered from the taxi and stood in the cold outside the motorhome. Gwen held out a key ring, a square plastic fob with a picture of the white statue of Venus de Milo, her face placid, her arms snapped off. 'Well, here we are, back home.'

Vivienne was blubbering again. 'I just want to say thank you to you both – Mary, Gwen, you've made me a better person, no, really, you have.'

Gwen laughed aloud. 'What about me? I cried in the petrol station as soon as we left London. I was a shadow of the person I am now. But now I've sung for the whole world on a film.'

'And as for me...' Mary's face was sad. 'I've shared a secret that I've never told anyone. I'll never forget this. It's been the best time of my fecking life – ah, sorry, Gwen.'

The three women opened their arms and clung to each other, laughing, and crying and talking at the same time. It had been a holiday they'd never forget.

41

Gwen and Mary dropped Vivienne off at the film location at eight o'clock in the morning and, after tears and promises to meet soon, Gwen reset the satnav and drove the motorhome towards London, watching through the driver's mirror as Vivienne waved, until she was out of sight. The weather was chilly, but Gwen and Mary were snug inside the cab; Mary insisted on having the radio on, blaring rock music as they crossed Yorkshire and drove onto the M1 at Doncaster, where it started to drizzle. The windscreen wipers swished rhythmically all the way down to Watford Gap, where they stopped for lunch and Gwen messaged Vivienne to let her know their progress. As she checked her phone, she noticed that she had several missed calls.

'Is it Clifford again?' Mary pulled a face. 'I'm sorry I landed him on you, Gwen. I shouldn't have given him your number, but I just assumed he was the letter C in your teacup, the one with all the hearts?'

'I don't know this number at all.' Gwen was puzzled. 'Do you think it's a scammer?'

'Likely as not,' Mary muttered as she munched cheese on toast.

'What time will we get home? I'm exhausted and it's you who has been doing all the driving.'

'We've driven quite slowly, and the traffic's been fairly heavy, and we've stopped for an hour so – we should be home before five.'

'That's good. I think I'll have an early night.'

'Me too,' Gwen agreed. 'I'll drop you off, then I'll take Jason the motorhome for a quick valet and get him back to Vicente, then I'll get the bus home, then I'll go straight to bed.'

'Do you want me to come with you to see Vicente, Gwen?'

'Oh, I don't think so, Mary. He has the lovely Cherilyn. Besides, I can take care of myself now.' She glanced at her phone. 'Shall we make tracks?'

* * *

Back at 104 Drayton Mews, the basement flat smelled musty, so Mary lit several joss sticks, filling the room with curling smoke and the sweet scent of jasmine. She dumped her case on the floor: she'd unpack tomorrow, put her clothes in the washing machine, find a place for the knick-knacks she'd bought on their travels. There was little food in the cupboard, but she found a tin of tomato soup and heated it up, muttering, 'This is the 80 per cent from now on. I think I used all of the 20 per cent for the whole of next year on that holiday.' She laughed. 'And most of it during the meal last night.'

She decided she'd pop down to Chandra's Convenience Store tomorrow and buy a few groceries from Ravi, ask him how the twins were. She hoped the babies were sleeping better, and that Ravi was putting a few drops of lavender in his own bath so that he'd sleep well too. A good night's sleep was important for a parent. Mary thought about Ravi's grandfather, Deepak. She hoped she'd see him in the shop, and they could have a conversation about cooking ingredients. She had enjoyed her holiday but, she decided, soup spoon in mid-air, that it was nice to be home. She realised that she was smiling.

* * *

Gwen sat downstairs on the bus, staring through the window at the busy streets. It was still drizzling, raindrops squiggling down the grimy glass, partially obscuring the view. Shops and houses rolled by, a block of flats. Gwen replayed her visit to Vicente, twenty minutes ago. He had looked fragile when she'd parked the freshly-washed and valeted motorhome in his drive with a full water tank and a new gas cylinder, and returned the keys; he had stood at the front door, his chest heaving as he breathed, and accepted the box set CD of Pavarotti that she had bought him as a thank you gift. He had smiled weakly; he was pleased to see her and had said how healthy she looked. Then a smart, bubbly woman in her fifties had appeared at his shoulder and greeted Gwen politely before fussing over Vicente, shepherding him back into the house. He leaned on her gratefully as she closed the door with a firm clunk. Gwen assumed that she'd just met Cherilyn and she hoped they'd be happy together. Vicente had appeared gaunt, and Gwen was glad he had someone to care for him. Then the rain started and Gwen walked to the bus stop, deciding that she'd come back the following week and bring some grapes. She'd lend him a CD of Mario Lanza singing *The Student Prince*. She'd build new bridges; it would cheer him up.

The bus slowed down, stopping; people clambered on, finding seats, shaking drops of water from their hair and coats. The sound of her phone buzzing tugged Gwen from her thoughts. She didn't recognise the number. 'Hello?'

An American voice answered, a friendly man who spoke as if he knew her already. 'Is that Gwen?'

'Yes, this is Gwen Prichard. Who's that?'

'I'm Chad Sorokin from New York. I got your number from Ştefan Davidescu, a friend of mine who says he knows you. He said it'd be okay to give you a call.'

'Oh?' Gwen liked the gravelly sound of the voice. 'I remember; he said you might ring me.'

'The thing is, Gwen, I'm setting up an opera school in London and I hoped you might be interested in finding out a little more about it. I'm recruiting some teachers and I could do with someone with your background knowledge to advise and maybe help me out a little. I don't have any other contacts in England and I know you'll be a great place to start, with all your experience. Ştefan says you blew him away with your voice.'

'Oh, it wasn't much, not really,' Gwen protested.

'I've been involved in opera for years. I sang with the Metropolitan on Broadway for some time. Do you know the place, Gwen? It's in Lincoln Square on the Upper West Side of Manhattan.'

'I've never been to New York.'

'Oh, you'll have to come visit, maybe even sing there. You'd be very welcome.'

'I might like that...' Gwen began.

'I started putting opera schools together when I got divorced, ten years ago. I've got three schools in New York now, which isn't bad for an old guy in his seventies. It's my passion, getting kids to understand opera, getting them to find their own voice.'

'Oh, I know exactly what you mean, Chad.' Gwen was thinking about Elinor. 'I've just done some work with the *cerdd dant*, where you improvise over a harp, at an eisteddfod in Wales. I love teaching young people to sing opera. It's such a gift to see them develop confidence and sing with passion.'

'You sound remarkable, Gwen.'

'Oh, I don't know about that...'

'The thing is – I've just gotten off a plane from New York – I arrived yesterday. I'm in London, at a hotel in Mayfair and I wondered, could we maybe meet up and have lunch tomorrow, then we could talk through my plans for the school and you can let me know if you're interested in the project?'

Gwen had a picture of Chad Sorokin already: it was as if she knew what he looked like. He'd be a big bear of a man, broad shouldered, with neat hair and a tidy beard. She imagined them sharing lunch together: he'd be a fascinating conversationalist. They'd discuss music with a shared passion, then he'd ask her to show him around London; they'd take a ride on the London Eye, sit at the top and gaze at the whole of the city in its vast sparkling glory. Then he'd take her small hand in his large one.

'So, lunch, Gwen? Tomorrow?'

'That would be lovely,' Gwen breathed. 'By the way, do you have a beard?'

'Yes, I do, as a matter of fact.' She heard his rich throaty laugh. 'So, is lunch at one o'clock okay? Can you get a cab to the Connaught Hotel? I'll pick up the tab, of course.'

'That sounds brilliant.' Gwen was already planning what to wear.

'And then afterwards, if we've time, I've always fancied a ride on the London Eye. We could see the sights. How does that sound?'

'It sounds heavenly, Chad,' Gwen replied, thinking that the baritone singer with the lovely accent had a name that began with a C.

* * *

The following day, Gwen brought two bowls of muesli down to the basement and shared breakfast with Mary as she chattered excitedly about her phone call with Chad Sorokin and the prospect of lunch and a ride on the London Eye. Mary pressed her lips together when she heard his first name and noticed the way Gwen's eyes shone. Mary knew exactly what would happen next.

Then Vivienne rang Gwen and they both listened to her good news. The dinner with Ştefan had been wonderful. He was planning on a TV film about a married couple whose relationship is floundering, so they rent a house on the coast of the Isle of Wight to reignite their passion. But the house is a powerful place, and it sucks the woman into its evil past, and she becomes psychotic. Vivienne was thrilled that Ştefan wanted her to consider trying for the role, with Lennie as her husband. She said it was a role to die for, in more than one way! Vivienne promised to tell them all about it next weekend when she would be back in London.

Then, two hours later, Mary rushed out to wish Gwen the best of luck as she stood in the hallway preparing to leave. She watched from the doorway as Gwen stepped into a taxi and waved her hand, dressed in a smart jacket and trousers, a pretty blouse, glossy hair and lipstick. Mary rubbed her hands gleefully; she couldn't wait to hear all about Gwen's date when she returned.

Then she had a cup of tea and vacuumed her basement flat from top to bottom. She washed the clothes from her holiday, arranged the knick-knacks she'd bought and set about making a shopping list. Mary concentrated on the 80 per cent first, adding yogurt and cereals and tins of beans to the list, then rice. Then she pulled on her jacket, dabbed the patchouli oil she had bought in Totnes on her wrist and made her way down to the arcade of shops on the main road. She stepped into Chandra's Convenience Store, where Ravi was delighted to see her.

'Mary. I wondered where you'd been, I hadn't seen you for three weeks...'

Mary shrugged. 'I've been on a holiday, Ravi. I've been all round

England and Wales. It was lovely. How are the twins, little Naira and Shanaya? Are they sleeping now?'

'Much better, since I put the drop of oil of lavender in their bath. And the heartbeat CD works like a dream.' Ravi smiled. 'So, what can I get you today?'

'I'll have some onions, tomatoes, lentils, and some rice, some yogurt, some chickpeas, please.'

'No problem, Mary. All very healthy foods.' Ravi busied himself, placing groceries on the counter. Mary handed him some money and placed the shopping in her bag as she chatted.

'Well, have you heard of the 80:20 lifestyle plan, Ravi? That's me from now on. I'm after doing the healthy eating on Monday to Friday. So, what can you recommend?'

He scratched his head. 'No gulab jamun, no heavy carbs, no fried parathas. What about a nice chana masala with roti bread? A brown lentil dal? A nice aubergine curry?'

'The lady needs a paneer lambabda.' The quiet voice came first, then a tall man in his eighties with white hair, a neatly clipped snowy beard and dark-framed glasses appeared in the doorway.

'Hello, Deepak,' Mary smiled.

'Have you been away?'

'Yes, I was just telling Ravi that I've been on holiday.'

'Well, I'm glad you're back. I have been searching out some of my old recipes for you.' Deepak glanced at his grandson. 'Ravi, take some time off, go and put your feet up, have a cup of tea. I will look after Mary.'

'Oh.' Ravi glanced at his grandfather, then back at Mary. 'All right.' She watched the younger man disappear into the back of the shop.

Deepak took his place at the counter. 'I missed you while you were away. I have been sorting out some of my wife's old recipes, traditional ones. I wanted you to have them.'

Mary met his eyes. 'How long has she been gone, Deepak?'

'She died eight years ago.' His shoulders slumped sadly. 'All I have now is her recipes. She was a wonderful woman and a wonderful cook.'

'I'm sorry...'

Deepak shook his head. 'So, I wanted you to have her recipe book, written in her own hand. I have it under the counter. I wrapped it in tissue but then you didn't come in and I wondered what had happened to you.'

'I'm back after the holiday and determined to get fitter and healthier.' Mary beamed. 'So, tell me about this curry...'

'Paneer lambabda, with lots of mint, chillies and tomatoes. The recipe is in Amina's book. And also, you must try the dhansak, with lentils, ginger, cloves, turmeric.'

'I want to try them all.'

Deepak inclined his head. 'I will give you the book. Then you can work your way through from page one to the end.'

'Do you make your wife's recipes, Deepak?'

'No.' Deepak's hands came together. 'I live here with Ravi and his wife and the children. I eat what they cook. The bhajis are very good. I will get some for you next time you come in.'

'Thanks.' Mary clapped her palms twice, thinking – an idea had come to her. 'What are you doing this evening?'

'I will watch the television; sometimes I read, then I eat and go to bed.' He seemed sad. 'My life now is a routine.'

'Right, you're coming round my house for a good curry. It's 104A Drayton Mews, the basement flat. We can cook it together. Make sure you write that down – 104A.'

Deepak's eyebrows rose. 'You're inviting me round your house? For a curry?'

'And why ever not? I always make too much for myself. And, sure, you can help me cook it.'

Deepak reached under the counter and pulled out a book wrapped in white tissue paper. He held it out to Mary. 'It would be an honour to visit you, to dine in your home.'

Mary took the book. 'Okay, then I'll see you around half six, shall we say?'

Deepak nodded, his face shining. 'And then perhaps I can invite you here, to share a meal with me and my family.'

'I'd just love that.'

'It's a pity I don't have my own place, Mary – then you could visit me whenever you wanted, and we could talk about curries and listen to some of my favourite music.'

Mary smiled. 'Well, for tonight you're just going to have to put up with the Dubliners.' She turned to go, then she twisted back to look at him. 'Although if you ever do need a flat of your own, I know a very good one not far from me that's coming up for rent soon.'

Mary waved a hand and set off towards Drayton Mews, carrying her shopping bag and humming a little tune. She was looking forward to cooking a curry and sharing it with Deepak. Things had improved so much in her life: she had made firm friends, she had been on holiday, and now she had a new friendship to look forward to. So, she thought to herself as she wandered along, she had the best people around her; she was healthy, she was wiser, she was happier. She knew she'd survive. No, she'd do better than that now. Much better.

REFERENCES

Brit Stop camping guide for motorhomes, camper vans, etc.
www.britstops.com
Camping in fields, etc.
www.wandering-bird.com/wild-camp-uk-motorhome

Music

'All Through the Night'/ 'Ar Hyd y Nos'
www.youtube.com/watch?v=yWUo7oVhF_4&
ab_channel=StarfallLeyline
How to pronounce the song 'Ar Hyd y Nos' in Welsh www.youtube.
com/watch?v=fRzJGM9o9HA&
ab_channel=MerthyrAloudWorldMusicChoir
'Myfanwy'
www.youtube.com/watch?v=jqo8pcQU-hs&ab_channel=nonwatcyn
'Myfanwy' with both languages subtitled www.youtube.com/watch?
v=tj3DIwQbocA&ab_channel=Ingen
The meaning of the song 'Myfanwy'

www.felinfach.com/blogs/blog/myfanwy-words-and-meaning
'Ty Coch Caerdydd' dance
www.youtube.com/watch?v=raI9WmGcIG4&
ab_channel=CardiffMorris
Thomas Tallis: *Spem in Alium* www.youtube.com/watch?v=
QmHInZSGIyY&ab_channel=AVROTROSKlassiek
Giovanni Capurro: 'O Sole Mio' www.youtube.com/watch?v=
ERD4CbBDNI0&ab_channel=corellono1
Mozart Requiem: *Lachrymosa*
www.youtube.com/watch?v=kI-TrAvp_xs&ab_channel=RosaMusic
Rossini: 'Cat Duet' www.youtube.com/watch?v=QNyR6rsGDyg&
ab_channel=KiriOnLine-DameKiriTeKanawa
Mozart: 'Voi Che Sapete' www.youtube.com/watch?v=
FdmGBFTB3z0&ab_channel=WarnerClassics
Purcell: 'Nymphs and Shepherds'
www.youtube.com/watch?v=x-oK-s3jpzE&
ab_channel=MyrnaTennant
Edwin Hawkins Singers: 'Oh Happy Day' www.youtube.com/
watch?v=EfGDvDGE7zk&ab_channel=maumau1968
The Dubliners: 'The Irish Rover' www.youtube.com/watch?v=
7otIK_5rpB8&ab_channel=brummydubliner
The Dubliners: 'Seven Drunken Nights' www.youtube.com/watch?
v=5CWIIoSf4nw&ab_channel=PaddyBarry

ACKNOWLEDGMENTS

Thanks to my agent, Kiran Kataria, for her kindness, wisdom, humour and integrity.

Thanks to Sarah Ritherdon, for being so brilliant and so insightful.

Thanks to Amanda Ridout, Claire Fenby and Nia Beynon for the magic they create, and to the hugely supportive community that is Boldwood Books team and writers. It's a privilege to be part of such an inspirational group of people.

Thanks to everyone who supports my writing: writer friends of the RNA, Rachel Gilbey and the fantastic team of bloggers.

Thanks to Erika, Rich, Rog, Jan, Jan M, Ken, Trish, Lexy, Shaz, Frank, Ian, Susie, Chrissie, Kathy N, Julie, Martin, Steve, (and Steve's mum,) Rose, Nik R, Pete O', Dianne, Mart, Cath, Stephanie, Slawka, Katie H, Ellen, Norman, Angela, Robin and Edward.

Special thanks to Jonno for all the music support.

Thanks to Ivor at Deep Studios for the tech.

So much thanks to Peter Blaker, Avril Silk and Solitary Writers, my writing buddies.

Love to my awesome neighbours and to the local Somerset community, especially Jenny, Claire, Paul and Sophie.

Eternal thanks to our Tony for being there, to Kim, and to my mum and dad, always in my thoughts.

All the love in the world to Liam, Maddie, Cait and Big G.

And finally, hugest thanks to anyone who has read and enjoyed any of my books, a heart-felt thank you. You make this journey wonderful.

MORE FROM JUDY LEIGH

We hope you enjoyed reading *The Golden Girls' Getaway*. If you did, please leave a review.

If you'd like to gift a copy, this book is also available as an ebook, digital audio download and audiobook CD.

Sign up to Judy Leigh's mailing list for news, competitions and updates on future books:

http://bit.ly/JudyLeighNewsletter

Explore more fun, uplifting reads from Judy Leigh:

ABOUT THE AUTHOR

Judy Leigh is the bestselling author of *A Grand Old Time* and *Five French Hens* and the doyenne of the 'it's never too late' genre of women's fiction. She has lived all over the UK from Liverpool to Cornwall, but currently resides in Somerset.

Visit Judy's website: https://judyleigh.com

Follow Judy on social media:

facebook.com/judyleighuk
twitter.com/judyleighwriter
instagram.com/judyrleigh
bookbub.com/authors/judy-leigh

ABOUT BOLDWOOD BOOKS

Boldwood Books is a fiction publishing company seeking out the best stories from around the world.

Find out more at www.boldwoodbooks.com

Sign up to the Book and Tonic newsletter for news, offers and competitions from Boldwood Books!

http://www.bit.ly/bookandtonic

We'd love to hear from you, follow us on social media:

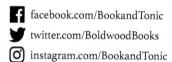

facebook.com/BookandTonic

twitter.com/BoldwoodBooks

instagram.com/BookandTonic

Printed in Great Britain
by Amazon